THE BLACK
ARRIVAL

TITLES BY PAUL E. COOLEY

THE
BLACK
ARRIVAL

Paul E. Cooley

SHADOW
PUBLICATIONS

Second Edition

Paperback ISBN: 978-1-942137-10-8
eBook ISBN: 978-1-942137-11-5

Visit our website at https://shadowpublications.com

To stalk Paul on social media:
  Mastodon: @paul_e_cooley@vyrse.social
  YouTube: https://youtube.com/paulecooley
  Email: paul@shadowpublications.com
  Mailing List: http://mailinglist.shadowpublications.com

Printed in the United States of America

Originally Published (First Edition):
  First U.S. Paperback Printing: Severed Press (May 21, 2015)
  First U.S. eBook Publication: Severed Press (May 21, 2015)
  First Audiobook Publication (Audible): Paul E. Cooley (November 19, 2015)

Second Edition Published by Paul E. Cooley and Shadow Publications (February 14, 2023)

Cover art, cover design, and internal layout by Scott E. Pond
Scott E. Pond Designs: www.scottpond.com

10 9 8 7 6 5 4 3 2 1

In memory of Indiana Cooley—
I shall forever miss you.

ACKNOWLEDGEMENTS

I wrote this novel during a pretty turbulent time in my life. I started a new job, had to say goodbye to my furry son Indiana, and was finally forced to deal with mortality in a way I'd never expected. The fact I finished this book and have already started the third in the series is a testament to the support of my family, friends, and my readers. That said, I have to give a shoutout to the following folks without whom this book would not have been possible.

Thomas E. Cooley — As with *The Black*, my father, chemical engineer extraordinaire, tutored me (once again and with less shouting) in chemistry and analysis equipment. He was always there when I had a crazy idea and even managed to plant a few of his own. Any violations of physical laws are intentional on my part. Any discrepancies with actual chemistry, however, are mine and mine alone.

Carolyn Cooley — Her constant support and cheerleading has always kept me writing. I am proud to be her son.

As always, I have to thank The Fiendlings. They have supported my work since 2009 and continue their incessant clamor for more.

— *Paul E Cooley (April 2015)*

THE BLACK
ARRIVAL

PROLOGUE

The slate-colored ocean rippled. The sun glared down behind blankets of clouds. Vivian yawned into her mic and checked the instruments. In the service, she'd hovered just above the desert floor before dropping troops into remote fire bases. Now? It was water.

She enjoyed racing to the rigs. Flying execs to their meetings was boring. At least the ocean was a challenge. Rig-hopping was a blast. She wished the weather system threatening *Leaguer* was already in her way. That would make the trip more interesting. But as it was, the waves were large, the froth white as snow, and the winds were choppy. Smile on her face, Vivian checked her fuel gauge, and then pushed the throttle another notch.

"I know we're supposed to get this done quickly," her co-pilot said through the radio, "but you're really pushing it."

She grinned. "Hines? Why don't you worry about picking up the barrel and making sure you don't drop the damned thing?"

The co-pilot sighed. He was already in the cargo area and sitting by the door. "Yes, ma'am."

Vivian checked their position. "ETA 2 minutes, Hines."

"Yes, ma'am."

A black dot appeared on the horizon. It slowly grew in size and after a moment, she made out the blinking red lights at the top of the oil derrick. There it was: *Leaguer*. It wasn't the largest rig she'd ever flown to. In fact, PPE had a few other rigs in the area that dwarfed it. But *Leaguer* was an offshore platform, which meant in heavy weather, landing on it was like dropping atop a see-saw. She bit her lip. The waves were a little restless, but hardly dangerous.

She made out the landing beacon sticking out to the side of the platform. Four men waited for her on the deck, an orange barrel between them. Vivian clucked her tongue. "Hines? You ready?"

"Yes, ma'am." He sounded tired and annoyed. Hines hated riding in the cargo area. She didn't blame him. He should have been in the pilot cabin and watching the ocean slide by. Occasionally, she even let him drive, but they had three other rigs to hit on the way back. And at least one refueling stop.

PPE had expedited *Leaguer's* sample. But that didn't mean it was the only one heading to Houston. It was going to be a long day. After collecting the barrels and refueling at sea, Vivian and Hines would fly to the mainland. A cargo plane was already waiting for them. Vivian hoped there wouldn't be any problems with the two other rigs. As she'd said to *Leaguer's* rig chief, they had a tight timeline and getting the oil to the cargo plane was only part of it.

She slowed the chopper above the landing circle and descended. When the helicopter touched the metal platform, the aircraft hardly twitched.

"Nice landing," Hines said.

A warning light blinked when Hines had opened the door. She heard his voice through the headset as he told the roughnecks where to place the barrel. She stretched her back and tapped her foot. "Come on, Hines."

"Hold your water," he said. "No, not you."

She clicked off her mic and chuckled. Poor Hines. Paperwork. Barrels. No flying? She'd tell him to take a nap when this was done.

The warning light flashed green and then held steady.

"Clear," Hines said. "Let's get back in the air."

Vivian clicked her mic back on. "Roger." She pulled on the stick and the helo rose smoothly from the platform. She turned back toward the ocean and hit the throttle. As the chopper raced above the waves, she imagined *Leaguer* getting smaller and smaller in the distance.

"Vivian?" Hines said over the radio.

"Yeah?"

"We hitting turbulence or something? Damned barrel is vibrating."

She cocked an eyebrow. "Um, no, Hines."

"Fucking bizarre."

"You need a nap. And now. We have another forty minutes before we touch down again. Close your eyes. I got this."

"Good," Hines said. "I'm still a little hungover."

"Yeah," she said, "I noticed. Maybe put your back against that barrel and get a massage."

He laughed. "Maybe I'll try just that."

Vivian didn't bother to respond. He could sleep. She would fly. The ocean spread to infinity in all directions. It was the kind of view she loved. Another four hours of flying today, and then she could rest. Maybe she'd even let Hines do some of the work for once.

BOOK 1: The Barrel

CHAPTER ONE

The tinted windows did little to keep out the sunlight. That's why the blinds were down and the office lights were off. Simpson sat behind his desk. The widescreen monitor cast blue-white light across his face.

The report on the screen was…interesting. PPE's exploration rig, *Leaguer,* had finally brought up oil from the M2 trench. After more than two years of preparation, the company finally had a stake. And it looked like a goldmine.

A single eight gallon test barrel of oil was in the air. The helicopter had picked it up from *Leaguer,* and then rig hopped to Port Moresby, Papua/New Guinea. The delivery company loaded it on a private plane and flew the barrel to Tokyo. And those were just the first steps in getting it to Houston.

Simpson stared at the map on his screen. The barrel still had several hours before it reached Tokyo. After customs and etc., the barrel wouldn't make it to Houston for another full day. And that's if there were no delays.

Delays. Simpson sighed and closed the travel map window. He brought up the email client, selected two emails, and brought them up side by side.

It wasn't enough to be the first company to drill M2. It wasn't enough to be the first company using new technology to explore the trench. And it wasn't enough that PPE was the first major offshore company to throw away the idea of contractors and subcontractors and use only corporate-owned and salaried assets. No, that wasn't enough. On top of that? He had a major personality issue going on.

Leaguer's Rig-Chief, Martin Vraebel, and the head of engineering, Thomas Calhoun, were not getting along. In fact, the two men seemed to hate each other. And on a rig that far out in the ocean, it was a little disconcerting. Both men were consummate professionals, yet they didn't seem to agree on anything.

In the past week, he'd seen nothing but gripes from Vraebel about Calhoun's team and their sense of entitlement. From Calhoun? Nothing but disdain for Vraebel's pomposity and micro-management.

Calhoun was an industry legend. That's why Simpson had hired his crew in the first place. Vraebel had to get along with them. He just had to. Some friction was expected, but Simpson had thought for sure that they were a good match. Now he wondered. This latest incident wasn't as much about personality conflicts as questions about expertise. And that was going too far.

Calhoun's team had performed the first cut analysis of the M2 oil. Calhoun's geologist, Shawna Sigler, had written up the report. If the shareholders saw the redacted report, PPE's share price would skyrocket. If, however, they saw the raw report, he didn't think the share price would do anything but plummet.

According to Sigler's analysis, the oil in M2 was pristine, perhaps the cleanest, lightest weight crude ever discovered. Refining it would cost next to nothing. Regardless of how far the price of oil dropped, M2 would provide PPE an incredible amount of revenue for decades to come. But there was a catch.

There always is, Simpson thought. Sigler had also included some startling, if not downright hinky, conclusions. She'd found a strange substance in the core sample that may be biological. She also suggested the oil might in fact be contaminated. While Sigler hadn't postulated what it could be contaminated with, she had put a warning in the report.

And that's when the shit hit the fan. Vraebel had sent Simpson an email along with the report. His assessment? Sigler and Calhoun were crazy. They were stalling for some reason and doing their best to inhibit the drilling. He wanted them off the rig.

That, of course, was out of the question. Without Calhoun and his team, *Leaguer* didn't stand a chance of mapping M2, much less finding the sweet spots. So that was a non-starter.

To make matters worse, Calhoun had sent an email telling Simpson that he'd happily leave the rig if that's what PPE wanted. The very idea sent a chill down Simpson's spine.

The oil industry was pretty incestuous. If someone screwed up, everyone knew about it. If there was friction? Everyone knew about it. And that meant the shareholders would discover it too. Oh, you could hide things from them, sure, but ultimately, the secrets got out into the world. There was no way to keep that from happening.

He swept his eyes from one email to the other. Acid burned in his stomach. They were less than a day away from drilling the next well. He had to make a decision.

God, he wanted a cigarette and a shot of Beam. But at ten in the morning, it was a bit early for either. He composed a different email to each man, but the content was essentially the same. Behave. Work together. Get the job done.

While he could be blunt with Vraebel, dealing with Calhoun was a bit trickier. The legendary engineer would bite if prodded the wrong way and Simpson knew it.

After he finished composing the two emails, he read each aloud ensuring they both said the same thing. When he was certain he was happy with the words, he clicked send on each email.

Simpson leaned back in his chair and clasped his hands behind his head. Sigler's raw report stared at him from the left side of the screen. The right side was the redacted version they'd forwarded to the testing facility.

He looked at the clock, saw it was nearly 1030, and sighed. He'd call Mike Beaudry over at HAL and make sure the testing department had the report. Maybe he'd even invite Beaudry out for lunch. Anything to make sure HAL did their best, fastest work on the incoming barrel. The shareholders had to know PPE was sitting on a goldmine. And HAL would prove it.

Simpson smiled to himself. Rise in stock price? Bonuses? Everyone riding the tide and making money? That's what they needed. Now he just needed HAL to put the final pieces together. By next week, Simpson, PPE Vice President of Drilling Operations, would be richer than he ever imagined possible.

* * *

The phone rang. Mike Beaudry stared at it until the caller ID lit up. He rolled his eyes, reached out, and picked up the black receiver. "This is Mike," he said.

"It's Simpson."

"Of course it is." Mike grinned. "And I'll bet you're calling to check up on us."

The receiver filled with laughter. Simpson was a drinker and a smoker and his gravelly voice was a stark contrast to his high-pitched belly-laugh. Mike couldn't help but smile.

"Well, yes," Simpson said. "Wanted to make sure y'all got the report and are ready."

"We did. And yeah, Cheevers is taking lead on it, as requested. They're going to work the sample all weekend. As long as it takes."

"I'm sure they'll do a fine job," Simpson said. "I talked to the CEO and he's green-lit a bonus on top of what we're paying if it's done by Sunday morning."

Mike blinked. "A bonus?"

"Call it goodwill money, Mike. I know you take care of your people and I know they're damned good at what they do. We just wanted to provide a little more incentive."

"Okay," Mike said. "I'm not going to ask about numbers. But thank you for the offer."

"You're welcome. You'll be there all weekend too?"

Mike sighed. "As always. If my people are working overtime, I'm working overtime. That's the deal."

"Not sure how you do that."

Mike laughed. "We're trying to grow the company. It takes what it takes. Call it my lack of a life."

"To that end, you available for lunch today? We could snort a shot or two."

He shook his head. "No can do. Too much work. We're still trying to get the new building online. And I have to spend the day yelling at the construction company. Not to mention getting my office ready to move."

"Okay. Rain check?"

"Definitely."

"The barrel should arrive early afternoon. By then *Leaguer* should be preparing to drill the second well. So the faster we get—"

"I get it. If we have the results fast, then you can bring up more samples, get more analysis, and start setting revenue projections."

"You know me all too well," Simpson said. "I'm glad you understand."

"I do. I'll be in touch if we have any questions."

"All right, Mike. Good talking to you."

"And you. Bye."

"Adios."

The phone went dead. Mike replaced the receiver and stared up at the ceiling. *Bonus? No one ever pays a damned bonus on top of a hot-shot. That's crazy.*

But money was money. He'd do his best to make sure they made the timeline. Mike tapped his fingers on the desk and then hit a button. The speakerphone sprang to life and immediately rang. Once.

"What's up, Mike?"

"We need to have a quick meeting."

"Okay. I'll be there in a second."

The line dropped. Mike heaved a sigh and swiveled his chair. Beyond the windows, the freeway stretched to infinity. Lines of cars sped through Pasadena on their way to Houston proper or points further south. Like most of his employees, he didn't live in Pasadena itself. It was just close enough to make the commute easy and far enough away from certain zoning restrictions to allow HAL to handle volatile chemicals.

With their new technologies, rigorous testing methodology, and the painstakingly chosen scientific team, HAL (Houston Analytical Laboratories, Inc.) was the most advanced testing facility in existence. Companies from all over the world sent their samples to HAL and the company was growing faster than anyone had dreamed.

Hence the new building. Back in the days before Mike took over and turned it into a world renowned lab, the company had quietly prospered with only two labs. The original building was old, dilapidated, and on the cusp of falling apart. Maintenance costs, fire inspections, permits…all of it was a hindrance. And the computer systems? The old building could barely handle the power necessary to keep the servers and equipment up and running.

But the new building was taking forever. Too many dips in the economy. Too many stalls on the labor front. But at least they finally had the new NOC up and running. Or rather, they would once Chuckles, their head of network operations, pronounced the facilities good to go. It would still be a few months before the new labs were ready. But Mike and the executive staff would begin moving to the third floor of the new building in the next two weeks. He hoped.

For now, though, the skybridge between the two buildings was finished. He could walk down to floor two and easily check on the progress of the new building without having to go outside. The old labs would continue to serve their clients until the new ones were ready. After that, they could get rid of the nightshift and have six labs running simultaneously. He was already vetting a new crop of petrol-chemists and bio-chemists to grow the staff. But Cheevers' team would be the first to move to the new building. He wished it was available for this PPE job. Would make life so much easier instead of having to manage the new building construction, his scientists working on the weekend, and the possible power outages.

Tapping at the door. Mike turned from the window. "Come on in."

The door swung open and Darren Strange walked in. The man was impeccably dressed in chinos and a black HAL dress shirt. His clean-shaven face glowed beneath the lights.

"What's up, boss?"

Mike snickered and pointed to the tablet in Darren's hand. "Have a seat. We need to discuss this weekend."

Darren sat down on the other side of the desk. He smoothed a possible wrinkle in his shirt and stared attentively with a smile on his face.

Darren. Always prompt. Always preened. Always ready to help. Mike didn't know how he'd run the place without him.

"PPE's barrel should be here tomorrow afternoon."

Darren tapped his fingers on his tablet. His eyes barely flitted from Mike's.

"We're ready for it," Darren said. "I already scheduled a meeting for you and Kate to go over the particulars later this afternoon."

"Good."

Darren swiped the tablet and brought up a document. "I've also made sure we have food coming for dinner, sandwiches for snacking, and a catered breakfast."

"So what exactly is my job?"

"Your job," Darren said, "is to keep us all employed."

Mike laughed. "Y'all do that yourselves. Hardly need help from me for that."

Darren waved a hand. "Now, what else do I need to know? What are you worried about?"

Mike shrugged. "Simpson just called me."

Darren groaned. "You know, you should never have given that man a direct number."

"True," Mike laughed. "But he is a friend."

"And a pain in the ass."

"And a pain in the ass," Mike echoed. "But Mr. PITA is offering HAL some extra money if we get this done by Sunday."

Darren raised an eyebrow and then laid the tablet on his lap. "That sounds interesting. Did he say the amount?"

"No. Thought it might be impolite to ask."

"Of course."

"But, knowing Simpson," Mike said, "it will be substantial. Would be nice to put a little extra in the Christmas bonus pool."

Darren smiled. "I'm sure the scientists would enjoy that."

"And Chuckles' team. That man has been working nonstop for weeks now on the new NOC. He says it could even be ready tomorrow."

"Yes," Darren giggled. "Every time I go to the new building to check up on things, he's in there fretting over cabling and power connections." Darren shook his head. "He's almost as bad as you are."

"Almost. So what can we do to make sure this weekend goes smoothly?"

Darren lifted up the tablet again. "I've scheduled their breaks. The mother's room is ready in case someone needs a power nap and they don't want to use their office. And, as I said, I have plenty of food and drink."

"Coffee?"

"Of course," Darren said. "Jay would cease to function without coffee."

"All right. Sounds like you have everything handled."

"But you're going to stay here with us anyway."

Mike said, "I'll work on packing my office, doing a bit of reading, and maybe take a few cat naps."

"Uh-huh." Darren looked expectantly at his boss. A moment passed. Darren finally spoke. "Is there anything else?"

"What time is my meeting with Kate?"

"In two hours. I think you should probably send her team home a bit early."

Mike nodded. "I think you're right. Okay. Anything that needs my attention?"

Darren rolled his eyes. "Only the construction reports you keep obsessing over."

"Right." He nodded to himself and slid his fingers across the trackpad. His monitors came to life. "I think I'm going to eat in. Too much to do."

"Okay, boss. Let me know what you want for lunch and I'll make it happen."

"Of course you will," Mike said. "Now, get out of here. Let the old man get some work done."

Darren stood, smoothed his shirt again, and walked back out of the office. He closed it behind him so gently that Mike barely heard the button catch.

* * *

As usual, the hall lights were harsh and garish. She walked down the hall to the stairwell. She passed the barely finished skybridge, nose wrinkling at the smell of fresh paint. The glass panes were still crisscrossed with tape and manufacturer stickers. Kate's laptop was beneath one arm. She barely felt its weight, but was all too aware of what Mike would want from her. Testing plans. Schedules. The usual.

He was a good executive, as far as those things went, but his lack of chemistry or biology education was terrifying. Running one of the premier chemical/bio testing labs should have required a damned PhD. But Mike Beaudry was one of those rare creatures that could look at facts, figures, personnel, etc., and somehow manage to make it work. Instead of pinching pennies and forcing the staff to do with the bare minimum, he was always willing to invest in new tech if it meant they could handle more work.

In addition, he rarely interfered with the scientific work. Except, of course, when it was a hot-shot job from a high-profile client. The impending delivery of the PPE sample certainly fit that bill.

A trio of construction workers were working on the other side of the skybridge. One of them held a slab of sheetrock and another ran the heavy drill to put in the screws. The third was already painting a finished section of wall with a base coat. The trio spoke Spanish and nothing else.

She opened the stairwell door and clomped up the stairs to the third floor. She looked forward to the day when HAL had elevators that actually worked. The new building wasn't ready for them yet. Maybe by second quarter. But that was a long way away. Until then, she and other employees had to put up with unreliable elevators, bad tasting water, and power outages. Not to mention the musty smell.

The insulation in the building was terrible. The stairwell was cold and moist. November weather had brought an unseasonable fall chill to Houston, accompanied by wind and outrageously high humidity.

The old building still had its ancient furnace and tons of air conditioning equipment to control the lab temperatures. It was always cold, but not like this. Kate wanted to rub her arms, but carrying the laptop made that impossible.

She swiped her badge in front of a glowing sensor. It beeped and then the door clicked. She readjusted the laptop, pulled open the door, and walked out onto the third floor.

Wooden-paneled walls shined beneath the fluorescents. Paintings hung from the wall every dozen feet or so. Mike was a fan of Dus. Some originals, as well as proofs and prints, stared at her as she walked toward the reception area.

She turned the corner. "Hey, Darren," Kate said.

The man behind the desk wore a black dress shirt with well-creased chinos. "Ah, Ms. Cheevers," Darren said. "Mike is waiting for you."

"Yes, I know," she said. "I looked in on the skybridge. It's kind of a mess."

Darren shrugged. He leaned forward and spoke quietly. "Between us girls," he said, "Michael is getting impatient with the workers. If he had his way, they'd be working all weekend too."

Kate rolled her eyes. "Considering how many months it took just to get the NOC done, I don't see how he thinks that's going to make things go any faster."

"Regardless," he sighed, "I had to cancel my date for tomorrow night. And I can't go to the big soiree." Darren pretended to sniff. "And I had a nice 70s, fire-red suit to wear. Ruffles and everything."

Kate laughed. "Oh, I want to see pictures!"

The droopy look on his face disappeared into a wide grin. "Oh, there will be pictures. I'll wear it for the pre-holiday holiday party. You're going to be there, right?"

"Of course," Kate said. "Assuming we don't get another hot-shot."

"Hot-shots." Darren thumped the desk with his knuckles. "You're working this weekend. Jay's working this weekend. Chuckles is working this weekend." He hissed through his teeth. "And I'm the one making sure you're all fed and watered."

Kate smiled. "What would we do without you?"

"Hopefully you'd get a boyfriend instead of being a fag-hag," Darren smiled.

"But you're so much fun to drink with."

"Of course I am," Darren said. "But at some point, dear, you need to get back on the proverbial horse."

She nodded. "If I ever get a night off, maybe I could."

"Your ex call in again?"

"Yup," Kate said. "And I can't wait to tell Maeve she's going to have to spend the weekend here."

"What an asshole," Darren growled. He ran his fingers through his greying hair. "What's the excuse this time?"

She grunted. "Work. But we both know what that means."

"New girlfriend?"

"That's my guess. We've been divorced more than two years and he's still dating strippers." Kate clucked her tongue. "How do you tell your daughter her father would rather get laid than spend the weekend with her?"

Darren shook his head. "No idea, darling. No idea." His computer dinged. Darren's eyes focused on the message on the screen. "Well, Michael knows you're here." He wrinkled his nose. "Guess you better go in."

"Okay," Kate said. "Sorry about your date."

"Thanks," he said. "Sorry about your weekend. This sucks."

"I just keeping thinking of the upcoming bonus. It's going to be a big one," she said with a grin.

Darren pointed to the wide door on the west wall. "Get in there."

"Yes, sir," she said with a mock salute.

Kate knocked on the heavy oak door. "Come in, Kate," Mike's muffled voice said.

She took a deep breath and swung open the door. Mike Beaudry's office was bright with white light. Instead of fluorescent tubes bathing his desk, two large halogen torches dispelled the darkness. Steel-colored mini-blinds hung down across the windows protecting the room from the sun's harsh afternoon glare. Mike was just fine without natural light.

He sat behind his desk. A large whiteboard hung from one of the walls. Jobs and schedules were marked on most of it. The far right side was clean of ink.

The words "PPE HOT-SHOT" glowed in large, red letters on the far left side. Below that was a scheduled arrival and due date for the report. Sunday. The barrel would arrive Friday afternoon and then the team would work through the nights to get it done. Kate choked off a sigh.

"Mike. What's up?" she asked.

His eyes flicked to the whiteboard. "Is that your crew? Is that everyone?"

She followed his gaze. Hollingsworth. Krieger. Cheevers. "Yup. That's us."

"Good," Mike said. "Neil's team will be in the bio-lab."

Kate blinked. "They have a hot-shot too?"

He growled. "No. They're still putting together that DNA study for the HMNS. For some damned reason, he can't seem to get ahead. And you know how his team is."

She smiled. "They work hard."

"When they work," Mike said.

"That's not quite fair, Mike, and you know it. The sequencers have been pretty finicky."

He rolled his eyes. "We spend all that money on their new equipment and they can't keep the damned things running more than a day before they hit a new bug in the software." He shook his head. "Next time, I'm making sure the support contract includes 24-7 on-site support."

"Right," Kate said. "Is that all you needed from me?"

He pointed to the chair across from him. Kate sat and placed her laptop on the desk. "I want to go over the tests for PPE. Simpson has been riding my ass for the past 48 hours making sure we're ready."

Kate hissed through her teeth. "Thought he was a friend of yours?"

Mike nodded. "Yeah. So imagine what a pain he'd be if he weren't."

She giggled. "One day, you're going to have to introduce us."

"Uh-huh," Mike said. "Considering his personality, I don't think that's such a good idea." He rapped a knuckle on the desk. "Show me."

She flipped open her laptop and initiated the wireless screen display. A projector whirred to life above Mike's desk. The white wall caddy-corner from the desk lit up with a spreadsheet.

Her mouse cursor turned into a large red dot. She moved it to the first entry and slid it down the column. "Normal tests. H_2S, moisture, sulfur content, the usual stuff."

"Timeline?"

She shrugged. "Depends on the sample, really. The report Shawna Sigler forwarded to us is, well, strange. The figures she came up with are a little off the charts. Shouldn't take very long for us to determine how far she's off. But if she's right," Kate licked her lips, "it might be a damned long night."

Mike frowned. "Why's that? I would think confirming them would be a good thing."

She pressed a key and the screen switched to a document filled with figures. She moved the red dot to the moisture content. "That really can't be right, Mike. And Simpson included in his email that if any of the figures are incorrect, he wants to know why they were incorrect. That might require us to do some deep digging."

Mike sighed. "Okay. So overtime." He shook his head. "Good thing we're charging the shit out of them so I can make this up to you."

"And we, um, appreciate that, boss."

"Of course you do. Go back to the tests."

She tapped a key and the spreadsheet reappeared.

"What's that 'light test'?"

"It's a strange one," she said. "We've been doing this for a long time, Mike, but I don't get that request too often. We've run it maybe four or five times in my entire career."

Mike's brows furrowed. "So what is it?"

"We bathe the sample in different spectrums of light. It shows the flow characteristics of the oil. Gives us some idea of how it will travel through the pipes over time, as well as through the reservoir. The pressure they cited, though, leads me to believe they'll have no problem. It's obviously not very viscous."

"Okay," Mike said. "And how long is that going to take?"

She shrugged. "A few hours. We have to find the right frequency. And every oil sample is different."

"Right. Goddamned snowflakes."

She grinned. "That's why they pay us the big bucks."

"Okay. You have everything you need?"

She nodded. "We've got it covered. Marie is going to start setting up the tests for us tomorrow afternoon and Jay and I are already calculating medians we expect."

Mike waved a hand. "Then you should go home. And I don't want to see you guys or hear from you until tomorrow afternoon. We should get a heads up as to when the sample will arrive. I'll make sure you get the call."

Kate closed her laptop and stood. "Darren said you and he will be here as usual?"

He nodded. "That's right. I'm going to help Darren bird dog you guys. This PPE contract is damned important and we can't afford any screw-ups. So if I need to bring you a kilo of coke to get you guys through it, I will."

She rolled her eyes. "I prefer meth."

"Or that," Mike said. "Now get out of here."

"Yes, boss," Kate said. She left him chuckling at his desk.

* * *

Cartoon music filled the office. Shoes off, Taz socks in full view, Jay Hollingsworth grinned at the tablet on the desk. He mimicked every word as Bugs Bunny and Daffy Duck argued about "wabbit season." When Elmer Fudd chimed in, Jay's voice flipped easily into the accent. Mel Blanc would have been proud.

He lifted the mug of tea and sipped. The computer screen was still dark. Jay sighed and tapped his fingers on the armrest. His system had been down for the last ten minutes. Reason? No clue.

A help desk message from his phone had resulted in an immediate response. But he knew damned well it would take the tech time to get off his lazy ass. Or it was possible, just possible, that Stevo was dealing with another issue. Jay smirked. Possible, but highly improbable.

The episode ended. "A bya-bya-bya-bya-that's all folks!" Jay echoed Porky Pig's sign off.

"Love to see a professional at work," Kate's voice said from the doorway.

Jay swiveled in his chair and pushed his glasses up on his nose. He gestured to the dark screen. "It's about all the work I can do right now." He sipped his tea. The liquid was lukewarm at best.

Kate smiled. "I take it you're waiting for Stevo?"

He nodded as his tablet's speakers belted out the Looney Tunes theme song. "If by waiting, you mean practicing my voice work, yes."

"Sounded good to me. Always does though."

"You're far too kind." He put his feet back on the floor and placed the mug on the desk. "So what's up, Doc?" he said in his Bugs voice.

"Mike said we should go home. The sample is arriving tomorrow afternoon. Wants to make sure we're fresh."

"And because the night crew doesn't have an assignment?" Jay asked.

She shrugged. "They finished their workload. Was an easy week."

"Until PPE's vaunted M2 barrel gets here," Jay said. "So they won't be joining us for the cluster fuck?"

Kate clucked her tongue. "I can call them in if we need a rest. But Mike would rather—"

"We handle it personally, yeah, I get it."

"Tough being a rockstar, isn't it?" Kate said.

"At least we're paid," he said. "PPE asked for us personally. So I guess that's something."

"Mike said something about a bonus, although I didn't tell you that."

Jay harrumphed. "At least we're getting paid," he said again. He tapped a finger on the desk. "Marie joining us?"

"Of course," Kate said.

Jay glanced at his mug with longing. Fresh hot tea sounded wonderful. But going home sounded even better. He slipped his feet into his closed-toe sandals. "Guess Stevo doesn't need me here to fix this piece of shit." He closed the tablet and cut off Yosemite Sam in mid-rant. "You have Maeve tonight?" he asked as he shoved the tablet into his satchel.

Kate nodded. "Yeah. Going to have her tomorrow night, too, unless I can find a sitter."

"What in tarnation?" Yosemite Sam's voice said.

"Exactly. I'll bet you can guess why."

"Shit," Jay shook his head. "Always knew that guy was an asshole."

"Wish someone had told me that before I married him." She looked up at the ceiling and sighed. "No, that's not true. Then I wouldn't have Maeve." Kate looked back at Jay. "I guess I came out ahead of the game."

A slow smile spread across Jay's face. "Probably the best way to look at it. Dare I ask the excuse?"

"New girlfriend."

Jay rolled his eyes. "And let me guess. You get to break the news. Again."

"Again," Kate said. "Come on, let's get out of here."

* * *

Rather than taking the elevator, Jay and Kate hiked down the stairwell. Laptop bags around their shoulders, the fabric straps groaned with the weight. Jay was quiet. Probably thinking about tomorrow's tests. Or maybe which Looney Tunes character he'd break out into next.

She sighed. Maeve was going to be pissed. Instead of getting time with her father, the girl was going to spend the weekend cooped up at HAL with no other children. Homework, video games, and the internet would pretty much be her world for at least 48 hours.

Maybe this would be a good thing for her. Time amongst the adults and a chance to see, really see, what her mother did for a living. It couldn't be that bad.

But she knew she could tell her daughter all the pluses until she was blue in the face. Maeve was going to reject them out of hand. She knew her daughter too well to imagine it going any other way.

They reached the bottom of the stairs. Kate swiped her badge across the reader. Without a card, you could exit the building, but not get back inside. The sensor beeped, the lock clicked, and she swung open the door.

The building didn't have many visitors. Mike, the CEO, met most of their clients offsite. The visitors they did have were escorted to the third floor by one of the executive team. Therefore Darren served as their receptionist and he was on floor 3.

The security desk was always helmed by at least one guard. Due to the sensitive nature of their work, HAL chose to hire security personnel as employees rather than employ a third party firm. It was simply easier that way.

As they rounded the corner, Kate saw Jakob Benjamin sitting at the desk. The twenty-something looked up and smiled at them.

"Done for the day?" He ran a hand through his curly, close-cropped hair.

Kate laughed. "For the day, not for the week."

Jakob nodded. "Yeah. I got the memo. I'll be manning things tomorrow night." He pointed at her. "Just. For. You."

She rolled her eyes. "Whatever. I'll have my daughter with me if you need some company."

He cocked an eyebrow. "How old is she?"

Jay cleared his throat. "Too young for you, horn dog."

"That's, um, not what I— I mean—"

Kate laughed. "He's messing with you. She's thirteen."

"Hmm," Jakob said. "She's going to be bored out of her mind. Unless you're planning on letting her blow stuff up in the chemistry lab."

"She'll be spending the weekend on the second floor. At least that's the plan for now. Unless I come up with a miracle." Kate tapped her foot. "Maybe you'll look in on her from time to time?"

He ran a hand down the front of his shirt. "Absolutely. I have to do rounds at night anyway. I can do that for you."

"Good." Kate looked at Jay. "Ready to beat the traffic?"

Jay scrunched up his face. "Darn'd tootin'."

"Okay, Yosemite Sam. Let's do this. See you, Jakob."

He waved a hand to them and went back to studying his computer terminal. She wondered exactly what he spent his time doing, but had always been too terrified to ask. As long as Mike didn't care, she shouldn't either.

She and Jay headed out of the doors and into the sunlight. A fast moving blanket of clouds left the world in twilight. "Shit. Big storm tomorrow?"

"Yup," Jay said. "Should make things fun."

"Right." Kate smiled at him. "Mike's going to page us with a delivery time."

He nodded. "Then I guess I'll see you tomorrow afternoon. If I can't nap tomorrow, I'll just come in and help Marie get ready."

"I figured."

"Until then, Madame," he said as Pepé Le Pew.

"Until then."

* * *

The new NOC. Chuckles flashed his badge at the black, rectangular sensor. A small green LED glowed above the panel. He grabbed the door handle and pulled. The heavy steel door swung open on silent hinges. The roar of air conditioning, blade fans, and power supplies slammed into his ear drums. He didn't flinch. Instead, he grinned.

Several pairs of full cover ear protection hung from the wall. Chuckles reached out and grabbed a pair. With his free hand, he pulled off his black flat-cap and placed it on the empty cart near the door. The thin strands of hair atop his head fluttered in the strong air flow. The roar died as he pulled on the ear protection.

The NOC. Servers. Network gear. Everything. Ten racks of blades, hundreds of terabytes of storage, and all the bandwidth the buildings would ever need. He walked down the row. The dim overheads slowly brightened. The construction company may have fucked up the rest of the building, but at least they got this one right. Exactly as he'd imagined.

Although the room wasn't yet networked to the new fiber backbone, he was able to control it from the piece of shit NOC in the other building. Not that it really qualified as a network operations center. It was more of a large closet with hellaciously loud machines, terrible cooling, and a network that could barely provide streaming speeds.

This was his baby. This room. These servers. All of this was his. Two years of planning. Two years of screaming at the CEO for the amount of money they needed. And two years of delays, promises, and vendor fuckery.

Chuckles nodded to each cabinet as he walked by. The storage appliances were lit up like a racing tree. Greens, yellows, but thankfully, no reds. Burn-in. He'd spend the past several days lovingly hooking up each piece of hardware with some help from Stevo. Now the racks of blades were all running an incredibly dense bio program. Neil's team had come up with this one to test their new DNA suite. It calculated mutation probabilities for the damned fruit fly genome. It was math he wasn't capable of comprehending and it didn't matter.

The virtual machines on each blade, 32 per blade, were tied together as a single, monstrous number-crunching unit. The CPU lights were pegged. An evil smile crossed his face. If they survived crunching the data through the weekend, he'd be happy enough to certify them as ready for action.

Which was good, because Neil's team was already chomping at the bit to use them for their DNA studies. The old servers in the other building were proving a little slow. Performing a single run on their molecular models was taking longer each time. When HAL first started offering the service, a single batch took more than eight hours. Now with all the data shared across 20 different Cassandra instances, batches took up to 24 hours. Basically, Neil was falling behind.

Chuckles petted the nearest cabinet, his skin tingling as it slid down the shining, black metal. "Tomorrow," he said in an accent somewhere between a Texas drawl and a New Jersey nasal grunt, "we'll see if you can handle some more load."

He turned his back on the cabinet and headed back toward the heavy NOC door. The hearing protection was excellent at muffling the server fans' jet-engine decibels and the crackling and crunching of spinning drives, but they were incapable of damping down the heavy vibrations of all those machines running in a tight space.

He was still grinning when he closed the server room door and replaced the hearing protection on its peg. He placed his cap back on his head, blew out a sigh, and walked back into the hallway. He knew the NOC lights would turn off in a few minutes. Once the motion detectors noticed stillness in the room, they automatically killed the lights to leave the servers doing their work in complete darkness, save for their blinking LED status lights.

His pocket vibrated. Chuckles reached into his jeans pocket and pulled out the phone. Five new alerts. "Fucking piece of shit," he said and walked back toward the skybridge. The old NOC was still the primary and still his problem child. He looked forward to pulling all of those old machines out into the loading dock and beating the ever loving shit out of them with a sledgehammer. Until then, he'd have to keep the damned system held together with chewing gum and baling wire. The phrase, one of his father's favorites, bounced around in his head. Face expressionless, Chuckles chuckled. If anyone had been in the hall, they would have thought him insane.

CHAPTER TWO

Bugs Bunny was getting the best of Daffy Duck. It was the episode with the abominable snowman. One of Jay's favorites.

He reclined in the chair and put his black sneakers up on the desk. Jay loosed a yawn and closed his eyes. As Bugs talked to the snowman, he spoke every line in tandem. Mel Blanc might have voiced the cartoon more than half a century ago, but Jay voiced it now. And dammit if his Bugs and Daffy wasn't spot on. Maybe even better than Mel's.

He knew every word, every nuance, every slight lilt or fall of the characters' speech. His wife had called him a mimic, but that was the wrong word. Jay didn't mimic; he recreated voices and sounds. And he constantly experimented. He heard the words in his head before he voiced them and his vocal cords followed suit. It wasn't particularly difficult.

Children, like Kate's daughter Maeve, always smiled when he used one of his voices. Didn't matter if it was Bugs, Scooby, or any one of the other hundred voices that weren't his. He could swing his voice from a guttural baritone to a ridiculously helium pitch.

The abominable snowman was melting on screen. Jay opened his eyes and grinned. When he was a kid, this was his favorite of the Bugs cartoons. It was still his favorite.

Speaking of Maeve, she and Kate would arrive soon. PPE's sample would too. Jay pulled his feet off the desk and paused the video player. He sipped from his large Taz mug and grimaced. The coffee was lukewarm. And that was being kind. He stared down into the brown liquid. Yup, time to throw it out and make a fresh carafe. It was going to be a long damned night.

He reached for the mouse and clicked open the PPE requisition document. The standard list of tests scrolled by. However, there was one oddity. "Light test?" he said to the room.

It wasn't the strangest thing he'd seen on a requisition. Offshore drilling often led to the odd test. When a company drilled an exploration well in thousands of feet of water, they wanted to run every test they could. PPE wasn't the first to drill in over 30k feet of water, but they were the company everyone was watching. The more test results they had, the more they could lie to the stockholders about what they'd found. Well, that was unkind. Not all assay releases were lies. Just most of them.

Every employee at HAL signed non-disclosure agreements. It didn't matter if you were the chief scientist or a janitor. The lawyers insisted on it. So did the industry itself. No one wanted their secrets getting out into the world. Not that it helped much.

Industrial espionage was rife within the oil industry. Offshore, onshore, didn't matter. The larger the possible find, the more interest by competitors. If a licensed area showed promise to one company, it was a safe bet others would try and muscle in as close to the find as possible. It was all a crap shoot, of course; one company could find a goldmine in one well and nothing but dead holes just a few hundred meters away.

PPE was exploring a newly discovered trench called M2. It wasn't actually "newly discovered," but that's how they were marketing it. It had been found over 2 years ago, but PPE hadn't gotten their act together until recently. The sample was from their first exploratory well. Jay knew all eyes would be on the lab now. PPE was paying a small ransom to get fast answers. He knew why, too.

Stockholders have little patience. They have even less foresight. If a company spends a billion dollars on licensing fees and the creation of a new rig, they want to see oil flowing. They want to hear how a production rig is going to be sent out immediately to drill, baby, drill. Only the black gold assuages their need for instant gratification. And corporate executives can only make so many "forward-looking" statements before The Street calls bullshit.

Jay watched the industry like a hawk. Didn't matter if it was something as cataclysmic as Shell restating the value of their reserves in Saudi, or Schlumberger inventing a new tool. The news mattered. It directly related to HAL's success.

One day, he'd actually want to retire. Maybe set himself up in Alaska at a fishing resort. Become a guide and fish the hell out of sockeye. Then in winter, he could come back to Houston to hide from the brutal cold. Jay smiled.

He rose from his chair, grabbed the mug, and headed toward the break room. Time to make more coffee. Time to prep the tests PPE had asked for. And more importantly, time to see what magic Marie had done.

Marie was his and Kate's assistant. She was only three years out of her PhD degree, but she was good. Not great, but good. She'd learn. Jay was sure that by the time he and Kate retired, Marie would be able to run the lab by herself.

He headed out of his office into the brightly lit, sterile hallway. Jay yawned. His clipped footsteps echoed off the tiled walls. HAL felt more like a morgue or hospital than a chem-lab. At least that's how Jay had always seen it. The new building would be better, but it was another few months before the company could relocate most of the staff.

HAL owned two buildings. The first, the one they presently staffed, was built to handle both biological samples as well as chemical. On the biological side, HAL had never handled anything virulent or inherently dangerous; the bio-side primarily focused on mineral and soil samples.

Once offshore drilling began in earnest, the company reorganized. The last decade had been a bonanza in terms of petrochemical analysis. Requisitions for oil assays had pushed HAL to run a 24 hour, five day a week business. But their building was busting at the seams.

The executives bought the nearby lots and started construction on a new, larger, more modern building. The recession and subsequent bankruptcy of several building contractors had put the schedule into hellish delay. So every day, the employees of HAL had to look at the mostly-built hulk of the new building while heading into their familiar, run-down home.

Jay entered the break room and sniffed the air. The ghostly scent of ground beans filled his nostrils. He smiled and headed to the coffee maker. Both carafes were empty. He knew that—he'd emptied both of them. But, being a bastard, he hadn't bothered refilling either. Since it was late afternoon, there was little need. Until now.

He pulled out the basket, popped in a fresh filter, and shook in the grounds. He placed one of the carafes below and punched the button. Lights blinked, water steamed, and Jay was in heaven.

When you spent most of your workdays around volatile chemicals, you learned to appreciate certain smells. The chemists wore masks and protective clothing when on the job, but that didn't mean you still didn't get the acerbic stench of chemicals up your nose. Especially if you were dealing with crude.

Sulfur, acetone, benzene, you name it, crude could have it. As bad as the oil might stink, some of the reagents used for testing were worse. Spend all day in that olfactory hell, and you came to appreciate the little things. For Jay, that was definitely coffee.

Light test. Right. He pulled his cell from his pocket and messaged Marie. *You got the test list?*

A few seconds later, Marie responded in the affirmative. Jay nodded to himself and pocketed the phone. The coffee was ready. He emptied his mug, washed out the crap, and refilled it. With a fresh 16 ounces of black, he left the break room and headed down the hall.

The stairwell was three flights of concrete and a steel railing. He took the steps to the lower level with care. The building had an elevator for the disabled and the just plain lazy, but he never used it. Jay glanced at the small glass windows high on the wall. Wan sunlight filtered through them. In no time at all, the sun would set and night would settle in.

Jay reached the fire door and waved his badge in front of the reader. The heavy steel door clicked. He pulled on the handle and walked into the first floor hallway.

The labs were located at the other end of the building. That way if there was some kind of fire or chemical leak, those in the offices on the second floor wouldn't be affected. Jay clomped down the hallway until he reached the entryway to the two labs. The phrase "authorized personnel only" was etched into the glass door. He flashed his badge in front of the card reader. The glass slid aside and he walked through.

Two metal doors stood on either side of the hallway. Jay sipped from the mug and then placed a hand on the fingerprint scanner. The scanner beeped as it took a photo of his fingers. He sighed and waited the requisite five seconds before the scanner beeped again and a green light appeared on the wall. Using his free hand, he pulled on the door handle.

The door swung open to the side and he walked into a small, glass walled room that faced the actual lab. It was a changing area as well as for brief breaks between long-running tests. Jay took another sip of coffee and let his nose linger over the cup. The steaming mug helped blot out the palpable scent of solvents and crude.

Jay put his coffee on the credenza. He eyed the row of lab coats hanging from metal hooks. Thursday night's crew hadn't had theirs cleaned yet. No wonder the place stank.

A sign on the wall said "NO FOOD OR DRINK." Jay wrinkled his nose at it and scanned the equipment cubbies. Masks. Check. Booties for footies? Check. Gloves? Check. Marie had no doubt already been through the checklist already. She was meticulous, even if she lacked the confidence to realize it.

He looked out into the lab. The floor tiles were stained with every color of the rainbow. No matter how many times they scrubbed it, the caustic chemicals had permanently marked them. The new building, thirty years newer than this one, would have stain-proof tiles and a much friendlier cleaning regimen. At HAL, the chemists were responsible for everything in the lab, including the "janitorial" side. Bringing in custodial staff was a security no-no.

Marie had prepped the area. Jay went through the tests in his mind. X-ray machine was ready. Slides were ready. Fluoroscope was clean. And in the back was the equipment for the light test. He pulled his phone out and checked the time. Maeve and Kate should be in the parking lot. He clucked his tongue, picked up his mug, and headed back out through the security doors.

* * *

The lab was completely empty, as she knew it would be. Marie's lab coat fluttered as she walked from station to station. She loaded the magnetic clipboards hanging from the steel tables with the testing parameters. Each station was for a different test. Once the barrel arrived, she, Kate, and Jay would start as many of the tests as possible. Especially the long running ones. While those proceeded, the team could run some of the short-duration examinations and then hurry up and wait.

The rush jobs were the worst. Marie had canceled her weekend for the M2 hot-shot. Not that she'd had much of a weekend planned anyway.

Alcos had once sent five barrels of oil from five different drill sites and demanded a 72-hour turn around. That was an all hands on deck situation. No one went home. No one left the building. Meals were ordered in. They slept on cots on the first floor near the labs. HAL smelled like a zoo for a week. But they'd finished the job in less than 48 hours. For that, HAL had been paid a LOT of money. And the execs were smart enough to pass on the good fortune.

There were other labs to work in. Her PhD wasn't even three

years old, but she could get a job almost anywhere. Kate and Jay were fantastic, if tough, mentors and the entire industry knew it. So why stay at HAL? Simple. She loved it.

Plus, Kate and Jay were good people. Despite how much she hated Jay's constant supervision, she learned something new from the man every day. It could be something as small as how he worked a pipette, drizzling the oil in a solution, or something as important as clearing up analysis anomalies. Jay knew what he was doing. And Marie wanted to know everything Jay could teach her.

With the stations ready to go, she started checking the equipment. For once, the night crew had done a good job of cleaning up after themselves. They usually left the lab somewhat clean, but far from spic and span. More than once, she, Jay, and Kate had had to clean equipment before beginning their daily runs.

Marie examined each of the analyzers. The digital readouts informed her the night crew had even run calibration tests before leaving. She smiled. When Kate's team got the call for a hot-shot, everyone pulled together. Yet another thing she loved about working at HAL.

She sat at one of the work stations and pulled up reports from the previous night's work. The night crew had been running tests on some oil captured from one of the seemingly million fracking operations in North Dakota. She wrinkled her nose as she went through the report. H_2S levels? Off the scale. Gravity? The same as absolute sludge. Refining it would be expensive. And given the price of oil was sure to drop to $40 per barrel by year's end, said fracking operation should just close up shop or they were going to lose their ass.

Marie closed the report and sighed. She pulled out her phone and checked for notifications. Nothing. Her phone had dinged nearly an hour ago that the M2 PPE sample was en route. The driver was supposed to call or text the moment he arrived. But at 1630 on a Friday afternoon, he was no doubt caught in hellish traffic.

The weather app on her phone said the polar cold front was stalled out near Austin, but was expected to drift east and south by midnight. Marie clucked her tongue. November in the Houston area rarely brought cold weather, but it often brought big storms. Wind, rain, hail, and fifty degree temperatures. Perfect, she thought. All we need is the power to go out too.

Marie's phone buzzed in her hand. A text message appeared. "Five minutes out" it read. She recognized the phone number as the courier's. She blew a sigh between her teeth. The lab was cold. At least getting out on the deck would warm her up for a few minutes. She cast a glance at the hand truck in the lab's west corner. Hopefully, she wouldn't need that old thing.

She walked to the side door and flashed her card at the card reader. A green LED lit and the lock banged in the slot. She swiveled the handle and walked into a wide, dimly lit hallway. Her footsteps echoed off the concrete walls as she made her way to the loading dock.

One of the few things HAL had done right when they designed the building was making it easy for the labs to take possession of potentially hazardous chemicals. Instead of the labs connecting directly to the outside, chemical shipments were unloaded at the dock and then moved into a containment area. Marie hoped the courier brought his own hand truck and knew how to use it. Otherwise, she might have to get some help.

The wide hallway led her to a large sliding door. Instead of opening it, however, she went left to the door marked with a glowing neon red "Exit" sign. She flashed her card to disable the alarm and then pushed on the solid bar. The door opened on to the thick, concrete dock.

The smell of exhaust and cigarette smoke stung her nostrils. Chuckles stood in the center of the concrete platform, a Pall Mall dangling from the side of his mouth. He glanced at her and nodded.

Marie's face flushed. "Hello, Stephen."

The corners of his mouth twitched upward. He exhaled a cloud of smoke and tipped his cap. "And how are you, Ms. Krieger?"

She swallowed hard and tried to say something, but her throat locked up. His subtle grin faded into a look of concern. She waved a hand and cleared her throat. "I'm ready for the hellish weekend, I guess."

"You getting a cold?" Chuckles' face was stony once again.

Marie shook her head. "No. Just— Been a long day."

"Hope not," he said. "You're going to be up for a long time."

She nodded. "How goes the new building setup?"

"Good. With any luck, we might be sharing the new network by next week. If," he said, "I can get some help from Stevo. And maybe Mark." Chuckles shook his head. "Goddamned lazy bastards." He blew smoke out of his nostrils, rolled his eyes, and then shrugged. "Sorry. My mouth tends to forget when a lady's present."

"It's okay. I'm really not easily offended."

The corners of Chuckles' mouth twitched again. "Still ain't right," he said.

"So you're going to be here all weekend too?"

He nodded. "Unless we somehow manage a miracle." Chuckles dragged again on the cigarette, his nicotine-stained fingers seeming to glow in the wan sunlight. A slight gust rushed by and obliterated the tendrils of smoke flowing out of his nostrils. "I imagine we'll run into one another in the break room. I do plan on taking breaks occasionally."

"Well that's—" The roar of a labored diesel engine with a less than adequate muffler split the relative silence. They both turned. A large panel truck bounced up and down as it navigated the speed bumps and uneven pavement. "Finally," Marie said under her breath.

The truck, its sides a mix of faded yellow paint and the nearly imperceptible remains of a company logo, turned around until its rear faced the concrete dock. A belch of black smoke erupted from the tailpipe. Marie wrinkled her nose at the exhaust's stench. The grind of old gears slipping into reverse echoed off the buildings. The truck paused, and then began moving backwards to the dock.

Marie and Chuckles watched in silence as the vehicle slowly

reversed until its rear nearly kissed the waist high concrete wall. The gears ground again and then the engine shut off. She felt Chuckles looking at her, but didn't turn. She knew he did that from time to time and it always made her smile.

"This your barrel?" he asked.

"Think so." Marie watched the driver open the cab door and step down to the broken and cracked concrete. He walked toward them, clipboard in hand. Streaks of sweat riddled his grey uniform. His eyes drifted upward to regard Marie and Chuckles. "Is this HAL?"

"Yeah," Chuckles said. "You got a delivery?"

Without answering, the man headed to the stairs and took them in a fast cadence. His feet hardly made a noise as he approached them. Marie glanced down at the heavy work boots. Despite the construction attire, the man moved with the grace of a predator.

When he was only a few feet away from her, he stopped. Chuckles had already moved closer to Marie. She was barely aware of his presence, but somehow felt better for it.

"I have a delivery for Kate Cheevers of HAL," the man said without glancing at the clipboard.

Marie tried to smile, but feared it looked more like a grimace. "She's not here yet. But I'm on her team."

The man grunted. "May I see some company ID?" Chuckles moved close enough to Marie to nearly touch her shoulder. "Ma'am?" he asked.

Marie struggled with the badge clipped to her white, spotless lab coat. Her finger finally found the fastener and lifted up the badge. It clicked as it slid off the tab and into her hand. She held it out toward the driver.

He plucked it from her fingers and held it nearly at arm's length. He squinted at the letters. Without a pause, he pulled the pen from the clipboard. The pen scratched the paper with a barely audible sound. When he was finished, he offered it back to her without looking up. His eyes focused on Chuckles.

"Sir?" the driver said.

Chuckles blew out another puff of smoke and pulled his badge from his shirt pocket. "After I show you mine, you'll show me yours." The words came out in a measured growl.

The driver's lips twitched into a smile. "Of course, sir. No need to get upset."

"Just want to see what you wrote and know you ain't a grifter," Chuckles said.

The driver laughed. "Grifter? I haven't heard that word in a long, long time." He took the card from Chuckles and wrote while his eyes scanned the letters and numbers. "You from back east then?"

Chuckles nodded. "Got here as fast I could, though."

"I know the feeling." The driver handed back the security card and turned the clipboard around so they could read it. Marie's eyes just saw lines of numbers and their names. It was all written on the "receiver" lines of the freight bill. "Okay?"

"Okay," Chuckles said. "ID?"

The driver grunted and pulled his own badge from his shirt. He handed it to Chuckles. Marie watched the man's eyes instead of the card. The driver looked tired, hot, and amused. But the uniform also didn't look like it was his. The fit around the arms and the shoulders was wrong. She shook her head. Paranoia. Hardly her best trait.

Chuckles handed back the card. The driver took it and put it back in the plastic protector on his shirt pocket. "Everything good?" he asked.

Chuckles nodded with a grunt. "Guess so."

"Good," the driver said. He stepped back down the stairs, placed the clipboard back in the cab, and then headed toward the rear door. He produced a key from his pocket and unlocked the heavy padlock. Chuckles and Marie shared a glance. The driver raised the door.

The remaining sunlight drove away the shadows revealing an orange barrel of oil secured within a rope nest. "Well," Chuckles said, "doesn't look like it moved much."

The driver ignored the comment, walked back up onto the

platform and headed inside. His dexterous fingers quickly undid the knots and released the barrel from its rope prison. Without saying a word, he unhooked the hand truck from its resting place and moved it to the barrel. The arms slid into place and the truck's forks lifted the barrel a few inches off the ground.

He moved the hand truck out onto the platform. Marie studied the wrapping on the top of the barrel. The stress strips were in place and untouched. If someone had tampered with the barrel, the strips would have flooded the plastic with red paint.

"Now," the driver said while he rubbed his shirt sleeve against the beads of sweat on his forehead, "if you would lead me to the destination?"

Marie exchanged a glance with Chuckles. "Um, only authorized personnel are—"

"Allowed in the lab. Yeah, I know." The driver pulled a piece of paper from his pocket and offered it to her. "Is that your CEO's signature?"

Marie read the document and blinked. "Yes. It is."

"What's it say?" Chuckles asked.

She locked eyes with the driver. "We're to escort him to the lab. HAL has agreed to it." She handed back the paper and sighed. "Follow me."

Marie walked down the platform to the delivery door. She touched her card to the reader and the heavy sliding door banged as the bolt slid back. She touched the green button on the wall and the door slid up with an echoing metal creak.

Strong fluorescent lights burst to life and dispelled the darkness. The hand truck squealed slightly as the driver followed her inside. Chuckles tossed away the filter of his cigarette. The breeze made it waver in the air before it landed in the butt bucket.

She led him to the west wall. A cylindrical stand sat beneath a number of rubber hoses. The driver stopped pulling the hand truck and stared up at the ceiling. "Doesn't oil eat through rubber and plastic?"

Marie nodded. "Yup. The rubber is just covering Pyrex tubes. Put the oil drum there please." She pointed at the stand.

The driver shrugged and pushed the hand truck to the metal cradle. He pressed a lever on the mechanized dolly and the forks lifted the barrel another two inches. When he was sure it was up high enough, he pushed the oil drum to the stand.

"There you go," Marie said. "Go ahead and lower it. I'll take care of the rest."

The driver pressed the release and the barrel slid into the cradle with a metallic clang. The oil inside the barrel sloshed against the metal. Something inside banged. Marie leaped back from the barrel and traded stares with the driver. "What was that?"

The driver shrugged. "Did that when I put it in the truck too."

Marie looked back at the barrel. "You're sure that's what came from the rig?"

He nodded. "Absolutely. I triple checked the paperwork and the serial numbers. This is what Leaguer sent you."

A prickle of gooseflesh covered her skin. The orange barrel didn't look so innocuous now. Something about it frightened her, but she couldn't put her finger on it.

"You done, sir?" Chuckles asked from behind them.

Marie blew a surprised sigh out of her mouth. "Yeah." She turned around and regarded the two men. "We're done."

The driver pulled the hand truck away from the barrel stand. "I'll see myself out. Sir. Ma'am." The driver pushed the cart back out to the dock. Chuckles followed until he was outside the rolling door. He pressed a red button and the door unfolded. It hit the concrete floor with a bang.

"Fucking douchebag," Chuckles muttered. He turned away from the door and blinked at Marie. "You okay?"

She rubbed her hands against her bare forearms. "Yeah," she lied. "That was weird."

Chuckles nodded. "Yeah. Think maybe PPE takes their security a bit too far."

"Maybe. Or that Simpson guy is certifiable."

"Ain't all executives sociopaths?" he said.

Marie stared at him and then started laughing. Chuckles' mouth twitched. "You know, you are the only man that can make me laugh when I feel like crying."

He raised an eyebrow. "Why you feel like crying?"

"Guy scared the hell out of me," she said. "Not sure what I would have done if you hadn't been here."

Chuckles' cheeks flushed. "Guess I'm glad I was here then."

"Thank you." Marie fought the urge to step toward him. What she wanted to do was hug him. "Stephen?"

He raised his eyebrows and the corners of his mouth twitched. "Yes?"

"You really are a nice guy. And I hate your nickname."

Chuckles smiled. It showed off the missing molar on his left side and his nicotine-stained teeth. On another man, it might look like a sneer, but on Chuckles, it was the brightest smile she'd ever seen. He cleared his throat and pointed at the barrel. "You need any more help with that?"

She shook her head. "No. Thank you. The machine will pretty much do everything else."

He nodded. "Have to get back to the NOC."

"Right," she said. "Big network switchover this weekend."

"Yeah." His smile disappeared, lips curling back down into a thin line. "Ya'll going to be here all weekend."

She wasn't sure if it was a question or a statement. "I think that's the plan."

"Okay." Chuckles cracked his knuckles. "Guess I'll see you around supper time." He tipped his cap and headed back into the main hallway.

Marie watched him go and let out a long breath. The man was enigmatic. He wasn't cute or handsome. And she had no idea why she was attracted to him.

Yes, you do, a voice said in her mind. *He's always polite and only smiles for you.*

Grinning, Marie turned to the oil barrel. Her smile disappeared. That creeping feeling started at the bottom of her spine and quickly rose to her neck. She bit her lip and walked to the stand. She pulled on an L-shaped piece of metal and it swung outward to the stand.

The rubber-coated steel led up to the ceiling and a series of pipes. The bottom of the L had a steel cap attached to it. When it was just above the cap, she let it go, and stared at the plastic shrouding the barrel's top.

Oil. All the way from M2 halfway across the world. She pulled the tab on the wrapping and ripped it forward. The shroud parted and exposed the metal cap. She frowned. The steel was dented outward as if it had been hit by something from inside. More likely, a roughneck hit it with a tool before realizing it was upside down. Or maybe a wave had rocked the rig while they were capping the barrel. No telling.

She walked to the shelves beside the barrel stand. A cylinder with a handle jutting from one side sat on the middle shelf. She picked it up and placed it over the cap. Three quick turns of her fingers and the cylinder snapped around the cap. She pumped the handle until she heard the barrel's cap snap.

Marie slowly unscrewed the remover from around the cap, but didn't raise it up. The design, one of Jay's, was nearly flawless. Except for this part. The magnetic bottom of the remover held the top of the cap, but she had to lift it in order to expose the hole in the barrel. In order to lessen any chance of contamination, she had to move the suction end of the L and place it over the hole as quickly as possible.

In the past year, she'd done this dozens of times. It was routine. The hairs on the nape of her neck stood on end. Her fingers trembled as she reached and lowered the L just above the remover. She took in a deep breath, moved away from the device, and then slammed the L metal coupling over the open cap. Metal clanged and the barrel seemed to groan.

She blew out a hiss of air and tightened the pump connection. When it was as tight as she could get it, she walked back and placed the removal tool back on the shelf. Marie returned to the barrel with a torque wrench and tightened the metal pump gasket until the wrench clicked.

Finally, she said to herself. Marie walked to the wall behind the L. She checked the vacuum gauges. No warnings. Smiling, she pressed a green plastic button. The pump started. She listened as the liquid flowed up the metal tubing and into the Pyrex rat's maze in the ceiling. The tubes led over the wall and into the chemistry lab. The chemists would then use the instrumentation to distill the exact amounts they needed for the tests.

Marie started to walk away from the barrel and then stopped. She turned and faced the shelf. She'd dropped Jay's famous removal tool before removing the lid cap from the barrel. The strong fluorescent lights showed her the muted gleam of oil stained metal. She could leave it there with the piece of metal still in the receiver end. She could. Marie sighed and walked back to the shelves. Get it done right, Jay always said.

She picked up the removal tool and moved her thumb to hit the button for the release. Something gurgled in the barrel. She whirled around as the lid popped from the tool. A jagged edge from the pierced metal cut into her skin. Marie yelped and studied her hand. The edge of her palm had a tiny cut. A thin streamer of blood welled out. The barrel gurgled again. She looked back at it. It wasn't moving. Nothing was banging to get out. It was just oil.

That's when her palm caught fire. Her nerves sizzled and she cried out. Her fingers shook and she dropped the remover to the ground. The metal lid from the barrel's cap dinged as it hit the concrete floor. The scream welling up in her throat died as the sensation passed.

She panted and brushed away a tear. That was pain she'd never imagined possible. Her hand throbbed. Marie picked up the tool, placed it back on the shelf, and walked as fast as she could to the lab.

Two card swipes and she was at the emergency shower. She pulled the chain and put her hand beneath the cold water. The throbbing slowed and then disappeared. She turned off the shower and put her hand beneath the iodine dispenser. A couple of pumps and the brownish-yellow liquid covered her skin. She gently rubbed it into the tiny wound.

Marie stared at her hand. The skin was stained from the iodine. She'd have to clean it up before she put on a bandage. When she and the team started the tests, she made a mental note to wear a glove.

* * *

The Honda raced through the light traffic. Kate took another sip from her coffee. Her daughter sang along with some annoying pop song on the radio. She didn't know who it was and didn't care. When Maeve was in the car, the teenager insisted on controlling the audio. Meaning, of course, it always ended up on the top 40 station. Kate hated it. Give her some hard rock anytime instead of this dreck.

She skirted around an eighteen wheeler and drove a significant distance ahead until pulling back into the right lane. Houston traffic was always crazy. With the increase in oil deliveries from the fracking operations in west Texas to the refineries in Texas City, the interstates and highways were constantly packed with the tanker trucks. It was good for her company and good for business in general, but the rise in accidents across the state weren't. She knew it was only going to get worse too.

The blessed "beep beep" of the phone muted the radio. Maeve groaned. Kate smiled at her daughter and then hit a button on the steering wheel.

"Cheevers," she said.

The sound of Bugs Bunny berating Daffy Duck was barely audible over the car speakers. "You on your way?"

"Well, hello to you too, Jay," Kate grinned.

"Hey, Uncle Jay!" Maeve shouted.

The voice brightened. "Hello, Maeve. I understand you're staying with us tonight?"

"Not by choice!" the girl yelled.

"Hush," Kate said. Maeve shut her mouth and went back to her phone. "Yes, Jay, we're on our way. Has the sample arrived yet?"

"No," he said. "Should be here within the hour, though."

Kate nodded to herself. "Okay. We're about twenty minutes out."

"Great. I'll have the coffee ready. I assume you brought a sleeping bag for the little girl?"

"Not a little girl," Maeve said.

There was a pause. "Did you bring the young lady a sleeping bag?" Jay corrected himself.

"That's better," Maeve said.

"Yes, Jay. Even brought a pillow for her."

"All right. I'll see you in twenty."

The speakers beeped and then another cheesy pop song shattered the silence. Kate hit the volume button and dropped the noise a hair.

"I'm old enough to stay home by myself," Maeve said.

"We've been over this. You are not staying at home alone all night. And since your father couldn't be bothered to take you, and I couldn't find a sitter, you're stuck with me."

"Not his fault he had plans," Maeve said.

"Right." Kate wanted to tell her daughter that was bullshit. Maeve didn't know about her father's recent obsession with a stripper. Nor that said stripper hated kids. It was his weekend. But like the three before, he hadn't bothered to show up and only called at the last minute to say it was impossible. Maeve hadn't cried, but this was the third time in a row. After the job with PPE was finished, Kate planned on talking to her lawyer again. Her ex needed a reminder about his responsibilities. Or a good, swift kick in the ass.

He had no problems telling his daughter what a worthless mother she was. Fortunately, Maeve ignored her father's tirades and saw them for what they were. Kate wondered if that's why he didn't want to be around her anymore. Allegiances had always mattered to Harry Cheevers. If you weren't on his side all the time, you weren't worth his time.

Still, a daughter needed a father. And Harry needed to get his shit together for Maeve, if for no other reason.

"The good news is we have a good network connection," Kate said. "You can stream to your heart's content."

Maeve brushed a stray lock of hair from her forehead. "Yay," she said.

Kate glanced over and saw the frown. "Don't be so bratty. It's going to be fun."

"Right," Maeve said. "Because anyplace that stinks that bad is fun."

"You'll be in my office, Maeve. The lab is air tight. You won't smell a thing."

Maeve wrinkled her nose. "Except for when you guys take breaks."

Kate laughed. "Won't be too many of those tonight. This is a rush job."

"It's always a 'rush job' on the weekends. Why can't these people just wait?"

"Because," Kate said, "they can't. And they're paying a lot of money. Do you know what that means?"

"I don't care."

"It means," Kate continued, "I'll get a good bonus. And that, in turn, means more money for college."

"Mom? That's years away."

Kate sighed. "It'll be here before you know it."

She pulled on the turn signal and took the next exit. A white-lettered green sign proclaimed "Welcome to Pasadena." She'd seen it so many times, it didn't even register. She maneuvered the car to the far right lane, caught a green light, and headed up the street. Warehouses lined the south side. A few leafless trees were scattered on the easements. It was late November and fall had finally chased away the summer heat. The pines still had their needles and they swayed in the gulf breeze.

"Finally," Maeve said as Kate turned at the next intersection. "The stinky, ugly building of Houston Analytical Laboratories." She turned to look at her mother. "Incorporated."

Kate hissed through her teeth and pulled the car into a covered parking spot. She put the car in park and clicked off the ignition. "You ready?" she asked her daughter. Maeve stuck out her tongue. Kate put her index and middle fingers together and reached for it. Maeve flinched. "That'll teach you." Kate clicked the button for the doors. "Come on. Let's get started."

Maeve locked her phone, stuck it in her fleece pocket, and opened her door. A cool breeze filled the car. She groaned. "I miss summer."

"Whatever. Thanksgiving break and Christmas will cure all of that."

The teenager turned to her mom with a smile. "Only if I get a new console."

"Out," Kate said with a shake of her head.

She grabbed her purse and slid out the driver-side door. Maeve followed suit from the passenger side. Maeve's blonde locks fluttered in the wind. Kate watched her daughter pull the black and purple pack from the backseat and the bedroll. The girl struggled to close the door.

"I've got it," Kate said.

"Nope." Maeve put her foot against the door and pushed. It slammed loud enough to echo in the parking spot.

"Dammit, girl," Kate said.

Maeve's cheeks flushed. "Sorry, Mom."

"Uh-huh."

They made their way to the concrete walk leading to the main building. The parking lot was mostly empty. During the week, HAL was a 24-hour operation. The weekends? Dead. Dead. Dead. Unless, of course, there was a rush job. And PPE wanted their new find tested. The timing was shitty, but Kate was glad to have been asked for by name. She'd helped HAL become the best in the business. The executives knew it, too. Maybe next year they'd make her chief scientist.

When they reached the heavy glass door, Kate pulled her badge and swiped it across the scanner. An LED flashed green and the lock clicked loud enough to echo. She pulled open the door and gestured to Maeve. "Ready for your slumber party?"

"Whatever," the girl said and shuffled into the building.

Kate fought the urge to sigh and failed. She left the cool breeze behind her. The door closed and the heavy lock slapped shut.

* * *

The hallway was cold and Maeve was already complaining. "It's colder in here than it is outside!" Kate ignored her and kept walking toward the stairs. "Mom!"

Kate glanced at her daughter. "You screw your face up any more, your mouth will turn inside out."

Maeve heaved a petulant sigh. "Upstairs?"

"Yes, upstairs," Kate said. "And since you're carrying so much crap, let's use the elevator."

"Good. Because my arms are already tired," Maeve said.

The whoosh of an automated door filled the hallway. Kate looked back. Jay was walking out of the labs. Smile on his face, coffee cup in hand, Jay looked as if the day was fresh and new. "Shhh," Kate said to Maeve, "we have a stalker."

"I heard that," Jay called from down the hall. "Hold up, ladies." Kate and Maeve stopped as the older man walked to them. When he reached Maeve, he tousled her hair. She pretended to flinch. "Keep that up, young lady, and I won't offer to carry your bedroll." He held out a hand to Maeve. She grunted and handed the rolled up blankets to him. "There. See? I'm good for something."

"Thanks, Uncle Jay," Maeve's teeth flashed in a grin.

Jay met Kate's eyes. "You said something about an elevator?"

Kate nodded. "Yup. Let's go."

They headed down the long hallway to the bank of gleaming steel doors. Jay punched the up arrow. Machinery groaned behind the door. "One of these days, that thing's just going to fall down and end up in our so-called basement."

"Why do you think no one uses it unless they're carrying something?" She gestured to the bedroll in his hands. "Hopefully the new building will be better."

"You been over there lately?" he asked.

She shook her head. "Nope. I know the skybridge is sort of open, but that's about it."

"Skybridge. More like the Alaskan bridge to nowhere. I mean why the hell did they need to build that to connect two second floors? It's ludicrous."

Kate shrugged. "Guess the execs wanted to be able to travel between them. Of course, that would require them to renovate this piece of shit."

"Mommy said a bad word," Maeve sang.

"She did indeed," Jay said. The elevator doors groaned open. Jay gestured to the door with his coffee cup. "Ladies first."

Maeve mocked a curtsey and stepped into the car. The elevator walls were textured, but the once bright Mediterranean colors had long since faded. Kate stepped in and Jay followed behind.

She stabbed the button marked "2." Nothing happened. "Dammit," she said and pressed it hard. The button lit up, the elevator dinged, and the doors did…nothing. "Piece of—" A motor rumbled and the doors slowly closed. Kate shook her head. "Well, at least the lab is still in good shape."

Jay rolled his eyes. "Right. As soon as the floor caves in, it'll be in the same shape as the elevators."

"Mom?" Maeve asked. "Why is this place always falling apart?"

The car lurched as it began to ascend the forty or so feet to the second floor. "Because we're waiting on the new building. And they don't want to spend any more money on this one until that one is finished."

Maeve clucked her tongue. "I don't think you guys should come to work anymore. Not until they fix it."

"Right," Jay said. "Because I've always wanted to be homeless."

Kate smiled at her reflection in the gleaming steel. The custodial staff wasn't allowed in the labs, but they did their best to keep everything else looking as new as they could. Pointless effort, really. Clients seldom visited the lab and HAL's employees certainly didn't give a shit one way or the other. But at least it made it seem like they were working at a real company that wasn't on a shoe-string budget.

Like Jay said, the labs were tip-top. Any time a new piece of equipment came on the market that Kate or the other lead scientists wanted, they got it. If something broke, it was either repaired or replaced in a matter of hours. That went for the computers too. The admins were always on call, even on the weekends.

The elevator lurched again as it came to a stop. Another ding and the doors struggled open. Maeve hurried through them and into the hall. When she was far enough away for Kate to exit, she turned around and pointed at the elevator with her free hand. "I'm not using that thing again."

Kate laughed as Jay exited. "I think Uncle Jay agrees with you."

Jay shook his head. "Next time, kiddo, you use the stairs. Even if I'm on your back." Maeve ignored them and headed to the office hallway. Kate and Jay followed.

"The sample here yet?" Kate asked.

Jay sipped his cooling coffee. "Marie hasn't texted me yet. So I'm guessing no."

Kate frowned. "But you checked the lab?"

"Yup," he said. "And it looks about as good as it's going to."

They reached the closed door marked "Cheevers." Maeve swiveled the knob and opened it wide. Kate's office was spartan, except for the picture of Maeve hanging on the wall and the leather couch beneath it. An LED in the corner of her computer screen blinked. Kate dropped her purse on the desk. Maeve was on the couch and unzipping her pack.

"Little miss? Where would you like your bed?" Jay asked.

She stuck her tongue out at him and then grinned. "Just drop it by the couch." Jay did. "Thanks, Uncle Jay."

He bowed and then turned to Kate. "What do we do until the sample arrives?"

Kate pushed her mouse and the computer screen lit up. She typed in her password, ran her finger through the thumbprint scanner, and then waited. "I think we should figure out the test order." The screen flashed and then displayed her desktop. She checked her email. "Christ. Chuckles is performing a maintenance update?"

"Oh, crap," Jay said. He took a long draught from his giant mug. "When's he going to start that nonsense?"

"If you ever checked your email, you'd know." Kate nodded to herself. "He's got a 10 to 4. I guess he'll be burning the midnight oil right along with us."

Chuckles. The most unpleasant man on earth. He was HAL's system administrator. When something went wrong with the network, their internet access, or any of the machines, Chuckles was the man to fix it. But if he couldn't fix your desktop remotely, he crawled out of his cave and stumbled into your office like a bear awakened during hibernation. Irritable, always muttering under his breath, and prone to screaming profanity in his cave, Chuckles was hardly her favorite person.

"At least we don't have to worry about the systems crashing and having to call him out of bed," Jay said. He sipped his coffee and scowled at the mug. "Dammit. This thing never stays hot long enough."

Kate said dryly, "Probably because it's made of thick ceramic and has no top. The heat just escapes too rapidly."

"You know," Jay gestured with his cup, "I'm a scientist too."

She dropped her eyes back to the computer screen. Simpson, Vice President of PPE, had sent her an email. She double clicked it, read the text, and hissed through her teeth. "You know, I'll take their money, but not their abuse."

"Now what?" Jay asked. He walked around her desk and read the email. "That's not abuse," he said. "He simply wants to make sure we let him know when the sample gets here. When we've started testing. When we've finished. When the report's done. And updates every five minutes." He took another draught of coffee and grimaced. "All very diplomatic."

Kate looked over the monitor at Maeve. She had unpacked. A sparkly colored tablet was on the couch along with her phone and the bedroll. A math book lay open beside her and she had a notepad in her hands. "Maeve?"

Her daughter looked over. "Yes?"

"Make sure you get plenty of light. Don't want those eyes going bad."

"Yes, Mom." Maeve reached behind her and touched the edge of the lamp on the end table. A cone of bright, white light dispelled the shadows. Maeve blinked at the sudden brightness. "Sheesh, Mom. You got the sun in here now?"

Jay laughed. "My gift. Your mom doesn't get much natural light in here." He pointed to the window. "Kate's office has such a great view of the building next door that she's nearly always in shadow. Hence the light."

Maeve shrugged. "Whatever."

Kate shook her head. "Sorry, Jay. She's, um, at that wonderful age."

"Is that recognition I hear in your voice?" Jay asked.

She tapped her finger on the desk and returned her eyes to the screen. "Something like that." Kate pulled up the report requisition from PPE. "Light test," she said.

"Yeah. I thought that was odd too," Jay said. "I mean it's not like we haven't seen that before, but still. I guess they're pulling out all the stops with M2."

"Stockholders want a clean bill of health." She smiled at Jay. "Else there's going to be hell to pay."

"Considering all the bullshit going on in the industry, I'm surprised anyone's trusting anyone's word," Jay said.

She shrugged. "If we—"

Yosemite Sam's voice started yelling from Jay's pocket. He raised an eyebrow and pulled out his phone. His lips turned upward into a smile as he touched the phone screen and raised it to his ear. "Marie. Where you been all my life?" Jay's grin widened as he listened. "Okay. Come to the break room when you're ready." He pulled the phone from his ear, touched the screen, and then pocketed it. "It's here," he said.

***

Nothing better than fresh coffee, Jay thought. *Unless it's a 15-year-old Macallan Fine Oak.* He sipped from the huge Taz mug and turned as Marie entered the break room.

Maeve and Kate sat at the table. Maeve had a glass of water. Kate sipped from her own cup of coffee. Their heads turned to follow Jay's gaze.

Marie stood in the entryway. Jay pointed with his free hand. "What happened to your hand?"

She glanced down at the bandage wrapping her palm. A blush rose to her cheeks. "Had an accident with your cap puncher."

"Ah," Jay said. "Yeah. I need to rework the design on that. I've done it before too."

"Did it feel like fire under your skin?" Marie asked.

Jay blinked. "Um, no. Maybe some mud fluid was in the sample?"

"Maybe," Marie said. "The sample is ready. It's hooked up and the vacuum pump is primed."

"Thank you, Marie. Have a seat," Kate said.

She entered the room and sat across from Maeve and Jay took a chair next to her. A paper spreadsheet was spread out on the table. The rows showed the tests to be run and their expected durations. Marie had already ordered them in an expected sequence.

Jay barely glanced at the sheet. Marie had taken care of putting all this together yesterday and he'd studied it more than once before Kate arrived. He imagined Kate had studied it too.

"I like this," Kate said. "You did a good job, Marie, and I think we'll run with it."

A shy smile lit Marie's face. "Th—Thank you." She turned to Maeve. "Hi, Maeve. How you doing?"

"Great." The teenager's voice was a desultory monotone.

Marie glanced at Kate. "Guess she's not happy about spending the weekend here?"

Kate shook her head. "Um, no. She's being a brat."

"Brat," Maeve echoed. "Right. Because what every teenager wants to do is spend their weekend here," she said, hands encompassing the room.

"Cut it out," Kate warned.

"It's okay," Marie said. "You know, Maeve, I used to spend weekends with my mom when she worked. Sometimes I even helped."

"Uh-huh," Maeve said. "She make you do your homework too?"

Marie's eyes flicked to Kate and then back to the girl. "Of course. But I didn't mind. Had plenty to read." She pointed at the tablet on the table. "But you have that. And we have a fairly fast network. Bet you can stream to your heart's content."

Maeve pushed a lock of hair from her face. "Yeah. That's at least something."

"Plus," Jay said, "I think Stevo keeps a console around here somewhere."

"A console?" Maeve asked, her face lit in a hopeful smile.

"Yeah." Jay said. "You're not the only kid who's been trapped here for a weekend. Neil's kids are here all the time. Especially lately."

"What kind of console?" the girl asked.

"Don't know." Jay sipped his coffee. "I wouldn't know the difference between a PS whatever or a X-thingie on pain of death. But I know we have one somewhere."

Kate looked at her daughter. "See? Not going to be so bad. Plus, our gracious CEO is making sure we have catered meals here."

"Cold cuts," Maeve sighed.

Her mother laughed and touched Maeve's arm. "No, girl. Mike pulls out all the stops."

"Won't be that bad," Jay said. "I promise. I'll email Stevo to help you get set up."

"Thanks," Maeve said.

The sour expression on her face had disappeared. Jay relaxed. The last thing they needed was for Kate to get distracted by her precocious daughter. "All right then." Jay knocked his fist on the table. "Let's get to work. Going to be a long night and might as well get started."

Kate smiled wide.

"What?" he asked.

"Haven't heard you make a single Looney Tunes reference."

Jay's mouth opened in a toothy grin. "Night ain't over yet."

* * *

The trio of chemists headed down the stairwell to the labs. When they exited through the secure door, the bright lights of the hallway made Jay squint. The lower floor of the building was more or less a large square bisected by the two labs. The chem lab on the west, the bio lab on the east. A wall of blast proof glass rose from floor to ceiling. Anyone in the hallway could peer through the wall and into either of the labs areas.

Jay swung his head. Neil and Bill were already in the bio-lab. Rather than being outfitted in safety gear, the chief scientist of HAL's bio-chem department wore a simple lab coat. His partner in crime, Bill Field, wore the same.

Must be nice not to have to worry about explosions, he thought, unable to stifle a snicker.

"What are you laughing about?" Kate asked.

"Just reminding myself how fun my job is," Jay said. Neil, tall, pale, and bald, waved at him through the glass. Jay returned it. Neil grabbed his crotch and then turned back to Bill. Jay shook his head. "They hardly ever need safety gear. Just ain't fair."

Kate punched him on the shoulder. "I think we have more fun."

"Only when we blow shit up," Jay said.

Marie hissed through her teeth. "Oh, let's not do that again."

"Don't worry," Kate said. "I won't ever let Jay near sodium again."

The trio walked past the bio-lab's decontamination area and to the chem lab's security doors. Jay glanced up at the camera embedded in the ceiling. A glowing red LED glared down at the heavy door set in the glass. Jay pulled his badge from his lab coat. Marie and Kate did the same. "Marie? Will you do the honors?" Jay asked.

Marie placed her badge on the black card reader. It toggled from red to yellow. Kate followed suit and the yellow light began to blink. With a sigh, Jay put his card on the reader. The light changed to green and the door clicked. Kate grabbed the handle and pulled.

A puff of air greeted them as the pressure inside the lab stabilized. The harsh tang of old chemicals greeted Jay's nostrils. "Phew. Place never clears out," he said.

Kate grunted. "Let's go. Mike's not paying us by the hour."

Jay gestured toward the door and winked at Marie. She walked in the lab without a word. He put his hand out to hold the door for Kate. She shook her head.

"Age before beauty."

Lips turned up in a sneer, Jay stared at her. "Genius," he said, "before mediocrity." Before she could reply, he walked inside the lab.

Kate hissed behind him. "That kind of talk's going to get you in front of HR, old man."

"Old man?" Jay said without turning around. "That's age discrimination."

A stainless steel table ran from just inside the glass to the other end of the room along the east wall. It stopped just before another wall on the north side. Shelves of flasks, beakers, test tubes, and other glassware were arranged against the back wall. Two large, tall cylinders rose in the middle of the room. On either end were several electrical instruments and LCD monitors.

The west wall had another long, gleaming steel table with various electronic analyzers. Doors closed, his ears popped as the room re-pressurized. Negative pressure in the chem lab kept potentially dangerous vapors from escaping if a seal ruptured or the glass managed to crack.

The negative pressure scenario always worried Jay a bit. If for some reason a cloud of say, H_2S, escaped during distillation or sulfur concentration tests, the lab techs would be locked in with the deadly vapors, unless they could shatter the glass or escape through the door. That was bad. But the idea the cloud would follow them if they managed to escape through the door was even more terrifying.

Jay watched Kate move to the computer workstation at the front of the lab. She sat down in the black, ergonomic chair, and pulled out her phone. She pressed the shift key, typed in her name and password. A dialog box popped up with the words "Enter Security Key."

Kate's fingers worked the phone until a number popped up on the screen. She typed the numbers into the box and clicked "Authenticate." The screen flashed and then filled with icons.

The "two-factor" authentication was annoying, but HAL's commitment to security was one of the reasons companies like PPE used their services. In many cases, that loyalty made for exclusive contracts.

"Okay," Kate said. "Let's go down the checklist."

Marie grabbed a small beaker off the shelf and headed to the sample dispenser. "500 milliliters?" she asked.

Jay took up a clipboard from one of the stations. He looked down through the bifocal goggles. "500 ML," he confirmed.

Marie pressed a few buttons on the controls. The machine beeped. She placed the beaker on the table below the dispenser. She pressed another button on the control panel and a pump activated.

* * *

It was trapped. *It* had no place to go. When the cap was punctured, it attempted to race upward through the steel pipes and gain leverage. But the vacuum prevented *It* from coalescing. At least *It* was in the dark, safe from *Its* enemy.

When the pump started, *It* streamed through the metal and Pyrex pipes toward the spigot. *It* had no thought other than escape. But with each particle siphoned off, *It* lost cohesion. *It* slept in the pipes as *Its* intelligence was slowly ripped away.

* * *

The electronic meter controlling the valve sent a signal. The valve opened and black oil flowed from the pipes. The first 400 ML of liquid rushed into the beaker. The sensors determined the amount dispensed and slowly throttled back the pressure. The sample's final 100 ML dropped into the beaker in fits and starts. As the last ML dropped into the beaker, the meter closed the valve. A single droplet of black clung to the spigot. Marie reached out and tapped the metal. The drop lost its grip and dropped into the beaker.

"Okay," Marie said. "500 ML."

"Good," Jay said. He'd moved from the distillation towers and stood near one of the tables. Marie picked up the beaker with her safety gloves and joined him. "Now, Leaguer's geologist, Sigler, claimed the API was insane. We just need to confirm it. Same with density and water content. Then we can get started on the fun stuff."

"I know," Marie said. She stared at him with a blank expression. "I did write up the testing order."

He raised his hands and said, "Sufferin' succotash, woman!" in Sylvester the Cat's voice, "I was talking more to myself." Marie blinked. Jay sighed. "Okay. I'll stop micromanaging."

"That'll be the day," Kate called from the back of the lab.

Marie smirked and placed the beaker atop a black circular stand.

Jay moved to assist and then stopped. "Marie? I'm just going to stand here unless you want help."

She grinned. "Stand there and watch. Make sure I don't mess this up."

"Uh-huh," Jay said. "Not likely."

The female chemist shrugged and dropped the temperature leads into the beaker. The metal ends disappeared into the black liquid. Marie turned to the digital controls. She pressed the up arrow until "75° F" appeared on the screen. She hit "heat."

The lab was kept cold to ensure certain chemicals didn't reach flashpoint or ignition temperatures. In order to properly test crude oil, however, the liquids needed to be kept around typical room temperature. The only exceptions were heat tests and distillation. Jay watched as the digital readout blinked 68°.

"You think Sigler is wrong about the API?" Marie asked.

"It's possible," Kate called from her station. "Like I said, her testing equipment may not have been properly calibrated."

Jay sighed. "Exploration rigs. Notorious for slipshod analysis."

"If they weren't," Kate said, "we wouldn't have jobs."

"True."

A bubble rose from the bottom of the beaker and popped when it reached the surface. Neither Jay nor Marie even noticed.

The readout beeped and Jay's eyes swung to the display. 72°. "This stuff heats fast," Jay said.

Marie nodded. "A bit faster than I expected. That's for sure." She looked over at Kate. "Light crude?"

"Very." Kate typed something into the computer and brought up a spreadsheet. She placed a finger on the screen and followed down the rows. "Got it. On par with the lightest stuff out there."

Jay and Marie traded a glance. "Well," he said, "guess Sigler wasn't so far off?"

The machine beeped three times. 75°. Three bubbles popped to the surface simultaneously, the sound lost below the din of the air conditioning.

"Let's get the API," she said. Marie picked up the hygrometer lead and put the bulbous end inside the beaker. The Pyrex sunk into the black liquid. Marie squeezed the plastic bulb at the other end. Oil shot up into the device. She pressed a button on a different control panel and waited.

Jay and Marie watched the API display. The counter started at 1, but quickly changed. In a matter of seconds, the LCD strip read 30. It hovered there for a second, and then rose.

When the display read "45," Jay and Marie exchanged a glance. The computer controlled equipment let out a beep and the display flashed.

"45 API," Marie said. "Guess Sigler was—"

A bubble popped on the liquid surface. The machine let out another beep and the number changed to 47. Then to 48. Then to 50. The machine beeped again and the reading stayed solid.

"What the hell was that?" Jay asked. His eyes weren't on the beaker, but staring at the machine.

Marie shook her head. "Never seen that before."

"What happened?" Kate rose from her station and walked to them.

Jay pointed at the gravity analyzer. "It just, well, it thought it was done and then changed. Also, something bubbled in the oil."

"Bubbled?" Kate frowned. "Temperature too high?"

He glanced at the thermometer. "Still at 75°."

"Well, that makes no sense." Kate rubbed her arms. "Final API is…" Her voice trailed off. The frown on her face disappeared into a flat line. "50? 50 API? Are you kidding me?"

Marie shook her head. "There's no way it's that high."

Another bubble popped to the surface. "What the hell is doing that?" Jay asked.

The trio stared at the liquid. The hygrometer beeped again and the three of them flinched. Jay finally said, "Guess we're supposed to take the reading now."

Kate shook her head. "Okay, so if it's 50 API, I think we can rule out any tests for heavy oil."

"No, kidding," Jay said as Yosemite Sam. "That varmint is about as light as it gets."

Marie nodded and pulled the hygrometer from the oil. The thick, black liquid clung to the bulbous Pyrex end. Marie gently shook the instrument and the oil drizzled off. The glass was clean. She frowned.

"Did you see that?"

"See what?" Jay asked.

"It just seemed to slide off," Marie said.

"What do you mean 'slide off'?" Kate looked closely at the hygrometer end. "That's—" She cleared her throat. "Strange. There's always oil left behind."

"Not this time," Jay said.

He took the hygrometer from Marie and headed to the hazard sink adjacent to the oil delivery system. With the device unhooked from its sensors and the analyzer, it was light and easy to handle. He placed it in the sink and started the water tap. He flipped a switch next to the faucet and heard the click of the glass and steel stopper popping into position. Jay pumped the cleaning fluid into the sink. When the foamy water swallowed the hygrometer, he turned off the faucet.

Kate and Marie had moved the gravity analyzer and replaced it with a hydrometer to measure the oil's water content. Jay walked back toward the station. Something burbled in the pipes above the dispensing unit. Jay glanced upward at the coil of steel leading to the metered faucet. A shiver ran up his spine. *Air in the vacuum?* That didn't make sense. And why was the goddamned oil bubbling at room temperature?

He shook his head and headed back to the other chemists. Kate tapped a few keys on the analyzer and the hydrometer shook in the beaker. Once again, clear glass disappeared as the instrument siphoned the liquid into its throat.

The analyzer beeped and then hummed as it started to process the oil. Jay clapped his hands together. "I think we can cross off half the tests in the assay."

Kate nodded. "I think you're right. All the heavy oil stuff can get dropped."

Marie waved a hand over the beaker and to her nose. She sniffed carefully and frowned. "This stuff doesn't have any smell."

Jay raised an eyebrow. "No smell?" He moved closer to the beaker and did the same thing Marie had done. The skin on his forehead scrunched and he stood back to his full height. "Suffering succotash. Marie's right."

She rolled her eyes at him. "Just because you talk like Sylvester doesn't mean you have to spit like him."

"Sorry," Jay said.

"No smell. A ridiculous API. What is this stuff?" Kate asked.

"I don't know," Jay said, "but I think it's safe to say M2 has crude the likes of which we've never seen."

"Or heard of," Marie mumbled.

The analyzer beeped again. Jay looked down at its rectangular, LCD display. "Result: N/A."

"What the—" Jay said. "Ladies?" The chemists looked at him and then followed his finger down to the analyzer's message. "You ever seen that?"

Kate bit her lip. "I think 'no' would be the answer you're looking for."

Marie growled in her throat and headed toward one of the computer terminals. "What's the model number?" she asked as she logged in.

"XJ-45C. Intac," Jay read from the labels on the analyzer.

Marie clicked a few keys and brought up the manual for the device. She quickly scanned through the documentation and then grunted. "N/A," she said aloud. "Not applicable, of course. Means there's either no water in the sample or a calibration error." She knocked the steel table with a knuckle.

"But you calibrated the machine this morning?"

"Yes. Like everything else," Marie said.

"The instrument has to be broken. There's no way there's no water in the oil," Jay said. "That just doesn't happen."

Kate clucked her tongue. "There is one possibility. Maybe the oil is so light that the water molecules just don't, well, cling to it."

"Cling to it. You mean the hydrocarbon rings somehow push the water out?" Jay shook his head. "Bullshit."

The chief chemist shrugged. "It's all theory, of course. We'd have to run a simulation on that."

"Right. But before we start treating it like some new compound," Jay said, "perhaps we should run through the other more pedestrian tests?"

Marie lifted the clipboard off the table, wrote down the results from the API and hydro tests, and then began crossing off test after test. "Well," she said at last, "that gets rid of a lot of time-consuming, useless analyses."

"So what's next?" Kate asked.

"Sulfur." Marie reached for the beaker and stopped. Several bubbles popped on the surface of the black liquid. "Jay? Why is it doing that?"

Jay and Kate exchanged a glance. A swarm of bubbles popped. He flicked his gloved finger against the Pyrex. The bubbling stopped at once. "I have absolutely no clue."

*　*　*

After hours in the chem lab, the break room smelled like heaven. Kate took another bite from a golden brown samosa. Her plate of chicken tikka was little more than bones and smears of sauce. She hated the fact she'd eaten it so fast, but it was just too damned good.

Maeve sat next to her, sniffling from the spicy curry she'd devoured. Her dexterous fingers dipped a piece of naan into the remaining curry and then disappeared into her mouth. "Wow, Mom," she said, "Mr. Beaudry pulls out all the stops, doesn't he?"

Jay laughed. "That's nothing. Just wait until breakfast arrives." He dabbed a napkin at the corner of his mouth and stifled a belch. "Hope you like omelettes, girl. Because they're great!"

"That was Tony the Tiger." Marie shot Jay a withering glance. "I thought you only mimicked Looney Tunes."

"I like all of them," Jay said. "Besides," he pointed at Maeve, "it made her smile."

All through the meal, Jay had made small talk with Maeve about games, school, music, anything to interrupt the silence between mouthfuls and chewing. As much as Jay loved kids, Kate wondered why he didn't have any. Then again, after working with him for so many years, she knew how much he hated awkward silences.

She turned to Maeve. "You get your homework done?"

Her daughter paused in mid-chomp on a popadom. "Sort of," Maeve said through a crunching mouthful.

"Maeve?" Kate said. "It's nearly ten o'clock. You should have everything done by now."

"Mom," the teenager said after she swallowed, "I have until Monday. It's still Friday. Cut me some slack."

Kate sighed. Marie was staring into the dab of saag paneer on the plate in front of her. "Marie? You okay?"

She looked up at Kate and frowned. "I'm fine. Just wondering about our samples downstairs."

Jay cleared his throat. "The break room is for breaks, Marie."

"I know," she said. "But—"

"But," Kate finished the thought, "you can't get it out of your head."

Marie nodded. "The report Sigler sent us from Leaguer mostly checks out. We thought her readings were off, or her equipment wasn't properly calibrated. But our tests prove her right."

"No," Jay said, "our tests prove hers *were* off. But not in the direction we thought they would be. This stuff is too sweet. Too perfect." Jay tapped a knuckle on the table. "Beginning to think they're fu—messing with us."

Maeve laughed. "Love how you changed that sentence, Uncle Jay."

Jay's cheeks flushed. "I sometimes forget there's a little girl sitting with us."

"Little girl? I'm 13!"

"Always going to be my little girl," Kate said and brushed a lock of Maeve's hair from her face. Maeve flinched away from her mother's touch, but smiled all the same.

"Messing with us," Marie said. "Right. That's what it's like. Either that or the sample was contaminated with something else."

"With what?" Jay asked. "I mean, what kind of contaminants would give us these kinds of readings?"

The table went quiet. Kate's mind filled with molecular chemistry, hydrocarbon rings, methyl attractors, and hydrogen stabilization patterns. She shook her head and looked at Jay. "I can't think of anything that explains this. Contaminants wouldn't change the bonds between the molecules."

Jay nodded. "Right. Unless there's something we're missing."

Maeve giggled. "You guys are studying oil, right?"

"Yes," Jay said. "It's, um, unlike anything we've seen before."

"So why do you think it's oil?" Maeve asked. "Because it came from an offshore rig?"

Kate's jaw dropped open. *Occam's Razor*, a voice said in her mind. "That's the craziest thing I've ever heard you say," she said. Kate beamed. "And I think you may be on to something."

"Not oil?" Jay said aloud. His eyes focused on the fluorescent lights. "That is crazy."

"We could perform a molecular study," Marie said. She tented her fingers on the table surface. "Stephen, I mean Chuckles, should have the NOC up tonight, right? We could run an NMR analysis on the makeup and then have the new programs model it."

Jay shrugged. "That would work. But since that'll take hours to run, we might as well first prove that it's *not* oil."

"Agreed," Kate said. "We need to check with Chuckles on the NOC status. I know the switchover is scheduled for tonight, but that doesn't mean he's going to get it done."

Jay giggled and then dabbed a paper napkin at the side of his mouth. "Considering the state of the new building, I wouldn't be surprised if those idiots screwed up some wiring."

Marie shook her head. "Stephen's a professional when it comes to that stuff. That's his baby. No way he'd let them screw that up."

Jay cast a suspicious glance toward the chemist. "'Stephen?' Not

'Chuckles'?" Marie blushed and Jay smiled knowingly at Kate. "I think our little Marie has a crush."

Kate laughed. "Good. Marie? Before we go back into the lab, I need you to check with him regarding the switchover. Let's see how soon he can get the computers up."

"Okay." Marie's voice trembled.

"You've got programs that can do that?" Maeve asked.

Kate nodded. "Yup. Neil and the bio-team have their software for pulling apart DNA and looking for analogs in the known gene banks. We have something similar."

"Similar, but not as powerful," Jay said. "Afraid no one cares what a hydrocarbon looks like."

"Except us. And except for now," Marie said.

Kate laughed. "We can perform a simple film test. Or let the machine do it. At least then we'd have an idea of the length of the molecular chain."

"All right," Jay said. "Sounds like we have a plan. But first we need to perform the distillation. I mean all this other sounds hypothetical and we're going to feel pretty stupid if it ends up spewing hexane at the first cut."

"Geek geek geek," Maeve mumbled.

"It's our job," Jay said. "And you might learn a thing or two if you listen."

Maeve's expression soured. "Right, because my grades in chemistry are *so* good."

Jay hissed through his teeth. "How can you have a chemist for a Mom and suck at chemistry?"

Kate threw up her hands. "Because she's incapable of listening. Oh, and her earth-science teacher is terrible."

"Tsk tsk. Obviously you need a better teacher." He pointed his thumbs at himself. "And I'm available."

"Right," Maeve said. She grabbed another popadom and crunched on it. "Because that will make me more interested."

"At some point, you're going to want to know how the world works.

And that's science," Jay said.

Maeve swallowed. "And what do you do when science doesn't explain things?"

The three chemists grinned.

CHAPTER THREE

The new NOC was on and Chuckles swaggered down the aisle of blade cabinets and storage arrays. Green LED lights shined from each slot. The hum of the fans was barely audible through the noise-canceling headphones.

Chuckles finished his walk of the aisles and returned to the NOC entrance. He closed the inner door, placed the hearing protection back in its cradle, and opened the outer door. He started to walk forward and then stopped. Marie stood a few feet away, an awkward smile on her face.

"Um, hello," Chuckles said.

She blushed. "Hi."

His brows scrunched together. "Can I, um, help you?"

She wiped a bead of sweat from her forehead. "We are running the analysis for PPE."

He waited for her to say more, but she didn't. "Okay," Chuckles said. She didn't look well. Her cheeks were flushed, but her skin was paler than usual. "Is there a problem?"

"Yes," Marie said and smiled. "We want to use the new molecular modeling programs."

For a second, Chuckles wanted to say no. He wanted to make comments about how the NOC hadn't yet been battle-tested. That he didn't know how it would perform. But that was bullshit. Chuckles had smashed the systems with several genetic analysis runs. The processors were burned in, memory tested, and all power supplies in the green. Plus? The new NOC was damned cold. In other words? There would never be a better time.

A lopsided grin appeared on his face. "We can make that happen," he said. "You guys give me an hour or two and I'll have it ready."

Marie nodded. "Thank you, Stephen."

"You feeling okay?" he asked.

"I think so. Probably got a cold or something."

Chuckles reached and touched her forehead with the back of his hand. Her flesh felt warm and clammy. "I think you need to take a break. Get some drugs. And maybe a nap."

She shook her head. "Not on a hot-shot. Sleep when you're dead and all that."

"Let's hope not." He put his hands on his hips. "What happened?"

"What?" She followed his gaze to her bandaged hand. "Oh, that. I cut myself opening the PPE barrel. Stupid mistake."

Chuckles frowned. "Any chance you got something on you? Like, what is that shit, fracking fluid?"

She giggled. "No fracking fluid. Not in offshore exploration, anyway."

He rolled his eyes. "You know what I mean. Something that ain't oil?"

"Don't know," she said. "I washed it in the emergency chem shower and covered it with iodine. And it's not like crude oil has a ton of bacteria or viruses."

Chuckles grunted. "You better go take something. That cold is creeping into your chest."

Marie nodded. "Okay, Stephen. I'll do that."

"Good," he said. "I'd hate it if you got sick."

"Really?" Marie's smile widened.

Chuckles' expression returned to a thin line. "Yeah. I'd like to, um, take you out some time. For drinks or something."

Marie blushed and looked away.

"Sorry," Chuckles said and stared at his feet. "Guess that was too—"

"No," Marie said. "I would like that."

He raised his eyes, cheeks hot with embarrassment. Chuckles shifted on his feet. "I have to get back to making sure the NOC is ready for you."

"Right." She stepped away from him. "And I have to get back to the lab."

"When's your next break?" he asked.

"Two a.m. Why?"

A smile tugged at his lips. "Just wondering when I'd see you again."

Marie opened her mouth to say something and then stopped. She swallowed hard. "See you then?"

"Hopefully," he said. She turned and walked back to the skybridge. He watched her head down the hallway, eyes straying to her perfect ass. *Beautiful. Smart. And not afraid of geeks.* He sighed. *And way above my station.* Chuckles shook his head and walked to the stairwell.

As he took the stairs down to the loading dock, he couldn't get her out of his mind. A cigarette or two and he'd be level again. Just talking to her had been a chore. He'd no idea what he'd say at break. He'd no idea he wouldn't get the chance.

* * *

As she walked to the skybridge, Marie stared upward at the exposed ductwork. The construction company still hadn't connected most of the ventilation for the second floor. The lights weren't all on either. Like the rest of the scientists at the company, she wondered if the damned building would ever be finished.

A sudden wave of fire hit her lungs. Marie doubled over, explosive coughs wracking her body. Tears squeezed from her eyes. Lightning bolts of pain shot through her skull. She lurched and placed one hand on the nearest wall to keep her upright as she gasped for air between each cough. Just when she was certain she'd suffocate, the fit abated. She spat a large wad of mucous to the concrete floor and wiped at her mouth. Marie didn't see the flecks of red in the yellow-green blob of mucous.

She panted in the gloom. *Sick. I'm sick.* Marie slowly stood and then leaned against the wall. Eyes closed, breath slowing, she whimpered as a flush of heat spread over her skin. Beads of sweat oozed from her forehead. Marie opened her eyes. The skybridge was no more than a few steps away. And in the break room? Drugs.

A wave of vertigo hit her as she entered the skybridge. She halted until it passed. A thin thread of mucous drizzled from her left nostril. She wiped it away and started walking again.

The skybridge portion in the older building was much brighter. As were the hallways. The normally soft, blue-white fluorescents burned her eyes. Through squinted slits, she made her way to the break room.

From inside Kate's office, she heard the sounds of music. Maeve must be playing a game. Or jamming out. Marie coughed again and another jolt of pain spread through her lungs. She shook her head to clear starlight from her mind and entered the break room.

The remnants of dinner had already been cleared and stuffed into the garbage cans. She'd no doubt Darren had done it. Whenever there were overnights, Mike and Darren took care of the food and making sure everything was as spotless as could be.

The medicine cabinet hung on the wall near the refrigerator. An emergency eye-wash station hung next to it. Marie opened the cabinet and sniffed back another snail-trail of snot.

Antihistamines, fever reducers, ibuprofen, bandages, antiseptic… She scooped up four anti-inflammatories and a blister pack of cold medicine.

Between sips of bottled water, she managed to swallow all the pills. As soon as her throat allowed her, she shotgunned the rest of the cold water.

That was all she could do. She couldn't leave Kate and Jay shorthanded. Not unless she was on her damned death bed. Marie tossed the empty plastic bottle into the recycling bin and headed for the stairs to the lab level.

***

Kate sat at the computer terminal. While she and Jay waited for Marie to get back, Kate decided it was time to enter some numbers. Not that there was much to enter.

The API, water content, and sediment readings were beyond bizarre. PPE was never going to believe the results. And if the strange nature of the oil continued to play out, she wasn't sure Simpson would even accept the report.

But first, they had to run distillation. The first cut would require them to heat the oil and then siphon off any gases present at different heights in the distillation tower. In a normal sample, any hexane, butane, or light hydrocarbons would evaporate from the crude and rise to the top of the tower. Heavier hydrocarbons would be captured by the trays set at different heights. Any heavy, nasty stuff would remain in the bottom of the tower. *In a normal* sample, she thought. *With this shit? No telling what's going to come out.*

Kate entered text in the fields on the form. She put notations for their observations next to the absurd numbers. *Absurd. Yes, that's the word.*

She looked up as Jay moved to the sample beaker sitting on the shelf. He was in profile, but she could still tell he was frowning at the Pyrex container.

"What's up?" she called.

He flinched and then turned to her. "The oil. It's still bubbling."

"Still small bubbles?" She hit the save button on the report and stood from the workstation.

Jay grunted. "Not exactly."

She walked toward him with quick steps as Jay backed away from the sample. "What's wrong with it? I know it's strange, but why do you look like you've seen a—" The words died in her throat.

Tendrils of dried oil clung to the sides of the beaker. But they no longer looked like liquid. Instead, the threads bore a strong resemblance to burned chocolate. In the beaker's center, the oil wasn't bubbling. It looked like it was boiling.

"Let's throw this shit out," she said.

"Yeah. Maybe we left it on the heater too long?"

"I don't care. It needs to go in the waste."

Jay grabbed a long pair of stainless steel forceps, put them around the beaker, and squeezed. He lifted the container from the shelf and carefully stepped toward the waste trap.

"If you'd do the honors?" Jay said. His voice quivered with nervous tension.

Kate moved to the bright red barrel inset into the floor. She pressed a handle on its side and the lid swung upward.

She stared down into the interior. The trap was still closed. "Okay, go ahead and pour it in."

"If it'll pour," Jay said. He walked until the beaker was above the hole and twisted his hands. As the container tipped, the oil slid free of the Pyrex and streamed into the barrel.

Jay kept twisting his hands, bending at the waist, until the beaker was upside down. Remnants of the oil dripped at a slow pace. "Sufferin' succotash!" Jay yelled. "Just go already!" Droplets of his saliva flew out of his mouth, some landing in the barrel.

"I think you got it all," Kate said.

"Okay." Jay began tilting the beaker back up again. When it was once again upright, he nodded to Kate.

She pressed a button and the lid slammed down atop the barrel. "Say goodbye to the sample, Jay."

"Bye, sample," Jay said.

Kate depressed the floor pedal with her foot. The trap opened and a vacuum pump whooshed. The apparatus was designed to suck any solids or liquids through the trap and into the waste container below. The container held up to 20 gallons of substance before it had to be emptied, but HAL rotated their traps between the day and night shifts.

That ensured the chemists knew what had been placed in the barrel so they could avoid mixing volatile chemicals.

"Now what do I do with this?" Jay gestured with the beaker.

She rolled her eyes and pointed. "What do you think you do? Put it in the damned sink."

Jay growled in his throat and followed orders.

The door at the front of the lab beeped twice. Kate turned and watched Marie step through the door. "And did you find Chuckles?"

"Stephen," Marie said. "His name is Stephen."

"Yes, I know, but—" Kate stopped. "Marie? You okay?"

The normally mocha-skinned woman was very pale. Marie shrugged. "Guess I got the flu or something. Started coughing pretty bad."

"Yeah," Kate agreed. "I can hear it in your voice. Sounds like you're breathing through cheesecloth."

"You need to go take something," Jay said.

Kate turned. Jay had left the beaker in the sink and was walking toward them.

Marie sighed. "I took a bunch of stuff. Just going to take some time to kick in."

"No." Kate pointed toward the door. "You are quarantined, young lady. Until you get a nap."

"But, you guys will have to do everything yourselves!" Marie's voice broke on the last word as she coughed into her arm.

"Uh-huh," Jay said. "So what we need is a chemist with the flu corrupting our samples."

"Give me a break," Marie smirked. "Like a little snot wouldn't do that stuff some good."

Kate giggled. "As chief scientist of the chemical analysis division of HAL, I'm telling you to get your ass upstairs and crash on a couch."

"Okay." Marie wiped a runner of snot on her sleeve. "I'll go to the mother's room."

"Good plan," Jay said. "Sit in that glider and sleep." He looked at

Kate. "You think we can get Maeve to check on her?"

Kate grinned and pulled out her phone. "Of course."

* * *

The waste container was clean. *It* moved as a tiny puddle. The constant assault of light and warmth had nearly destroyed *It*. Without nourishment, *It* could do little.

Before *It* dropped into the trap, saliva flew inside and dissolved into the puddle. *It* absorbed the material, broke down the DNA and biological components into their constituent atoms, and rearranged them to be part of *Itself*.

The energy was enough to sustain *It* a little longer. But without more, *It* would cease to be. *It* slowly slid across the metal, searching for something else to absorb. But there was nothing to consume besides the molecular film left by cleaning solutions and chemicals.

It ceased moving. *It* shrank in size as it pulled itself into a small, dense layer. *It* had to wait. Continuing to move would only weaken *It* further.

* * *

Ratchet and Clank were blowing the shit out of everything. Maeve maneuvered the cartoonish wombat-looking character from side to side as a huge creature flung missiles at it. Her thumb expertly pressed the four buttons on the controller in a sequence only she seemed to understand.

The boss' health bar disappeared and the creature fell into the virtual ground. Ratchet's world shook with the impact. Maeve smiled as the screen faded into a cut-scene. That's when her phone chimed.

She pressed the "Start" button and the screen froze. Her phone buzzed again. She dropped the controller and grabbed the phone off the table. Maeve rolled her eyes as she read the message.

"Bad enough I'm stuck here. Now I have to be a nurse?" she said aloud. The texts were from her mother. And they were pretty clear. Maeve sighed.

She stood from the couch and grabbed her glass of water. If she had to meet Marie at the stairs, at least she could get another drink while she was at it.

A gust of wind shook the window pane. With the console blaring the game's audio, she hadn't noticed the weather change. Rain was falling. The wind had picked up. And she'd little doubt the temperature had dropped. She sighed.

Maeve opened Kate's office door and stopped. The hallway was darker than before. The fluorescents that had practically shined off the off-white walls seemed dim and wan. She stuck her head out through the doorframe and looked from side to side. There was no one in the hallway.

A tremor of fear rose up her spine. Darkness. It was one of those childhood fears that still gnawed at her. She didn't believe in Hell, but if one existed, she knew hers would be endless darkness punctuated by alien sounds and the occasional slithery touch on her skin. She shivered and stepped out of Kate's office.

The hall was silent except for the sound of the air conditioner and the wind buffeting the building's exterior. Maeve walked with careful steps toward the break room. She froze as the overhead lights came alive with full brightness.

She squinted through the sudden illumination. Maeve swallowed hard. She tried to call out, but her voice came out in a guttural whisper. She cleared her throat. "Hello?"

There was no response. She cocked her ear to listen, but there was nothing to hear. Heart thumping in her chest, she continued walking.

When she reached the corner, she peered around it. Empty. She loosed an inaudible sigh and turned into the break room.

The fluorescents came on the moment she stepped across the threshold. With the exception of the garbage cans and recycling bins, it was impossible to tell a meal had been served an hour earlier. Maeve wondered if HAL had cleaning faeries on staff.

She opened the fridge and pulled out another bottle of water. She spun off the cap, filled her glass, and tossed the empty bottle into the bin.

A creaking sound caught her attention. She remained as still as a statue and focused on the sound. A soft click followed a squeal. "Hello?"

A wet, chest-rattling cough echoed from the hallway. She flinched and nearly dropped her glass. "Marie?"

A hand appeared in the doorway. Then Marie. Maeve sighed and then she saw the look on the woman's face. Marie was more than just sick. She looked...diseased.

Maeve put the glass on the counter and walked toward her. "You okay, Marie?"

The chemist pulled up her arm and coughed into her sleeve. "Yes," she managed in between gasps. "I think I need to lie down."

"You need some drugs?"

Marie shook her head. "Already took some. Think I just need some blankets and a place to crash." Marie tried to take a step and swayed on her feet.

"Let me help you," Maeve said. She walked to Marie and put an arm around her waist. "Where are we going?"

"Down the hall," Marie croaked.

Maeve took the slight woman's weight and they shuffled in awkward steps. Marie's lungs rattled with each breath, the next more labored than the last. Maeve felt trickles of sweat falling from Marie's forehead and into her hair. She wondered if Marie had somehow become infected by something in the lab. No, not infected. Contaminated.

They reached the end of the hall and Maeve turned them around the corner. A large room with an open door was at the end of the adjacent hallway.

"Is that where we're going?" Maeve chuffed. Marie didn't speak, but she felt the woman nod. "Just a few more steps, Marie."

Marie said nothing in return. She seemed to be growing weaker with each step. Maeve's back started to ache and she suddenly realized her arms were crying out from the effort. When they started, Marie was still holding up most of her weight. Now she was little more than a rag doll on sticks.

As she led Marie through the open doorway, the lights came on. After the stringing brightness of the hallway, the wan glow of the overheads was soothing. A glider sat in the middle of the room. A small bed was up against the west wall. A crib, of all things, was pushed against the east wall.

The walls of the other offices were barren and off-white except for whatever the denizens had hung themselves. The mother's room, however, was covered with bright landscapes. Starscapes covered the ceiling.

Maeve led Marie to the bed. When they were at its edge, the girl awkwardly turned her charge around until Marie could sit. Instead of sitting, Marie's ass plopped onto the mattress. Bed springs creaked.

Maeve let out a long sigh. Her arms and back ached and her heart raced in her chest. She turned her eyes to Marie's. The woman seemed unfocused and distant. "Marie? You okay?"

Marie turned her head and stared at Maeve with glazed eyes. A pained smile crossed her lips. "Need to sleep."

Maeve nodded and slid off the bed's edge while she unhooked Marie's arm from around her neck. Marie tried to shift her weight on the mattress. The springs creaked again. Marie lay backward, her legs still hanging off the bed. Maeve grabbed them and pushed them upward until they too were on the mattress.

She lifted Marie's head and put a pillow beneath it. "You cold?" Maeve asked.

Marie, eyes closed, nodded.

Maeve bit her tongue and looked around the room. Besides the glider, crib, and bed, the room was practically vacant of other furniture. A small chair was next to the door. Maeve saw what she was looking for.

Blankets were piled up on top of the chair. Maeve made a mental note to thank CEO Mike for giving a shit about his employees. She unfolded the thickest of them and covered Marie's feet, legs, and torso. Marie's weak hands pulled the blanket up to her neck.

"You need another one?"

Marie shook her head. "Not yet. Can you, put another one next to the bed? I'll grab it if I need it."

Maeve placed a dark blue comforter within Marie's reach. "There. You want some water or something?"

Marie shook her head. "No." She held out her hand. "Thank you, Maeve."

The teenager clasped her hand around the clammy, hot skin. Marie's pulse seemed to throb in her veins. "I think we need to get you a doctor."

"Will sleep. If I'm not a little better soon, I'll get someone to take me."

Maeve nodded. "I'll come back and check on you in twenty minutes or so, okay?"

Marie swallowed and her face screwed up in pain. "Thank you, dear."

Maeve forced a smile. "Sleep now. I'll be back soon." She let go of Marie's hand. The woman seemed to relax and immediately fall asleep.

She waited a few moments, her eyes focused on the rise and fall of Marie's chest. When she was sure the woman could breathe and appeared to be resting, she rose from the bed and headed to the door. As she reached for the light switch, she heard something crackle.

Maeve turned and looked back at the bed. Marie had rolled over on her side. Bed springs. That must have been the bed springs. Marie's leg moved beneath the covers. Maeve's face dropped into a sad smile. "Sleep well," she said and shut off the lights. She walked from the room, closing the door behind her.

She didn't hear the crack and snap of bones as tendons and ligaments dissolved. She didn't hear Marie's unconscious gasps of pain. Maeve headed back to Ratchet and Clank without a clue.

***

More oil. More goddamned oil. Or whatever this shit is. Kate punched buttons on the distillation console and set it up for a heating run.

The lab was kept at a constant 18.3°C. Once oil was placed in the stream, the distillation furnace would heat it to 350°C. At that temperature, the crude would flash into different hydrocarbons, with the lighter components turning into gas. In theory, anyway. The M2 oil was so light, she wondered just how many different types of hydrocarbon it contained.

"Think we can get away with just 3.75 liters?"

Kate flicked her eyes to the dispensing station. Jay had the distillation sample container set up below the spigot. "Better make it 5.5 liters."

She stared back at the screen and set the timers. Once the oil was in the distillation feeder, the gas furnace would heat it up. When the crude reached the target temperature, the computer would release the oil through the heat exchangers and into the tower.

The tower itself was composed of trays with coolant temperatures. As the oil boiled at the tower's bottom, gasses would rise toward the top. Hexane, butane, propane, and other light hydrocarbons would be trapped in the top trays while heavier hydrocarbons would condense at higher temperatures in the lower trays. Simple process, really.

Sensors at each tray in the tower would analyze the condensed gas and send the readings to the computer. After thirty minutes, they'd have their readings and know the true boiling point of the crude as well as its overall hydrocarbon content.

"Um, Kate?" Jay said.

She looked up from the computer. Jay stood a few feet away from the container with his eyes locked on it. "Yes?"

"Can you, um, come here and look at this?"

Kate rose from the chair and walked to the dispensing station. "What is it?" Jay pointed a finger at the container. She followed his gaze and her brows scrunched together.

The vacuum pump whirred as it loosed the crude from the pipes. The oil, however, flowed in a concentrated stream, much faster than it should have. "What the hell?" Kate looked at Jay. "How much pressure did you give it?"

"I didn't change the settings," Jay said. "It's like its struggling to get out through the pipe." He swallowed hard. "But that's not what I'm looking at."

Kate looked at the container. It was trembling. "What the hell?" She walked to the container and stared down into the hole. Without proper illumination, it was impossible to see anything other than darkness in the container.

"Move back, Kate," Jay said. "As soon as we reach 5.5 liters, I'm shutting this thing off."

She nodded. "I've never seen that before. Damned thing's made of iron. How the hell is it shaking like that?"

Jay shook his head. "No clue. But I don't like this stuff."

"Me neither." She stepped away from the rattling container. The rapid flow of oil slowed. The pump groaned as it decreased the pressure in the pipes. "We need to get this damned thing checked," she said. "That pump sounds like it's going to give out."

"No shit," Jay said. The oil falling from the spigot thinned and then turned from a stream into droplets. When the dripping ceased, he moved to the container and hit the lever. The top slid closed with a thump. The container ceased trembling.

Kate shivered. "What the hell kind of oil is this?"

"Let's find out," he said. He rolled the container to the atmospheric distillation machine. He placed the metal hose over the containers lid, screwed it down over the threads, and then hit the release. A metallic "chunk" sound echoed inside the iron container. Jay wiped his forehead. "Ready?"

"I guess." Kate walked back to the computer station. She checked the status lights on the screen. The distillation unit reported the system was closed and ready for a run. She looked up at Jay. "We're green."

"Good," he said. He stepped away from the container and peered over Kate's shoulder. "Let's see what this shit is."

She clicked "Run." The heater beneath the distiller whumped as natural gas flowed over the pilot light. A series of numbers in the upper right corner of the screen blinked as the temperature slowly rose.

Jay stretched. "Thirty minutes." He yawned. "What other tests can we run?"

She shrugged. "We can run the light spectrum test, I guess. But first, I want to make sure Maeve is taking of Marie." Kate pulled out her phone and texted her daughter. She placed the phone on the table. She watched as the readout continued its upward trend. "Guess we have about five minutes before the oil gets circulated through the heat exchangers."

"Then I guess I'll get samples prepared for the UV test. We still want to do the NMR?"

She tapped her fingers on the table. "Yeah. I want to know what the hydrocarbon bonds look like." Kate cleared her throat. "PPE's find is unlike anything I've ever seen before." She glanced upward at Jay. "Or you."

He nodded. "Got that right."

A sly smile lit her face. "This may be something for the scientific journals. Assuming, of course, PPE lets us talk about it."

"Good point."

Kate's phone buzzed. She picked it up and looked at the screen. Her smile turned into a frown. "Maeve says Marie is really sick. She left her in the mother's room. Guess she's sleeping now."

Jay bit his lip. "Maeve going to check on her?"

She nodded. "She says she's going to go in there in about twenty minutes. But she thinks Marie needs a doctor."

Sighing, Jay pulled out his phone. "Man, that flu came on fast. Wonder if she's got that shit the vaccines missed." He chose Darren's contact info and checked the bars on his phone. As usual, the lab was impenetrable for cell signals. He relocked the phone and walked toward the front of the lab. "I'll see if I can get Darren on the line." He shook his cell phone. "Useless for calls."

"That's why Maeve and I are talking over the WiFi," Kate said.

Jay shrugged and picked up the cordless phone from the desk. He dialed Darren's extension and waited. The phone rang twice before it picked up.

"Why, hello, lab," Darren said in his slightly effeminate voice.

"Hey, Darren. It's Jay."

"And what can I do for you, Mr. Hollingsworth?"

"We have a bit of a situation," Jay said. "I'm afraid Marie came down with something. She's pretty sick."

There was a pause on the line. "What kind of sick? Not food poisoning, I hope."

Jay laughed. "Nothing like that. It's the flu or something. She's running a fever and coughing her lungs out."

"Where is she?" Darren asked.

"Kate's daughter has her in the mother's room. I think she's sleeping now, but we might need to get her to a doctor."

"Ugh." Darren clucked his tongue. "I can take her to the emergency room. Is it really that bad?"

"I think so," Jay said. "It came on really really fast."

"Okay. Let me tell Mike what's up and I'll go down and see her."

"Thanks, Darren. If we need to, Kate and I can stop what we're doing and—"

"Absolutely not," Darren said. "Mike'll have my balls if you guys do that. Keep doing what you're doing and I'll be in touch."

Jay smiled. "Thanks, Darren. You're a life-saver."

"Remember that," Darren laughed. "Talk soon."

"Cheers," Jay said and hung up the phone. "Okay, Kate. Darren's got it covered."

"Good," Kate said. "If she's really that sick, we need someone other than Maeve taking care of her."

"Agreed." Jay hoped Darren and Mike would handle it. Mike was very protective of his employees and Darren was an extension of the CEO. Sometimes Jay wondered which of them really ran the company.

Kate ran a hand through her hair and checked the readout. "Vacuum is holding. The temperature is over 100°C."

"That was fast. That means the oil is pretty damned thin." He walked to the distillation tower and peered at the container. He frowned. "Kate? It's doing it again."

"Doing what?"

"Moving."

She looked beneath the table and at the sample container. Her skin popped into gooseflesh. The heavy iron container trembled. "Stupid question, but are you sure whatever came out of that spigot was oil?"

"Yes." Jay tugged at the lab coat's collar. "Which is why I'm suddenly wondering why we aren't burning this shit instead of trying to figure out what it is."

The container rattled again and then stood still. The computer beeped and she swung her eyes back to the display. "200°C."

Jay slowly stood. He wiped sweat from his forehead. "Jesus, Kate. What is going on here?"

"I don't know. But we need to figure it out."

                                    * * *

The hall lights rose in brightness as he walked to the mother's room. After he checked on Marie, he'd make sure Maeve was okay. But the way Jay spoke on the phone had him worried. Mike too. When he'd told Mike that Marie was ill, the CEO had paled considerably. Darren couldn't remember the last time one of the chemists, or the biologists for that matter, bailed on a hot-shot. And while Marie hadn't been with HAL more than a year, she worked hard. Jay and Kate consistently submitted her for raises and title promotion. For her to be absent from the lab, she had to be really sick.

Darren stopped. For a moment, he wasn't sure what he was hearing from down the hall. And then he smiled. Maeve must be playing a video game. In addition to the wind and rain pelting the sides of the building, the sounds of things blowing up and shots being fired sounded like crackling kindling. *At least she's keeping herself entertained,* Darren thought.

The hallway ended at the mother's room. The lights were off in there. Darren slowed his steps. If Marie was sleeping, he didn't want to wake her. He reached the mostly closed door and slowly pushed it open. Instead of the squeak and squeal of hinges, the building super had made sure this door was well oiled. Darren would have to thank him for that.

When the door was wide enough for him to see in, he stepped to the side to allow the hall light to filter in through the crack. A narrow, oblong ray of light started at the doorway and made its way to the wall. Darren frowned.

Marie was sleeping, all right. But something was very wrong. The covers were flung to the floor. The sheets were drenched with sweat. And her breathing sounded like a bellows.

"Jesus," he whispered. He hurried to the bed and placed his hand on her forehead. Her skin felt like it was on fire. Darren pulled out his cellphone and dialed 9-1-1.

"She okay?"

Darren nearly dropped the phone. Maeve leaned against the doorjamb.

"No, she's not." He put the phone to his ear. The operator picked up.

"9-1-1. What is your emergency?"

Without a beat, Darren told the operator the building's address and Marie's condition. She promised an ambulance in fifteen minutes or less and asked for Darren to stay on the line.

"Maeve?" he said while cupping his hand over the receiver. She blinked at him. "I'll need you to go to the front entrance and get Jakob to let the EMTs into the building when they get here."

She frowned. "I don't have a card key."

Darren reached down and unhooked his card from his chinos. "Catch." He tossed the card to her. Maeve caught it in the air. "That'll let you through the door if you get locked out."

Maeve nodded. "Okay. What else can I—"

"I got it, dear. She's very sick, but I don't think she's dying." The words sounded like a lie the moment they left his mouth. "Now go on and wait for them."

"You want me to tell my mom?"

Darren bit his lip. "No. Let's wait until after the EMTs get here."

"Okay," Maeve said. She hurried away from the door.

Panic. That was the real enemy here. If he panicked, Maeve would panic. And no one needed that. But his heart pounded in his chest and he felt damned hot. Of course, that could be because he was hunched next to a human furnace.

He turned away from the door and looked back at Marie. Her eyelids fluttered. Darren slid one of them up and looked into her eye in the dim light.

Flecks of something danced in the whites of her eyes. *What the fuck did you catch, girl?* Darren closed the eyelid. Her breath hitched and his heart stopped. It seemed like an eternity before her chest rose again in a shaky rhythm.

Seconds ticked off and turned into minutes. He held Marie's hand in his and whispered a prayer. Regardless of what he'd said to Maeve, Marie was dying. And he knew it. With his closed mouth moving as he spoke silent words and pleas, he didn't notice the movement in her leg. He didn't see the way her foot jerked and then turned sideways as the bone fractured and dissolved. But he heard the fracture's crack and crunch.

Darren opened his eyes and looked down at the bed. He didn't notice her foot was turned the wrong way, but he did see the blood seeping out of her skin. "Jesus." The word was barely audible even to him.

"Sir? Are you still there?" a tinny voice said through the phone.

He brought it back to his ear. "Yes. Yes, ma'am."

"The ambulance has arrived and they're heading to your location."

A relieved sigh escaped his lips. "Thank you."

"I'm going to hang up now. Please tell the EMTs everything you've told me."

"I will," Darren said. "Thank you." He ended the phone call and pocketed the phone.

"Hello?" a voice yelled from the hallway.

"Here. We're down here!" Darren yelled through the open doorway.

A moment later, two paramedics walked in, Maeve in tow. She flipped the light switch and the fluorescents bathed the mother's room.

One medic carried a large bag, the other rolled a stretcher. The first EMT asked what Marie had taken, how long she'd been ill. "What's her name?" the paramedic asked.

"Marie," Darren said. "Marie Krieger."

The medic crouched next to the bed. "Marie? Can you hear me?" He slid up an eyelid and shined an LED flashlight in her eye. "Marie?" He turned to Darren. "How long has she been unconscious?"

"Don't know. Didn't realize she wasn't sleeping until I called 9-1-1." Darren's lip quivered. "Is she——"

"She's non-responsive," the red-headed EMT said. He put a hand on her forehead. "Holy shit. Joe?"

The EMT named Joe raised his eyebrows.

"We have to get her out of here. Now." Joe nodded and unfolded the stretcher. The other EMT looked at Darren. "We're going to take her to the nearest ER. Do you have someone to come with us?"

"I'll go," he said. "I'll make a call from the ambulance."

"Good."

Joe reached for Marie's legs and stopped. "Holy shit. Is that blood?"

"Doesn't fucking matter, man," the red-head said. "She's going to die if we don't get her temp down."

Joe carefully put his arms beneath her legs while the red-head slid his under Marie's torso. As the two men lifted her onto the stretcher, Marie's body cracked and crunched. "What the hell?"

"Shut up, Joe. Let's go!" the red-head yelled. The two men rolled the stretcher from the room and to the elevator.

Darren stood, phone in hand. Maeve was just outside the door, face pale and eyes wild. He put a hand on her shoulder. "Maeve? You did good." She handed back his badge. Darren tried to smile and failed. "Let your mom know we're taking Marie to the hospital, okay? I have to go."

Maeve said nothing, only nodded.

He ran down the hallway. The EMTs had barely managed to get the stretcher into the elevator. Darren slammed the "G" button and the elevator began its descent. The red-head was on the radio telling the ER Marie's condition and that they were on their way. Darren hoped they'd arrive in time.

* * *

The temperature widget blinked. "350°C," she said to Jay. "Let's see what we're getting."

He stood next to her and peered over her shoulder. The pair of chemists watched and waited for the analyzers to display the results. The bottom of the curve blinked and showed the first cut range of 60°C.

Kate sighed. "What the hell? We should have something here."

Jay hissed through his teeth. "Remember how light the oil is? Maybe there's no lighter hydrocarbons in it."

"Maybe." Kate tapped a finger on the keyboard's edge.

"What are you thinking?" Jay asked.

She shrugged. "I'm thinking we need to try another cut."

"Okay. Let's reset the analyzer and get the next—"

The analyzer graph changed. A tiny curve appeared. Jay and Kate waited for it to move again. It didn't. Frowning, Kate zoomed in on the graph.

"What. The. Fuck." Jay's voice was a guttural whisper.

Kate shook her head. "Tell me that doesn't say what it's saying."

"Goddammit." Jay stood to his full height and stretched. "Explain to me how a hydrocarbon changes to water?"

"Does anything with this shit make sense?" Kate asked.

At 60°C, they should be catching hexane and light gasoline. Instead? Water vapor.

"Boiling oil turns into water vapor." Jay shook his head. "That's just not possible. Chemically speaking, it's just not goddamned possible."

Kate saved the analysis to the RAID drive and swiveled in the chair. She clasped her hands together and stared at her partner. "This isn't oil," she said. "I don't know what it is, but it's not oil."

"No shit." Jay scratched at his scalp through thinning hair. "So what do we do now? Seems to me the only things left are NMR and a light test."

She nodded. "If Chuckles has the computers ready, NMR will at least give us some idea of the molecular composition. A light test?" She bit her lip. "That will show us what it reacts to. How it flows." She thought for a moment and then nodded. "Okay. I agree. Let's get set up for those."

Jay shook his head. "Not yet. We need to see something first."

"Which is?"

A grin slowly spread over his face. His white teeth gleamed in the light. "We need to see what's left in the reflux. The oil boiled. So what's it look like now?"

Kate opened her mouth to reply, and then stopped. Analyze the reflux? If the oil produced water vapor, did it break down under the heat? Did the chemical composition somehow change? "Okay. Yeah. Let's take a look at this stuff. But I think we need to stop calling it oil."

Jay said, "M2. It's M2."

"Yes," Kate said. "M2 it is." She moved the mouse and clicked a few icons. The gas heater whumped as the flames went out. "It's going to cool down now. Let's give it—" Kate's phone chirped. She pulled it from her pocket and stared at the screen. "Shit."

"What is it?" Jay asked.

Kate looked up from the phone. "Marie. Darren called an ambulance for her. Maeve said they're heading out now."

Jay shook his head. "Goddammit. You think we should leave? Follow or something?"

"Hang on." Kate texted Maeve and waited. Her phone lit up with a new message. "Maeve doesn't even know where they took her. I guess Darren will call Mike and let him know."

"What the hell kind of flu takes her down in a few hours and sends her to the hospital?" Jay clenched his fists. "They better have taken her to the med center."

Kate sighed and looked back at the screen. "She'll be okay." Even as the words came out of her mouth, she knew she didn't believe them. Something was wrong. The oil. The goddamned oil. It had to— "Jay?"

"Yes?"

She swiveled in her chair. Jay flinched from her stare. "She cut herself, right? When she opened the barrel?"

Jay frowned. "Yeah. That's why her hand was bandaged. But—" He chewed the side of his mouth. "What? You think she got infected by something? Like mud fluid? Or—"

"Or something else," she said. "Maybe some bacteria from a volcanic vent somehow got in the oil. Or something like that."

"Hmm…" Jay thought for a moment and then shook his head. "That's crazy. You punch down into the trench. If they'd hit a volcanic vent, the drill string would have been vaporized."

"Okay, I get that," Kate said. "But what if the oil reservoir congealed around one? Or the vent went dormant? There's anaerobic bacteria down there. It could have sat in the oil for, well, who knows how long."

"Kate, that kind of bacteria feeds on particles of organic life. Usually. I know some of them can feed on sulfur and other chemicals, but if it fed on the oil, it would have eaten the oil. M2 is a closed system. There wouldn't be any left."

She spun in her seat and stared back at the monitor. "Yeah. You're right."

"But," Jay said, "there could have been something else on the container cap. Like maybe it picked up something on its way here?"

Kate picked up her phone, unlocked it, and went through her address book. When she found Darren's number, she stood and walked to the control console. "I'm calling Darren."

"Good idea," Jay said. "I'm going to go talk to Neil. Maybe see if he can get something off the cap."

Jay touched her shoulder as he walked out of the lab. Despite the contact's brevity, it felt reassuring. As she dialed Darren's cell phone number into the cordless land line, she hissed a sigh through her teeth and wondered how the night could get any worse.

* * *

The hallway was brighter than the lab. Jay squinted as he walked between the two labs and headed for the secure holding area. He swiped his card at the heavy steel door. The reader beeped and the lock clicked open.

He pushed on the door and it swung wide. Jay walked into the room and shivered. Although the area was secure and as airtight as the construction crews could make it, it wasn't well insulated. The dropping temperature outside had left the room colder than usual. On top of that, the wind must have been blowing the rain sideways. He heard it slamming against the building's steel walls.

The bright light shined off the steel shelves, but he saw what he was looking for through the glare. The tool, the one he designed and put together, sat on one of the shelves. Jay started walking toward it and then slowed. *What if it's infectious? What if it's airborne?* He paused for a moment and then grunted. *If it's what made Marie sick, then it's definitely infectious. But airborne?* All the talk in the lab about anaerobic bacteria living on volcanic vents thousands of feet beneath the ocean surface had his mind racing.

He checked his gloves. The corrosive/chemical resistant protection would keep him safe from anything that had been in the barrel. He hoped.

He pushed his glasses up with a gloved knuckle and stared through the bottom of the progressive bifocals at the metal tool. Marie hadn't detached the lid. It was still there, its bottom stained with a black film.

Jay looked around the storeroom and found what he was looking for. The supply cabinet was ajar. He smiled and opened the door. A small box of heavy plastic zipper bags stared back at him. He pulled out a fresh bag. The plastic slipped easily from its container. Jay grabbed a black marker from the shelf and marked it "M2" with a barely legible scrawl.

Opening the bag was much more difficult than he had expected. The glove's fingers weren't exactly thick, but they were thick enough to make the task more difficult than it should have been. Jay sighed. When he finally managed to open the bag, he headed to the shelf with the remover.

A drop of oil sat on the shelf next to it. Jay's eyebrows raised. Had that been there before? He frowned and then looked at the plastic. What if the barrel hadn't contained oil after all? What if Kate was right and something else was in the barrel other than crude? Would it eat through plastic?

Jay tapped his foot. Yosemite Sam's voice screamed "Tarnation!" in his mind. *Well, genius, besides breaking down its molecular structure, how are you going to know? Simple. Test it.*

He fought a shiver of fear and moved a step closer to the shelf. The black, teardrop shape didn't move. He had expected it to. He really had. But didn't understand why. *Kate has you completely freaked out,* he thought. *There's nothing to be afraid of. It's just some goddamned sludge from a goddamned trench in the goddamned ocean. It might be strange, but it's just another fucking hydrocarbon. GET OVER IT!*

An embarrassed grin lit his face. He felt stupid, knew he was being stupid, but that didn't stop his hands from quivering. He put his thumb inside the bag so he had some leverage and kept his palm and fingers on top of it. Jay took in a deep breath and then pressed the plastic bag down atop the black drop.

The smell of burning plastic wrinkled his nostrils before his mind accepted what he was seeing. The plastic in contact with the oil curled and boiled. He pulled the plastic bag off the shelf, but held it in front of him like a shield. The droplet had burned through the first layer of the plastic bag. He stared at the droplet. It was no longer tear-shaped. Instead, it had become a tiny, circular dome.

Jay stepped away from the shelf, eyes still focused on the black. "Sufferin' succotash," Sylvester whispered from his mouth. Flecks of spittle flew with the words and landed next to the little blob of black.

Well, plastic isn't going to work. What's next? He turned back to the supply cabinet. He clucked his tongue and scanned the well-organized trays and boxes. Wrenches, hammers, plastic, socket sets, fasteners...

He turned around and faced the shelves. The blob seemed... bigger. A shiver ran down his back. He took a deep breath and laughed at himself. This was asinine. There was no reason to be afraid of it. It dissolved plastic. Lots of chemicals did that. Hell, even some common hydrocarbons could eat through certain plastics.

Melt, idiot. Not burn.

Jay tried to ignore the sarcastic voice in his head. Tried, but failed. It was right. Melting wasn't the same as burning. And that shit had burned through the plastic like a flame.

He needed something. Pyrex. Metal. It obviously couldn't eat through either substance. It had traveled all the way from Leaguer in a regular old oil drum and they had transferred it using Pyrex. The oil... *No*, he told himself, *the M2*. The M2 hadn't dissolved any matter with densely packed molecules.

Jay eyed the door leading back to the lab hallway. He didn't want to go all the way out there just to come back in. But what else was there he could use to get a sample of what had infected Marie?

Fuck it, he said to himself. He walked to the shelf and picked up the cap-removal tool. The lid still had a film of M2 on it. That should work for what they needed. He'd worry about cleaning up the blob later.

He picked up the tool by the handle and held it away from his body. Something twitched in the corner of his vision. Jay's eyes flicked back to the black blob on the steel shelf. It was still a dome of impossible darkness. A small, circular patch of shining steel was next to it. Jay blinked at it.

The metal was old. The rest of the shelves looked weathered and, in some places, rusted. The gleaming circle of brightness was as out of place as the black blob.

Jay stepped back from the shelving, stripped off a glove, and palmed his phone from the lab coat pocket. He pressed his naked thumb against the sensor and it unlocked. Afraid to lose eye contact with the drop of M2, he held the phone up so he could keep it in the corner of his eye while he scanned the icons on the screen.

He found the camera icon and pressed it. The phone's screen flashed and then showed the shelves. Jay focused the phone on the blob and the shining metal next to it. He took a step forward to get them both in the frame, and then pressed the shutter icon.

The phone's impossibly bright LED flashed. Just to be sure, he hit the icon again and the phone took another photo. He didn't think anyone would quite understand the importance of the shining metal. Hell, he wasn't sure he understood it. But at least he had some photos.

Jay turned from the shelf, pocketed the phone, slipped on the glove, and made his way to the security door. He pressed his key card against the reader and it beeped. A slight push and the door was open. Before he entered the hallway, he turned once more and stared at the shelf.

From this distance, he shouldn't have been able to make out the blob. But there it was, sitting on the shelf. Something so black that light seemed to slide off its surface. Shaking his head, Jay closed the door and headed for the bio-lab.

* * *

She listened as the ringer buzzed on the other end of the line. *Pick up, Darren.* Ring. Ring. *PICK UP!* Finally, the ringing stopped.

"You have reached the voicemail of Darren Strange. Please leave your name, number, and a brief message, and I'll get back to you as soon as possible."

Kate sighed. When the line beeped, her voice came out in a rush of words. "Darren, this is Kate in the lab. We forgot to tell you that Marie may have been infected by something in the barrel from PPE. She cut her hand. Tell the EMTs to check it and call me back here in the lab." She left the number for the lab's landline and hung up the phone.

She tented her hands on the desk and stared at it. How long ago had the ambulance left? Ten minutes? Less? What had happened?

Stop panicking, she told herself. If Darren was in the back of the ambulance with Marie and an EMT, he probably couldn't even hear his phone ringing. She hissed between her teeth. Or maybe he was talking to Mike.

Mike. She sighed and picked up the phone again. She dialed Mike's extension and waited.

The phone picked up on the third ring.

"This is Mike."

Kate smiled. It didn't matter how tired he was, how pissed he was, Mike always sounded like an old friend you'd missed talking to. On the phone, anyway.

"Mike, it's Kate."

"Hey, Kate. Can I call you back? I'm on the phone with Darren."

She blew a sigh between her teeth. "Well that explains why he didn't answer my call. We need him to know something."

"What's that?" Mike asked.

"This may sound crazy," she said, "but Marie cut herself on the PPE barrel. We think she may have been infected by something on the cap."

There was a pause. She imagined him in his office, leaned back in his chair, and studying the ceiling while his mind raced around in circles. "Infected," he repeated. "Okay. I'll tell him. Let me call you back in a few minutes."

"Thanks, Mike."

The line went dead. Kate hung up the phone and pulled out her cell. She made sure the WiFi signal was still strong and it was. Kate typed out a message to Maeve and sent it. She just wanted to make sure her daughter wasn't freaking out.

When Maeve replied with a goofy face emoji, Kate couldn't help but smile. She was proud of the girl. Maeve took care of Marie the best she could, and sounded the alarm when things went bad.

Bad. The word kept echoing in her skull. What if Marie died? What if whatever was on the cap of the barrel was airborne? What if they were all infected? What if—

She caught movement out of the corner of her eye. Kate turned to the glass wall. Jay walked down the corridor between the two labs, the removal tool held in his hands. He was white as a sheet. She moved to leave the chair and head out into the hall, and then remembered Mike was going to call her back.

Whatever Jay had seen in the secured area had obviously frightened him. Or maybe he was just scared of catching whatever Marie was infected with. Or maybe—

The phone buzzed. Kate flinched. It rang again and she picked up the receiver. "This is Kate."

"Kate. Mike. Darren says Marie is in bad shape. He's going to call me again as soon as they get to the ER."

"You tell him about the barrel? About the cut?"

"Yeah," Mike said. "I did. He told the EMTs and they've made the ER aware as well."

"He going to call you when he knows something?"

Mike cleared his throat. "Yes. And as soon as I can speak with the doctors at the ER, I will. For right now, though, I think it's best if your team uses all caution with the PPE sample until we figure out what happened with Marie."

"Jay took the top of the cap to Neil and his team. They might be able to at least see if there's some kind of bacteria on the lid that cut her."

The line went silent.

"Mike? Still there?" she asked.

"Yes." He sounded tired and frustrated. "If you have any worries about continuing your tests, then stop. I'll tell Simpson he can wait."

Stop the analysis! A voice said in her mind. *Quit fucking with this stuff until you know what's going on!*

"I'll think about it, Mike. Let me talk to Jay and I'll get back to you."

"Okay. Just be damned careful. I don't want anyone else going to the ER tonight."

She grinned. "Yes, sir."

She heard a beep on Mike's end. "Fuck. Call me when you guys make a decision. I have another call."

"Will do," Kate said. But the line had already gone dead.

She swung her head toward the sample delivery spigot. Between the barrel and what had been vacuum-pumped into the pipes, they still had gallons of M2. *Gallons.* If the oil itself was the cause of the infection, they were sitting next to a goddamned bomb.

Kate stood from the desk and looked through the glass. In the other lab, Jay stood next to Neil's bio-chemists. Neil was sitting at a workstation with a microscope. She wondered how long it would be before they knew something. If anything.

She glanced at the distillation tower and wondered if the oil was cool enough to take a peek. The computer console announced the temperature of the oil. It was only 24°C. Time to see what the stuff looked like after it had been heated up.

***

Neil pushed his horn-rimmed glasses up on his aquiline nose and peered into the microscope. Jay stood a few feet back next to Bill Field.

Just getting the remaining oil off the lid and onto a slide had been a chore. When Jay had brought the sample in and explained to Neil how corrosive it was, the bio-chemist had merely blinked. Neil and Bill, however, hadn't bothered asking questions. Instead, they appeared welcome for the distraction.

Neil sat back in the chair and swiveled so he could face them. "I can't see anything."

Jay cocked an eyebrow. "What do you mean you can't see anything?"

Neil scratched at the remaining hair on his scalp. "Not enough light, maybe. I don't know. This stuff… Light just seems to fall into it."

"And we can't use an electron microscope," Bill said.

One of Neil's team, Bill was probably the oldest person working at HAL. He had three PhDs and seemed only happy when he was in the lab. Jay had beers with him once or twice a month. In addition to his love of the lab, the old fart was also an incorrigible dirty old man.

"Why's that?" Jay asked.

Bill shrugged. "We need a biological sample. Or something we can freeze. Unless—" Bill's words trailed off.

"Unless, we create an emulsion," Neil said. His smile displayed his crooked, dingy teeth. "We can suspend the oil in water and create a slide the SEM can actually analyze."

"Yup, that'll work," Bill said. He turned to Jay. "Shouldn't take us too long to prepare it and fire up the SEM to take a peek."

Jay nodded. "Okay. But I want to tell you again how corrosive this stuff is. I know the sample is small, but one drop of this crap ate through a plastic bag."

"We'll be careful," Neil said. "You really think this will help Marie?"

Jay shrugged. "I don't know. But the more information we can send to the hospital, the better off she'll be."

Neil clucked his tongue. "Okay. Mike will have a heart attack. I mean we're already late on the analysis for the museum. But I think this takes priority."

Jay clapped Neil on the shoulder. "Thanks, man. And if there's any flak from Mike, just send it my way."

"Will do," Neil said. "Give us about an hour," he wiped at his bloodshot eyes, "and we should have something for you."

* * *

When Jay re-entered the lab, Kate was pulling apart the bottom distillation tray. "Don't!" he yelled at her.

She flinched and turned to him. "Jesus, Jay. What the hell?"

He walked to her in quick steps, his mouth set in a grim line. "Look. I just got the lid from the secure area."

"So?" She stood up and faced him.

"There was a drop of M2 on the shelf," Jay said. He gulped as he remembered the inexplicable fear he'd felt when facing it. "I tried to pick it up with a plastic bag and it melted the plastic."

Kate blinked. "What?"

"Yeah. It melted it."

Her eyes tilted toward the ceiling and then flipped to the dispenser station. "Melted?" Kate flipped her eyes back to his. "So what kind of hydrocarbon melts plastic?"

"Gasoline can melt certain plastics. Toluene, hexane."

She nodded. "The lighter hydrocarbons can damage thin plastics. Right. And M2 is damned light."

"And," Jay said, "it might have something else in it. I mean, we haven't exactly been able to determine what this shit really is."

Kate thought for a moment. "Okay. But I want to see what it looks like after the distillation run. We boiled it. Nothing came out. No gas, no particles, nothing. So what happened to it?"

Jay opened his mouth to reply and then stopped. What *did* happen to it? Did it break down into other components? Did it still have corrosive properties? A grim smile lit his face. "If we're going to examine the remains of the distillation, we need to be damned careful. I suggest we get all the safety gear we use for acids and toxic gases."

She cocked an eyebrow. "You worried M2 turned into sulfuric acid? Or H_2S?"

He nodded. "Why not?"

"The analyzers didn't pick up any changes like that."

"Why would they?" Jay asked. "If it didn't actually turn into gas under heat, M2's molecular structure could have changed into something toxic. Maybe not in a gaseous form, but it's certainly possible it turned into an acid."

She rolled her eyes. "No, Jay. We would have seen evidence of the chemical breakdown in the heat signatures."

"Exactly," Jay said. "And how fast did this stuff heat up?"

Kate thought for a moment. She fingered the distillation table's metal surface. "Okay. I still think you're wrong, but let's do it your way. Regardless, I think we need to run the light test as well as the NMR."

"Agreed," Jay said. "Neil's team is going to use a scanning electron microscope to analyze the sample I brought back from the secure area."

"How soon they going to have results for us?" she asked.

"He said in less than an hour."

Kate's eyes dropped to the floor. "Shit."

"What's wrong?" Jay asked.

She bit her lip. "I was hopeful we'd have something sooner than that."

"You talk to Mike yet?"

She nodded and raised her eyes. "He was on the phone with Darren when I called. He told Darren about a possible infection from M2. Last I heard, they were nearing the hospital."

Jay blew a sigh between his teeth. "Good. Man, I hope she's going to be okay."

"So do I," Kate said. She turned her gaze back to the distillation tower. "Let's gear up and see what we can see. We can't help Marie until we have as much information as possible."

"True," Jay said. He eyed the rack of safety equipment on the wall. "Let's do this."

CHAPTER FOUR

The ambulance was screaming through the intersections and passing the sparse vehicles on the Pasadena streets. After Darren told the EMTs that Marie may have been infected by a biological agent, they scrapped their plans to head to the nearest ER. The dispatcher insisted they take their patient to the medical center.

Ever since Ebola-stricken people had entered the country, major hospitals had been trained in rapidly deploying quarantine protocols. Darren had no idea what that entailed, but the blond EMT had explained it as he hooked up another IV bag.

Marie was in bad shape. Her skin was so white, it was impossible to tell she'd ever been anything else. Strands of long, kinky hair had fallen out of her head. She looked as though a three-year old had given her a haircut with a pair of pliers.

"Okay. We're almost there!" the driver yelled from the ambulance cabin.

Darren was still holding Marie's hand. The flesh was so hot, she might as well have been boiling from the inside. The heart monitor hooked up to her chest beeped in an arrhythmic beat. "Stay with me, Marie," Darren said. He didn't know if she could hear him, but it made him feel a little better to talk to her. When they first entered the ambulance and started their journey to the ER, he'd felt stupid talking to her. Now, he wondered if his voice would be the last thing she ever heard.

The heart monitor flatlined for a second and then resumed its stumbling beat. "Hang on, girl," Darren said.

The ambulance took a sharp turn. The metal stretcher rattled along with the other gear. "Jesus, man, don't kill us in getting there!" the blond EMT shouted.

Darren listed backward and then snapped forward as the vehicle came to a stop. "We're here!" the driver yelled.

The doors opened and bright light streamed into the ambulance. Darren blinked as his eyes adjusted. He stifled a surprised yelp when he saw what had opened the doors.

Three figures, dressed in blue hazmat suits, stood outside the doors. Their faces, full of concern and concentration, stared at the stretcher. The blond EMT groaned. "You fucking kidding me?" he said to no one.

Two of the hazmat suited figures strode forward and grabbed the stretcher's edge. They pulled it out of the ambulance and the wheels unfolded as it hit the concrete. The two figures quickly rolled the stretcher out of sight.

Darren moved to get out of the ambulance, but the remaining hazmat suited figure held up a hand.

"Mr. Strange?" a woman's voice said through the helmet.

Darren nodded. "Yes."

The fiftyish woman in the suit frowned at him. "I need to get some information from you before we put you in quarantine."

"Fucking quarantine," the EMT murmured.

The woman shot him a glaring stare and he immediately shut up. "Are you feeling any symptoms? Fever? Joint pain?"

His heart hammered in his chest. Did he feel anything? Had he? He'd been so focused on Marie that he hadn't—"

"Mr. Strange?" the suited figure asked.

"Sorry," Darren said. "No. I'm fine."

"You look pale."

"Of course I look pale," Darren said. "One of my coworkers is very sick and you fine folks ambushed us wearing fucking moon suits!"

The woman in the suit cracked a ghost of a smile. "Sorry for the dramatics," she said. "But we need to make sure this isn't an airborne microbe."

Airborne? Darren cringed. "If it was, everyone at the lab would be sick. Well, except for the bio-lab."

"You have a bio-lab at your company?"

He nodded. "Yeah. They work on animal strains and DNA analysis."

The woman frowned. "Do they work with any biologically hazardous specimens?"

Darren let the words sink in. "Um, no. Nothing like that. They just look at animal and plant samples from drilling sites and occasionally do work for the museums."

She nodded. "Okay. Mr. Strange? I'd like you to follow me." She turned her laser stare at the EMT. "You and the driver stay put. Another member of my team will be with you shortly."

The EMT sighed. "Yes, ma'am."

"Come with me." She stepped aside so Darren could exit through the rear.

He shuffled out of the ambulance and put his feet on the ground. The rain pounded the pavement beyond the overhang and a cold wind tore at his clothes. *Should have worn a jacket*, he said to himself.

He turned to follow the blue-suited woman and stopped. A large plastic tunnel led from the ER entrance and into the hospital. "What the hell?" he asked.

She turned back to him. "If you please, Mr. Strange."

"Darren," he said. "Please call me Darren."

"Okay, Darren." She gestured to him and walked into the tunnel. Darren followed.

The plastic was translucent enough for him to see the scared, dazed faces in the ER waiting room. Nurses and doctors continued their walks through the halls, but every one of them paused in their steps to look at him through the plastic.

His flesh erupted in goose bumps. He wanted to think it was the cold biting through his thin sweater, but he knew it was fear. Plain and simple fear. Did Marie have Ebola? Or maybe some devastating form of bubonic plague? Darren's head filled with scenes from zombie movies. He shivered and continued following the blue moon-suited figure.

His shoes crunched on the plastic and for a moment, he thought he would slip. Darren gritted his teeth and continued down the long tunnel. Up ahead, he made out an impossibly bright room. As the blue-suited figure stepped out of the tunnel, the brightness intensified. Darren shielded his eyes and stepped out.

When his eyes adjusted, the shivers returned. They were in an operating room. Marie's body twitched beneath glowing blankets. Strong lamps were pointed at her face while another hazmat suited figure checked her eyes.

"Darren?"

He turned to his escort. She had a pen and clipboard in her hands. "Yes?"

The woman's face was once again hard as stone. "I'm Doctor Harrel from the CDC."

He gulped. "CDC? What the hell is—"

"Please. I have a couple of questions for you and then you can ask me some. Okay?"

Darren nodded.

She asked him if he worked for HAL. She asked him if he'd been exposed to any biological contaminants. She asked how Marie had been exposed. When he mentioned the barrel from PPE, she raised an eyebrow.

"So she cut herself opening the barrel?"

Darren nodded. "That's what the other chemists told me."

She wrote something down on the clipboard. Darren wondered

how she could write while wearing those thick gloves. "So you didn't see her get cut?"

"No. Hell, I don't even know what the barrel looks like. I just know where it came from."

She blinked. "And where did you get it?"

He rolled his eyes. "It's a sample. From an offshore oil platform called Leaguer."

She scribbled. "And where is this platform?"

Darren shifted his feet. "I don't know. Somewhere in the vicinity of Papua/New Guinea."

Her eyes flicked up from the paper. "Okay." She pointed to a bed against the other wall. "We need you to pull that curtain, undress, and put on a gown. As soon as you're ready, we'll examine you for contaminants."

"Contaminants?"

Dr. Harrel frowned. "Yes, Darren." She gestured to Marie's stretcher. "We need to make sure you don't end up like her."

His lip quivered. "Is she dying?"

"Yes." She placed a gloved hand on his shoulder. "We're doing everything we can, Darren. We're close to stabilizing her, but we don't know how much damage the infection has done."

Darren wiped a tear from his eye. Marie. Marie had been the youngest scientist HAL had ever hired. She was sweet, shy, and barely talked unless it was about chemistry. At least with other people. With Darren, however, she'd opened up. He glanced at her twitching form on the stretcher.

"Can't let her die," he mumbled.

Dr. Harrel nodded. "We're doing our best." She pointed at the bed. "Let's make sure you're not infected, okay?"

He wiped another tear from his eye and nodded. On numb feet he headed to the bed and pulled the curtain closed. He took off his sweater and the room's cold bit through his undershirt. By the time he pulled off his underwear, he was shivering. And this time, not from fear.

Socks, gown, and blankets lay on the bed. He dressed as quickly as he could. He could hear the doctors talking to one another as they tried to keep Marie alive.

"This is Dr. Harrel. I want a quarantine team set up at ground zero immediately." Darren peeked around the corner and saw Dr. Harrel staring at Marie's blanketed body. She cocked her head as she listened to a voice on the other end of the radio. "Yes. Full quarantine. No one in or out without a suit. And I don't want anyone inside until we make contact with those labs." She paused again. "No. We don't know if it's airborne. I'll have to finish examination of Mr. Strange and the EMTs before I determine that."

Darren pulled on his socks. His stomach churned with nervous fear. The doctor kept talking into the radio, but he'd stopped listening. HAL was being quarantined. He was quarantined and the ambulance crew would be as well. It was past midnight, and he'd never felt more awake and terrified in his life.

* * *

Kate's skin itched. The comfortable lab coat hung on a hook next to Jay's. She had stripped off her normal lab gloves and replaced them with a heavier pair. While the others were designed for possible interactions with toxic chemicals, these were made for probable encounters. In other words, she was counting on getting M2 on her.

The suit she wore zipped over the gloves. Her comfortable running shoes had been replaced with heavy booties made of the same substance as the gloves. A heavy hood covered her head and hung down past the top of the suit. The faceplate was made of Pyrex.

The chem-lab, unlike the bio-lab, didn't have oxygen hoses for the suits. Instead, the chem suits had filters for short term exposure to toxic substances. But really, if something like hydrogen sulfide gas broke out in the lab, the chemists would have to hit the purge fans and get the hell out of the lab as quickly as possible. The suits would protect them for a minute or two, but beyond that, death was certain.

"You hear me okay?" she asked.

Jay nodded. "Yup," his voice said through the radio. "Hear you just fine. And you're panting."

"Damned suit is hot."

"Yeah. I noticed. It's ball-sweat bayou in here."

"I'll take your word for it." Kate walked to the distillation tower. "How do you want to do this?"

Jay stood next to her, his eyes focused on the bottom tank. "Like we always do. Just goddamned carefully."

They locked eyes for a moment. Jay looked calm, but she knew better. The color in his face was off and his eyes sparkled with nervous energy. "You ready?"

Jay gritted his teeth and then nodded. Kate nodded back to him and then put her hands around the top of the boiler assembly. Jay grabbed the bottom and twisted.

The click of the lock disengaging echoed in the lab. Kate looked down as Jay slowly lowered the boiler section. She drew in a deep breath. "Oh. My. God."

Jay quickly put the iron bowl on the floor and stepped back. Kate stepped back too.

"What the hell is that?" The color had completely drained from his face. Kate barely heard his words as she stared into the remains of the oil.

It's not oil, she told herself. *Oil doesn't do that.*

Threads of burned, black material rose up the sides. Each thread ended in a hook like shape. That was bad enough. But it was the center of the bowl that chilled her to the bone.

The oil in the middle of the iron bowl was burned into a solid shape. Kate's mind struggled to put it into context and finally succeeded. She wished it hadn't. An appendage. It was the only word that came to mind to describe the tentacle-like shape rising from the bowl. Its end was razor sharp and curled into a hook like the threads on the bowl's sides.

"What the hell *is* that?" Jay asked again.

Kate raised her eyes to his. "I don't know," she said at last. Her mouth had gone dry and the words came out in a croak. "It's not a liquid anymore."

"No," Jay agreed. "It's not." He lowered himself to his haunches, but stayed a few feet away from the bowl. "At least not on top. But from the coloring, I'd say the M2 became a solid through and through." He looked up at her. "Boiling it changed its structure."

"But into what?"

Jay stood, eyes flicking to the equipment hanging on the wall. "Let's find out. We can take a sample and put it in the NMR. Maybe even get a slice for Neil's team. That electron microscope might tell us a few things."

"Okay. And how do you propose we get a sample?" She took another step away from the bowl. "I don't think I want to get near that shit."

"Yeah. About that." Jay walked to the shelves housing dozens and dozens of different sized beakers as well as various sized forceps and other lab tools. He picked the longest and smallest pair of forceps and turned back to Kate. "I might be able to grab a chunk with this."

Kate rolled her eyes. "You're crazy."

"Sufferin' succotash, lady! We have to do something!"

Kate saw flecks of spittle cling to the inside of Jay's faceplate and laughed. Jay blushed. "You might want to try Elmer Fudd when you're wearing that suit."

"Um, yeah," Jay said. He walked toward the bowl, forceps extended. He had to get on his haunches again, only much, much, closer to the bowl. His faceplate fogged from his rapid breathing.

Kate walked until she was behind him. "Calm, Jay. Calm." She placed her gloved hands on his shoulder. His raspy breathing in her headset slowed and diminished.

For a moment, she wasn't sure he could muster the courage. And then, without warning, his hands reached forward and the tool closed around the tip of the brown, crusted shape. The material crunched as the metal prongs tightened. Both she and Jay flinched at the sound. Particles of the substance crumbled into the bottom of the bowl. Jay slowly pulled the tool backward.

"You got it," Kate said. She hissed a sigh between her teeth as Jay lifted the pincers. The bottom portion of the hook-like shape was between the metal prongs.

Kate stepped back and Jay stood with his prize. He walked in slow steps to the stainless steel examination table.

She made her way to the equipment shelves and pulled a deep, stainless steel tray into her hands. Then she turned and put it on the table. Jay lowered the sample.

"Here goes." He released pressure from the handles.

The sample thumped into the tray. Bits of mass crumbled like dried mud and peppered the tray's gleaming surface. The hook, however, remained mostly intact.

Kate grabbed a magnifying glass from the collection of tools on the table. She focused it on the sample and leaned over to get as close as she could. The soft light made it nearly impossible to see. "Jay? A little more light?"

He reached for the gooseneck lamp and swiveled it until the bulb was above the tray. He flicked the switch.

A cone of bright, white LED light shined down on the tray. The exposed steel reflected the light back into her face. She blinked as her eyes adjusted and then held the magnifying glass back to the sample. She took in a deep breath.

The material looked like a burned brownie or sedimentary rock. The hook and its base were little more than crumbs still clinging to one another. Kate looked at Jay and offered him the magnifying glass.

Jay took it and studied the sample. "Hmm." He lifted the magnifying glass and then reached across the table for a pair of tweezers. "Let's see just how fragile this shit is."

Kate held up a hand. "I don't think that's a good idea."

His teeth flashed in a grin. "No such thing as good ideas, Kate. Only varying shades of bad."

"What?"

Tweezers gripped in his fingers, he closed the metal tines around the base and then pinched. The base crackled and then crumbled into chocolate colored grit.

Kate let out a deep breath. When Jay had touched the sample with the tool, her heart rate spiked into a sprint. A bead of sweat ran down her cheek. "No liquid."

Jay looked up at her. "No liquid," he echoed. "Which means it underwent a phase change."

"That's not possible. It would have produced gas. The analyzer would have picked that up."

He placed the tweezers down on the table next to the tray and put his hands on his hips. "Science explains everything. Until it doesn't."

"Bullshit," Kate said.

"You misunderstand." Jay raised his gloved hands. "Ancient man thought the sun rising every day was magic. The starlight, mere pinholes in the blanket of night. That was the extent of their science." He peered back down at the tray. "Maybe we just don't have the tools to understand this."

She took the tweezers from the table and clicked them between her gloved fingers. "I haven't given up yet. We still have the NMR." She jerked a thumb toward the glass partition separating the chem lab from the bio lab. "And maybe the SEM will show us something too."

Jay said, "Then let's see what else our science can figure out. Because right now, I feel like we're in the damned twilight zone."

* * *

After all of Jay's warnings about the substance's corrosive qualities, Neil had decided to treat the sample like a bio-contaminant. The protocols in place for dealing with potentially hazardous chemicals were essentially the same as with hazardous biological contaminants. The difference? Neil's team wore positively pressured suits. The oxygen hoses attached to their backs made movement awkward and Bill had more than once nearly pulled his out of the ceiling. Neil just hoped Bill remembered their bio-hazard training.

Bill was stooped over a stainless steel table with a syringe. Because they only had the underside of the metal lid to work with, they'd suck up what they could into a Pyrex syringe and then create an emulsion with water. If it reacted to the water, then they'd have to try something else.

"Okay, here we go," Bill said. Neil watched his colleague touch the thin, metal needle to the jet-black film on the lid. With his free hand, he pulled back the plunger.

The metal needle squealed against the lid. Neil was afraid it would snap, but it held. As Bill's fingers pulled the plunger further back, obsidian liquid entered the glass enclosure. "Got it," Bill said.

Neil hissed through his teeth. "Not much."

"But enough." Bill held the syringe upside down, the needle pointing toward the ceiling. "You ready to create an emulsion?"

Neil nodded. He'd already put out the glass dish used for the SEM and coated it with water. "Just make sure you don't put too much of that crap in there."

Bill chuckled. "Wouldn't worry about that. It's not like there's much M2 in the syringe." He placed the needle into the shallow water and slowly pushed the plunger.

A viscous, black drop oozed out of the needle and into the dish. Neil watched as the drop floated atop the water. When there was no reaction, he blew a sigh through his teeth. "Okay. So far so good."

Bill clapped him on the back. "Told you. Nothing to worry about."

"Whatever, man. If Jay's not on crack, that shit eats plastic. If it eats plastic, there's no telling what else it will dissolve." Neil glared at his partner. "Take this seriously."

Bill raised his hands, the syringe pointed at the ceiling. "Okay, okay."

"Good." Neil lifted the glass dish in his gloved hands and turned to the scanning electron microscope. The sampling case, a large cube of beige-painted metal, sat on a table next to the actual microscope. Neil touched a button on the side and the sample case split in the center. The front moved silently forward. He placed the glass dish in the sample case, made sure it was snug, and then pressed the button again.

The sample case shut with a barely audible click. A green LED started to glow on the side of the case. Neil walked to the keyboard and display next to the SEM. He touched the screen and it came to life. By tapping and sliding his fingers, he quickly went through the various screens to set up the sample. He labeled it "M2-Emul-01." The screen flashed and a dialog box appeared. Neil glanced at Bill. "We ready?"

Bill grinned behind his faceplate. "Should I get the fire extinguisher?"

Neil rolled his eyes, shook his head, and stabbed the green "run" button. The SEM motors whirred to life. The word "Scanning" blinked on the screen.

*   *   *

Two tests. There were only two tests he and Kate could think of: NMR and light fluoroscopy. At least while the NMR was running, they could get the fluoroscopy test prepped and see what kind of funky colors M2 gave off.

But first, they had to get the distillation tank washed as well as the other glassware. Between her, Marie, and Jay, the lab was usually spotless after every test. But she had to admit that Marie was the OCD member of the trio. Any spec or stain was enough to drive her into a whirlwind of frenetic action. Provided, of course, she wasn't watching, prepping, or analyzing an experiment.

And instead of helping Jay and Kate, Marie was possibly dying somewhere in an ER. Her lip quivered. Kate took a deep breath and suddenly wished she could take off her helmet and wipe away the tear squeezing from her eye.

"You okay?" Jay asked.

Kate's voice came out in a croak. "Yes."

Jay had gathered all the equipment that had been in contact with M2. A pile of the stuff sat beside the chemical sink. He picked up the tray they'd used for the inspection of the boiled M2 and then stopped. "Um. Kate?"

She broke out of her fugue and walked to the sink. "What is it now?"

Jay stepped back from the sink. "I think we may have a problem."

She stood next to him and followed his gaze. A beaker sat in the sink. It was completely clean. But that's not what Jay was staring at. The sink was made of stainless steel, but it was nicked and marked by years of abuse from toluene and other cleaning fluids. The metal was dull and in need of a good polish. Except for the amorphous shape leading from the beaker to the drain.

"What the hell did that?" she asked, already knowing the answer.

Jay cleared his throat. "You think maybe Marie poured M2 into the sink before we went on break the first time?"

Did she? Sounded like something she would do. Kate tried to remember, but it seemed like that had happened a thousand years ago.

"I, um, don't know, Jay."

He pointed at the shape. "I've seen that before." He shivered and his breath huffed into the mic.

Kate scrunched her eyebrows. "Where?"

Jay gulped. "In the secure area. Where I found the lid." He turned to her. His eyes twinkled with manic energy. "There was a tiny drop of M2 on the shelf. I tried to scoop it up using some plastic, but it melted it."

"Right. You told me that."

"What I didn't tell you," Jay said, "is that when I turned back to get the lid, the drop seemed a little bigger. And I think it moved."

"Moved?" Another shiver dripped down her spine. "How could it move?"

He shrugged. "I said it seemed to. I don't know that it did. But there was a, well, a polished shape next to it. Like it had eaten through all the shit staining the steel."

Kate slowly turned and stared back down into the sink. There was no sign of any M2, but she could see her own reflection in the shining area of metal. "I don't get it," she said at last. "They bring this shit up from below the ocean floor and it looks like oil. But it's obviously not." She looked at the equipment piled next to the sink. She frowned. "Jay?"

"Yeah?"

Her face paled. "Um, where's the M2?"

He cocked an eyebrow. "What do you mean?"

She gestured to the various instruments. "I don't see any traces of the oil. None."

He clucked his tongue. His faceplate fogged. "Maybe it slid out like it did when we put it in the waste. It all moves together, or not at all."

"Huh?" she asked.

Jay rolled his eyes. "What I mean is that the stuff sort of, well, attracts itself. The molecules must bond in some way. Like glycerine. It moves like a liquid, acts like a liquid, but has some kind of, I don't know, magnetism to itself?"

She thought for a moment. "So that's why it wouldn't come out of the beaker easily? When you put it into the waste?"

He nodded. "I think so."

Biting her lip, she stared back into the sink. "We need to drench this with toluene. Now."

"Right," Jay said. "Breaks up normal heavy hydrocarbons. Might work on this shit too."

"We hope."

Jay leaned forward and turned on the tap marked with a "T."

If not for the faceplate and hood, their noses would have burned from the gasoline-like stench of the liquid. Toluene, in conjunction with other solvents, poured out of the faucet and bathed the sink. More importantly, they went down the drain and into a waste tank. Although the solvents could destroy small amounts of hydrocarbons, it wasn't enough to handle large quantities. Neither chemist heard the sizzling sound as the chemicals streamed into the drain.

They quickly washed and drained the Pyrex and instruments. When they'd finally exhausted the pile, except for the tray containing the boiled black, they glanced at one another.

"What do we do with the solids?" Jay asked.

Solids. Phase change. Kate thought for a moment and then said, "We can perform an experiment."

"Experiment? What kind of experiment?" Jay asked.

"How much M2 do we have left?" Kate pointed to the spigot.

He shrugged. "Probably somewhere around 12 liters. Why?"

She clasped her hands at her waist. "We have M2 in solid. We have M2 in liquid."

"Uh, I already don't like where this is going," he said. "I don't want any more shit out of the barrel than necessary."

"Agreed," Kate said. "But follow my logic. We clean the tray with toluene and see how it reacts. If it does, then we take a sample of the liquid and try the same."

Jay licked his lips. "You want to experiment on this crap when we don't even know what it does?"

"Science hates cowards," she said.

"And hell loves fools." Jay clucked his tongue and then nodded. "Okay. So how do you want to do this?"

"Let's take a small sample of the solid, put it in a clean beaker, and then pour the solvent into it." The terror, fear, and worry she'd felt earlier was gone. Instead, her stomach churned with excitement. "After that, we set up the fluoroscopy and NMR tests. And while they're running," she pointed at the sample spigot on the wall, "we do the same test with the pure M2."

Jay stared up at the ceiling. For a moment, she was certain he was going to say no and call her crazy. When he finally smiled, his eyes were more manic than ever. "Brilliance. That's all I can say, sheer unadulterated brilliance." The words came out as Wile E. Coyote.

"Then let's do this," Kate said.

He grasped the edge of the tray and placed it in the sink. The corner of the metal clanged. The remains of the hook section crumbled. Kate and Jay exchanged a glance. "Fragile."

"No shit," Kate said. "Turn on the tap and stand the hell back."

Jay nodded to her, took in a deep breath, and turned the tap. The solvent solution rushed out of the faucet and consumed the remains of the boiled M2. When the toluene covered the layers of sediment, Jay killed the solvent flow and stepped back.

Kate sucked in a breath as the lab filled with the sound of frying bacon. A cloud of steam rose from the sink as the toluene dissolved the particles. The sizzling sound faded and then disappeared. The vapor dissipated. They exchanged another look and then Kate peered over the sink's edge.

The tray was empty save for the toluene. There was no sign of the M2 solids. Kate frowned. "What the hell?"

Jay joined her, looked in the sink, and said, "Well, that's not what I expected."

"It catalyzed it."

He nodded. "Or something akin to that. But there should still be some remnant of it."

"Not if it dissolved. I mean," she licked her lips, "that cloud of steam? That was heat, Jay. It reacted pretty violently."

"That worries me," he said. "If it reacted that way to, um, the boiled M2, what's the liquid going to do?"

She sighed. "Good question. I think we need to answer it. But first,

I want to set up the other tests."

"Okay," Jay said. He looked up at the clock on the wall. "Jesus. It's late."

Kate nodded. "Yes it is. And we haven't had a break in a long time. Do you want to take one?"

He shook his head. "No. We can have the samples ready for testing pretty fast. Once the NMR starts, we'll have time. Plus, the fluoroscopy shouldn't take long. The NMR won't require any supervision. We can get some coffee or take a nap. I'll set up the NMR to alert us when it's ready."

"Fair enough," she said. "Then let's get it done. I need a nap."

* * *

The comfy chair wasn't so comfortable anymore. Ever since Darren had left with Marie and the ambulance, his stomach had been turning cartwheels. Mike's eyes were closed, but all he kept seeing in his head were flashing lights.

He had to call Simpson. He had to call him and tell him that HAL couldn't possibly get the analysis done in time. They were down a chemist and he'd no doubt Jay and Kate were less than focused on the task at hand. And he had to admit—he didn't blame them.

From what Darren said, she probably wouldn't survive the night. Darren, normally unflappable and always in control, had barely been capable of coherent speech. Whatever had infected Marie had put her into some kind of coma. Darren said he'd seen blood on the sheets in the mother's room.

After getting off the phone with Darren and Kate, he'd looked up the symptoms for hemorrhagic fever and dozens of other nasty illnesses. None had the rapid incubation time this had shown. Whatever had infected her was faster than anything he could find on the web.

What the hell did your people do, Simpson? What the hell did you bring up?

The phone buzzed. Mike opened his eyes and stared at the LCD caller-id strip. The word "UNKNOWN" blinked at him. He didn't want to answer it, but he had to. It could be Darren calling from the hospital. Or the hospital itself.

It buzzed again. Mike let out a sigh and leaned forward in his chair. The leather creaked on well-worn springs. He lifted the plastic receiver and strangled the buzzing sound.

"Mike Beaudry," he said into the phone.

There was a pause. "Mr. Beaudry. This is Doctor Hutchins from the Houston Center for Disease Control."

He sat rigid in the chair. "Ok. Can I help you?"

"We haven't confirmed it yet, but we believe your facility was the origin point for an extremely hazardous bio-contaminant."

Mike closed his eyes. "What kind?"

Pause. "We don't know. We are continuing to treat your employee, Ms. Marie Krieger, and would appreciate your cooperation in the meantime."

"What do you mean cooperation?" Mike's skin prickled.

"The CDC is sending a team to inspect your lab. We ask that you allow no one in or out of the facility until we have time to investigate the pathogen as well as ensure no one else from HAL has been infected. Do you understand?"

No one in, or out. "You're putting us under quarantine." It wasn't a question.

"Yes, sir. That is correct."

Mike tapped his finger on the desk. "Doctor Hutchins, how do I know all this is on the up and up? How do I know you are who you say you are?"

Another pause. "Mr. Beaudry, do you have access to a computer?"

"Yes."

"Then lookup the number for the CDC. Call it. Ask to be transferred to Houston and ask for me. Until then, please allow no one in or out of the facility. Our team should be there in the next twenty minutes."

Mike nodded. The acid in his stomach boiled over into his throat.

He loosed a bile-tasting belch and sighed. "Okay, Doctor Hutchins. I'll put the facility in lock down. Expect a call from me shortly to verify your identity."

"Thank you, Mr. Beaudry. Please alert your staff to stay clear of the, um, barrel of oil. It is vitally important they not come into contact."

Mike nodded. "I will, Doctor Hutchins. I'll call you in a few moments."

"I look forward to it." The line went dead.

* * *

The SEM whined as it continued to scan. Neil sat in front of the monitor and watched as the computer generated a picture line by line. With each passing nano-second, the SEM bombarded the sample with lines of electrons. The "optics" registered the brief illumination of the sample and translated them into hi-definition pixels.

With the sample safely in the SEM, they'd decided to take off their suits. Until they had to manually handle M2, there was little point in getting hot and sweaty and wasting any more of the lab's O_2 supply.

Neil tapped his fingers on the table's edge. "Bill?" He swiveled in his chair and stared across the room. Bill was at his own computer, no doubt watching porn. "Bill!"

The bio-chemist groaned and then turned around. "What do you want? The scan done yet?"

"Um, no," Neil said. "And that's the problem. Come here."

Bill loosed an epic sigh and rose from his chair. The crackle of old bones echoed in the lab as he flexed his knees. "Too old for this shit."

"Right," Neil grinned. "Stop bitching and take a look at this."

"Okay, okay." Bill walked until he was behind Neil. "What the—" He pulled his glasses from the front of his lab coat and put them on. His bushy, grey eyebrows scrunched together. "That's not right."

Neil hissed through his teeth. "No shit."

The screen's edges were filled with grey. The water molecules were clearly visible. That was, until the computer started to render the center of the emulsion. The screen should have been displaying molecules of M2. Instead? Black. Nothing but black.

Neil smacked the table's edge. "So what the hell does it mean?"

Bill shrugged. "No clue. I'll have to go look at the operating manual. But I've never even heard of something like this."

Neil nodded. "Maybe what we should—"

The phone on the wall buzzed. The two men exchanged a glance. Bill sighed again and walked to it. He caught it on the third ring. "Lab. This is Bill." Neil watched the man's displeased frown disintegrate into confusion. "Okay, Mike." He stabbed a button on the phone and the intercom went live. "You there?"

"Neil?"

The head of the bio-lab looked up at the speaker on the wall. "Yeah, Mike? What's up?"

"We have a bit of a problem. Marie was infected by something in the chem-lab. Or rather, may have been."

"Jay told us," Neil said. "She doing any better?" There was a pause. He and Bill exchanged a glance. "Mike?" Neil asked.

"I don't have an exact status on her condition, but from what the CDC said, I don't think so."

"Shit," Bill said.

"Shit is right," Mike continued. "Jay said you two are running tests on the PPE sample"

"That's correct. But—"

"Then stop. Now. The CDC has asked we quarantine anyone who has been exposed to the PPE sample. They're afraid the contagion will spread."

Bill and Neil exchanged another glance. Neil cleared his throat. "Okay. We'll, um, leave it where it is. Not much luck anyway."

"Good. One more thing. You have to stay in the lab."

Bill frowned. "What? What do you mean stay in the lab? We've been in here for—"

"The CDC is sending in a team. They want to make sure the labs are kept in lockdown and any and all staff that have been exposed remain there."

Neil shook his head. "Mike, we've got nothing down here. No restrooms, no water, no food—"

"Look, Neil, they'll be here soon. If they find us breaking quarantine, it might get a lot worse. Stay put. Please."

It was the "please" that struck Neil. Mike sounded scared. Neil turned to the finished SEM picture. The sample was black. No other color. No other details. Just black. "Okay, Mike. Understood. And we'll stay away from this shit."

"Good. I'll give you an update as soon as I get one. Stay safe." The speaker squawked and then buzzed with the sound of a dead line.

Bill turned off the speakerphone. The lab descended into silence save for the gentle, nearly inaudible whoosh of the A/C.

Neil chewed his lip. "Now what do we do."

"I don't know, but—" Bill broke off. His eyes stared at the glass wall separating the bio-lab from the chem-lab. Color drained from his face. He raised a gnarled finger.

"What?"

Bill didn't answer, but his body started to shake.

Neil rose from his chair and looked into the other lab. His blood turned cold. "Jesus Christ! What the fuck is that?"

***

Just approaching the sample delivery system was enough to make his stomach flutter. They needed two samples, one for each test. The NMR didn't require a lot. Just 50 ml. The fluoroscopy? A liter. Another goddamned liter of M2 out of the barrel and into the lab. While Kate prepped the NMR for the scans, his job was to gather the samples. Approaching the faucet, he was beginning to have second thoughts.

What if he spilled that shit? Would his suit protect him? Or would it melt through and turn his skin into vapor while it sizzled through his bones?

He shook off the thought. He grabbed two of the largest beakers from the wall. Each would hold 2 liters of liquid. For the fluoroscopy sample, it was acceptable. For the NMR? It was absolute overkill. *Coward*, a voice said in his mind. *Afraid of a little hydrocarbon.*

"Fuck off," he whispered. He glanced at the NMR station. Kate hadn't noticed his words. Jay sighed. He put one of the beakers next to the dispensing station. The other? It was shaking in his hands. He gritted his teeth and typed in the amount of liquid he needed. The crimson digital display flashed 50ml. He placed the beaker beneath the spigot and moved his index finger to just above the "dispense" button.

Images raced in his mind. A rushing river of black that ate light and everything in its path; tentacles with hooks that slashed and destroyed anything they touched; the crackle of dissolving bones and burning fabric. Jay closed his eyes and shook away the horror film rolling through his imagination.

Imagination. That all that it is, Jay. Get over it. He stabbed the button.

The vacuum growled as it sucked the viscous fluid through the metal and glass tubes. Air burst from the spigot and then M2 began to flow. Jay stood at arm's length, the beaker cradled in his hands. The impossibly dark liquid plopped into the beaker's base. Before he knew it, the vacuum pump shut off and the controller beeped. A final drop of M2 blooped into the tiny pool at the beaker's bottom.

Jay stared at the small amount of M2. He waited for it to do something. To move. To burble. To explode. He blinked. The substance did nothing but sit there. He blew a hiss through his teeth and turned to Kate. "Your NMR sample."

"Thanks." She looked up from the control panel and saw the beaker. She cocked an eyebrow. "Is there actually anything in that beaker? Or did you decide you needed ocean-sized glassware for a raindrop?"

"Ha-ha," Jay said. "I don't know about you, but I don't want to give this shit a chance at my suit."

She opened her mouth and then closed it. Kate stood and took the beaker. "Good point." She glanced at the other beaker on the table. "You think that one's big enough?"

Neil stared at the wall with the glassware. "If you see one that's bigger, I'm all for it."

"Yeah," Kate said. "I guess you're right." She touched his shoulder with her free hand. "Be careful." She walked to the NMR.

A sound caught his ear and Jay turned back to the dispensing station. Something in the pipes burbled. Another shiver raced down his spine. *Get a hold of yourself. You've heard that sound before. It's just the vacuum.* He reached for the other beaker and then stopped. His hands were shaking. Jay clenched his fists. When he relaxed them, the shaking had stopped.

His stomach growled. Food. Dammit, they hadn't eaten in a long time. Much less stopped to drink something. As soon as they got the tests up and running, he was heading upstairs for a snack and at least two bottles of water. And he'd drag Kate out of the goddamned lab if he had to.

Jay grabbed the beaker. He entered 1 liter into the dispenser keypad. The display flashed the amount. He took a deep breath, placed the beaker below the dispenser, and hit the button.

The pump hummed. This time, he was sure he heard something in the pipes. Something more like a growl than the spitting of air.

A thick stream of M2 poured out of the spout and into the beaker. Jay kept his hands around the glassware, but once again stood back as far as he could. The liquid quickly filled the beaker. Bubbles rose from the bottom and popped at the surface even as more liquid flowed in on top of it.

Jay's hands started to shake, and not from the added weight. The stream slowed as the dispenser pinched off the flow. It turned into a trickle, and then a few drops. Then? Nothing.

The liquid in the beaker bubbled some more and then stopped. His skin puckered into gooseflesh in the hot suit. As if M2 wasn't strange enough, the idea he held nearly a liter of a corrosive substance similar to sulfuric acid was terrifying. He wished he'd never gone into the secure area and never seen what he'd seen. At least then he wouldn't be so damned afraid.

Jay turned from the dispensing station and headed toward the fluoroscopy machine. He walked with slow steps, his eyes flicking up to watch where he was going and then quickly down to look at the beaker. With each step, a bubble rose from the bottom and popped at the liquid's surface.

When he finally reached the machine, he placed the beaker on the table. He studied the glassware. There was no M2 clinging to the sides. "What the hell are you?"

"What was that?" Kate asked.

An embarrassed smile lit his face. "Nothing," he said without turning. He slid aside the cover of the sample reservoir. It could hold up to four liters of liquid, but a single liter was enough. He hoped. He didn't want to go through this madness again.

He lifted the beaker and slowly tipped it toward the reservoir. The M2 sample poured out of the container in a rush. He nearly dropped the glassware in surprise. The beaker was empty. No strands or tendrils of liquid remained on the sides. The stuff had acted like a solid rather than a liquid. Jay stared into the reservoir, but saw nothing but darkness. Another shiver wracked his spine and he pressed the button on the control panel. The reservoir panel locked into place.

He exhaled long enough to fog his faceplate. The M2 was in the machine and no longer in his hands. The beaker had no trace of the oil. He put it aside.

"Jay?"

He nearly jumped. Chuckling, he turned to Kate. She stood next to the squat NMR machine, hands on her hips. "Yeah. We're ready to start the fluoroscopy. You ready too?"

Kate nodded. "Of course. We should—" She stopped. "Jay, you okay?"

"Yeah," he said. "Just— I don't like carrying that much of that shit."

"Don't blame you. I didn't like handling 50ml of it." She stared at the machine in front of him. "What do you think we're going to find?"

He shrugged. "Don't know. But that shit was bubbling again."

"You think it will hurt the test?"

"I doubt it. But I want to know what's in this stuff. Or what it really is."

"Well," Kate said, "let's get things started."

She turned back to the NMR station. Jay watched her for a moment while she punched buttons on the computer keyboard. *Get things started*, he thought. *Yeah, let's do that.* The fluoroscope screen was dark. He touched the monitor and the screen lit up.

He typed on the on-screen keyboard with his index finger to enter the label for the sample as well as the parameters. Once the machine was ready, the screen turned green. A dialog box appeared with the words "Cancel" and "Start." He took a deep breath, and pushed his finger on the "Start" button.

The machine hummed as it drained the reservoir and pushed it into the pipes. The monitor flashed and showed a wheel of color. A camera inside the machine took digital video of the oil as it flowed through the pipes. Different wavelengths of light shot out and bombarded the M2 sample.

The oil glowed with different hues before swallowing the wavelengths. "The hell?" He leaned closer to the screen. He couldn't believe what he was seeing. The color wheel shifted as it rapidly flipped through all the shades of red. He flicked his eyes back to the view of the oil. Normal crude would absorb some of the light, sure, but all of it? No.

A soft humming noise caught his ears. Jay shifted in his chair. Kate was starting up the NMR. The powerful magnets in the portable machine would start pulling and imaging M2's molecular structure. With any luck, the process would model M2 and they'd finally find out what it was made of.

"Everything okay?" he asked Kate.

She nodded. "Yup. I'm ready to fry this sucker."

"Good. While it's being poked and prodded at the atomic level, you can come over here and tell me what you see."

Kate cocked her head. "Oh." She stabbed a key on the keyboard and the humming sound increased. "I can't wait." She touched a few more buttons and a bright yellow dialog box appeared on the screen.

"If you do'd it, you get a whipping!" Jay called in Bugs Bunny's voice.

She giggled. "I do'd it." Her gloved finger touched the screen. The lights in the lab dimmed for a millisecond and then recovered. The humming of the NMR increased into a constant drone. Kate rose from her chair and walked over. "Okay. What's it doing now? I mean—" Her voice trailed off.

The color wheel had turned again. This time the M2 sample was bathed in various shades of green. As the light hit the liquid, it reflected for an instant before it was swallowed. All that remained between flashes was the impenetrable darkness of the black.

Kate groaned. "Why can't it just be normal?"

"Good question," Jay said. The light wheel spun again. This time, to yellow. The lightest shade vibrated against M2's lack of color. The picture flickered. "What the—" The yellow moved to a darker shade and the image lay still. "What was that? What made the camera do that?"

Kate shook her head. "I don't think that was the camera." Her voice came out in a barely audible croak. "I think that was M2 moving."

"Bullshit." Jay watched the colors deepen toward a bright orange. Had it moved? He was certain the camera had jittered. Or vibrated. But had it? And what if it *was* the M2? What if it *had* moved? "Maybe we should stop the test."

She shook her head. "No, Goddammit. We're getting somewhere. It moved in the yellow range, right?"

"The lightest, yeah."

She pursed her lips. "What if it doesn't reflect anything back but full spectrum light?"

Full spectrum light. He peered up at the soft fluorescent bulbs. Those always cast a bit of blue and were far from full spectrum. Halogens? Much closer to real sunlight. "ROY-G-BIV," Jay said, nodding. He turned to the other lab stations.

The light above the dispensing station was much brighter than the fluorescent bulbs. That's because it was an ambient halogen. The other lamps at the stations, including where they'd run the first few tests, also had bright white lights. The bubbling. "Shit," Jay said. "I have a theory."

Kate grimaced. "What might that be?"

He cleared his throat. "The M2 didn't respond much to the fluorescent lights. But it bubbled when it was near the halogens. Halogens create something more akin to natural light, but still far from the real thing. Can't remember the numbers, but it's in the 3,000 kelvin range. I think natural light is closer to 5,000 kelvins."

"So?" Kate pointed at the color wheel as it shifted into green. "Nothing else has made it twitch."

"Right," Jay said. "What if we take out the prism? Instead of having it split the light into the different wavelengths, we just hit it with a full spectrum and see what happens?"

She stood straight and stretched. "I think we need a break, Jay. My stomach is crying for food and I'm thirsty."

Jay's stomach growled on cue. "Me too. But let's try this. The NMR is still going to take a while."

She sighed. "Okay. Fine. Stop the test. Reprogram it for full spectrum."

"Thought you'd never ask," Jay said. He touched the red stop-sign icon and the machine's gentle whirring halted. He canceled out of the program and returned to the main screen. Although the machine wasn't made to use full spectrum light, it had a test mode for that very purpose. Jay selected diagnostic mode.

A warning popped up. Jay growled at the screen. "Yes, I know it's not a real test, dumbass." He punched the ignore button and continued. He set the timer for 60 seconds and brought the color temperature to its maximum color. When he started the program, 4,000 kelvins of white light would flood the chamber and hit the M2 sample.

He looked up at Kate. "Ready?"

"Hit it.".

Jay hit the button. The vacuum pump started circulating the oil. Two seconds later, the camera image flared to life. White light bathed the circulating oil. As they watched, the liquid bubbled and boiled.

The pump groaned and the machine started to shake. "What the—"

"Turn it off!" Kate yelled.

A tendril of smoke rose from the pump mechanism. Inside the vacuum of the recirculating pipe, M2 sloshed against the sides in a silent, furious scream. Jay blinked as the oil started to disappear. Tendrils of dirty gray gas gathered inside the pipe.

"Turn it the fuck off!" Kate screamed.

Jay moved a gloved finger and touched the "Stop" button on the screen. The machine groaned again as the pump was silenced. The light died and the camera image faded to black.

Even though the analyzer had stopped and the light was turned off, a high-pitched whine started from inside the machine. A red dialog box popped up onto the screen. "Shit," Jay said. "The pressure. There's too much pressure in the pipe!"

"Release it!" Kate yelled.

"If I do that, it's going to fill the lab with whatever that shit was."

Kate turned and ran as fast as her suit allowed. The atmospheric purge box sat on the far wall. The bright red handle was encased in a heavy plastic box. She reached it, clicked open the release, and pulled the red handle.

The lab exploded with sound. Heavy fans in the ceiling started turning. They spun backwards to pull air up into the purge system. A klaxon alarm pierced the air. "Hit it!" Kate yelled.

Jay stood, stabbed the "Release" button on the screen, and then quickly moved away from the machine. He was glad he did.

A valve turned inside the machine and broke the pipe's vacuum.

A heavy cloud of white burst from the pipes and rose up into the air vents. But that wasn't the scary part.

Tendrils of black squirted out of the pressure hole. They streamed onto the floor and pooled. Jay's entire body shook. The separate little pools moved toward one another. The oil, or whatever the hell this shit was, gathered itself into a single pool of smoking black.

"Oh, shit," he said. "Kate! We have a problem!"

The remaining sample of M2 slid backwards into the shadows. As he watched, it seemed to grow in size, although it could have been a trick of the light.

He stepped backward until his ass hit a table. "Kate?"

"Hang on," she said.

Jay kept his eyes on the place where the M2 flowed. He wasn't going to let it out of his sight.

The klaxon silenced, but the fans continued whirring. "Okay," Kate said into the mic. "Tell me what just happened. And please get your breathing under control. You sound like a panting dog."

Jay gritted his teeth. His heart beat raced at light speed and pounded in his ears. *Calm. Calm. Calm.* Kate was right. He was on the verge of a goddamned stroke. He took a deep breath and exhaled through his nose. "Okay," Jay said. "Better?"

"Better. What the hell just happened?"

It was still there, in the shadows. An inky pool against the dull floor. The place where the sample had landed was clean. Shiny. It glimmered even in the wan light.

"We need to get out of here," Jay said. He lifted a finger and pointed at the shadows. "Do you see it?"

She walked from the controls and stood next to him. He didn't bother turning to look at her face; he didn't want to risk missing any movement.

"What am I looking at, Jay?"

"See the shadows?"

Kate grunted. "Beneath the fluoroscope?"

"Yes."

"Jay. Those are just shadows."

He jumped as the phone rang. Kate sighed and walked back to the control desk. She picked up the handset. "Chem-Lab. We're fine. We—" Her voice paused.

Jay wanted to turn, but didn't. No fucking way was he imagining what just happened. And no fucking way was he going to stop looking at whatever it was. It had moved, dammit. He knew it had.

"Okay," Kate said. Jay heard the beep in his earpiece as the phone was patched into their headsets. "Go ahead, Mike."

"First off, are you two okay? Really? What happened?"

"One of the analyzers had a meltdown. The M2 sample reacted and caused a critical pressure problem. Had to purge it in case it was toxic." Kate sounded a little out of breath herself.

"Have you been able to determine toxicity?"

For a moment, neither he nor Kate made a sound.

"Hello? You still there?" Mike asked.

"Yes," Kate said. "Sorry. No. We don't know what it was."

Mike sighed into the intercom. Jay immediately knew their boss was under more stress than from just a lab incident. "Okay. Here's what I want. I want you two to get on respirators. And I want you to stop all tests on the PPE sample."

"Mike? What happened?" Kate asked.

"Marie is very ill. The CDC is on their way to quarantine us and they've asked that you stay in your labs. Both teams."

Jay fought the urge to tear his eyes away from the shadows. "They think it's contagious?"

"They don't know," Mike said. "But they're going to quarantine us to make sure."

"How long before they get here?" Kate asked.

"Fifteen? Twenty minutes? Look, you and Jay just need to stay the hell away from the samples and stop whatever tests you're running.

Understood?"

Something twitched in the shadows. "That could be a problem," Jay said.

Mike grunted. "What do you mean, Jay?"

"It moved." Jay's words were little more than a whisper. "And we can't stop the NMR."

"What? Why can't we stop the NMR?" Kate asked.

Jay pointed to the shadows. "Because we have to go through it to get there."

Mike groaned. "Jay? Have you lost your mind? What are you talking about?"

The shadows moved again. He heard Kate's sudden intake of breath through the headset. She'd seen it now. And no, he wasn't hallucinating.

"Mike? Let me call you back." Kate killed the line. "Jay?"

"What?" His eyes watered. He'd barely blinked since he'd first seen the puddle of M2 move.

"What do we do?"

"Good question. I'm ready to hear some ideas."

Kate cursed under her breath. Jay wondered how long they had before the thing in the shadows decided to do something.

* * *

Panic. He knew that's what he should be feeling. Instead, he was too tired to feel much of anything. He'd been in the ER long enough to lose track of time and any semblance of order. He was hungry, but didn't feel like eating. He was thirsty, but didn't want to ask for water. Why? Because Marie was dead.

While he sat on the portable hospital bed and they drained vial after vial of blood from his arm, the steady, but slow rhythm of the electrocardiograph beeps provided a constant backdrop of sound. He heard it below the speech of the doctors and the clinking of medical equipment.

The CDC docs looked like astronauts in their gear. The only differentiating features among them were the name tags taped to their suits and their height. Disaster movies kept playing through his head. There was always high drama, people with strained voices, and some kind of invisible clock ticking down. This was nothing like that.

Instead, it was boring. The CDC doctors spoke in technical jargon and in slightly disinterested voices. They were professionals, sure, but Darren expected at least some excitement among them. Maybe it was fatigue. Maybe it was because they already knew their patient was dying and there was nothing they could do to stop it.

When the beeping sound's gentle rhythm skipped into dubstep, he peeked through the paper curtains. Two doctors were already dragging a crash cart to Marie's bed. Although a sheet covered her legs and torso, it was easy to see something bad was going on beneath it. The sheet's normal white was crusted in places with dark red and yellow stains. Darren would have retched if he had anything in his stomach.

The dubstep beat disappeared into a flat line of sound. The doctors looked at one another. Three other doctors stepped into view. They pulled away the sheet. Darren wanted to scream.

The flesh on her legs looked like spoiled cream cheese. Large swaths peeled off as they lifted the sheet. Blood wept from the wounds, but it was too dark. Too black. Her face was little more than a pale bruise. Her breasts, not large to begin with, had shrunk into themselves. Darren wanted to look away, but couldn't.

A doctor lifted the paddles and placed them on her chest. "250 joules," a muffled voice said. The defibrillator whined as it charged.

"Ready," one of the docs said.

"Clear!" the one holding the paddles yelled. The doctor pressed down. The sound of electricity arcing from the machine and into Marie's still form echoed in the room. The machine maintained its steady flatline buzz.

"Charging," another voice said. "Ready."

"Clear!" The doctor placed the paddles on the chest and pressed down. A loud ripping sound vibrated Marie's body. "What the—" the doctor had time to say before the paddles, along with his hands, sank through the woman's chest.

The room filled with the sound of sizzling fat on a hot-plate. The doctor screamed in agony and lifted his arms away from the bed. His hands were gone at the wrist. A primal scream started in Darren's mind. The doctor wobbled on his feet and started to fall backward.

A tentacle, blacker than deepest space, flew out of the chest cavity and wrapped around the doctor's neck. His scream died as he was pulled into Marie's chest. The sizzling sound was deafening. The doctor's body disappeared into the table's void.

Doctors yelled in surprise. Marie's body melted away as a black pool of viscous liquid flowed over the sides of the table and onto the floor. The metal beneath gleamed as if polished. The pool moved across the floor toward the doctors still frozen in terror.

Darren finally found his voice and the scream locked in his throat pierced the air. He stumbled toward the room's exit. A uniformed security guard pelted toward him through the plastic tunnel. He held up a hand and yelled for Darren to stop.

A chorus of shrieks made Darren turn back toward the room. The black pool spread across the floor and covered the doctors' feet. One of the suited figures fell forward into the black pool. The body immediately dissolved.

Another doctor fell backwards onto the floor, legs raising into the air. His feet were missing below the ankle. The last in the trio screamed and screamed as tendrils of black fluid rose up his suit; he dissolved feet first into the floor.

"What the fuck is that!" the guard screamed.

Darren didn't want to know. He sprinted past the man and reached the tunnel's edge. Behind him, he heard more screams and cries of pain. When he found himself in the parking lot, he kept running. He barely noticed the cold sheets of rain drenching his skin or the freshening wind.

＊

Visitors. That's what Mike said. Only that's not all he said. The visitors? The goddamned CDC.

Jakob stared at the display on his left. The screen was split in four, giving him two views of the parking area, and a view at each of the emergency exits. The images showed swirling rain and not much else. It was incredibly difficult to make out shapes, let alone details.

Jakob sighed. What a shitty night. He'd had to let EMTs into the building, watch them take Marie away, and calm down Maeve. And now? The freakin' CDC?

He glanced at the other monitor. The split screen cycled between the lab hallway as well as the second and third floors. With the exception of Maeve and Darren coming down with Marie, there hadn't been much to see.

Maeve was back in her mother's office. Mike hadn't left his. And now that Darren was gone, he couldn't even look forward to the man coming down for a chat.

Well, at least he had a book to read in between checking the monitors. Probably best to do that after the CDC showed up though. Wouldn't want to get caught—

One of the screens twitched. He cocked an eyebrow, blinked, and then stared at it. It was in the parking lot. The camera image distorted, flickered, and then went dead. It wasn't conscious, but his hand drifted down to the butt of his pistol.

Jakob stood from his station and peered into the darkness beyond the heavily tinted glass doors. Something moved in his peripheral vision. He swung his eyes back to the monitor. The other view of the parking lot displayed nothing but black. Just like its twin.

He unsnapped the holster and tapped a finger against the pistol butt. Jakob quickly scanned the other screens. The scientists were still doing their thing in the lab. Nothing moved on either of the upper floors. So whatever was going on—

Then he heard it. A roaring sound followed by the shriek of sirens. Something moved outside the glass doors. He walked to them. They should have auto-locked after the EMTs left with Marie. No one should be able to get in here without a key card. Behind the bulletproof glass, he was completely safe. So why were his nerves sizzling with trepidation?

The sirens were closer.

That's the CDC. And the cops. And—

Something banged outside the doors. He walked closer to them, pistol halfway out of its holster. The dim glow of the streetlight lamps had disappeared. Everything was black through the glass.

What the hell is going on?

He walked closer, the pistol almost fully out of the holster. He put his nose to the glass and held his free hand over his eyes to block the glare from the overheads.

The entrance to the building was covered. Blocked. Something yellow or orange flapped in the wind. Jakob gritted his teeth.

What the hell is—

A gloved hand smacked into the glass. Jakob jumped back, heart pounding in his chest. A figure pressed itself to the entry doors.

"CDC!" a muffled voice said. "Let us in! Now!"

Jakob released the pistol and it fell back into the holster. He didn't bother snapping it. Until he knew for sure who this clown was, he wasn't taking any chances.

He reached next to the door and hit the red "Open" button. The door locks clicked. The figure remained where it was. Rolling his eyes, Jakob pushed open the door.

Beneath the sounds of wind and rain, he heard the growl of engines and the clanking of metal on metal. Distant excited voices yelled at one another, but he couldn't understand what they were saying.

The figure walked inside along with two others. Jakob stood aside to give them room, hand back on his holster. He blinked at the invaders.

Dressed in green moon suits, they looked like strange aliens dropped into his universe. The trio looked at one another and then one walked back to him.

Through the faceplate, he saw the face of a less than homely woman. Her eyes shined with excitement. She held out her federal ID.

"My name is Dr. Melanie Hoyt. I'm with the CDC."

He blinked at her.

She tapped her foot. "What's your name?"

"Oh, I'm Jakob."

"You the only guard?" one of the more stout figures behind Hoyt asked.

Jakob nodded and took the badge from Hoyt. He stared at it. CDC. Yeah. Her picture? Yeah. She looked much better without that moon suit. He looked up at her, smiled, and handed it back.

"Have you been exposed to the agent?"

Jakob blinked again. This was just too goddamned surreal. "What agent?"

The woman rolled her eyes. "The contagion. Were you exposed to the barrel, the oil, the labs, or Ms. Krieger?"

"No." The woman continued staring at him. "I mean, I opened the doors for the EMTs to get her and take her to the hospital, but I didn't like get breathed on or anything."

"And you haven't had contact with the oil?"

He shook his head. "No, Dr. Hoyt. I'm just the schlep who guards the door."

She nodded and then looked around the foyer.

He cleared his throat. "And who are they?"

"Dr. Glaze and Dr. Dugger," she said. "Is this foyer the biggest public area?"

He snickered. "It's the only public area. Everything else is locked off."

She nodded again and looked at her companions. "This will do for a quarantine area. Will make it easy for us to get supplies too."

"Quarantine?" Jakob rubbed his hands together. "Mike said something about that, but I didn't think he was serious."

Hoyt turned and looked at him. "Mr. Beaudry told you we were coming. He told you there would be a quarantine. And you didn't believe it?"

"Surreal," he mumbled.

"Where are the labs?" she asked.

He pointed to the security doors. "Back there. The only way into the labs is through those doors."

She nodded to herself and clicked something on her belt. "Control? Hoyt. Bring the supplies to the front. We'll bring them in. Over."

Jakob heard a staticky reply, but it was too low for him to understand. "Supplies?"

She held up a finger to shush him, and then tapped the radio again. "Yes, Jakob. Supplies. We need to get into the lab. Now."

Jakob nodded. Mike had told him to get them whatever they needed. He walked to the security doors and then stopped. He turned and looked at Hoyt. "Did you take out my security cameras?"

A sneer appeared on her face. "Yes."

He nodded dreamily. "Good. Because I thought I was having a stroke." He turned back to the door. Through the heavy steel, he heard a crash and someone yelling. Jakob slid his badge across the sensor. He jerked open the door and peered in.

* * *

The NMR was still running. Neither Jay nor Kate was interested in seeing the results now. They had bigger problems. The first was simple: figuring out what to do.

Jay suggested they move to the front of the lab. Kate thought that was a great idea. Backs against the glass wall, just inches away from the hallway, the pair watched the shadows. The hunger she'd felt before the fluoroscopy had dissolved into heartburn. And, dammit, she needed to pee.

"I'm, um, still waiting to hear an idea," Jay said.

Idea. Yeah. Right. CDC coming in, quarantine, they were trapped with *something* and Jay wanted ideas. Great. Like some magic light bulb was going to pop into existence over her—

"Jay?"

"What?" he asked without turning around.

"We have lots of powerful lights in here."

"Yeah, so?"

She opened her mouth to say something sarcastic and then stopped. Jay's hands were shaking. He was terrified. She hissed through her teeth instead. "What happened when we bathed it in full spectrum light?"

"Shit. Sorry. I guess my genius took the night off." He looked around the lab. "The halogens."

"Yes, the halogens," Kate said. "If we turn all the table lights on, we might be able to keep it cornered."

"Yeah, that could work."

"You don't sound convinced."

Jay turned to her. His face was pale and he looked exhausted. In other words, he looked exactly like she felt. "We can point some of the lights toward it. But, just where the hell do we try and drive it?"

She bit her lip. He had a point. Kate scanned the lab, much as Jay had done. Her eyes focused on the waste drain in the far corner of the room. "Jay, we are idiots."

"What?"

She lifted a finger and pointed to the far corner. The shadows were extremely thick in that area. If M2 was afraid of the light, It would be the perfect place to make it feel safe. "The waste drain. We could drive it down into the waste tank. We just have to open the seal and drive it down."

"And it'll be trapped," Jay said to himself. He clucked his tongue. "Great horny toads!" Yosemite Sam said. "I think we got us a plan!"

She was scared to death, sure, but that didn't mean she wasn't chuckling. She punched him in the arm. "Try and be serious. That wascally wabbit," she said pointing to the shadows, "isn't a damned cartoon."

"Sorry. You're right. So how do you want to do this?"

"First, we need to point all the halogens at the floor. Create some kind of barrier."

"Yeah. And I think we need to turn up the overheads." He pointed to the rectangular lights in the ceiling. "The fluorescents may not hurt it, but at least we'll be able to see it."

"Good idea," she said. "Keep watch."

"Yes, ma'am."

Kate tapped his arm. Through the suit's protection, she barely even felt the impact. She walked sideways toward the door. Finally, she turned away from the lab itself and stared at the stainless steel control panel. Two dimmer switches along with a keyed power cut-off stared back at her. She placed her fingers on the first dimmer switch and turned toward the lab interior. She spun the knob.

Half the lab's fluorescent lights quickly brightened. The deep shadows by the tables disappeared. The table with the fluoroscope remained clothed in dim light. "Let's see what you think of this," she said and spun the second knob.

The lights in the ceiling blazed down. The stained tile floor reflected the light back at her eyes and she had to squint. Jay lifted a hand to his faceplate to block the glare. After blinking several times, she was finally able to see. But she wished she had a pair of sunglasses.

The shadows were gone. Except for the furthest recesses of the tables and equipment, there was only the gleam of metal and light bouncing off every surface. And there it was. Right where they'd last seen it.

Stains led up to the side of the fluoroscope, but where M2 had touched the floor, the tile surface was immaculate and shining. With the lights blazing down, the pool of M2 was obvious. The shadows where it had hidden were no longer dark and foreboding, but just a dimness of the light. Against the bright white of the surrounding tile, it looked blacker than anything she'd ever seen.

Jay cleared his throat. "Well, there it is."

"Yeah." Kate stepped to the nearest table. "You grab the other one."

"Point it where?"

"Let's make a path," she said. "Make sure it can't come after us."

"This is nuts." He walked to one of the tables, pointed the gooseneck lamp to the floor ahead of him, and flicked the switch.

A bright rectangle of light appeared on the floor. It was slightly diffused, but more than enough to cast a broad spectrum. She hoped. Kate did the same with the table lamp nearest her.

They made their way down the row. Each time they turned on a new light, they made sure to point it at the floor and targeted so it continued the barrier. When they were only a few meters away from the fluoroscope, Kate stopped. The M2 hadn't moved since they started their experiment. Could it see them? Could it hear them?

"Jay?"

He turned to her, his hand on the next lamp. "Yeah?"

"What do we do if it moves past the lights?"

His face paled. "I guess we run."

She shivered. Maeve was on the floor above them. Hopefully asleep. And hopefully unaware any of this shit was going on. They had to make sure the M2 stayed in the lab. The idea of that stuff getting out of here and loose in the building was terrifying.

The last two tables. They were down to the last two tables. Kate switched on a lamp, and followed the routine of aiming it. Jay was still a meter away from the last table on his side. Why? Because it was the fluoroscopy table.

The suit made it difficult, but Jay squatted, his eyes focused on the pool of deep black. "All we have in this lab are LED flashlights."

Kate giggled, but it came out more as a shuddering wheeze. "We have everything aimed." She tapped her foot. "What we need is a long extension cord."

Jay groaned into the mic and stood up. "Keep your eyes on that thing."

"I will. What are you going to do?"

"You'll see," Jay said.

She heard his gentle footfalls as he headed back to the front of the lab. Kate swallowed hard and then focused her tired eyes on the pool of M2. It was an amorphous shape. Instead of a circle or oval, the pool had the occasional runner jutting out from its center. It reminded her of something she'd seen in biology class. Something bacterial. Or viral.

Her life consisted of carbon rings, methane units, and chemical bonds. Crude oil, atmospheric samples, waste water from manufacturing plants, sewage runoffs… Nothing biological. This was a whole new ball game.

So what was it? Her mind raced over their experiments. Low gravity. Hydro-carbon characteristics. Anaerobic. Broad spectrum light sensitivity. Hell, she didn't even know its actual flashpoint. It bubbled and boiled when it came in contact with any source of illumination that approximated sunlight, but could it actually burn? And if it did, what would it release?

In the fluoroscope's vacuum, there was no oxygen to make flame. Would it have caught fire if it had been in an aerobic environment? She didn't know. And what was it going to do when they hit it with the halogens?

Jay's tongue clucking brought her back to the world. In what little peripheral vision the faceplate provided, she could see something in his hands.

"You found an extension cord?" she asked.

"Yes, ma'am. Just don't tell anyone I pilfered it from my boombox."

"Boombox?" She snickered. "What the hell did you have a boombox down here for?"

"Hey, not all of us went out and replaced our tape collections with CDs and mp3s." Jay flipped a plate on the floor and connected an end of the extension cord. She saw his hand out of the corner of her eye. He disconnected the lamp from the table near the fluoroscope machine and plugged it into the extension cord. He flicked the switch and a cone of light appeared. "We're in business."

She took a deep breath. "Okay. You've got light in your hands. Your knees okay?"

"Cracking and clacking, but yeah. I can do this."

"All right." She put her fingers on the gooseneck of her lamp. "I can drag this one out a little bit. Give you some cover."

"Okay." Jay sounded less than ready, but he squatted down again with an "oof." He pointed the lamp's light a half-meter in front of him. "I'm ready."

Kate wasn't. Not really. But they had to get the M2 into the drain. She wouldn't feel safe until it was in the waste tank and incapable of hurting them or anyone else. "Here we go," she said. She knew her hands were shaking. She just hoped she could give Jay cover in case it moved toward them. "Go." Jay exhaled a nervous breath and duckwalked forward.

The strong light bobbed up and down slightly with each step. Jay grunted into the mic. The M2 was still, its surface seemingly as solid as metal. The bright halogen light edged forward bit by bit. When he was half a meter away, Jay slowly raised the light from the floor and toward the pool.

As the rectangle of light obliterated the remaining shadows, Kate took in a deep breath. It was now or never. Jay paused, the light mere centimeters away from the M2. He exhaled loudly and then shined the light directly at the black.

The surface bubbled immediately. The pool moved backward out of the light leaving smoke in its wake. "Jesus," Kate said. "Okay. Drive it toward the drain."

Jay said nothing. She heard his breathing turn to panting. She couldn't imagine how hot it was inside that suit. He dropped down to his knees and shuffled forward. The pool smoked and vibrated as the light touched its edge. It moved backward again. The tendrils that strayed from the center had disappeared back into the pool. When it moved, it moved like a single organism.

The drain was still several meters away. Kate crept forward. She had enough slack in the lamp's cord to cover Jay for another half-meter. After that, he was on his own. She squatted down and pointed her lamp at the pool as well.

Tendrils of smoke rose from the viscous fluid and it slid backward to get out of the light. Each movement revealed more impossibly clean tile. Jay crept forward another step. The black moved backward. The middle of the pool started to quiver. "Jay?" Kate licked her lips. "What is it doing?"

"I don't know," he said. He lifted the lamp's neck a few centimeters and focused the light on the middle of the pool. A white spot appeared on the quivering mass. The liquid bubbled and then a hole of clean tile appeared. The mass of black had hollowed itself out like a doughnut, the rest of its mass distributed around it. Jay moved the light to one of the edges. The black responded by filling the hole it had left and pulling back once more. The quivering radiated outwards.

"What is it doing?" Kate said into the mic. "It's almost like—"

Something rose from the middle of the pool. Even with the lab lights turned up to full, the shape was difficult to make out. After another second, she knew what it was. "Jay! Get back!"

A thin tentacle that ended in a hook shot out of the middle of the pool. The edges receded as it focused its mass into the appendage. It wavered in the air and then started slashing. Jay fell backwards on his ass. The lamp slipped from his hands and smashed into the tile floor. The bulb shattered. The bright spot on the pool of black disappeared. "Jay!" Kate yelled.

The appendage grew in length. The top of the hook swiped at the table. Jay tried to shuffle backward, but the suit was too bulky. Kate gritted her teeth and moved as far as the cord would let her. She pointed the light right in front of Jay. The tentacle lashed out and into the rays of light.

Smoke billowed out from the hook's end. The appendage flew back into the pool with a slurp. The black moved backward away from the light. A new appendage grew out and grabbed the table leg. It pulled.

The table rattled and then started to tip. The fluoroscopy machine wobbled. And then the table came crashing down. Kate shivered with fear. A sizzling sound started behind the trashed piece of furniture. Kate's hands shook, but she kept the light facing a half meter in front of them.

"Fuck me," Jay panted into the mic. "We have to get out of here."

"You got that right."

"And what the hell is that sound?"

The sizzling hadn't stopped. If anything, it had grown louder. A puff of smoke, or maybe steam, rose into the air from behind the overturned table.

"Get up!" Kate grabbed Jay's hand and lifted. He was heavy and for a moment, she wasn't certain she could help him to his feet. He finally grasped her other hand and pulled himself up. Both of their faceplates were fogged from the exertion.

They stumbled backwards. Kate jerked as the cord from her lamp ran out of slack. "Shit."

"Leave it!" Jay yelled.

She put it down on the floor, the bright light casting a halo a meter in front of them. They continued moving backwards toward the glass partition separating them from the hallway.

The sizzling sound slowed and then disappeared. "We have to get out of here," Jay said. "Like now."

"Mike said we have to——"

"Fuck Mike! Fuck the CDC!" Jay's panting chuffed into the mic. "Oh, shit. What the hell is that?"

Kate followed his gaze. Something peered at them over the top of the table. A black stalk with a scorpion's dead eye stared at them. "Did it grow?"

The table wobbled. Something appeared at the side of it. An

impossibly black, three-toed claw scratched at the floor.

"Oh. My. God." Jay's voice shivered. Another puff of smoke rose from behind the table.

The eye stalk waved in the air. The sizzling sound ramped up. "Fuck the CDC," Kate said. She bolted for the door. Jay followed.

Something squealed along the floor. She was afraid to turn and look. Her gloved fingers fumbled with the door handle.

"Hurry!" Jay shouted.

Kate finally got her grip on the handle and pulled. The door opened and a rush of air whooshed into the room. She scrambled out of the lab and held the door for Jay. Her headset filled with gibbering as Jay shut the door behind them. When she looked through the glass, her heart stopped.

The table the M2 had hid behind had been thrown into the wall. Several other tables lay on their sides as well. Broken lab equipment was scattered across the floor. In the middle of the room, a squat, black thing stood on several legs of differing sizes. Some had three toes, others five. Two eye stalks waved in the air, dead eyes staring at her.

The thing scrambled over the broken and smashed equipment. Smoke rose from the floor where it touched plastic and circuit boards. They melted into its grotesque body and it grew larger before her eyes.

"Hey!"

Kate jumped. So did Jay. She turned and saw Neil and Bill. They had come out of their lab as well. The two men were still in their clean-room suits sans hoods.

"What the hell is that!" Bill yelled.

She didn't want to see what it was doing now. "Did you see it?"

Neil nodded. "We saw it through the glass in our lab. Right after we talked to Mike. Is that the M2?"

Jay pulled off his hood and tossed it away. He ripped out the headset and dropped it to the floor. "Yes, Goddammit. That thing is the oil!"

"We—" Kate pulled off her hood and held it by one hand as she struggled for breath. Her hair was a matted, drenched mess. "We have to kill it. It's eating anything that's not metal or glass."

"Jesus," Bill said.

His cheeks were pale beneath his 5 o'clock shadow. He looked as though he'd been awake for years. It made her wonder how she looked.

"It's afraid of the light," she said.

"Bull. Shit." Bill shook his head. "It's not having any problems tearing the hell out of the lab!"

"No," she said. "Only broad spectrum. Sunlight. Or halogens."

All four of them started as someone banged on the door at the end of the hallway. Kate turned toward it. "I hope that's the CDC," she said.

The door banged again. There was a murmur of voices and then the banging stopped. The beep of the card-scanner echoed in the hall. The door squealed open.

Jakob stepped aside as three people clad in green moon suits walked into the hall. "CDC! Stay where you are!" one of them yelled.

A crash from inside the lab made the four scientists turn. Kate caught a glimpse of something moving on the ceiling. And then it was gone.

"Where did it go?" Jay asked.

Kate shivered. "Into the air ducts."

BOOK 2: Quarantine

CHAPTER FIVE

The three moon-suited CDC specialists corralled them in the bio-lab. Before walking them inside the enclosed room, Kate and Jay placed their removed hoods in a large yellow bag marked with a bio-hazard symbol. Anything that had been inside either lab was considered to be contaminated and would be destroyed.

You mean studied, was what Kate thought. No way they were simply going to burn that up. Not without a chance of figuring out what infected Marie. At this point she didn't much care either. She wanted food. She wanted to pee. And she wanted to get the hell out of HAL with her daughter. And what did the CDC want? For none of them to leave.

Those feds hadn't seen the thing in the lab, hadn't watched it move and devour. All they'd seen was four terrified scientists in the midst of a complete freak-out. And instead of getting the hell out of the building, they were quarantined in the goddamned lab.

Still in her chem-suit, sans hood, she sat in one of the rolling chairs near the computer station. Jay was slumped against the wall. He looked as though he was going to nod off at any moment, but she knew better. He might be exhausted, but after what they'd seen, she wasn't sure either of them would ever sleep again.

The leader of the CDC crew, Dr. Melanie Hoyt, had a tablet in her gloved hands. She tapped the screen as she spoke. "So what was the extent of your exposure?"

Jay and Kate looked at one another. Kate shrugged and stared at the woman in the moon-suit. A single lock of Dr. Hoyt's hair had come loose and dangled inside her mask. Her voice was muffled, but perfectly understandable.

"Well, neither Jay nor I had direct contact with the M2," Kate said.

Dr. Hoyt raised an eyebrow. "M2?"

Jay cleared his throat. "It's what we call the oil. It's from a trench called 'M2.' It's located near Papua/New Guinea."

The doctor nodded. "Where PPE drilled."

"Right," Kate said. "The sample arrived yesterday afternoon in a typical oil barrel. Marie—"

"Ms. Krieger?"

"Yes, Dr. Hoyt." Kate felt like slapping the woman's hands every time she looked back down at her tablet. "Marie hooked up the barrel to our vacuum pump system. She cut herself on the barrel's lid when she perforated it."

Dr. Hoyt frowned. Her green eyes bored into Kate's. "And what's the procedure when that occurs?"

"Excuse me?" Jay asked. "You implying something?"

"No," Dr. Hoyt said, clearly implying something. "Just wanted to know what the procedure is when you are contaminated by the oil."

"Oil is not contamination," Jay said. "If it was, you wouldn't be putting the shit in your fucking car, lady."

"No need to be defensive," Dr. Hoyt said.

"Look, Doc," Jay said, his finger pointing at the other lab, "you didn't see what just happened. You weren't in there with that thing! It's loose in the goddamned building and you want to give us the third degree about procedure?"

The moon-suited doctor dropped her hands, the tablet tapping against one knee. She glared at Jay. "We're getting to that, Mr. Hollingsworth."

"Doctor," he corrected her.

"Excuse me," Hoyt said, "*Doctor* Hollingsworth. A young woman is dying at Ben Taub and we need to know why." She tapped her foot. "And I don't understand why you're making up some story about a monster."

Jay opened his mouth, but no words came out. Kate knew exactly how he felt. "Look, I don't expect you to believe us. But if we just sit here, that thing is going to come back here and kill us. And we need to get everyone the hell out of the building!"

Dr. Hoyt's foot stopped tapping. She turned to the other CDC personnel. "I'm sure these fine scientists will stay here with me. Go cordon off the area. Do a search and sweep and find any other people. We need them quarantined as well."

"I need to get my daughter," Kate said. "Now. Please let me go—"

"No one leaves unless they're in a suit," Dr. Hoyt growled. "And not contaminated."

"We're not contaminated!" Kate yelled. "We never touched it."

"It could be airborne," one of the CDC drones said.

Kate stood from the chair and walked up to Dr. Hoyt. "If it's airborne," she said, "we're already screwed. Because this will have broken out on Leaguer. And if it's airborne, the chopper pilots who took it off the rig infected more people. And so on." Kate swallowed. "You'd already have thousands of dead bodies. It's. Not. Airborne."

Hoyt flexed her fingers. Kate didn't drop the stare, but she saw them in her peripheral vision.

"Okay," Hoyt said. "But we can't prove that right now. We have to treat this like it's airborne until we're sure."

Kate's lip quivered with anger. "Fine. Then do your job and get our people safe." Hoyt said nothing, but her eyes hardened. "Now," Kate hissed.

"Dr. Cheevers. Where should we look for the others?" Hoyt asked.

"Second and third floors." Kate pointed at the phone. "We can call Mike and get him to tell everyone in the two buildings to meet at a common place."

Dr. Hoyt blinked. "Adjoining buildings?"

"Yeah," Jay said. "Connected with a skybridge. It's supposed to be ready for us in a couple of months."

"Mike is in this building. There's at least one more employee as well," Bill said. "And a security guard."

The doctor's moon-suit crinkled as she turned to her team. "That big foyer at the main entrance. That's where I want all the employees." She glanced at Kate. "All the non-contaminated personnel. Glaze? Dugger? Retrieve Dr. Cheevers' daughter and bring her here. Then sweep the building and stay in contact. We'll call Mr. Beaudry and get the message to everyone else."

"Okay, Mel." A short, heavy beard graced the CDC man's chin and his voice dripped with a Texan accent. "Come on, Glaze. Let's do this."

The two CDC men walked to the door and headed out into the hallway.

Hoyt turned back to the scientists. "They'll get your daughter and then they'll do their jobs. Can you call Mr. Beaudry for me?"

Kate nodded. "I'll do it. But you need to do more." She took a deep breath. "That thing dissolves anything that isn't metal or glass. And that's not all. It started out as just a few liters. Now it's huge!" The CDC doctor's lips twitched. "Oh. You still don't believe us."

"No," Hoyt said, "I don't."

Kate's face flushed. She was so angry, her body sizzled. "I'm calling Mike. Then you're going into the chem lab. And maybe you can tell us what happened. In the meantime, Neil? Show our CDC friend the SEM image."

Dr. Hoyt raised an eyebrow. "You scanned it?"

"Yeah. We scanned it." Neil said. "Want to see something you've never seen before?"

* * *

Dugger waited until they'd left the quarantined hallway before snickering. He looked at his partner. Glaze's face was locked in a grimace. Dugger pointed at him. "You believe that crap?"

Glaze shook his head. "I don't know, man. I mean, they sound insane."

"Yes, they do," Dugger said. Houston CDC might not be Atlanta, but as the fourth largest city in the USA and one of the busiest ports in the world, the Federal government had made sure the presence was adequate. After 9/11, the worry had been anthrax or weaponized small pox. After Liberia, it'd been Ebola. And after Florida? Dengue Fever. The possible diseases entering the country were skyrocketing. Hell, if people didn't start vaccinating their kids again, something like polio might kill an entire generation. Dugger hoped he'd be dead long before something like that happened.

"How do you want to do this?" Glaze asked.

"What do you mean?" They walked toward the foyer where Dr. Hoyt wanted them to set up triage. "Get the other team in here. Get them to set things up and meet me upstairs. Easy peasy."

Glaze grunted. "Easy— What does that even mean? Something redneck related?"

Typical. Just what he expected from a damned Midwesterner. The man didn't understand that swamps and mosquitoes and ridiculously uncomfortable heat were all part of the Houston experience. He whined during the summer, froze during the winter, and was a general pain in the ass. Maybe Glaze would head back to Chicago soon. Dugger certainly hoped so. The guy was talented, but Christ, you could only put up with so much bitching.

"Look, partner," Dugger drawled, "it means no problem. Comprende?"

"Whatever, man." Glaze rubbed at his arm. "We might need beds in here."

"Beds," Dugger said. Enough of this shit. He wanted to find Dr. Cheevers' kid and wait for the rest of the HAL personnel to get their asses down here. Sooner they had the place contained, the sooner everybody could go home. "Ain't gonna need beds, Glaze." He turned and walked toward the elevator bank.

"Wait!" Glaze said. "Where you going?"

Dugger twisted his hand into the shape of a gun, index finger pointing toward the ceiling. "Up. Isn't that where the kid is?"

"Yeah," Glaze said. "But we shouldn't use the elevator."

Dugger sighed. "We don't have security keys to get through the fire stairs."

The other CDC man shook his head. "Bullshit. We can get one from the security guard."

"Yeah," Dugger said and stabbed the up button, "but I ain't walking up the stairs in this getup unless forced."

"Lazy bastard," Glaze said.

Dugger grinned. "That's fat lazy bastard to you. Now get those guys in here and meet me on the second floor. I want to sweep this place before the sun comes up."

"Right," Glaze said. "Because you have plans."

"Hey, now," Dugger said. "I always plan a little pickle tickle for the wife in the morning."

"Pickle tickle," Glaze echoed. "See you upstairs."

The elevator dinged. "That you will," Dugger said. When the doors opened, he walked inside, and pressed the button marked "2." He waved at Glaze as the doors closed. The radio in his helmet belched a stream of static. He winced. Hoyt was probably trying to get a status report. The status was they were going to get the kid, get the rest of the folks out of here, and then he could go back to sleep.

The elevator dinged. Dugger watched the doors slide open. His grin faded. "What the—"

***

A smell. Her nose wrinkled and she snorted herself awake. Maeve opened her eyes and regarded the dark office. The hallway lights were off. With the office blinds closed, there was no ambient light filtering in from outside. The game console's single, green power light glowed like a cat's eye in the darkness. Rain touched the windows; gusts of wind rattled them. She blinked a few times and then sat up.

The smell. It was a combination of cooking meat and something rotten that had been in the sun too long. With a yawn, she reached behind her and clicked on the light.

The strong halogen lamp exploded with brightness. She shut her eyes against the glare, and then slowly opened them. The table was still clogged with drink cans, an empty coffee mug, and the wrappers from candy bars. She had to clean that up before her mom showed up. And where was she anyway?

And what the hell was that smell? She yawned and gathered up the cans and wrappers. She glanced at the coffee mug, decided it was too much to hold, and left it on the table. If Mom was still in the lab, she couldn't call, but she could text. Maeve hit the power button on her phone. The display was blank sans the weather alert in the notifications. Oh well. She'd see Mom soon enough.

Maeve walked to the office threshold and stopped. The smell was stronger. And there was a sound, something she barely made out against the central air's hum. Darkness. She hated it. She always had. Despite the wan rectangle of light that streamed into the hallway from the office, it was too damned dark. She took a deep breath and walked into the hallway.

An overhead fluorescent immediately came on. Well, she thought, at least the motion sensors still worked. The smell. Jesus, did something go bad in the break room? Was there a power outage? She hadn't been asleep long enough for that to happen.

With her hands full of wrappers and cans, each step was a trick in holding on to it all. With every few steps, another set of lights streamed on. Before she rounded the corner, the lights came on in the adjoining hallway. A shadow appeared on the wall. Maeve's brows furrowed. "Hello?" Her voice echoed in the empty hall. The shadow disappeared, but the lights remained.

Heart thumping in her chest, the back of her neck crawling with goose flesh, she walked to the corner and peered around. An empty hallway stared back at her, but the stench was much more palpable. Her gorge rose in the back of her throat. She let out an acidic burp and turned the corner.

The hall was still empty, but something was...wrong. The smell was stronger as she approached the break room. It was definitely coming from there. "Hello?" she called again. No answer.

Maeve reached the break room and looked in. The lights came on in the room. The tile floor shined as though it was freshly mopped. In fact, it was impossibly clean. Even the stains were gone. She dropped the aluminum cans in the recycle bin and threw away the wrappers. And that's when her sleep-hazed mind made sense of the table and chairs. The plastic was stripped off. The seat backs, once vinyl, had disappeared. The table was bare metal, shining, and spotless.

Something sizzled. Maeve scanned the room. The counters were clean, but not sparkling clean. Darren had done a good job cleaning up after dinner, but he sure as hell didn't mop the goddamned floor. And the table? The chairs? Who would do that?

The bacon sizzle was louder, the smell stronger. She retched, but didn't toss dinner. Something was burning. And it wasn't just meat. Plastic. Vinyl. Rubber. And it was behind her.

Maeve slowly turned. The sheetrock in the walls was dissolving. Her eyes slowly rose upward. Wisps of smoke escaped through the gaps in the metal supports. She stepped backward.

One of the ceiling tiles was gone. Just...gone. A thin, black stalk slowly descended through the hole. A serpent's black eye popped forth from its end. It blinked at her.

Maeve screamed and ran through the other side of the break

room. Behind her, she heard the smash and crash of something large falling to the tile floor. She turned the corner and pelted down the hallway. With every hurried step, another fluorescent light popped on.

The sizzling sound rose in volume and something's heavy steps pounded into the floor. Maeve reached the next corner and turned left. Something crashed into the wall. Maeve spun around, panting from the run. A squat, black creature with five legs, and three arms twirled away from the burned wood and sheetrock. It made no sound other than the sizzling of its feet dissolving the carpet. The thing's eyestalks pointed at her and a large maw appeared in the center of its body. A hooked tentacle shot out in her direction.

Maeve screamed and ran. Heart thumping in her ears, she barely heard the sound of sheetrock cracking and burning as the thing chased her, its tentacles smashing into the walls. The elevator bank dinged, but she didn't even hear it. She nearly lost her balance when the carpet switched to tile in front of the elevator. Her left sneaker's toe hit the transition lip. Maeve stumbled, but managed to keep her feet. Within a second, she was past the bank when one of the doors opened.

"What the—" a muffled voice yelled.

Maeve turned around. A moon-suited figure had walked halfway out the door when it saw the monstrosity. The thing didn't turn. Instead, its tentacled arms seemed to skate across its surface. The mouth too. The hooked appendages shot forward and ripped through the fabric. A new smell, cooking flesh, added to the olfactory assault.

The man screamed. A mixture of smoke and steam erupted from the torn suit. The man's heavily gloved hands clutched at his ruined chest. One of the thing's appendages rose to the man's shoulder. It hesitated in the air and then whistled as it ripped sideways. The hook smashed into the man's head just behind the temple.

A rotten melon squelch echoed in the hallway. The top half of the man's head flew to the ground. Blood, brains, and bone scattered across the tile floor. The figure sagged and then fell forward. Two tentacles reached behind and dragged him into the creature's massive maw.

The sizzling of frying meat stung her ears. Smoke billowed from the thing's mouth as the figure slowly disappeared inside. Maeve, mouth open, eyes wide, turned and ran.

She made it to the other hallway, swiveled her head, and saw the bright crimson glow of the exit sign. Barely keeping her balance, she bounced off the opposite wall and sprinted toward the fire door. A ripping sound followed her, but she didn't turn around. She hit the fire door's push bar. The heavy steel and glass fire door resisted her at first, but then slowly swung open. The ripping sound increased in volume. Whatever it was, it was closer. Maeve screamed and forced the door wide enough to slink through. She turned and shut it behind her.

Something crashed into the door. The stairwell echoed with the sound. Maeve pressed her hands against the steel, hoping against hope the creature couldn't open it. Panting, her eyes filled with starlight, she looked through the glass. There was nothing but impenetrable darkness on the other side of the door. But there was nothing dead about it. It rippled against the glass. Something knocked against the door's bottom half. The door shuddered, but didn't budge.

The darkness retreated. When the thing was a few meters away from the door, Maeve froze. Her heart seemed to stop in her chest. It was larger. It barely fit in the hallway. Extra legs jutted out from its base. Two eyestalks waved in the air. Two more stared directly at her. Its hook-ended appendages dragged across the sheetrock walls. She knew the hallway was filled with that sizzling sound.

"Miss?"

She jumped and whirled. Another man in a moon-suit stood a few steps down from the landing. His heavy hands clutched at the bannister.

"Are you okay?" he said in a muffled voice.

Maeve nearly knocked him over when she grabbed him around the waist and started to cry.

***

In the past several hours, he'd been called by the CDC, discovered Marie was mostly likely going to die, and PPE was up shit creek without a paddle. Their oil wasn't going to get analyzed and their rig, for all he knew, was now filled with infected people.

Because Simpson, PPE Vice President, was a good friend of his, Mike had called him shortly after he told Kate and Neil to cease work and prepare for quarantine. Simpson hadn't exactly been thrilled.

"The fuck do you mean you've been quarantined?"

Mike had sighed. "A Dr. Hutchins from the CDC called me. Told me one of my employees was on death's door and they were worried that whatever she caught, she caught from here. Also, your oil from Leaguer is under suspicion. Or at least the barrel is."

"How is that possible?" Simpson's voice bellowed into the phone. "This has to be some trick. The Saudis are trying to sabotage M2. They must have——"

"Simpson? Calm down." Mike took a deep breath. "I didn't believe it either. I called the CDC in Atlanta. They verified his identity and put me right through to him. It's for real."

Simpson snorted. "Goddammit. Look, if that was the case, wouldn't Leaguer be infected? I mean, there's no way they'd have been able to keep themselves away from it. Shit, cleaning out the damned mud traps could expose them, let alone the drilling and filling the barrel. And the engineering team? Calhoun's team were the ones running the damned tests!"

Mike tried not to sigh. He failed. "I don't know how, Simpson. I only know what they told me."

"Goddammit. You know how far behind this puts us?"

The relative numbness he'd felt suddenly departed. The idea Marie might not ever work again at HAL bounced around in his head. A wave of anger replaced the vacuous feeling of incredulity. "I don't give a fuck about your oil," Mike growled into the phone. "In case you forgot, one of my employees might be dead even as we speak."

There was a long pause after Simpson's deep intake of breath. When he finally spoke, his voice was calm, and apologetic. "Right. Sorry. I should tell my people to stop drilling until we figure this out."

Mike nodded to himself. "Yes, you should. If you don't, the feds might."

"Goddammit," Simpson said. "Okay. Mike? Keep me updated. And I'm sorry this happened. If we track it back to the shipping company, I'll have someone's ass."

"As will I," Mike had replied.

Their goodbyes had been cordial, but strained. The exhaustion of the night had finally hit him. The sun was just a few hours away from gracing the horizon. Not like they'd be able to tell with all the cloud cover and the storm pounding the building.

Mike had dozed off when the phone rang again. He opened his eyes and stared at the caller-id strip. "BIO-LAB" it said. Instantly awake, he reached out and took the receiver. "Beaudry. What's up, Neil?"

"It's Kate."

"Sorry, Kate," Mike chuckled. "I— Wait, what are you doing in the bio-lab? CDC told you guys to stay in your lab."

She sighed. "That's what I wanted to tell you. We have, um, a little issue. Actually, fuck that. We have a serious problem, Mike. We need everyone in the two buildings to meet in the foyer of building 1."

Mike stared at the receiver in his hands and then put it back to his ear. "What?"

"Don't ask why. Just do it. The CDC is here and they want everyone in the foyer."

"Okay," Mike said. "I'm pretty sure Chuckles is the only one in the new building. Unless one of the security folks is strolling around."

"Round them up and get them down here. Oh, do you have a halogen flashlight?"

Mike opened his mouth and then closed it. "What?"

"Do you have a halogen flashlight?"

"Um, I don't know. I might."

Kate's voice turned cold. "Listen to me very carefully, Mike. You're not going to believe me. And I don't care. But something got out of chem-lab. And—"

"Something?"

"Yes. Shut up and listen! It doesn't like natural light. Or anything close to it."

He frowned. "Are you high?"

"I'm not fucking kidding!" she screamed into the phone. "Just… Just find a halogen light if you can. Maybe Chuckles has one or knows where some are. Check with him. Keep them handy. And if you hear a sizzling sound? Run from it. Okay?"

"Um, okay. Kate, what the hell is going on?"

"Just do what I told you, okay? We'll see you down in the foyer as soon as you get here."

"Okay."

"Be safe, Mike."

"You too, Kate."

He hung up the phone and stared at it. Something *escaped* from chem-lab? This had to be a joke. No. She wouldn't do that. Jay? Hell yes. Bill? Absolutely. But Kate? No.

The office lamp was a halogen. The amount of heat and light the thing produced was why it was in the far corner of the room. If…well, if *whatever* it was she was afraid of came in here, it was in for a shock. But it wasn't like he could carry the damned lamp around with him.

The server room had strong lighting. Might be a good place to hole up if… "This is stupid," he said to the empty room.

Mike rose from his chair, stretched, and walked toward the door. He stopped. Chuckles.

He picked up the phone and dialed the NOC. The phone rang and rang. Mike frowned and then sighed. Chuckles must be out of NOC1 and traipsing around the new NOC. He hung up the phone. He'd at least have to check and see if the surly tech was in the new server room. That meant going to the second floor. Oh well, he was heading there anyway.

Rounding up all the staff was easy. Darren was at the hospital, Marie was...at the hospital, and all that remained were Chuckles, Jakob the security guard, and himself.

Mike stood from his desk and looked at the heavy wooden door leading to the reception area. Normally, Darren would be out there. He wished Darren was there now. Mike might be the CEO, but without Darren, he was barely functional. Besides, Darren would know where the goddamned flashlights were.

He reached into his office drawer and pulled out a Glock. The 40 caliber would stop whatever the hell had "escaped" the lab. He checked the magazine, racked the slide to put one in the throat, and jammed it into his waistband.

"Ok," he said as he opened the door, "let's do this." By the time he got to the elevator, he was too far away to hear the phone ringing.

* * *

This isn't happening, was what kept echoing in his mind. He didn't know how far he'd run or in what direction. Soaked to the bone, shivering, and terrified, Darren was close to passing out.

His feet struck the pavement grinding the glass in his heels deeper and deeper. The heavy socks he'd worn in the hospital were little protection against the litter in the gutters and on the street. The only upside was he was so cold, he didn't even notice the pain.

With the hospital far behind him, he slowly dropped from an awkward run into a stumbling walk. He put his arms around himself. The shoulder was lined with parked cars. Darren bumped into the side of one and stopped. He leaned his lithe body against the cold metal. He couldn't go any further. Just couldn't.

"Hey!" a voice called.

Darren barely heard it over the sound of the wind and the pattering of the rain against the cars and pavement. "Help me?" His voice was a nearly inaudible croak.

A strong hand touched his shoulder. "You okay, buddy?"

Darren shuffled as he turned to look at the man. Dressed in a trench coat hanging down to his knees, umbrella extended to cover his exquisitely coifed bedhead, a tall, barrel-chested man stared at him.

"You need to get out of the rain, man. You're gonna freeze."

Darren's teeth chattered so hard he could barely speak. "Need phone." The two words dropped in jittery syllables.

The man nodded. "Okay, buddy." The man moved the umbrella so it covered the two of them. He turned Darren toward the sidewalk and gently marched him onto the pavement.

Darren didn't remember much else until he found himself wrapped in a blanket and on a leather couch. His soaking wet gown and bloody hospital socks were puddled on the floor. He was naked and a steaming cup of something was on the end-table next to the couch.

The man stood a few feet away. His trench was gone and he wore a red-checked house-coat. His face turned into an uneasy grin. "What's your name?"

"Darren."

"I'm Richard." He pointed at Darren. "Do I need to call the police?"

Darren shivered beneath the blanket. His feet were starting to burn. He didn't know shit about frostbite, but he thought he might have it. Either that or his heels were screaming because he had two tons of glass in them. "Need to call my office. Then need to call 9-1-1."

Richard frowned and pulled a cell phone from his pocket. "What's going on, Darren?"

Everything hurt. He just wanted to sleep. But he had to call Mike. The rest of the lab was in big trouble. "The end of the world," Darren said.

***

Hoyt stood motionless and breathless as she peered at the image on the screen. She'd checked the settings on the SEM twice and still couldn't believe her eyes. "That's not possible."

Kate ground her teeth. "Where's my daughter?"

"She'll be fine," Hoyt said. She wished the chemist would calm down. Hoyt made a mental note to call the hospital and see if any of the other contaminated personnel were also delusional. She pointed at the screen. "I don't understand."

Neil nodded. "Now you're getting it."

"It's just...black."

"That's the point," Bill said. "It's just black. No molecules. No electrons. It's not possible. And yet you don't believe," he said and pointed to Jay and Kate, "what they're saying? Call your people and get us the hell out of here!"

Hoyt sighed. All four of them were crazy. The SEM was obviously broken or the calibration was wrong. She didn't know how that was possible either, but it was the only thing that made sense. Still, she needed to check in with the hospital anyway.

She clicked the control box attached to her belt. "Dr. Harrel? This is Hoyt. Over."

A jolt of static came through the line and made her wince. Somewhere out there in the world, a bolt of lightning had come down. God, but she hated the radios. "Harrel? Come in." No response. "This is Dr. Hoyt at HAL. Is anyone reading me?"

She frowned. The storm could have knocked out comms, but she doubted it. She looked down at the radio frequency to double check. Yup, she was on the right one. She clicked the knob over another spot. "Dugger? Glaze?"

"Melanie!" a voice shouted back. "I've got the kid. But we are seriously fucked."

Her eyes narrowed. "Keep your head, Glaze. Where's Dugger?"

"We're heading back your way. Be there in a few. Melanie? We need to get the hell out of here and now."

She sighed. Maybe the crazy was contagious. "Report when you get here. And get Dugger back down here. We have—"

"Dugger's dead," Glaze said.

Hoyt's mouth dropped open. "Just get here." She flicked the radio switch again. "Control? This is Dr. Hoyt at HAL."

"Go ahead, Hoyt."

"We've lost communications with Ben Taub. Have they reported in?"

"Negative, Hoyt. HPD is on the scene outside the building. Nothing's moving."

"Get them in there and find out what's going on."

The radio crackled with static. "We don't have suits for them."

She growled into the mic. "Then get them suits! Get them in there and figure out what's going on!"

"What's your situation, Hoyt?"

"Glaze reports we have casualties. We'll need more personnel in as soon as possible."

"Casualties? Do you have an outbreak situation?"

Hoyt licked her lips. Her next words might condemn her team to staying in the building. "Unknown, Control. Will report back ASAP. Glazer will be reporting to me in a moment."

"Understood, Hoyt. Report situation as soon as possible. Control out."

She stared at Kate. "Dr. Glaze has your child. He's heading here now."

A flush of color rose in Kate's cheeks. Hoyt was actually glad about that. When they'd first entered the now broken quarantine area of the labs, all four scientists had looked as though they were in shock. Especially Kate and Jay. Those two looked like they'd seen a nightmare. Something in Hoyt's stomach started to flutter. This was starting to seem a little too real.

"Well?" Kate said. "What's going on? How's Marie?"

Hoyt put her hands on her hips. "We've lost contact with the hospital."

Jay and Kate exchanged stares.

"What?" Hoyt asked.

Kate opened her mouth as the phone rang on the desk. She glared at Hoyt and then walked to the desk and punched the speakerphone button. "Bio-lab. This is Kate."

"Kate! Thank God!" Darren's voice yelled through the speakers.

A shiver of confusion rose up Hoyt's back. "Mr. Strange? Aren't you supposed to be in—"

"Shut up, you twat! Kate! It was in Marie! It ate everything! People, plastic, oh Jesus, it ate everything but—"

"Darren, slow down," Kate said. "What are you talking about? What do you mean—"

"Something burst out of her. Some kind of creature. Just all black goo and—" He started to cry. "It ate the doctors."

Kate put her hands on the table and leaned over. "Where are you, Darren?"

"I don't know," he said. "We have to call the cops! We have to call somebody!" Something banged on the other end of the line. The entire room echoed with the tinny sounds of Darren sobbing.

"Hello?" Kate said.

The receiver crackled. "My name is Richard. Darren is at my house. Who is this?"

Kate took a deep breath. "Hello, Richard. Can you keep him safe? And tell me where you are?"

The man gave his address. Kate wrote it down on a slip of paper. "I think he needs a doctor," Richard said. "I can take him to an ER. I'm right near the med center—"

"Don't go to the med center!" Kate yelled. "If he needs a doctor, take him to a 24-hour doc in the box. But make sure it's away from the med center."

"Okay, lady. Okay. I get it."

Kate hissed through her teeth. "You have a cell number, Richard?"

"Yes."

"Give me the number, please." Kate scribbled it down on a piece of paper. "Okay. Get him to the doctor. I'll call you as soon as we can get someone to help you. And Richard? Thank you."

"You're welcome," the voice said.

The speakerphone dropped to a dial tone. Kate hit a button and the speakers went silent. She looked at Hoyt. "You believe us now?"

A beeping sound caught her attention. Hoyt turned and looked through the glass to the same door she and her team had come through. Glaze led a teenage girl into the hallway. She was barely walking on her own. Her hands gripped Glaze's moon-suit.

Kate looked up and saw her daughter. She sprinted toward the door.

"No!" Hoyt yelled. "You're in quarantine! You could infect—"

Kate pushed her aside and headed into the hallway. The teenager dropped her hands and ran to her mother. They embraced. Hoyt heard sobbing, but wasn't sure which of them was crying.

"Glaze?"

The man walked into the room. His eyes seemed vacant and dazed. "Yes, Mel."

"What happened to Dugger?"

Glaze stared down at the floor. "It ate him. At least that's what the kid says."

"Ate him?" She walked to Glaze and grabbed his shoulders. "John? What do you mean it ate him?" He didn't respond. She shook him. "John! Snap out of it. What happened?"

He blinked twice and then met her stare. "I saw it. Dugger took the elevator. I got things prepped in the foyer. I walked up the stairs and saw the girl." He coughed and cleared his throat. "I looked through the window in the fire door." He squeezed his eyes shut.

"John?" Hoyt's voice dropped into a whisper. "What did you see?"

His eyes flicked open again. What she saw in them was terror. "It. I saw it."

CHAPTER SIX

The rain was dying down, but he knew it was damned cold outside. At least for November. With the central heating set to 68°, the new building was normally comfortably cool, but the heater seemed to have stopped working. When he walked down to the second floor, the temperature must have dropped at least five degrees.

Mike headed to the new NOC. If he found Chuckles there, they could gather some gear and get the hell over to building 1. If he didn't, then it'd be up to him to try and find Chuckles. That could take some time. And Kate didn't seem to think he had any.

Her words played over and over in his mind. Something was loose in the building. From the barrel? That made absolutely no sense. But he'd known Kate for nearly a decade. There was no way she'd say something like that unless it was true. He patted the Glock in his waistband just to make sure it was still there.

As he walked toward the NOC, his eyes drifted up to the exposed ceiling. Some of the duct work hadn't even been connected yet. No wonder the goddamned heating wasn't working down here. Mike hissed a sigh and continued down the hallway. The fluorescent lights dispelled the darkness, but they somehow seemed less than bright. Maybe it was the fact at least a third of them were out. Or maybe it was the time of the morning. Didn't matter.

He reached the door to the new NOC and pulled his keycard from his front pocket. He flashed it in front of the sensor. It beeped, a green LED lit up, and the door clicked as the lock slid back. Mike pulled the door open and a wall of sound hit his ears.

With the inner door still closed, the sound wasn't ear-crushing, but it was still loud enough to be annoying. He peered into the NOC control center. Empty. Mike went in anyway. He checked the camera displays. The server room was blanketed in darkness. If he remembered correctly, the lights were supposed to go on if anyone walked in there, or if there was any motion. With the room in pitch black, it was obvious Chuckles wasn't in there either.

The security displays showed nothing but darkness. A monitor high on the wall displayed temperature and power readings of each rack. If they ever got the damned building finished, HAL would have the most advanced computational system in the chemical and bio-chem industries. His teams could couple nuclear magnetic resonance and scanning electron microscope analytics and model molecular structures faster than their largest competitors.

Mike pulled a sheet of paper out from one of the log books. He scrawled a message on it telling whoever read it to head to the floor 1 foyer in the old building. He signed the piece of paper and left it on one of the consoles.

With one last look at the server room's impenetrable darkness, he turned to leave the room. He stopped in mid-stride and stared at the wall. Tool belts, filled with screw drivers, ratchet sets, and chip removers, hung from hooks. But that wasn't what caught his attention.

Several headbands with built in lights hung below them. He grabbed one of them and put it in his pocket. He took another, said a prayer that the gods of fashion never noticed this sleight, and put it on his head. He snapped the plastic switch on the top and a bright white cone of light hit the wall. He smiled.

A few emergency flashlights were plugged into a power strip. He took one of those as well. He slid the heavy cylinder into his belt. He wondered how much more his pants could take before they simply slid down to his ankles.

Mike walked out of the control room and headed back into the hallway. The door closed and locked behind him. The growl of the servers immediately disappeared.

He made his way across the skybridge and then stopped. When he'd come down from his office on the third floor, he'd taken the stairwell that dropped him near the skybridge. He hadn't paid attention to the rest of the floor. But he was now.

The floor's carpet was gone. Just gone. The sheetrock walls were ripped and burned. Wooden studs, metal fasteners, and piping were visible through the ragged holes.

The old NOC was down the hall and to the left. He hoped Chuckles was still in there. If they could evacuate everyone to the first floor foyer, they could get the hell out of here before, well, before whatever did *that* came back.

Mike looked up at the ceiling and stopped in mid-step. He fingered the Glock on his belt. Several of the ceiling tiles had disappeared. Exposed wires, pipes, and metal gleamed. "Fuck me," Mike whispered.

He moved to the wall and stepped past the holes in the ceiling. The rational part of him knew there was nothing up there, but the reptilian part of his brain refused to believe that.

By the time he reached the door to the old NOC, he'd seen more destruction in the interconnecting halls: no carpet, holes in the walls, missing ceiling tiles, and broken fluorescent lights. Whatever roamed the building wasn't screwing around.

The area around the NOC, however, was untouched. That was strange to say the least. Mike pulled his badge again and swiped it across the card reader. It beeped and the door unlocked. Mike slowly pushed it open.

The room was its usual dark cave. The server fans were loud as hell and Mike winced. There at the back of the room, dim lights bathing his workstation, Chuckles sat at his terminals. His displays were lit up with code and the output from monitoring software. His headphones were clamped on his skull.

Mike moved so he was in view of the glass mirror attached to the wall. If Chuckles saw the movement, maybe he wouldn't be startled. Mike continued walking to the workstation and stopped. Chuckles' body stiffened. The head of network operations pulled off his headphones, placed them on the desk, and then slowly swiveled in his chair.

His eyes were bloodshot and he looked like he hadn't slept in weeks. "What's up, Mike?"

Mike barely heard the words. "We need to get the hell out of here."

"You need to what?"

"The CDC wants us to evacuate to the first floor foyer."

Chuckles blinked and stood from his chair. The left side of his face twitched. "Um, okay."

"Let's— Wait, do you have any halogen flashlights?"

Chuckles cocked an eyebrow. "Halogen lights?"

"Yeah. Do you have any?"

"Um, we should. More shit we were planning on recycling." He left his desk and walked to the makeshift storage closet. He opened it. Coils of network cords, network cards, stacks of drives, both dead and new, stared back at him. Chuckles bent down, his cap staying put on his bald head, and pulled out a heavy cardboard box. He reached into it and brought out two small lights. "These should work," he said. He clicked the power button of each and a strong cone of light flashed out. He nodded. "Perfect. Good batteries." He turned to Mike and held them out. "You need these?"

"More like *we* need them. You hang on to one. Give me the other."

Chuckles blinked and handed one of them to Mike. "We getting ready for a blackout or something?" Chuckles asked. "I have plenty of LED—"

"LEDs won't do it." Mike lifted his phone from his pocket. "Come on. Let's go."

"Why is the CDC—"

"Let it go, man. We have to go."

Chuckles stood, closed the supply cabinet, and stared at Mike. "What the hell is going on?"

Mike raised an eyebrow. "Please. We need to get out of here. Come on."

The tech straightened his cap and blew a sigh through his teeth. "Okay, boss."

Chuckles walked to the door, opened it, and stopped. "Did someone pull up the carpets? And what the hell is that smell?"

Mike walked up behind him and peered over his shoulder. The carpet that had been intact when they entered the NOC was gone. "Oh, shit," Mike said. He pulled the Glock from his waist. "Chuckles? I think we're in trouble. Turn on your flashlight."

"What? Mike, this is bullshit. What's—"

"Shut the hell up," Mike whispered. "Look, just do it. Turn on the flashlight, and keep it ready. If you see something moving, point your light at it. Okay?"

Chuckles shrugged. "Fine. Where's Kate's team? Marie down there with them? I didn't see them at their break."

Mike bit his lip. "Let's talk about that when we get to the foyer, okay? Just believe me when I say we have a problem."

"Sure." Chuckles sighed. "Lead on."

"Vamanos," Mike said. With the pistol in his right hand, the emergency flashlight in his left, he stepped into the hallway.

Chuckles was right about the smell. His nostrils singed with the stench of burned meat and something fetid. The skin at the back of his neck crawled with tension. His flashlight wasn't very powerful, but the one Chuckles held was. The tight cone of bright white light waved around the walls and cut through the fluorescent's blue-white light.

As they walked toward the emergency stairwell, the only sounds were of heavy breathing behind him, and the storm outside the building. Even the central heating's soft hum seemed to have disappeared.

With the carpet missing, their footsteps formed a strange clumping cadence. Mike winced with every step. Chuckles had obviously never learned how to walk in the woods. They were making too much noise. *It*, whatever *It* was, would no doubt hear them. And then—

He felt silly. This *had* to be a joke. Or a misunderstanding. Or both. But the CDC call hadn't been a joke. And neither had Kate's.

He continued walking, Chuckles' stomping feet behind him. The red "EXIT" sign glowed at the end of the hall. As they walked, his eyes flicked upward to the ceiling. The fluorescents were still flicking on as they walked, but all they showed was the damage to the sheetrock, exposed plumbing and ductwork, and the all too clean concrete.

The fire door shined beneath the overhead light mounted next to the "EXIT" sign. Mike gulped. Whatever was in the building, he hoped like hell it wasn't behind that door. If it was, they were in big trouble.

They came to a hallway intersection. Mike held up his hand and peered around the corner. The tile in front of the elevator bank was clean. The metal doors shined brighter than any steel he'd ever seen. Carpet on either side was gone as were entire sections of sheetrock. Pieces of metal were scattered across the floor. A zipper, buttons, and a smartphone stripped to the bone lay on the tile. Bits of wire connected to a metal disc stared back at him. Was that a headset?

Mike ignored the elevator bank. They weren't going that way. Just needed to get to the stairwell. Just needed to get there.

He waved his hand forward and continued walking. Chuckles' flashlight pointed up at the ceiling and Mike's eyes followed the cone of light. Something up there moved. Or maybe it was his imagination. The tickle of nervous tension in his spine switched to a freezing shudder. His mind raced with scenes from horror movies. The thing in the ceiling. The serial killer behind the door. Mike's feet moved faster. By the time he'd taken five steps, he was sprinting to the door.

Chuckles followed suit. Mike reached the door and slammed into the push bar. The door swung wide. He held it open while Chuckles rushed through it.

Mike closed the door and peered through the glass window. The fluorescent lights down the hall turned off one at a time. Mike's breath fogged the glass, but it didn't matter. There was nothing to see.

Mike turned from the door. Chuckles' face was set in its usual disinterested line.

"Did you see something?" he asked.

Mike clicked off his flashlight and stuck the pistol back in his waistband. "I don't know. I thought I did."

Chuckles nodded, but his face was absent emotion. "I thought I did too."

"Okay," Mike said after catching his breath, "let's go." He walked across the landing and took the steps two at a time. Chuckles did the same. Neither of them noticed the eyestalk peering at them through the fire door's window.

*　*　*

When they exited the stairwell, Chuckles finally felt he could breathe. He'd known Mike for years and he'd never seen the man this stressed out. He didn't think Mike really knew what was going on either, but the stripped down hallways, the detritus of metal zippers, fasteners, even the phone, was enough to hit Chuckles in the gut. Something was wrong. He didn't know just how wrong until they reached the bottom of the stairwell.

The door leading to the street was blocked. The window was a strange shade of red and he knew there should be wan streetlamp light streaming through it. Chuckles walked to the other door and tried to peer out the darkened window.

He pulled up his flashlight and shined it through the glass. Red corrugated steel stared back at him. Chuckles raised his eyebrows. Who the hell would block the door?

"Chuckles!" Mike yelled. "Let's go, man."

"Why is the door blocked?"

Mike cleared his throat. "Because we're under quarantine. They're not letting us out of here, man."

He took one last look at the window, shrugged, and then followed Mike out the interior door to the first floor.

The foyer was empty of people save for Jakob. He stood from his desk and stared at them.

"Hi, Jakob," Chuckles said.

The security guard was pale and looked almost stoned. Evidently he'd already had an interesting night too.

A few portable stretchers lay on the floor near the front doors. Boxes of disposable blankets, meds, and surgical gloves were laid out near the beds.

Jakob pointed at the clutter. "They brought all that stuff in here, Mike. I feel like a damned door man for the CDC."

Mike laughed. "You did fine, Jakob. Where are they?"

"In the labs," he said.

Chuckles glanced at the security doors. They were locked and the sensor glowed red. At least that was something. He turned, cast his eyes to the front doors, and froze.

A yellow, person-sized tunnel was connected to a large stand of red metal. The tunnel left just enough room for the doors to open. He walked to the glass and looked up. A metal housing covered the top. No one was getting in or out except via the tunnel. *Quarantine*, Mike had said. Until he saw the tunnel, he didn't really believe it. Now it was undeniable.

"Mike?" Chuckles asked as he turned around. "What the hell is going on?"

Mike's phone was in his hands. His thumbs played over the virtual keyboard. "Something about the oil from PPE. Marie got infected."

"Infected?" Chuckles walked to him. "Infected by what?"

Mike looked up from the screen as his phone made a whooshing sound. "I don't know. They had to take her to the hospital."

"She okay?"

Mike put the phone in his front pocket. "I honestly don't know."

Chuckles clicked off his flashlight. "Mike? What the hell are these for? There's plenty of light. It's not like we're facing a blackout."

Mike yawned. "Kate said we needed them. So we have them."

"Need them for what?"

"I guess whatever escaped the lab doesn't like light."

Chuckles snorted. "That makes about as much sense as anything else." He pointed to the ceiling. "Light there. Lights on the walls. Lights everywhere. So how do these flashlights do anything different?"

"Look, man. I don't know. I just did what she told me. And you saw what happened upstairs."

"Yeah," Chuckles said. "I did. And if I hadn't seen that, I sure as shit wouldn't have followed you down here. You do know I'm trying to bring up the new NOC and—"

"You listening to yourself?" Mike asked. His cheeks flushed crimson. "We are under quarantine. Marie is in the hospital. The CDC has us completely locked down and you're worried about the goddamned servers?"

Chuckles opened his mouth to reply and then stopped. Dammit. Mike was right. "Okay. Sorry."

Mike stared out through the front doors and to the yellow tunnel. "I wouldn't believe me either," he said. "Still not sure I do. What I—" He stopped in mid-sentence as his phone dinged. Mike pulled it from his front pocket and read the message. He typed a quick reply and smiled at Chuckles. The smile was strained, but it was better than an exhausted grimace. "The CDC is bringing Kate and her team out here. We'll get some answers soon."

"Great," Chuckles said. He pointed at the door. "Any guesses on what happens if we walk out there?"

Mike grunted. "I've a feeling we don't want to know."

"Was afraid you'd say that." Chuckles sighed and pulled out his phone. His email box was filled with alerts. The air conditioning in the old NOC was failing. He blinked. "Uh, I think I know where our intruder is."

Mike's eyes went wide. "Where?"

"The goddamned server room."

* * *

Glaze was clearly in shock. So was Maeve. While that bitch Hoyt grilled her coworker, and Maeve refused to let go of her mother, Jay listened. Whatever the M2 had become, it was more dangerous than ever. He kept fighting the urge to stare back across the glass partition at the chem-lab. That thing might come back through the hole in the roof. But they had a bigger problem just now.

Jay stood at the computer console and bought up a terminal. He logged in and brought up the testing control panel for the chem-lab. Results from their tests scrolled across the screen. All but one—the NMR.

When the hell had they started that test? He knew it couldn't have been more than an hour, but it seemed like days. Of course, the fact he hadn't slept in forever didn't exactly help.

Regardless, the test should be finished. Or at least close to it. He collapsed the test results until he found the one he was looking for. "NMR," he said to himself. Jay clicked on the results tab.

A graph of colored lines appeared on the screen. He blinked at them. Jay turned around and nearly ran into Neil. The bio-chemist's eyebrows were raised.

"Jay? You okay?"

He shook his head. "Look at the screen." Jay stepped aside. Bill joined them at the desk. The three men stared at the display.

Neil scratched at the grey in his temples. "Um, that's not possible."

"Oh, man," Bill chuckled. "That's just awesome."

"What are you gentlemen discussing?"

Jay turned to Hoyt. She'd sat Glaze down in a chair. Her CDC team member didn't exactly look like he knew where he was. Jay knew the feeling. "Know anything about chemistry, Dr. Hoyt?"

Her eyes narrowed. "More than you think." Her voice was knife-cold.

Jay flashed a grin. "Then take a look at that," he said pointing to the screen, "and tell me what you think."

She glared at him and then moved forward. Bill and Neil stepped aside and made space. Her suit crinkled as she bent down to look at the screen. Jay watched her expression change from annoyance to confusion.

She pointed a finger at the screen. "Shouldn't that be, um, varied or something?"

"Varied?" Bill laughed. "Lady, that graph should show all sorts of shit. Mainly hydrocarbon rings. But that ain't what I see."

She glared at Bill and then looked at Jay. "What am I looking at?"

Jay cleared his throat. "The spikes in the graph. Those are atoms made of heavier elements."

"And?"

He tried to hide a smirk, but couldn't. "Dr. Hoyt. Please look at the bottom of the graph."

She did. He smiled when he saw her eyes widen. "That's not possible."

Neil and Bill laughed. Jay thought they both sounded on the verge of hysteria. "No. It's not possible. Especially considering what we saw on the SEM." The bottom of the graph showed the scale in atomic weight. "There's no hydrogen in this stuff. No carbon either. Whatever it is, it's way off the periodic chart. By miles."

"Um," Bill said, "shouldn't that be radioactive as hell?"

Jay shrugged. "I look like a goddamned physicist?"

"Bill's right," Neil said. "We should be fried. That stuff shouldn't exist in nature. No way it can be stable."

"Unless it is." Jay rubbed his eyes. "If it's got the same number of electrons, protons, and neutrons, it should be as stable as anything else."

Hoyt stared at Jay. "Dr. Hollingsworth? Was the oil…heavy? As in actual weight?"

He shook his head. "No. Quite the opposite. All of our tests showed it to be what we call high gravity crude. The sweetest I've ever heard of. No crap in it. Just pure hydrocarbon goodness."

Hoyt shook her head. The moon-suit crinkled again. "Then how is that possible? If the primary components are an element with that high of an atomic weight, it'd be impossible to even bring out of the ground."

"True," Jay said. He rubbed his hands together. "Exciting, isn't it?" The dour look on her face made him grin wider. Mania was at the threshold. Any second, he knew he was going to lose it. Too many hours awake. Too much insanity. And too many unanswerable questions. "An oil that acts like oil, but isn't. A substance that doesn't have excitable electrons. A liquid that consumes any material that doesn't have tightly packed atoms? And," he pointed to the chem-lab rubble, "something that can change state from liquid to solid and is dangerous as hell." He laughed and wasn't surprised at how insane he sounded. "Like I said: exciting."

Maeve had finally stopped crying. Kate was rubbing her daughter's shoulders and looking up at Jay. "We have to get out of here. All of us. Now. Before that thing comes back."

Jay nodded to her. "Agreed." He turned back to Hoyt. "As much as I'd like to sit here and convince you that we're in trouble, HAL employees are getting the fuck out of here. And you can shoot us if you like." He nudged Bill in the arm. "Let's go."

"No, you can't leave," Hoyt said. She grabbed Jay's shoulder with her gloved hand. "This is a quarantine situation."

Neil snorted. "Lady? One of your own people just got devoured by the same thing that destroyed the lab next door. You want a quarantine? Fine. Lock the building up, set it on fire, but we're getting the hell out of here."

She moved to block their way, but Neil pushed her hard enough to knock her back against one of the tables. "Gentlemen!" she yelled.

It didn't matter. Jay had had enough. He shrugged off her attempt to grab his arm and headed into the hallway. Neil and Bill were right behind him. Hoyt, cursing under her breath, regained her balance and started to follow.

Kate stood and pulled Maeve up with her. Her phone buzzed. She looked down at it, read the message, and then looked at Jay. "Mike and Chuckles are in the foyer."

"Good." Jay pointed to the door at the end of the hall. "Let's go see what Mike knows."

* * *

Phone still in hand, Chuckles looked up as the security door to the lab area beeped and then opened. Kate and Jay, still dressed in their protective suits without the gloves and face-shields, walked out. Maeve's arm was around her mother's waist. The kid looked terrified. Bill and Neil followed them. Two people dressed in moon-suits popped out last. The security door closed and latched behind them.

Chuckles looked back down at his phone. The alerts for the NOC kept streaming in every five minutes. The temperature was over 90° and still rising. If they didn't want to lose the entire NOC, he'd have to go up there and shut down the systems. The auto-shutdown obviously wasn't working. Big shock. It'd never been tested.

He locked the phone and put it back in his pocket. Mike was already walking toward his disheveled scientists. Chuckles glanced at the glassed-in front doors again. Beyond that tunnel and the metal stand blocking their way, sunlight would no doubt be pounding the concrete in a few hours. Even if it was only through clouds. He rubbed his eyes. Like the rest of the crew, he hadn't had any sleep in a long time.

"Okay," Mike said to the group, "someone tell me what the hell is going on."

The woman in the moon-suit glared at him. "Mr. Beaudry? I'm Dr. Melanie Hoyt. Are all of your employees down here?"

Mike tapped his foot and crossed his arms. "As far as I know. I checked the new building too. But," he gestured to Chuckles, "he's all I was able to find. And no one else has come down."

Hoyt bit her lip. "Okay." She gestured to her partner. "Dr. Glaze and I are part of the Houston CDC office. We're the first response team."

"And there used to be three of them," Kate said.

Hoyt glared at her and then looked back at Mike. "The rest of our team is outside this building. They have cordoned off the area and there is no way out of here until we have isolated the infection."

"Infection?" Chuckles asked. The woman looked in his direction. "Mike said Marie was infected."

Hoyt nodded. "Ms. Krieger was taken to the Ben Taub ER. She was isolated, as were the EMTs that brought her in and Darren Strange."

The knot of stress that sat in Chuckles' stomach tightened. "How is Marie? She going to make it?"

"We don't know," Hoyt said. "We've lost contact with the hospital team."

Kate shook her head. "Bullshit. Chuckles? Mike?" She waited until their gaze met hers. "Darren called. He said—" She cleared her throat and Chuckles saw a single tear form in her left eye. "He said everyone's dead. That something came out of Marie."

The walls upstairs. The missing carpet. The incredibly clean elevator bank tile. The images flashed in his memory. A spike of heartburn hit his stomach. "What we saw upstairs," he said, "wasn't pretty." He gritted his teeth and then forced himself to relax. "Whatever is in the building, it's eating through everything."

"That's not metal or glass or concrete, yes," Jay said. Chuckles looked at him, but he wasn't the only one. The entire group watched Jay. "It doesn't seem capable of eating through those materials. But it likes grit and grime just fine. And anything porous like sheetrock." He scratched at his arm. "I imagine it likes skin as well."

Chuckles pursed his lips. "Well, I know where the damned thing is. Or at least where it was."

Hoyt swung her head. Her fierce eyes locked with his. "Where?"

"The NOC."

"What is that?" she asked.

He rolled his eyes. "Network Operations Center. It's where we keep all our computer equipment. The A/C is dead up there. The servers are starting to overheat. I doubt it's a coincidence." He pulled out his phone and unlocked it. "Yup," he said as he read the latest text. "100° and rising."

Kate and Jay traded a glance.

"What?" Chuckles asked.

Kate looped an arm around Maeve's neck. The girl was still too pale, but he thought she was looking better.

"It doesn't like heat," Kate said. "Heat. Natural light. Halogen light. From what we saw during the distillation test, it'll catch fire at certain temperatures."

Chuckles pursed his lips. "Any idea how hot it has to get?"

"No," she said. "But it's probably not much over 120°."

"This is all very interesting," Mike said, "but it doesn't tell me how we're getting out of here."

The CDC woman shook her head. "Did you not hear me, sir? We're not getting out of here until I can tell the teams outside the infection is isolated."

"Isolated?" Mike sneered. "Lady, if you saw what I saw upstairs, you'd know it's not airborne."

Hoyt sighed. "Sir. You have to understand. What Ms. Krieger had was extremely virulent. Her body was in an accelerated state of decay. If something like that was communicable, a city like Houston could go into an epidemic in a matter of days, if not hours."

"Well," Mike said, "that doesn't exactly do us a goddamned bit of good right now, does it? I want my people out of here. And I want them out of here now. Call whomever you need to, but get us—"

Something crashed on the second floor. The group jumped as

one, their eyes immediately scanning the ceiling. No one moved. All Chuckles could hear was the sound of everyone's breathing. And that was only a distant whisper compared to the pounding of his heart.

Hoyt's radio came to life. Her body stiffened and then slowly relaxed.

"Dr. Hoyt?" a tinny voice said in her helmet. Chuckles could barely hear it.

"This is Hoyt."

"What's your situation?" the voice asked.

"All known personnel are located in the evac area. We have one team member missing, presumed dead."

"Presumed," Glaze whispered.

She glared at him as she spoke. "No known disease vectors at this time. However, we have a situation with an unknown assailant. Over."

There was a pause. With each passing heartbeat, the sinking feeling in his stomach increased. Chuckles was absolutely certain the next thing the voice said wasn't going to make him or anyone else happy. He was right.

"Dr. Hoyt. This is a code red situation. I repeat, code red. Ben Taub has experienced an outbreak of some kind. The entire first floor of the hospital is deserted, but there is an extensive amount of damage to the interior as well as equipment. We are moving to evacuate the higher floors. Until we know what caused the damage in the hospital, HAL is under forced quarantine. Do not try and leave the premises. Over."

Chuckles shook his head and muttered "Fucking assholes."

Hoyt blinked at him. "Control. Code red acknowledged. However, we need more personnel—"

"There will be no one in or out of HAL until the situation is resolved. Over."

She took a deep breath. "Understood, control."

"We are in contact with the personnel aboard the PPE rig Leaguer. They have a similar outbreak ongoing. We are hoping we will have more details soon. Give us a sitrep every thirty minutes. Over and out."

"Hoyt out," she said.

"You work with some real douchebags," Chuckles said.

Hoyt said nothing.

"Well," Mike said, "want to tell us what a 'code red' is? Or do I just take it to mean we are royally screwed?"

Glaze giggled. "Mr. Beaudry? Your instinct is dead on."

"The fuck does that mean?" Chuckles asked.

Glaze continued to giggle.

"Get a hold of yourself, John," Hoyt said.

The man in the moon suit lifted his gloved hands and pulled off his helmet. Air hissed out of his suit.

Hoyt grimaced. "Dammit, John!"

"Like it matters," Glaze said in return. "If they're not already there, the cops will be outside." He pointed at the exit. "They'll be told to shoot anyone that comes out the door. And before long, soldiers, army and marine reservists, will get here from Ellington Field. And trust me," Glaze said, "they *will* kill you if you step outside that door."

Chuckles laughed. "Great fucking weekend."

"We can't leave?" Maeve asked in a choked whisper.

Kate gritted her teeth. "So, Dr. Hoyt. What do we do now?"

Hoyt's cheeks flushed. "We stay here where it's safe."

Chuckles glanced from the CDC woman to the others. Everyone looked exhausted and frightened. He turned to Jay. "You say this thing hates strong light?"

Jay nodded. "Yeah. Anything that approximates natural light."

Chuckles grinned. "Then we should head to the new NOC. It's got damned powerful lights. It's going to be cold, but it will be a good place to hide out."

Mike shook his head. "To do that, we'd have to go upstairs. Remember what the second floor looked like?"

"Well, what about a distraction?"

"No," Kate said. "We know it can see, but we have no idea if it can hear."

Chuckles held up his flashlight. "This is a good old, power-chewing, heat-creating halogen flashlight. And we have more of them upstairs. If we see it, we can make it move."

"We'd be better off somewhere with windows," Jay said. "Take down the blinds when the sun comes up, let the light drive it away."

Glaze laughed. "And where the hell would that be?"

"Conference room," Mike said. "New building. Floor three. It's in the corner and covered with windows. And they actually face east." He checked his watch. "And that means we'll have several hours of good light. At least until the sun goes down."

"We should just stay here," Hoyt said. "When they determine the infection isn't a threat, they'll let us go."

"Look, Dr.," Kate said, "you missed the show in the lab. The M2 attacked us. It's going to figure out a way to come down here. And when it does, it's going to absorb us just like it did to the other member of your team."

"She's right," Glaze said. "I saw it in the hallway. Mel, it'll kill us."

Hoyt opened her mouth and then closed it. Chuckles thought the woman was going to slap her colleague. She rubbed her gloves together. The crinkling sound was loud in the quiet foyer. "Then we need a plan."

Something was sizzling. Cooking.

Chuckles sniffed the air. The stench of rancid meat cooking over an open flame stung his nostrils. He raised the flashlight toward the ceiling and clicked it on.

Mike's light joined his. The ceiling tiles were still in place, but the sizzling sound increased.

Hoyt grunted. "What is that—"

"Shut up, lady," Chuckles said. He cocked his head to one side. The sound wasn't all that close, but was growing louder. He turned around toward the building's interior and walked forward until he could see the elevator bank. He froze.

Beneath the harsh blue-white fluorescent lights, a stream of thick, black liquid squirted through the crack in the elevator doors. A curl of smoke or steam rose from the floor as the goo devoured everything on the tile. The puddle of black grew before his eyes. Chuckles stepped backward. A crunching sound joined the sizzling as a solid branch rose from the liquid. A black orb popped out. The insectile eye stared straight at him. The pool shuddered as a tentacle formed into a leg.

He pointed the flashlight at the thing. The pool shuddered violently, but the stream of fluid kept coming. "Move!" Chuckles yelled.

He ran away from the elevator bank and toward the emergency stairs. Chuckles didn't wait to see if the others followed. The image of the staring eye and the blacker than black arachnid-like leg was all he could see as he pushed through the door and into the stairwell.

* * *

Chuckles was yelling and running for the stairs. Kate heard crackling and spitting coming from the elevator bank around the corner. She knew that sound all too well. She grabbed her daughter's shoulder and pushed her toward the stairwell. "Move!"

At first, Kate wasn't sure Maeve would or could. But the girl got her feet under her and started to run. Kate pushed her forward and kept a hand on her shoulder. The emergency door started to close when Maeve smashed her shoulder into it. Kate heard something pop. Maeve cried out, but didn't stop running.

Maeve took the stairs two at a time, her right hand holding her left shoulder. Kate wasn't sure, but she thought her daughter was screaming. It was difficult to tell over the pounding of her heart and the sounds of yelling and terror behind her.

When the stairs turned at the platform, she snuck a peak toward the door. Bill and Neil were halfway up the steps, Mike close behind them. Kate felt Maeve pull her arm and her attention snapped back to the stairs. Maeve was moving faster and Kate struggled to keep up. Her daughter was in pain, but she was nearly on Chuckles' heels.

When they reached the second floor platform, Maeve slammed into Chuckles' back. He yelled in surprise, but didn't turn. Instead, he pulled out his security card and flashed it front of the reader. It beeped. He opened the door and held it. "Go!" he yelled.

Maeve ran through, Kate right behind her.

* * *

Dr. John Glaze. A PhD in immunology. An MD with a specialization in virology. He was qualified to serve in any bio-lab on the planet and at any pharmaceutical company's R&D. What he wasn't qualified for? Fighting a goddamned oil monster.

When the man called "Chuckles" pelted out of the foyer and to the emergency exit, his already overloaded mind did what it always did—it turned over the problem. Which, of course, led to the first rule of scientific curiosity—observation.

Instead of following the panic wave and listening to the alarm bells going off in the back of his mind, he walked toward the elevator bank. The sizzling and crackling sounds barely registered in his forebrain. They were just more noise lost in the panicked yelling and screaming. His protective suit crinkled with each step. Somewhere in the universe, someone was screaming his name. The sound was coming through the radio, but it was just static compared to the maelstrom in his mind.

The elevator bank came more into view. Something black slammed into the tiled floor. John stopped in mid-step. An obsidian multi-jointed leg with a three-taloned claw crunched as it took weight.

He took a step backward. The sizzling sound faded into nothing, but the crackling sound intensified. His brain finally started to process it. The leg moved. Another leg appeared. And another. And another.

John's mouth opened in an O. His eyes widened. He stared at the thing in the elevator bank. The word "black" was incapable of describing its color. Supported by seven legs, a ragged, oval shaped torso came into view. Eyestalks rose from its top. The blacker than black orbs at the end of the stalks stared at him with alien malevolence. He took another step back as tentacles sprouted from its sides. A serrated maw opened in its middle. The creature, silent except for the crackling as more tentacles burst from its middle, moved toward him. Its taloned feet clicked on the tile floor.

The ancient reptilian part of his brain screamed in terror. More adrenaline rushed into his blood stream. John finally realized something—he needed to run away. But his feet remained firmly planted on the floor as the creature approached him.

The monster's open maw clicked open and closed in a death-metal rhythm. John tried to scream, but there was no air in his lungs. His vocal cords, like the rest of his body, were frozen in place.

The thing extended its legs and rose to its full height. John craned his neck upward. The three-meter tall thing loomed over him, its mouth nearly level with his head. He managed another step backward before the tentacles streamed out past him and then met behind his back. The creature's mouth puckered from the slick, fluid torso. Jagged black spikes jutted forward. John fell backwards. The tentacles behind retracted.

A tremendous force slammed into his spine. The smell of burning fabric hit his nostrils just before he saw one of the tentacles bursting from his chest. A gout of blood jetted into the thing's mouth. John screamed in pain and raised his eyes. The thing's mouth was darker than anything he'd ever dreamed possible. His eyes wide with pain and wonder, reflected nothing but the absence of light. When the thing dragged him into its crunching maw, the pain was bright, but brief. Metal fasteners, the innards of his radio, and fillings pattered to the floor.

* * *

When the thing attacked Glaze, he'd been frozen in place. When the man's body dissolved into its maw, Jakob's brain finally kicked into gear. He could run. He could fight. Unfortunately, he tried to do both.

He skinned the Glock from its holster and backed away from the creature. He jerked the trigger. The concussion in the closed space instantly deafened him. From five meters away, every bullet hit the nightmare.

An impossibly sharp, hooked tentacle twitched as its end disappeared. The next round went through the creature's middle and into the wall. Another round severed an eyestalk. The rest of the bullets missed the solid protrusions.

Another eyestalk popped out. The severed tentacle crackled as it lengthened and a new sharper hook appeared. He was still walking backwards when he hit the wall. The creature gathered itself. And then it charged.

Jakob's finger kept pulling the trigger, but the only sounds in the foyer were the clicking of the thing's taloned feet on the floor. No more rounds. No more weapons. The creature opened its maw and then it was on him.

* * *

She watched John walking toward the elevator bank. Dr. Melanie Hoyt screamed for him to stop, but he kept going forward. She moved to restrain him and then stopped in her tracks. A black spidery leg came into view and her resolve shattered.

Dr. Hoyt turned and ran as fast as the suit would allow. She kept screaming Glaze's name and hoped he was following, but didn't turn around to look. Whatever the thing in the elevator bank was, she didn't want to know. She didn't want to know anything more about possible infections or quarantines. She just wanted the hell away from it.

They had to let the world know. They had to inform FEMA. They had to—

The emergency door was swinging back on its hinges. She slammed into it and it opened back up. The latch caught a loose fold of her suit. Melanie came to a dead stop as the tough fabric held her fast. Screaming, she grabbed the suit with her hands and pulled. The strong Tyvek fibers resisted at first and then started to part. Air rushed out of the suit.

She jerked her arms as hard as she could and the suit finally came free. She twirled around and her eyes caught sight of the horror walking out of the elevator bank toward her partner.

As its tentacles rushed forward and through John's torso, one of its eyestalks craned toward her. Melanie screamed and slammed the door behind her.

Someone was shooting in the foyer. And screaming. She had to get out of here.

The suit's boots were hardly the best for running, let alone up stairs. She more waddled than ran up the metal and concrete. When she reached the first landing she peered down at the door. She could see movement through the pane of shatter proof glass inset into the door. The thing was there. Waiting. She didn't know if it could get into the stairwell and didn't want to stick around to find out.

She continued up the stairs and came to the fire door. Her hands scrabbled at the door handle. She pulled, but nothing happened. The door was locked.

She screamed and banged her hands on the door. It was like punching stone, but she barely felt the pain in her knuckles.

They weren't going to let her in. They were just going to leave her for that thing. She could hear it down there, smashing into the door. She was their escape plan. It would break through the door, through the walls, and climb the steps on its taloned feet, to pierce her with its hooked tentacles until its impossibly black teeth crunched her—

The door opened and nearly knocked her down the stairs. A hand reached through and grabbed her arm. She fell through the doorway and crumpled into a heap on the bare floor.

She looked up into Mike's bright eyes. He looked scared to death.

She knew how he felt.

She turned toward the door. It was closed up tight. A hand touched her shoulder and she screamed. She whirled around. Mike raised his hands. "You okay?" he asked.

Melanie shivered as she tried to get hold of herself. "Yes," she managed to say. He offered his hand and she let him help her to her feet.

"Let's go," he said and pointed down the hallway. She blinked at him. With a frustrated sigh, he grabbed her hand and pulled her. A moment later, they were both running.

* * *

They stopped in the middle of the hall. Mike was out of breath. No matter how much time you spent in the damned gym, running for your life took it out of you. And dragging Hoyt's stunned weight hadn't helped. Hands on his knees, he couldn't help but smile as he dragged in deep breaths. He'd have to talk to his trainer. He was obviously not getting the proper exercise for life-threatening situations.

Kate leaned up against the wall near the skybridge, her arms circled around Maeve's neck. The girl's left arm hung limply at her side. Tears of pain and fear had stained her face. Mike knew how she felt.

Chuckles looked ready to pass out. And then he did something Mike didn't think possible. He pulled a cigarette from his front pocket and lit it. "That's better," he wheezed.

"You have to be kidding me," Mike panted.

"Nope," Chuckles said. His emotionless face betrayed little. He exhaled through his nostrils in jittery streams. He gestured to the bare walls. "Was that what did this?"

Jay nodded. The chemist was as pale as the lab coat he wore beneath his chem suit. To Mike, he looked like he'd aged a century since Friday afternoon. "Had to be." He swung his eyes to Kate's. "Yeah?"

She nodded and looked at Mike. "That's what we were trying to tell you."

Mike shook his head. "That thing came out of the goddamned barrel of oil?"

"It's not oil," Kate said. "I don't know what it is. We have no clue." She looked at Neil. "What do you think?"

The bio-chemist grimaced between sharp breaths. "Chuckles. Give me a damned cigarette."

Chuckles raised his eyebrows, but said nothing. He pulled out the pack and handed it to Neil. Neil's shaking hands popped open the pack and slid one out between his fingers. He put it between his lips. The flick of the lighter wheel echoed in the hallway. A teardrop flame appeared in front of Neil's face. He dipped the cigarette into the flame, took a deep drag, and coughed.

Bill laughed. "Been too long for you, Neil."

Neil choked back another cough and then dragged again. He held the smoke in his lungs for a moment, and then blew out a cloud. "Yup. That's just what I needed."

"After a panicked run up the stairs? Are you out of your mind?" Kate asked.

Neil laughed. "When you've seen a goddamned oil monster, all bets are off."

"Knock it off," Mike said. "What do you think, Neil? What the hell is it?"

The bio-chemist shrugged. "I don't know. But I think we need to get somewhere safe."

"The new NOC," Chuckles said. "That's my vote. Just grab a damned parka first."

"How long until the sun comes up?" Mike asked.

"A few hours," Jay said. "Although the goddamned clouds are going to make it a bit dim."

"Mom?" Maeve asked. "I want to go home."

Chuckles' phone made a klaxon sound. The tech pulled it out

of his pocket and stared at the message. "Okay, Mike. You have a decision to make."

"What's that?" Mike asked.

Cigarette between his lips, Chuckles breathed deeply. He blew the cloud of smoke to the ceiling. "The old NOC might be on fire in a few minutes. And if that happens, we have to rely on the halon system. And there's no telling if that fucking thing damaged it."

"Let it burn," Neil said. "Maybe then the goddamned assholes outside will get us the hell out of here."

"Don't bet on it," Dr. Hoyt said. "They'll let this place burn and be thankful for it."

Bill shook his head. "No, no, no. They won't. Why would they let—"

"Code Red, Mr. Field. It means we are expendable in order to keep an unknown biological infection from spreading." Hoyt bit her lip. "And I can't say I blame them."

"Mommy, I want to go!" Maeve yelled.

Kate cooed in her daughter's ear and then looked at Mike. "I'm taking my daughter to the new NOC. Now." She turned and started through the skybridge.

"Kate! Wait!" She didn't turn. Mike shook his head. "Goddammit. Okay, Chuckles. We need to turn off the security so we can move around. Get to the new NOC and get that done."

Chuckles dropped his cigarette to the floor and crushed it beneath his shoe. "I can do that in the old NOC too. And I can just yank the goddamned plug on the server room. Keep us from getting a fire in there."

"Okay. Move it."

Chuckles saluted and then ran down the hallway.

Mike watched him go and then turned to the others. "All right. Let's go. We need to get to the NOC." Bill and Neil left the hallway and headed across the skybridge.

Dr. Hoyt shook her head. "We're still going to be trapped. In a small space. There won't be anywhere to run."

Mike nodded. "Yup. Got any better ideas?"

The CDC doctor thought for a moment. "No. No, I don't. But how long can we stay in there?"

"Until we freeze to death." Mike's smile looked like a sneer.

* * *

His heart thumped in his chest. Another cigarette was already between his lips. A trail of smoke followed his quick steps down the hall. The comforting voices of the group had dissipated leaving him alone with only the sounds of the building's labored heating system and rain pelting the exterior.

It wasn't until he was in sight of the door to the old NOC that the fear actually hit him. His mind filled with what he'd seen. The black fluid coalescing. The strange thing rising out of its center. The impossibly dark orb that seemed to stare at him. He shivered hard enough to grind his teeth. He'd noticed that the other CDC member, *was his name Glaze?*, wasn't in the hallway a few minutes ago. Had that, that thing, eaten him?

Chuckles walked to the door and held his hand against its surface. The steel-reinforced door was warm, but not hot. No fire. Yet.

He swiped his card across the reader and it beeped. He crushed out his cigarette, exhaled, and then swung open the door.

The usual blast of chill air was absent. Instead, it was a scorching desert wind. His face immediately flushed. After the cold of the hallways, the warmth was refreshing. For about fifteen seconds.

He closed the door and hit the overhead lights. The sudden and intense illumination pounded his retinas and for a moment, all he saw was the after image of their glare. He closed his eyes and waited. When the bright flash faded into a dim glow, he opened his eyes. His mouth fell open.

The server room was an absolute disaster. The heavy plastic stand-up supply closet was gone. Just. Gone. The only thing that remained of it was piles of metal computer parts. Melted circuit boards, prongs from chips, exposed copper wire, and dozens of other parts he couldn't even identify were strewn across the floor.

The ceiling tiles were all but vaporized. The shining, naked metal supports jutted out into space with nothing holding them. The light fixtures had mostly escaped unharmed, but bundles of fried network cables hung in a heap from the ceiling.

His computer desk was gone except for skeletal, metal bands. The monitor had crashed to the floor. All the plastic from the display, his workstation, and everywhere else in the room had been vaporized. "So much for turning off the security," he said to the empty room. Chuckles blinked at the mess. Light shined off the floor. He'd never seen it so clean. A mad laugh escaped his mouth and then stopped as he turned to the server racks.

The metal was still intact. The plastic clips holding the shelves in place were gone, but none of the old machines had slid out of the racks. The air conditioning units were dead. The power cables had shorted out after the plastic and rubber surrounding them disappeared. Or dissolved. Or whatever the goddamned thing did.

The eyestalk entered his mind again. His spine crawled with imaginary legs. Chuckles shook away the image, but the sensation stayed.

He looked at the control box on the wall. The thing had eaten just about every other goddamned piece of plastic or rubber in the room, but the breaker box was encased in steel. He smiled at it and then pulled it open.

The relatively new switches stared back at him. Before they were able to put all the servers in the room, HAL had an electrician in to reroute some cabling and bulk up the breakers. Chuckles stared at the big red handle. It was locked in the "ON" position. He reached out and put his fingers on it. He took a deep breath, said a silent prayer, and then flipped it in the other direction.

The servers died and the lights went out. The fans and the myriad of RAID arrays slowly spun down leaving the room in utter silence. Chuckles took another deep breath and then reached for the flashlight in his pocket. He turned it on. The halogen beam ripped through the complete darkness. He turned back toward the door to get back to the hallway and stopped in his tracks.

That sizzling sound. That smell of cooking, rancid meat. It was back. He shined the light at the door. It was still intact. A sinking feeling hit his stomach. He knew where it was now. The only question was if it would let him reach the door.

He slowly raised the light to the ceiling over the doorway. The tiles were gone and exposed pipes shined back at him. Chuckles slowly walked to the door. He heard something creak at the back of the room, but ignored it. If it was, well, that thing, he was pretty well fucked anyway. He was more afraid of the damned thing ambushing him as he tried to get out.

Step. Step. Step. He was just a foot from the door. Just one more step and…

Something sizzled. Chuckles spun around. The cone of bright light danced in his hands. A piece of metal fell from the ceiling and crashed to the floor. He shined the light upward and saw *it*.

The creature was wrapped around the pipes. It had eaten through the supports holding one of the light fixtures. A curl of smoke rose from its liquid form where his light stabbed it. He stepped backward, but kept the light focused on it.

The creature didn't make a sound. It contracted and then slithered away from the light. He adjusted his aim and kept hitting the black form. It slithered further and further away until the light no longer reflected off its surface.

Without changing his aim, he felt for the door handle with his free hand. He found it, swiveled it, and the lock clicked. Chuckles gently pushed and heard the welcome drone of the heater in the hallway. A sliver of ambient light filtered through the crack in the door. He pushed harder and slowly walked backward.

He crossed the threshold into the hall. Something crashed down from the ceiling in the room's far corner. Chuckles slammed the door, turned, and ran. The fluorescent lights that still worked came on as he pelted down the hallway. The hall echoed with the sounds of sizzling. He turned around, but kept walking backwards.

The door to the old NOC hung off one hinge. A cube of black moved through the doorway.

"Fucking douchebag!" Chuckles yelled. "Can't dissolve it, so you'll just knock it over?"

An eyestalk sprouted from the middle of the moving black shape. As it squeezed through the space, legs, tentacles, and more eyestalks pushed out of its surface.

Chuckles gulped. It was between him and the skybridge. Goddammit. How did he take a wrong turn? He laughed in the hallway and was surprised at how insane he sounded. He turned back around and resumed running.

It was giving chase. He knew it was. *Have to shut off the security,* he reminded himself. But how the hell was he going to do that without a network? With the old NOC down, there was no WiFi, no internet backbone, nothing. He needed a terminal. He needed something he could login via VPN and get it done. What he needed—

Chuckles took the next left and then headed into building one's main conference room. The automatic lights came on. He cursed and killed the switch. Chuckles gently closed the door and locked it. He didn't know if the thing could hear. But he had to take the chance.

As fast as he could, he ran to the other side of the table and dropped to the floor. The heavy table was supported by a wooden cylinder on either end. Chuckles scrunched into the fetal position and held his breath.

The conference room's west wall, made of translucent glass, faced the hallway. He didn't know if the creature was smart enough to actually look for him, but he wasn't taking any chances. Chuckles closed his eyes and held his breath.

He focused. And then he heard it–the click of taloned feet on the exposed concrete floor. Even through the glass wall, he could smell it too. Except for the click of its feet, the creature was completely silent.

Knock. Knock. Scratch.

As silently and slowly as he could, he exhaled and then sipped a long breath.

Knock. Scratch. Knock.

It was at the door and trying to get in.

He silently cursed. He wanted to look. God, how he wanted to look. Was it there outside the glass? Eyestalks waving and trying to catch a glimpse of its prey? Did it know he was even in here?

The sounds stopped. Bolts of pain rose up his spine and he grimaced. He couldn't hold the position for long, but dammit, he wasn't stretching until he was sure that thing was gone. Time crawled. He tried to keep track of the seconds, but lost count. Finally, blessedly, he stretched out his legs and straightened his back.

He reached into his pocket and pulled out his phone. It had plenty of battery, plenty of signal. Thank God he wasn't in the damned labs. He'd have no network, no cell, nothing. Shit, not even a landline. Chuckles smiled at the phone.

A few taps and he turned the phone into a WiFi-hotspot. If Mike had let him choose the right goddamned VPN provider, he could have done this shit on the device. He exhaled another breath and then peered around the cylinder. There was nothing on the other side of the glass. The lights in the hallway had already gone dark.

Chuckles sighed and finally realized how fast his heart had been beating. He inhaled and exhaled slowly through his nose. The thumping in his ears subsided. When he thought he could breathe normally again, he pulled himself to a crouch.

The workstation was at the end of the conference room. He checked the angle from the glass. Unless someone was standing adjacent to the door and looking in exactly the right direction, he'd be hidden.

Forty-five seconds, he told himself. *That's all you need.*

As he duckwalked to the workstation stand, he went over the steps in his mind. He reached the end of the table and stopped. He checked his phone one more time. The hotspot was live. When he reached the machine, he'd have to select the WiFi, type in his password, and use the web-browser to login into the virtual private network.

The VPN was the one damned piece of technology he'd already clustered into the new NOC. He clenched his free fist. He just hoped the connections from the NOC could talk to the building's security system. If not, they were screwed.

He raised his head over the table just high enough to look at the door one last time. The lights in the hall were still off. Wherever it had gone, it wasn't there and that's all that mattered.

Standing up was a bad idea. He knew it. And he sure as shit wasn't going to do it. He duckwalked past the table and to the workstation. With every step, he was closer to the pulsing HAL logo on the screen.

He swung his head back to the door. The lights were still off. Chuckles gently pressed the spacebar and the HAL logo melted into a login screen. He typed in his username/password and waited. The system thought for a few seconds and then flashed an error message. "Unable to authenticate."

"Just fucking awesome," Chuckles whispered. Without the network, the computer couldn't contact the authentication server to look up his credentials. He typed in the root password. The login screen disappeared and dropped him to the maintenance interface.

A few clicks and he added the computer to his WiFi hotspot. Seconds later, he was logged into the VPN and bringing up the security system UI. While he waited, he snuck another look around. The lights in the hallway were on. His breath caught in his throat. As he watched, the lights flicked off. He blew out a sigh and focused on the terminal.

He navigated to the security software. As fast as he could, he killed the card readers in the labs, the loading dock, and the readers on the second floor. That would allow everyone access to building one without restriction. Building 2? That was trickier.

With the switchover half-done, the software could only access the main offices and not the lower floor or the new NOC. Chuckles brushed a sheen of sweat away from his forehead, readjusted his cap, and pulled out a cigarette. He lit it and checked the window again. Nothing there. Lights off. Everything good.

He opened a terminal, typed in his credentials, and started grepping the security processes for the floor. The new building's software was radically different than the old. It took him a few minutes to find them. He stared at the process responsibility list.

The new NOC and its halon system were controlled by the same goddamned thread. Killing the NOC's security access would take out its fire system too. Chuckles scowled at the screen. If they made it out of this, he'd have to change that right after he strangled the tech who set it up that way.

Something creaked in the ceiling. Chuckles looked up in the darkened room, but saw nothing. He went back to the screen. The first floor of building two wasn't even open yet. The fire doors worked, but that was about it. With a few keystrokes, he eliminated the card readers in the new building.

His phone buzzed. He swung his eyes over and looked at it. The system had sent him several texts saying security was offline. That was fine. He brought up the daemon list once more, and double checked it. If he forgot anything, they'd all be—

Chuckles stopped in mid-exhale. A small stream of smoke crawled from his nostrils. Something was sizzling. And even through the acrid taste and smell of tobacco, that sweet and sour stench of cooked rotted meat stung his nostrils. The sizzling was louder.

He looked at the terminal one more time to make sure everything was off. It was. He turned around and froze. The ceiling at the far end of the room was melting. A large, thick column of black ooze slowly drained from the ceiling onto the carpeted floor.

As slowly as he could, he inched his hand toward the flashlight still in his pocket. It wasn't there. His eyebrows rose and he frantically searched the room with his eyes. There it was, by the table. Must have slid out of his pants when he was curled up like a baby. He flung the cigarette to the floor and dove for the flashlight.

Chuckles grabbed the light and rolled to the right. His finger clicked the button and he shined it at the wall.

The column of black was already spreading. Two eyestalks stared at him beneath the halogen's glare. Curls of smoke rose from where the light touched it. The creature moved to the right. Chuckles followed it with the light.

Dark curls of foul-smelling smoke belched from the eyestalks. Burning particles danced in the air before dropping to the floor. The eyestalks crackled and retracted into the mass. At the same time, a smaller eyestalk rose from the center of the amorphous shape.

Chuckles slowly backed up. He didn't dare take his eyes off the thing and kept the flashlight pointed at the new eyestalk. Acrid smoke curled from the appendage. The tall black blob jiggled and then shifted to the wall.

He saw the door out of the corner of his eye. The lights in the hallway were still off, but that didn't matter. He had to get the hell out of the room. The halogen seemed to keep it from rushing forward, but the beam wasn't powerful enough to really hurt it. What asshole suggested this would work?

When he felt he was far enough from the table, he shuffled sideways. His left foot connected with the leg of a chair. He cursed and slowly retracted his foot. The blob was still jiggling, smoke continuing to rise from the appendage.

He rounded the table and cursed again as one of his feet hit the end of a power cord. Goddamned conference room douches always dicking with the cables. With each step, the cone of light was more faint against the impossibly black shape. The smoke had damned near ceased.

The thing crackled and a leg appeared. Then two more. The creature expanded. Hooked tentacles popped out of its middle. More eyestalks appeared.

He ran to the door, swung it open, and pelted down the hallway. From behind him, he heard a crash, tumbling metal, and the sizzle of it melting through something.

Chuckles rounded the corner and sprinted to the skybridge. Just had to get to the new building. Just had to get there.

The next corner would lead him to the skybridge. Lungs burning, Chuckles sprinted. He reached the corner, turned, and then screamed.

The thing stood before the skybridge, a wall's worth of rubble behind it. It was goddamned huge! Its bulk of tentacles, mouths, legs, and eyestalks filled the entire hallway.

He stumbled to a stop. One of the mouths flashed its black fangs. He pulled up the flashlight and pointed it at the thing while he backed away.

Smoke belched upward. It backed off a step, but the tentacles seemed to be getting longer. Chuckles' heart raced in his chest and his mouth filled with the taste of bile. The creature had backed off enough to show a narrow sliver of the skybridge entrance.

Chuckles took a step forward, the flashlight alternating between the eyestalks. The creature backed off a bit more. He sneered at it. "Don't like the light after all, do you?" he said to it.

The creature responded by growing two more mouths. The eyestalks bent toward him. The incredibly black orbs at the end glared at him. He could feel the hunger in them.

Chuckles took another step forward. More smoke belched upward. He jumped as a klaxon alarm started up. Water sprayed down from the ceiling and the hall became a dizzying kaleidoscope of crimson and blue-white light.

The rain from the sprinklers washed over the creature and the rest of the hallway. The water streaked across his glasses and he could barely see through them.

The creature's mouths grinned. Either that or it was the drops of water skewing his sight. Either way, the damned thing seemed to be laughing.

Chuckles aimed the light at the end of one of the eyestalks. The orb burst into flame and was immediately doused by the sprinklers.

Chuckles gritted his teeth. "Goddammit!" He took another step forward and immediately regretted it.

The creature's tentacles had been growing, but he'd been too distracted to realize it. One of them flung outwards and smashed the hand holding the flashlight. The snap of his broken wrist was punctuated by the light flying into the wall where it shattered. The halogen light went out.

He screamed and held his ruined hand. The creature pulled back its tentacles. They thumped on the floor in an alien rhythm. Chuckles backed away.

The thing walked forward on its legs, its talons clicking on the concrete as the sprinkler system continued its incessant shower.

"You piece of shit!" Chuckles screamed at it.

The thing pressed forward. Dozens of tentacles streamed out of its midsection. They lengthened and lengthened until they were behind him. Chuckles, still cradling his wrist, smiled at the thing through the pain.

"I hope you get a fucking sunburn!"

He barely felt the pain when the hooks smashed into his back, but he was conscious enough to scream as three of the mouths crunched down on his head and shoulders.

CHAPTER SEVEN

The skybridge had been vacant. The thing obviously hadn't visited much of the new building. The sheetrock and carpet was still intact. That much, at least, had gone according to plan.

Mike had ushered Hoyt to the new NOC, his head constantly swiveling so he could look behind them. He hoped Chuckles was successful. Not to mention okay. He'd never forgive himself if he'd sent the man on a suicide mission.

When they reached the NOC, a haggard looking Bill, Neil, Kate, Jay, and Maeve were waiting outside the door. They stood in a less than organized line looking down the hallway.

Mike frowned as he approached them. "You tried the door?" he called out.

"Yeah," Neil said. "No dice. Our cards don't work."

Mike walked to the door, produced his key card, and swiped it. The LED light turned green and the lock beeped. He winked at Neil. "Being the boss has privileges."

He swung the door open and noise immediately filled the hall. The environmental lights came on and showered them in brightness. Mike pointed to the NOC control room. "Get in there."

Kate and Maeve went first, followed by the rest. Mike closed the door behind them and then stopped. The control room was packed shoulder to shoulder. "Shit," Mike said. "Well, guess I didn't think about how many people we had."

"Room was built for three people," Neil said. He was standing as far away from Kate and Maeve as he could to give them room. But mother and daughter still looked cramped.

Mike grinned. "Well, I hate to say it, but the folks with the most clothes are you science types. Including Dr. Hoyt here. So maybe y'all could get your ass in the server room."

Mike walked to the inner door and swiped his key card. The lock beeped and he swung the door open. A tremendous wave of sound filled the small chamber. Fans, spinning drives, and the deafening A/C system were enough to make him wish he was at a Motorhead concert.

He pulled the sets of hearing protection off the walls. They had three. Mike cursed. He could send Bill, Neil, and Jay in there, but no one else. At least not for too long.

"Dr. Hoyt? Can you go in there without these?" he asked raising one of the sets of headphones.

She nodded. "Have hearing protection in my helmet. Not a problem."

"Okay, good. The room isn't all that loud for short stints, but I guarantee you're going to want it if you're in there a while." Mike pointed inside the server room. Bill muttered something he couldn't hear as he grabbed a pair of the heavy headphones and put them on. The older man walked into the room, immediately grabbing his arms to stay warm.

Jay and Neil followed suit, as did Hoyt. When they were all in the room, Mike shut the inner door, walked into the control room, and shut its door. The sound of the server room immediately ceased.

Mike sighed and then forced a smile. Kate and Maeve were looking at him. He slapped his hands together. "Well, folks, let's settle down for a long wait."

Kate sat against the wall, Maeve practically in her lap. The girl wasn't yet thirteen, but she was already taller than her mother. Her hurt shoulder slumped and the top looked swollen. Not good.

Mike knelt and looked at the tool chests beneath the consoles. Tools, parts, cables. That was it. "Why the hell didn't Chuckles requisition a goddamned fridge?"

Kate rolled her eyes. "Probably because a little spill would fry your wonderful new computer system."

He sighed. "Yeah, okay. Fine. You're right." The goddamned NOC didn't even have a first aid kit. If they got out of this, he'd make sure that was addressed.

The heavy metal table creaked as he leaned against it. He swung his head toward Kate. "You want to tell me what the hell that thing is?"

Maeve whimpered. Kate shushed her and stroked her hair. "I honestly don't know. The M2 didn't react to the scanning electron microscope. And we didn't exactly have a chance to study the NMR."

He cocked an eyebrow. "Is that test still running?"

She shrugged. "No clue. Unless Chuckles sent the data here. If he sent it to the old NOC…" She didn't bother finishing the sentence.

"Right." Mike sighed. "Goddammit. If I see Simpson again, I'm kicking him in the balls for sending us this shit."

Kate shook her head. "Those people on the rig. I wonder how many of them are already dead."

"Probably a lot of them. Not exactly any place for them to go." Mike looked through the glass window into the server room. The four scientists were huddled together on the hard tile floor, backs against the server racks. He could see their mouths moving, but the sound proofing in the control room made it impossible to have any idea what they were saying to one another.

"It didn't start out this big, did it?"

Kate bit her lip. "No, Mike. It didn't. It was a couple of liters. That's it. And once it started consuming matter, it just kept getting larger."

"What the hell could do that?"

"Monster from outer space," Maeve said. Her eyes were scrunched in pain. "Something not from our world."

"Certainly not something our science can explain," Kate said. "But you're right, dear." She kissed the back of her daughter's head. "It's not anything we've ever seen in nature."

Mike clucked his tongue. "You say Marie got infected from a dollop of this crap?"

"Yup," Kate said. She wiped a tear from her exhausted face. "Spread through her entire body in a matter of hours. Consumed her."

"I could be wrong," Mike said, "but that sounds like a virus or bacteria, doesn't it?"

Kate nodded. "Yeah. But didn't act like anything biological. Shit, its atomic structure didn't even react to the SEM. It was like we were shooting energy at a black hole."

"Black hole," Mike mused. Sounds about right."

"That Hoyt woman said they were already talking to PPE and the rig." Kate cleared her throat. "Wonder if they're going to try and save anyone from there. Or if it's already too late."

The lights went out in the server room. Mike's jaw dropped open and then he closed it as the lights came back on. Jay was waving his hands at the motion sensors. "I forgot the damned lights go off when there's no movement."

Kate sighed. "You heard from Chuckles?"

Mike pulled out his phone and looked at it. He had an email. He narrowed his eyes and unlocked the phone. The security system had sent him a message telling him it was offline. "All right, Chuckles!" He grinned at Kate. "The security system is offline. He got it done."

She smiled. "Make sure that asshole is on his way over here."

Mike laughed and typed up a new text. "With any luck, he'll be able to hear his phone in the old NOC. God that place is loud." He clicked "send" and put the phone in his shirt pocket. "Going to be crowded in here."

Maeve hissed in pain. "Mom? Did I break my shoulder?"

Kate sighed. "Maybe. Just try not to use it, baby."

"Don't call me that," Maeve said, but there was no angst in her voice. "I'm not a baby."

Kate kissed the back of her head again and then looked up at Mike. "How long are we going to stay in here? We can't stay here forever."

Mike nodded. "I know." He tapped his foot. "Maybe Hoyt will get an update from her people."

"We have landlines in here?" Kate asked.

He glanced at the console, saw the cordless phone, and picked it up. He pushed the talk button and listened. "No. Nothing." He slammed it down back on the console. "Cell phone only."

"Well, at least we have that," she said. "So we don't have a real plan."

Mike shook his head. "This was my plan. You come up with something better, you tell me."

She sighed. "There's no place that's safe. Not even in here."

"You said this thing can't eat metal, right?"

"Right."

"Well, this room is shielded. Sheet metal in the walls, a ton of sound-proofing." A grin spread across his face. "If we could get downstairs into the lab area, we'd be behind metal walls."

"Mike, the new labs aren't even ready yet. They don't have the damned ceilings up. Too many exposed ducts. Too many ways for that thing to get in." Kate sighed. "Besides, you think the cops or soldiers or whatever the hell is waiting outside hasn't already got that covered?"

"Good question. And a good point." The light in the server room went out again. It flicked back on, catching Jay in the middle of an impressive impression of an airplane marshal. When he finally dropped his hands, Jay was still moving them around, but in excitement. Mike saw the looks on the other scientists' faces. They all looked excited. Except for Hoyt. She just looked pale. "What the hell?"

"What?" Kate asked.

"Either Jay had an epiphany, or he's about to stroke out."

* * *

Why in the hell did it have to be so damned cold? Jay understood that servers needed to be kept cool, but this was overkill. He didn't know if it was because the building wasn't finished and the temperature had dropped outside, or if it was because Chuckles had designed the room to double as a meat locker.

Hoyt sat next to him, Bill and Neil across from them. Hoyt had her arms crossed and sat cross-legged. Bill stared at the ceiling, his legs spread out. Neil's loafers were mere inches from Jay's running shoes.

"Might be time to get some new soles, Neil."

"Been hearing that for years," Neil said. "Besides, Jay, when's the last time you bought a new pair of shoes?"

"Well," Jay shrugged, "you have a point."

Bill sighed. His eyes drifted down to look at Hoyt. "How long are we stuck here?"

Jay glanced at him and fought back his own sigh. Bill was too goddamned old to be playing the "are we there yet?" game. She'd already given that answer. Asking it again wasn't going to be much help.

"Until they tell us we can leave," Hoyt said. Her voice was barely audible through the hearing protection.

"You tried contacting them?" Bill yelled.

Hoyt looked up at him. Her face was lined with exhaustion and she looked like she was in shock. She opened her mouth and then closed it. She reached down and clicked the radio on her belt. She swiveled a knob and the radio beeped loud enough for Jay to hear through his ear protection.

"Control, this is Hoyt," she said into her headset.

Jay barely heard the response. He pulled off his headgear and the angry sound of fans and drives punished his ears. He leaned toward Hoyt so he could hear.

"Hoyt. This is control." A wave of static hit the channel. "What is your situation? Over."

She looked up and regarded the three men before clearing her throat. "We have a hostile organism, repeat, hostile organism in building

1. We have moved to the NOC in building 2. Second floor, far down the hall from the skybridge. Over."

There was a pause. "Acknowledged. We have received communications with PPE rig Leaguer, source of the infection. We have very few resources available to help you at this time. Ben Taub has been overrun. Repeat, Ben Taub has been overrun. Over."

Hoyt frowned. "Hostile organism at the hospital? Over."

"Affirmative, Hoyt. We have no way to extract you to a safe quarantine area at this time. Hole up and stay safe. Over."

She growled. "Control? What the hell are we supposed to do? Light a campfire, sing some songs?"

Another pause. "We will update you as soon as we have more information. Over and out."

"Acknowledged." Hoyt hit another button on the radio and the static died from the speakers. "Fucking acknowledged," she said.

"Great," Bill said. "Just great. I have to piss, I'm hungry, and these assholes aren't going to do a damned thing to help us." He glared at Hoyt. "Our tax dollars at work."

She sighed and then her eyes bored into Bill's. "Mr. Field? Did you hear what they said? Ben Taub has been overrun."

Bill rubbed his hands together. "So the hell what?"

A sinking feeling hit Jay's stomach. "Shit."

"What?" Bill asked.

Jay turned to Hoyt. "Does that mean what I think it means?"

She nodded. "Yup. It means that as far as they know, everyone in that hospital is dead."

Bill gulped. "That's a huge hospital."

"No shit," Neil said. "Like over 500 beds big. Not to mention the ER, the support staff, nurses, doctors, and visitors." He shook his head. "Jesus, we are so screwed."

"Worse than that," Jay said. "Think about how much that thing had to eat? We have the little one."

The color drained out of Bill's face. "We have the little one?"

Jay nodded. "If the progression of growth is consistent. I don't know if it gets as much nourishment from inorganic versus organic material, but think about how much of both it has in a hospital. I can't imagine how large it is."

Neil giggled. He sounded half-mad. "Always thought Houston would get eaten by a hurricane, not some goddamned blob."

"You're oversimplifying it, Neil," Jay said. "By a lot. It started it out as a bit of oil here. How long did it take it to start, well, behaving like an animal? It didn't have to eat much to be able to grow limbs."

Neil frowned. "Yeah. You're right." He bit his lip. "Maybe the oil is actually some kind of larval stage for it."

"Larval?" Bill asked. "Fuck me. If that's the larval stage, I don't want to know what the final growth stage is."

Hoyt kicked her legs out. "If one drop of that shit was enough to not only kill Ms. Krieger—"

"Her name was Marie," Jay growled.

"Sorry," Hoyt said. "If one drop was enough to not only kill Marie, but use her body for exponential growth, there's no telling how damned big that thing is. Or what it could be once it reaches critical mass."

Jay hissed through his teeth. "Critical mass. Maybe that's the key."

"What?" Neil said. "What are you talking about?"

The lights went off. Jay waved his hands and they came back on.

"Just, well, listen. Leaguer drilled into M2. They obviously hit oil or something they thought was oil, right?"

"Yeah, so?" Bill asked.

"What we've seen from the M2 substance is that once it reaches a certain size, or accumulates some level of mass, it's able to transform itself," Jay said. "Produce limbs, for instance. But it can also reabsorb them, right? Those appendages, they weren't as dark as the rest of its body. It was like—" He searched for a word. "Whatever it transforms looks different. Not as rich. Reflects more light. Whatever."

Hoyt sighed. "I'm waiting for a point, Dr. Hollingsworth."

"The point, my dear Dr. Hoyt, is that maybe it's actually transitioning to its final form. Perhaps its pseudo-limbs are some kind of, I don't know, shell?"

"Shell?" Bill said. "I think you've been smoking weed again."

Jay shrugged. "I don't know enough biology to say it right."

"Oh, shit," Neil said. His eyes glowed with excitement. "You're thinking of seashells."

Jay blinked. "I guess."

"If this, um, creature," Neil said, "can synthesize proteins, then it could in theory produce solid layers of matter."

Bill laughed. "No animal on earth can produce protein structures and minerals that fast. Nothing like that exists in nature! You're nuts!"

"When science doesn't make sense, we keep digging until it does," Jay said. "But think about it. This, whatever it is, burrows beneath the ocean floor and sits there for, who knows how many millennia. It surrounds itself with hardened matter and more or less becomes one with the ocean floor."

"And then leaguer drilled through that layer?" Hoyt asked.

Jay nodded.

"I think you're in shock, Dr. Hollingsworth," she said. "That's about as far-fetched an idea as I've ever heard."

"Of course it is," Jay said. The buzz in his brain was nearly impossible to contain. He knew he was on to something. Just knew it. "If it could synthesize that fast, why couldn't it reabsorb as well?"

"To what end, though? That doesn't make evolutionary sense," Bill said.

"Without knowing the lifecycle, it's impossible to tell," Neil said. "I mean, we've never seen anything like this in nature. It replicates like a virus, can consume an animal exponentially larger than itself, change its form at will, and consume anything that's not metal, concrete, or glass."

"That we know of," Jay said. "It might be able to chew on a lot more.

Or," he licked his lips, "there may be more things it can't eat." The lights went out again. Jay waved his hands and the lights returned. "If it can't eat densely packed atomic structures, what else couldn't it eat?"

Bill blew a sigh between his teeth. "Who cares? It's going to eat *us!*"

Neil opened his mouth and then closed it. "Oh, man."

"What?" Jay asked.

"If you're right and it needs protein to reach its final state," he gulped, "then it's going to want all it can get."

Hoyt turned white as a sheet. "We're the prey?"

Neil nodded. "We're its preferred food source."

* * *

The building was a devastated hulk. *It* had consumed all the ancillary materials *It* wanted. But *It* still didn't have enough of what *It* needed.

The creature made circuits through the hallways as *It* searched for food. *It* occasionally smashed a tentacle through the remaining sheetrock in frustration. There had to be more food.

It didn't want to slide down the elevator shaft again. Doing so would require *It* to change shape, and *It* was happy with *Its* current configuration. Besides, *It* had already tried to get out that way and there was no way for *It* to leave.

It found the skybridge and squeezed *Its* bulk through the entrance. Plastic and rubber melted, but the glass stayed intact. *It* halted halfway through. One of *Its* eyestalks gazed out the window on the darkened world. *It* already felt the stirrings of its enemy. The light was coming. *It* knew this. And there was nothing to be done. *It* had to become whole before that happened.

* * *

She shifted. Maeve's elbow had dug into her breast far too long. God, the girl was getting heavy. With her eyes closed, Kate grinned. Not too many years ago, Maeve had been little more than a crying thing in diapers. Now? She was growing up and entering high school next year. *If she makes it there*, a voice said in her mind. Kate's smile disappeared into a thin line. *Fuck off*, she said to it. *She'll make it. We will make it.*

Mike was more fidgety than she'd ever seen him. He kept checking his watch, his phone, and then peering through the window into the NOC. He was searching for a way out and no doubt hoping Chuckles would text him back. She knew how he felt. Every time she managed to avoid the swirling desperation in her brain for a minute, it returned with a vengeance. And there was little more to do than wait.

Tap. Tap. Tap.

Maeve's body went rigid. Kate peered around her daughter's hair. Mike stood straight, eyes focused in the direction of the control room's inner door.

Maeve sniffed. "It's— It's not coming in here, right Uncle Mike?"

He didn't turn around. "Y'all be still and quiet. I'll be right back." He opened the door and stared into the small hallway.

Bang. Bang.

Everyone in the room jumped. Maeve stood, her left arm hanging at an odd angle. Kate followed suit.

"Mike?" she called. "Was that the outer door?"

He held his hand up in the air.

Bang. Scratch. Bang.

Her pulse, relatively calm to begin with, was off to the races. She put a hand on Maeve's right shoulder and squeezed. Her daughter leaned back into her.

It was there. In the main hallway. Waiting. Trying to find a way in.

Kate's mind filled with the image of tentacles that ended in sharp talons and maws of incredible black. She shook away the image.

The creature was nothing like the movies. Instead of yowling, growling, and snorting as it chased its prey, it was completely silent except for the click of its claws on concrete or the sizzle of its body dissolving matter. Her skin prickled with gooseflesh. She wanted to tell Mike to shut the goddamned inner door. Just shut it. Play dead. Make it come for them. Don't give it a way in. Don't give it a way in. Don't give—

BANG! BANG! SQUEAL!

Kate felt as though she couldn't get enough air in her lungs. They could die in here. It could find a way in, and they'd have no way out.

Mike stepped into the inner hallway. He closed the door behind him.

The room held its breath. The seconds crawled. Kate stared at the metal door, afraid it would move. Or when it opened that an eyestalk would peer straight at her with those beyond dead obsidian eyes. The handle jiggled. She sucked in a long gulp of air preparing to shatter the world with her scream.

The door swung open. A very pale Mike entered the room and gently closed the door behind him. He put a finger to his lips and continued walking until he was just a few feet away from the group.

His voice was barely more than a jittery whisper. "It's out there. It can't get through the door."

"What about beneath it?" Maeve asked.

He opened his mouth and then closed it. The remaining color in his face melted away. "I—There's a metal plate at the bottom. And I think some rubber gaskets. That's what makes the room somewhat air-tight." Despite the obvious fear on his face, he managed a slight smile. "Don't worry, girl. We're safe."

Something rattled under the floor. Kate dropped her head and stared at the tiles. The control room sat a half a meter or so above the actual floor. She raised her eyes to Mike's. "I think it's in."

* * *

No one had said a word for several minutes. Jay was too busy trying to formulate molecular structures in his mind to want to talk. Besides, they had a theory. He wasn't sure it was a good theory, but it fit.

For most of his life, he'd lived in a painstakingly black and white reality where science made sense. Chemistry wasn't like biology. It wasn't prone to mutations or other strange phenomenon. Atoms bonded. Atoms formed chains. They just, well, did. Sans environmental forces such as temperature, pressure, and interaction with other chemicals, chemistry was about as pure science as you could get. Until now.

What the hell did this thing secrete that was capable of dissolving anything but metal, glass, concrete, and other densely packed structures? How did something like that fail to respond to electron beams? How? How?

Jay gritted his teeth. Maybe "how" was the wrong question. Maybe "why" was the question they should be asking. He knew he was right about the thing creating its appendages like a snail creating a shell. The speed, though, was what was insane. How the hell was it doing that?

And there was that word again. "How." Jay shook his head. He wished he was at his desk, Loony Tunes in the background, while he attacked his whiteboard. He'd have the NMR results, the molecular models, everything. He'd have—

Jay's mind stopped racing. The NMR. Chuckles shunted the processes over to the NOC. Surely it had finished the run by now. I mean, how long had it been since the CDC entered the building?

He stood with a groan and readjusted the hearing protection on his ears. Through the control room's glass, he could see Mike staring at the inner door. Kate was too. Jay raised an eyebrow. Did they hear something?

Mike slowly crept forward and opened the inner door. Jay lost sight of him, but could see the door closing behind him. Mike must be checking on something in the hallway. Jay's heart started to beat faster.

It could be Chuckles, he thought. But somehow that didn't feel right. If Chuckles was smart, he'd hidden himself away where the M2 couldn't get to him. But where the hell was that? The lab? No. It had broken out of the lab area. Easily too. By way of the—

Jay looked up. The ceiling wasn't even tiled. Wide, painted PVC pipes carried power and network cabling through the room. Jay tapped his foot on the floor and felt it give a little. They were on risers. There was a probably a goddamned rat's nest of cabling beneath the floor as well. At least the room didn't have a sprinkler system. There were no sprinkler heads in the ceiling, but there were plenty of vents.

He caught movement out of the corner of his eye and glanced toward the control room. Mike was back in the room. He and Kate were talking. A tremor rattled the floor risers. Jay stared down. The tile he stood on was shaking. He turned to the others. They were all staring at the tiles they sat on as well.

"No." He shook his head, eyes widening. "No!" Jay yelled. "Get up! It's in the floor!"

The three scientists stared at him. Jay rushed forward and grabbed Hoyt's arm. He screamed at the others to get off their asses and pulled the CDC doctor to her feet.

Beneath the sound of the fans and drives, he heard the creature's crackle and sizzle. Bill and Neil scrambled to raise themselves. Jay wasn't waiting. He dragged Hoyt to the inner door. He grabbed the handle and swung it open. Jay pushed Hoyt through and turned around for Neil and Bill.

One of the server racks began to lean. "It's coming through the floor!" Jay yelled.

The leaning server rack fell over with a tremendous crash. The next one in line leaned as an eyestalk poked through the tiles. Neil stumbled as he ran, Bill right behind. A tentacle slashed through the tile floor. Particles of foam and plastic flew into the air. The tentacle wrapped around a server rack and pulled. They fell like dominos. Jay's feet trembled from the crash. Electricity sparked and Jay's nose filled with the smell of ozone and burning plastic.

Bill and Neil tumbled through the inner doorway. A klaxon alarm wailed. Jay shut the door. The NOC control room was already empty and the outer door to the hallway was open.

Jay launched himself through and shut the door behind him. Even the heavy sound-proofing did little to mask the sounds of destruction within the NOC.

"Goddammit!" Jay yelled. He pulled himself up. The hallway was filled with the survivors. "Where the hell do we go now?"

Mike blinked at him. "We can go down, or we can go up."

Another loud crash filled their ears. The outer door shook as something smashed against it.

"Move! We can't fucking stay here!" Mike yelled.

Jay didn't need to be told twice. He reached out and grabbed Kate's hand. She looked up at him with wild eyes. "Now!" he yelled.

The fog cleared from her face and those wild eyes narrowed. She clutched her daughter's undamaged shoulder and gently pushed her toward Jay. The three of them scrambled down the hallway.

"No! Not that way!" Mike screamed behind them. Neither Jay nor Kate heard him.

Maeve was crying. It didn't sound like fear, but something more primal—pain. Jay slowed and turned. Kate nearly slammed into him. He gestured to Maeve.

"Hold your other arm, girl." She did as she was told. "Here we go." He bent down and lifted her by the waist until he could get his hands beneath her. Once she was situated in his arms, he continued down the hallway. Kate ran past him.

Jay couldn't help but smile. Momma bear was scouting for her cub.

The overhead lights weren't on. In fact, they weren't even hooked up. Kate pulled out her phone, hit the flashlight setting, and scanned ahead of her as she jogged.

The carpet ended as they turned the corner.

"Fuck!" Kate yelled.

The hallway ended in a clutter of stacked wooden planks and a collection of tools. Heavy plastic created a makeshift wall behind the mess. The plastic rippled from the outside wind.

"Nope nope nope," Jay said in Beaky Buzzard's voice. "Kate?" He gestured with his head toward the large opening in the wall.

She turned and pointed her phone's light toward it. The wan light barely broke the thick darkness. A naked, filthy concrete slab stared back at them.

Jay puffed air from his mouth. His arms were starting to burn. He readjusted Maeve and she whimpered. "Sorry, girl."

"It's okay, Uncle Jay," she said, teeth gritted.

A scream echoed in the halls followed by a crash. Jay jumped and nearly lost hold of Maeve.

Kate's flushed cheeks drained of color. She turned the phone's light back to the entrance to the unfinished room. "No choice," she murmured and crossed the threshold.

Jay turned slightly and brought Maeve safely into the room. When he was sure her feet wouldn't hit the walls, he pivoted until he faced forward again. His eyes were slow to adjust, but there was still enough illumination from the hallway to make Kate's silhouette easy to follow.

Gravel, remains from the concrete pour no doubt, crunched beneath his feet. The air grew colder as they headed further into the room. Kate's light turned in a slow arc. The dim glow exposed sawhorses, stacks of sheetrock, and metal.

Jay quickly realized where they were. This was the floor for the chemistry and biology departments and this room was to be their new workspace. He suddenly wished he'd paid more attention to the construction plans. At least Kate looked like she knew where she was going.

The far end of the room was pitch black. There was no glass. Kate's light illuminated large wooden sheets pasted against the outer wall. If he ever found the construction moron running the project, Jay would kick his ass.

She panned the light against the opposite wall. They were nearing the middle of the building. Maeve's breathing was barely audible, but every few steps, a small whimper escaped her lips. Jay didn't know how much longer he could carry her. He wasn't young anymore. If he could put her in a fireman's carry, that would be one thing. But with her shoulder? Just wasn't going to work. Twinges and pinches of pain rippled up his back. He gritted his teeth and kept moving. Just had to keep—

Something rumbled in the ceiling. The acrid smell of burning plastic and fabric hit his nostrils.

Kate slowly panned her light upwards. PVC and metal pipes snaked from one end of the room to the other before disappearing behind an inner wall. A wide rectangular metal duct stretched from the building interior to the middle of the room.

A/C? Heat? He nodded to himself. Definitely the kind of ducts used for air flow. But that meant—

"Kate," Jay hissed.

She turned to him, but her light was still pointed upward. "What?"

"We have to go back. Now." He may have been whispering, but his voice sounded way too goddamned loud. He didn't know if M2 could actually hear, but he wasn't willing to take the chance.

"Why?"

He started backing away toward the hall. "I think it's in the ducts."

She paused for a moment. Even in the darkness, he could see the stress in her body language as she finally realized what he was saying.

The light hit his eyes as she began to move. She wasn't running, wasn't jogging, but she sure as hell wasn't just walking. Gravel crunched beneath her running shoes.

Jay turned back to the hallway and hurried across the threshold. He heard her on his heels when the tinging, pinging of stressed metal hit his ears. A groan escaped the room as screws failed beneath the mass of what had crawled inside. He was already running down the hall. If it was still in the room, they might be able to make it back to the skybridge. Or hell, maybe the—

They turned the corner. Jay's mouth dropped open. The door to the NOC was bent in half. What little carpet had been laid down in the hall was gone. The sheetrock above the NOC had disappeared save for burned fragments and edges.

A bent duct exchange above the wrecked NOC door drooped at an odd angle. Thick black smoke wavered from the far end near the skybridge.

All the saliva disappeared from his mouth. "Kate?" Jay's voice was little more than a croak.

"I see it," she said. "We have to get to the stairs."

"They're blocked off, aren't they?"

"I don't know," she said. "But we have to try. We can't go down there."

The sound of sizzling, frying bacon hit their ears. Kate cast a glance behind them.

"Move!" she yelled. Jay followed her to the fire door. He hoped like hell they wouldn't be trapped.

* * *

Mike couldn't think. As Jay, Kate, and Maeve ran down the hall toward the construction area, two thoughts managed to break through the fog in his brain: Kate was leading Jay and Maeve to a dead end, and he had to get the others the hell away. The NOC door began to buckle from whatever was trapped in the NOC.

"This way!" he yelled and ran toward the skybridge. He didn't wait to see if the others followed. A pang of guilt rose in his conscious mind. He was supposed to be the leader, the person in charge, and here he was running for his goddamned life without giving a shit about the people depending on him.

He reached the skybridge entrance and turned. Neil and Bill were hot on his heels. Hoyt stumbled along as if she was barely conscious and in control.

"Move it!" Mike screamed at her. Bill and Neil headed into the skybridge. The woman stumbled again and fell to the floor. Mike cursed and ran to lift her up. The door to the NOC buckled, one corner bending outward. A black tentacle shot out through the gap and curled around. It smashed into the wall just above Hoyt's head. She screamed, but didn't get up. Mike reached her, bent at the waist, and grabbed her feet. He dragged her as fast as he could toward the skybridge.

Her suit rubbed against the exposed concrete. The fabric ripped and tore. She was screaming. He could barely think through the red fog that filled his mind. The tentacle reared back, shortened, and then punched into the buckling door. The impossibly strong hook tore through the metal as easily as a knife through a soda can.

Can't dissolve metal, a voice said in mind. *But sure as shit can fuck it up.* Mike threw the thoughts away and continued dragging the screaming woman.

Another tentacle flicked out of the gap in the door. Its hook sheared upward through the hole the other had made. The middle of the door ripped. Flakes of metal exploded outward like shrapnel.

Mike dropped her feet, grabbed her arms, and lifted Hoyt off the ground. "Run, goddammit!"

Her left hand in his, he pulled her forward. Hoyt's feet finally moved in cadence with his. Together, they stumbled into the skybridge. Something crashed behind them, but Mike didn't dare turn. They had to get someplace safe. And right now, that was anywhere but here.

Bill and Neil waited on the other side. The two scientists huffed and puffed as they tried to catch their breath. "Stairwell!" Mike yelled at them as he passed. Hoyt's hand let go of his. She'd finally come to her senses and was moving on her own. In the harsh light of the overhead fluorescents, a rectangular piece of metal and the remains of a pair of glasses sat on the floor. Anger rushed through his mind. Now he knew what happened to Chuckles. And it was all for nothing.

The stairwell was around the far corner. There was no carpet remaining and the walls were scorched and smashed. The creature had more or less destroyed the entire second floor.

He turned at the elevator bank and nearly stopped. The door to one of the elevators had buckled. It shined incredibly bright beneath the overhead lights. *So that's how it got to the first floor*, he thought.

Mike reached the stair well and swung the door open. He stood beside it, gesturing wildly to the others. Hoyt ran past him to the landing. Neil followed on her heels. Bill's face was flushed and pained. The man couldn't run anymore. Mike reached out and grabbed him, saving him from face-planting onto the concrete landing. He led the older man into the stairwell, pushed him against the wall, and then slammed the door shut.

The security locks were disabled, but the door clicked shut just the same. He stared through the porthole in the door. The lights in the hallway clicked off one at a time. Chuckles may have disabled the security, but the eco-systems were still on. He gritted his teeth and turned.

There was barely any room on the landing. Hoyt had moved a few steps down, as had Neil.

"Where now?" Neil asked.

Mike stared into his frightened eyes. He glanced toward Hoyt. She had the same wild look. Bill held a hand to his chest and wheezed.

"We're not safe in the foyer," Mike said through a pant. "We can lock ourselves back in the bio-lab."

Neil shook his head. "Are you kidding? That thing busted out of the chem-lab back when it was small! How the hell do you think we're safe in the bio-lab?"

"Got a better idea?" Mike asked. He knew Neil was right, but he was angry just the same. There was no place safe. And if they went outside, they might be shot by whoever was running things out there. If Hoyt was right, they were all considered expendable; they were already casualties.

Neil dropped his head. He looked up at Bill. "You okay, man?"

Bill nodded, but the movement was weak and barely perceptible. His panting slowed, but his cheeks were too pale. "Will be," he said.

"How the hell did it get into the NOC?"

Mike shrugged. "Let's talk about that when we get some place safe."

Hoyt turned and took the stairs two at a time. Her left leg had obviously stiffened on her, but she was fighting through the pain. Neil took the steps a little more slowly. Mike put his arm around Bill's waist and led the old scientist carefully down the stairs.

Bill cleared his throat. "You think the others made it?"

"I hope so," Mike said. "We can't help them now. They're on their own."

"That poor kid," Bill said.

Mike didn't reply. Kate and Jay were smart, but they didn't have the flashlights. They were defenseless. He prayed they were safe.

CHAPTER EIGHT

They'd made it to the stairwell without incident, but they could still hear the creature tearing through the second floor. Kate wondered how long it would be before the thing figured out where they had gone. She hoped *It* would remain confused until they could get the hell out of the building.

The new building was still under construction. The stairwell led down to an emergency exit that had already been blocked off. The door wasn't locked, but it barely budged against whatever the authorities had put in front of it. Again, there was no way out.

Maeve held her arm at an odd angle. Jay stripped off the remains of his contamination suit. The crinkle of the fabric echoed in the concrete stairwell. Kate stared at him until he raised his eyebrows.

"What?" he asked

She managed a grin. "I guess we don't need these after all."

"Nope," he agreed. "Useless. M2 will eat right through it."

"Maeve?" Her daughter looked at her. The girl's teeth were locked together in pain. "Would a sling help?"

"Don't know," the girl said.

Jay stared down at the remains of his suit and smiled. "Let's do something about that."

The stairwell was silent except for the sounds of movement, sirens beyond the emergency exit, and their own breathing. Jay started to form a makeshift sling out of the suit. Kate stared at the door leading to the first floor interior. She blew out a sigh between her teeth.

"Jay? I'm going to go scout the lab room. See if there's anything we can use."

He shook his head. "Let me get Maeve situated first. You shouldn't be going in alone."

"That's exactly why I'm going alone. Take care of her." She tried to keep the fear from her voice, but knew she had failed. Kate stroked her daughter's undamaged arm. "I'll be right back."

"No," Maeve said. "Don't go."

Kate cleared her throat. "It's upstairs. And if something happens and we have to move, I can't carry you. But Uncle Jay can, right?"

Jay nodded. He looked less than happy about the situation. "I can. I will."

"Just stay here until I come back. If that thing comes through the stairwell, get your asses into the lab area, okay?"

"We will," Jay said.

Kate bent down and kissed her daughter's cheek. She managed a smile. "I'll come back for you. I promise."

"Isn't that what all the stupid white people say in horror movies?" Maeve asked.

Kate giggled. "Don't worry, daughter of mine. I've seen them all."

She turned from her two companions and faced the inner door. Kate took a deep breath, and swiveled the handle. It moved easily beneath her hand. She pushed it open and headed inside.

Darkness. Pure, uninterrupted darkness. No windows. No way for ambient light to even think about coming in. The door swung closed behind her with a bang. Kate jumped and then chuckled. She didn't know how it was even possible, but the first floor was somehow even darker. She pulled her phone from her pocket, turned on the flashlight mode, and swept the light in front of her.

The floor was strewn with tools, sawhorses, stacks of sheetrock, metal supports, and bundles of wood. Just like the old building, the room had a wide hallway that faced the labs. Unlike the old building, there were four different lab areas instead of two. The two new chem-labs had already been piped. Drains leading god-knows-where sat in the middle of each room. The metal gleamed dimly in the wan light.

The workers had yet to put up the glass enclosures or even put in the electrical cabling. She glanced around as she searched the floor. Debris crunched under her feet.

At least it hasn't been here, she said to herself. *Or the floor would be completely clean.* That was a good sign. Maybe M2 didn't know there *was* a first floor. A shiver ran up her spine. *What if—*

She killed the thought as she raised her light to point at the ceiling. In the less than bright light coming from the phone, she could still see unfinished air ducts and pipes. "Fuck," she said to the empty room. Even at a whisper, her voice echoed off the concrete walls.

It could get in here. It wouldn't have to bother with doors or stairs. If it found its way into an adjoining duct, it would just pour into the room. The thought of the black ooze raining down upon them made her sick to her stomach.

She pointed the phone to the far wall. Was that what she thought it was? A tripod?

Kate walked forward until the shape solidified. A grin spread across her face. A large rectangular light-head stood atop the tripod. Light. The workers had to have light to work in here. She looked for a switch on the tripod, but didn't find one. Cursing, she followed the extension cord leading out of the light-head.

The cord led to a portable transformer against one of the walls. She knelt down and studied it. Four red, rocker switches stared back at her. She looked at the labels. One was marked "Master" and it was in the off position. Kate took a deep breath and flicked it.

The world exploded with light. She shut her eyes and waited for the retinal afterimage to fade. The room hummed with the buzz of electricity through the heavy halogens. When the afterimage dimmed, she slowly opened her eyes to slits.

The incredibly large room was lit in each corner. The area for chem-lab 1 was the brightest. The construction crew had put up several halogen tripods to illuminate plumbing and piping they were still connecting.

She turned off her phone's flashlight mode and studied the ceiling. Ductwork stretched from the walls to the building interior. There were a number of exchanges leading upward. If the creature somehow entered the main vent, it could drop on them from anywhere.

But if it tried to get to chem-lab 1, it'd be burned alive. That was the answer. They could sit in the middle of the lights and they'd be safe for as long as there was power and the lights didn't burn out.

Best option, she thought. Kate turned and walked to the stairwell entrance. Just for giggles, she looked at her phone. "No Signal." Well, that was as expected. With the heavy stone walls, insulation, and half of the floor beneath the actual ground, cell phone reception would be shit. She already knew Mike had planned to put a repeater on the building.

A little late now, she thought. If they stayed in here, they'd be safe, but cut off. No internet. No cell. Nothing. But at least they'd have light.

She knocked on the stairwell door. "Jay? Maeve? Come on in."

Someone murmured through the heavy metal door and then the door handle turned. The image of a tentacle tearing open the door flashed in her mind. She knew it wasn't in the stairwell, but her heart was off to the races anyway.

The door opened wide. Maeve stood next to Jay, her left arm wrapped and slung. Jay glanced at Kate. "You like my ER skills?"

Kate sighed. "Maeve? Is it better?"

The girl nodded, but said nothing. She walked past her mother and into the room. Jay shrugged and followed her.

Kate closed the door behind them and tested to make sure it would stay closed. She blew a sigh between her teeth and turned to watch Jay and her daughter.

Jay studied the ceiling much as she had. Maeve walked directly to the intersection of light in the unfinished lab.

"Sufferin' succotash," Jay said. "This is one big ass room."

"Shut up, Sylvester," Maeve muttered.

Jay made a farting noise with his lips. "Kate?" He pointed to the ceiling. "Those ducts lead out and up, am I right?"

She nodded. "I think so. If I remember correctly, they'll be positively pressurized so air only goes out, not in."

"Right." Jay shook his head. "Too damned bad all this isn't ready. But hey," he clapped his hands, "at least we have light."

Maeve put her back against the wall near the lights and slowly slid down. She used her good hand to steady herself, but still managed to make a dull thud when her ass touched the floor. She let out a small cry of pain.

Kate looked at Jay. "We need to see if we can find a med-kit. They have to have one around here somewhere don't they?"

Jay blinked. "Only if you think illegal immigrant labor follows OSHA rules."

She glared at him. "Let's look anyway."

He shrugged and moved off to the far wall. Kate watched him go and then headed to Maeve. She knelt next to her daughter. "You going to be okay?"

Maeve's head rested against her chest. "Really hurts." She looked up at her mother. "Next time? Get a babysitter."

Kate's mouth opened and then closed. She giggled and stroked her daughter's hair. "Stay still. I'll try and find something to make you more comfortable, okay?" She rose to leave.

"Mom?"

"Yeah, hun?"

Maeve stared at her with level eyes, but the girl's lower lip trembled. "How long do we have light?"

"As long as we have power, baby."

"And what if…it…decides we don't need power?"

Kate fought to keep her expression level, but the flesh on her arms prickled. "It's not smart enough for that."

Maeve sniffed back a tear. "How do you know that?"

"I don't." The words were out of her mouth before she thought about them. She shook her head. "I don't, baby, but if it was that smart, I don't think we'd be standing here."

Maeve put her head back on her chest. Kate watched her for a moment and then began searching the unfinished labs.

*   *   *

It took both Mike and Neil to get Bill through the doors and into the chair. He slumped in it like a tired kid, but his breathing was an old man's wheeze.

Hoyt had managed to get herself into a chair. She stared at the wall as though it was something interesting. Neil was sure she was in shock. He didn't know what to do for her or if there was anything that could be done.

Mike stood next to the computer. When he cleared his throat, Neil looked at him, eyebrows raised. "What?"

"Can you get on this thing and see if we have network?"

Neil rolled his eyes. "If the old NOC was destroyed, I'm not sure we're going to have anything."

"Try." Mike's voice was a low growl. His expression was flat, but his eyes were full of panic and anger.

"Yes, sir," Neil said. He marched to the computer desk and brought up the interface. He typed in his username and password. The computer thought for a moment and then a red dialog box appeared. He sighed. "Can't authenticate. No network, boss."

"Goddammit," Mike hissed. He slammed a fist down on the

computer desk. The monitor jumped and so did Neil. "We have to—"
He stopped and then turned to Hoyt. "Dr. Hoyt?"

The woman kept staring at the far wall. She hadn't even twitched
at his words.

Mike walked to her, placed a hand on her shoulder, and gently
squeezed. "Melanie?"

Hoyt blinked. Her head swiveled toward him as if it were on
rusty hinges. She blinked again. Her eyes glittered a little. That was
something.

"Do you still have communications with your people?"

"My people?" she asked in a dreamy, far away voice. "My people
are dead, Mr. Beaudry."

Mike winced. "Can you communicate with the CDC? Your radio?"

"Radio." Dr. Hoyt stared down at the floor.

Neil walked forward and knelt in front of her. "Can I have your
radio, Melanie?"

Hoyt raised her head and stared into his eyes. "They won't talk to you."

He forced a gentle smile. She was cracking up, but anything he
could do to humor her might bring her out of her daze. He hoped.
"Maybe they will. I'd like to try."

"Okay." Dr. Hoyt pulled the radio from her belt and offered it.
"Control won't be happy."

"I'm sure they won't be," Neil agreed. "But I will be. And I'm
going to get us out of here."

"You are?" She sighed and stared again at the floor. She finally
spoke in a whisper. "We are going to die here."

The words hung in the air. Neil glanced up at Mike. His face was pale,
but his eyes still glittered with energy. Mike nodded at the radio. "Do it."

Neil stared down at it. He turned the volume dial until he heard
static and pressed the talk button. "Control. This is HAL. Over."

The static continued. Beneath the layer of white noise, barely audible
excited voices wavered in and out. Neil blinked and tried again.

"Control. This is HAL quarantine area. We have an update on our situation. Over." He depressed the talk button. The room seemed to hold its breath.

"HAL. This is quarantine control outside building 2. What's your status? Over."

Neil grinned at Mike. That was good. They were talking to the folks just outside the walls. Fifty feet from where they sat was freedom. Now if only they could get there.

"This is Dr. Neil Illing from HAL. We are trapped in the lab on floor 1 of building 1. We need help. The creature is roaming freely through the building and there is no place to hide. Over."

There was a pause. Neil's heart pounded in his chest. He was sure he heard Mike's doing the same.

"Dr. Illing? Where is Dr. Hoyt? Over."

Neil took a deep breath. "Dr. Hoyt is indisposed. She is unable to communicate at this time. Over."

Another pause. The seconds dragged out like minutes. Neil suddenly wanted to scream at the radio. What was taking so goddamned long?

"Dr. Illing. We have the buildings surrounded. There is no way out, no way in. We cannot assist you until the biological entities are contained. Over."

Finally, blessedly, he lost it. "Are you fucking kidding me?" he shouted into the radio. "We have no weapons! We are unable to hide, let alone fight! At least give us some fucking weapons! Over!"

Pause. Pause. Pause.

"Dr. Illing. Your situation is understood. We cannot take the chance any of you are infected. Ben Taub is a war zone. The biological entity there has killed most of the hospital personnel and patients, as well as many military resources. We have it contained for the moment. We cannot risk another entity escaping. Over."

The radio's plastic cover creaked beneath his grip. His white-knuckled fingers trembled. "Control. Have you tried halogen light?

Anything besides bullets and bullshit?"

Pause. Pause. Pause.

"Dr. Illing. Can you update us on your entity? How large is it? What are its characteristics? Over."

Neil felt like he was going to explode. He took in a deep breath to scream at the asshole on the other end of the radio, but stopped himself. He exhaled through his teeth and waited until he felt like he was in control of himself.

"Control. Our entity is large. It has consumed all the carpet, most of the sheetrock, and other non-metallic, non-glass materials. It has also killed at least three people. Probably more. But we haven't seen it fully formed. It is large enough to easily fill a hallway. It sprouts tentacles and legs and is becoming increasingly fast. Over."

Pause.

"Dr. Illing. Do you have any samples of M2? Over?"

He glanced at the electron microscope. "Mike. Go over there and look through the eyepiece. You should see nothing but black with a blue glow around it."

Mike rolled his eyes and did as he was told. He peered into the microscope. "Uh. Neil? All I see is a glow. There's no black."

Neil opened his mouth and then closed it. He turned his head and looked over at the SEM. "Uh, Mike? Step away from the scope."

The boss stepped back. "Where is it?"

"Get out your flashlight," Neil hissed. "Turn it on and pan the floor. Look for anything that gleams where it shouldn't."

"Dr. Illing? Are you there?" the voice said from the radio.

"Control. Stand by," Neil said.

Mike pulled the heavy safety light from his pocket and turned it on. The white light glared into the floor, easily visible against the fluorescent blue from the overheads. He stood next to the SEM and trained the light around the area.

"Focus on the sample container," Neil said. He couldn't keep his voice steady and his heart thumped in his ears. If it had escaped the slide, where the hell did it go?

Mike pointed at the SEM. "Here?"

Neil nodded.

"Shit." Mike's light hit an impossibly clean, impossibly bright trail on the metal. He took another step away from the SEM as he followed the trail with his eyes.

"Dr. Illing?" the radio squawked.

He thumbed the speak button. "Control? We have a sample loose in the lab. I think there's more in the chem-lab's sample system. Plus whatever is left in the barrel. Over."

"Um," Mike said, "the trail just wraps around the machine." He killed the light and looked back at Neil. "Where the hell did it go?"

"Understood, Dr. Illing. Leaguer's encounters with the substance indicate it is highly flammable. If light doesn't fight it off, you may need to resort to more drastic measures. Over."

Neil stared down at the radio. Fire. Light. Extreme heat. Maybe there was a way to fight this thing.

"Neil?"

Mike's shaky voice pulled him out of his thoughts. Mike's face was milk pale. Neil raised his eyebrows.

The CEO pointed down at the floor. Neil followed his gaze. There. In the shadows beneath the microscope sat a tiny shape. Something amorphous. Something so dark it was like a hole into another universe.

Neil tried to speak, but his voice came out in an unintelligible croak. He cleared his throat. "Mike? Get your flashlight back on."

"Yeah." Mike gulped and flicked the switch. He slowly trained the cone of white light toward the shadows.

As the light chased away the darkness, the black shape twitched. When the halogen light came within a few centimeters, the shape trembled and slowly flowed backwards further into the shadows.

"Mike?"

"Yeah, Neil?"

"Blast it." Neil took a deep breath and was a little relieved to see Mike doing the same.

Mike slowly lowered himself to his haunches. He flicked the off switch. The halogen's cone disappeared. He adjusted his aim and then flicked the switch.

A bright, white spot appeared in the middle of the amorphous shape. Bubbles burst across its surface and the room filled with the crackle of green kindling. A sewer smell combined with burning rubber stung Neil's nostrils.

The shape's edges split off from the burning center. Neil's mouth dropped open. Two individual tendrils formed as their parent burned. Less than a few millimeters in size, they stayed in the shadows.

The original, larger puddle had disappeared. The floor was scorched where it had been. "Mike?"

"I see them," Mike said. He pointed the light at the larger of the two stragglers. It exploded in a puff of smoke and fire. He switched targets with the same result. Three smudge marks were all that were left.

"Dr. Illing?"

The radio made them all jump. Neil thumbed the talk button without moving his eyes from the scorched floor.

"Control, this is Illing. We have destroyed the sample loose in our lab. Over." Mike kept his light focused on the floor. He seemed to be in a trance. "Mike?"

The man turned to him. A little color was slowly coming back into his cheeks, but he still looked on the verge of passing out.

"You okay?"

Mike nodded. "Yeah. I mean—"

"Dr. Illing. Are there any other samples loose? Over."

He shook his head and then winced. It wasn't like they could see him. "No, Control. Nothing else loose. We have the large entity roaming the building, the sealed barrel, and whatever is in the dispensing system. Over."

Mike blew out a sigh and then laughed. "We need to just set fire to the whole goddamned place."

Neil cocked an eyebrow. "I'd say that's a last resort." He pointed to the secure area behind the labs. "There's enough flammable chemicals back there to blow a hole in the goddamned universe."

Mike nodded. "I know. That was the point."

"Dr. Illing. Is there any way to secure the barrel? Over."

Neil opened his mouth and then closed it. "What the hell is he talking about?"

Mike shrugged and looked at Hoyt. The CDC doc was staring at the floor as if nothing had happened. Neil wasn't even sure she was breathing.

"Dr. Hoyt?" Mike said. She didn't look up. Mike walked toward her and tapped her shoulder. She flinched, but did not break her stare with the tile. "Dr. Hoyt? Melanie?"

It was the first name that seemed to snap her out of it. At least a little. She slowly raised her head and met his eyes. "What?"

"What do they mean by secure?" Mike asked.

She shivered. "Sample. Any virulent pathogen samples have to be collected."

Mike looked at Neil. "You tell them to fuck right off."

Neil nodded. "Control. There is no way to secure the barrel, the lab, or anything else. The M2 entity roaming the building can come back here at anytime. Over."

"Dr. Illing. It is imperative we have samples to study. Please find a way to protect the barrel and whatever remains in the dispensing system. Over."

"Fuck you," Mike growled.

Neil clicked the talk button again. "Are you out of your mind? This stuff destroys damned near everything it touches! You can't take it out of here!"

"Dr. Illing. If you do your job, we'll get you out of there. Over."

"Job." Mike spat out the word with a stream of saliva.

"Control? Get us out of here. Now. And you can have your damned sample."

Pause.

"Control?"

No response.

Neil looked at Mike. "You're right. We have to blow this place. They're going to let us die in here anyway and we can't let that shit out in the world."

Mike turned toward the chem-lab and Neil followed his gaze. The room was a wreck of smashed equipment. When the M2 had escaped into the ceiling, it had left the place a ruin.

"You know how to run the dispenser?" Mike asked.

Neil nodded, although his boss wasn't looking at him. "I do, yeah."

Mike turned to him. "Then let's figure out how to torch this place. If nothing else, it'll keep the big beasty upstairs from coming down here. I hope."

"That's going to be tough," Neil said. "We have halon systems in both labs as well as the secure area. They'll put out a fire in no time."

Mike smirked. "Then I guess we'll have to get creative." He looked at Bill. The older scientist was still slumped in his chair, a look of pain on his face. "Still with us, Bill?"

He raised his head and winked at Mike. "I ain't dead yet." The words came out in a huff of air.

Neil put a hand on his friend's shoulder. "All right, Bill. Let's start brainstorming."

* * *

A quick search resulted in finding a white, plastic box emblazoned with a red cross. Jay swiped it up and brought it back to the unfinished chem-lab area. Kate followed him, her face a mask of concern.

He handed it to Kate and she put it on the floor. She pressed her thumbs on the latches and the kit opened. An EpiPen, bandages, a tourniquet, and several packages of meds stared back. Kate sifted through the tough paper packs until she found what she was looking for.

"There we go," she said. She tore open the paper and shook out two caplets. "We don't have any water," she said as she offered the meds to her daughter. "So do your best. I know how much you hate pills."

Maeve groaned and then picked the caplets out of her mother's hand. She popped them into her mouth, her face set in a rigid grimace, and then swallowed. She choked once and then exhaled.

"Should take the edge off the pain," Jay said. He smiled at the girl, but he was still shaking inside. What good were meds if that…thing came down here? They had to find a way out. They had to find some part of the building the CDC or FEMA or the goddamned military didn't know about. Regardless of what awaited them outside, there was no way it could be worse than what they were trapped with. If they could just—

"Jay?"

Kate's voice cut through his river of thoughts. "I'm sorry," he said. "What did you say?"

She gestured to the tripods. "These are all we have. If they get damaged, we're screwed."

Jay nodded. "Also means we don't have a way to drive it off. Can only stay in the circle of light."

"I've been thinking about that," she said. "Remember what happened during the distillation test?"

Jay shuddered at the thought. "It turned solid. And all the, well, all the life went out of it."

"Right. The distillation test is performed in a vacuum. So if there was no air, there was no way for it to burn."

Jay nodded. "Okay. So you think it's flammable?"

"Why not?" She glanced toward the shadows outside the semi-circle of light. "It shares some properties with regular hydrocarbons.

And Sigler's tests aboard Leaguer showed a very low boiling point. Maybe a flame will destroy it. Catch it on fire."

Jay thought for a moment. What she said made sense. If only they had a way to test it. He shook his head. "Doesn't matter. We don't even have a goddamned lighter."

Kate rolled her eyes. "We're chemists, Jay. And humans have enjoyed the privilege of fire long before they figured out how to write. I think we can manage."

He stood and looked out into the shadows as Kate had. The afterimage of the strong lights made his night vision non-existent. He clucked his tongue and walked beyond the circle. It took a moment for his eyes to adjust, and the entire time, he kept imagining a long tentacle sliding across the floor toward his feet.

He shook away the image, but couldn't stop the shaking in his bones. The afterimage finally faded. In the shadows and dim light cast by the glare of the halogens, he made out saw-horses and tools. They had electricity. They could create a short-circuit, true, maybe some sparks. But what the hell could they set on fire with that?

He suddenly wished Chuckles was down here with them. He might know how to overload the panels. Shit, he'd have a lighter. Then Jay frowned. "Kate?"

"Yeah?" she said from behind him.

"We can create a short circuit, maybe. But that might take out the lights entirely." He slowly turned and blinked at her. "And then we'd have nothing."

Kate opened her mouth and then closed it. She nodded. "You're right. That's a bad plan."

He turned back to the room. There had to be *something* they could do. Some way to defend themselves.

Something in the ceiling creaked. Jay looked upwards. Nothing moved. The vents and ducts were still and nothing black was hanging up there. At least not yet.

A concrete saw sat against one of the walls. Drills and pneumatic hammers lay on the sawhorses. A metal stand held a jigsaw. The blade was sheathed in protective rubber.

Jay continued walking forward. Something blocky lay at the bottom of the far wall. He pulled out his cell-phone and turned on the flashlight mode. He scanned the shadows. If it was down here, he was already dead—he was too far from the circle of light. He knew it, but the light made him feel a little better.

Several rectangular shapes jutted from the box. He walked closer and then a grin slowly spread across his face. When he was close enough for the cellphone to illuminate the shape, he snickered.

"What is it?" Kate called from across the room. Her voice bounced off the concrete walls, words barely discernible in the impossibly long echo.

Jay looked down. LED lights. All green. He pulled on one of the rectangular shapes. It clicked out of its slot. Heavy, he thought. He examined it beneath the light and started to laugh. "I got it," he said.

"What?" Kate sounded concerned.

Jay turned to her and then found himself sprinting across the filthy, debris covered floor. When he reached the circle of light, he was out of breath, but damned near hysterical with laughter. "A battery," he panted. "A goddamned power-tool battery."

She blinked. "So?"

He wanted to yell at her in frustration, but instead his grin widened. "We can make this thing into a lighter. Sort of."

"How?" she asked. "You going to overload it or something?"

He showed her the exposed contacts. "See those? We just need to connect some metal to them. It'll throw off sparks. If we have something pretty flammable, we can create a little fire."

She shook her head, a smile appearing on her face. "Where the hell did you get that idea?"

He laughed. "Boy Scouts. We used steel wool for fire starter when it was too wet to catch kindling. The stuff burns pretty well. Got it from SOS pads."

"Oh, man," Kate said. "We don't have any steel wool."

He shook his head. "No, we don't. But what we have is a room full of dust, wood chips, and," he said pointing at his shirt, "threaded fabric. We cut the thin t-shirts into strips, unwind the threads as best we can, and then," he licked his lips, "we pray."

"And what are we going to use for metal?"

Jay frowned. "We could try folding some aluminum or something like that." He turned back and looked around the floor. "Someone has to drink soda down here."

Kate looked lost in thought. Jay knew how she felt. Materials. They had plenty to start a fire. But what they hell were they going to use to create the circuit?

She glanced over at her daughter and then smiled. "I've got it," she said. "The suits. They have metal woven into them."

Jay smacked his forehead. "That will work. Metal threads."

"Okay. We have a plan. So let's get moving on it."

Their shared grins disappeared as the ceiling creaked. Something banged in the ducts. They traded stares. And then they started working.

* * *

It didn't take long to come up with a plan. The only difficult part would be making it out alive. Neil didn't have high hopes for that.

The secure area had halon systems that would be nearly impossible for them to sabotage. Even if they managed to get on a ladder and smash the sensors, he wasn't sure that would keep them from going off. Hell, the system might read their tamper attempts as an actual incident and gas them all to death.

Of course suffocating can't be any worse than being eaten alive, Neil thought. He shivered. The whole situation was ludicrous. If he hadn't seen the

M2 first hand, he'd never believe such a thing was possible. An organism that acted like a hydrocarbon, but was capable of absorbing damn near anything as food and changing form? Not possible. Something that could hide its atomic form from an electron microscope? Again, impossible. No one would believe it. If he pinched himself enough times, maybe he'd wake up. *You are awake*, he told himself. *You just wish this was a nightmare.*

He, Mike, and Bill had brainstormed how to accomplish their task. Hoyt was still lost in her own little world and only answered if they called her by her first name. Neil didn't think she was ever going to snap out of it. In a way, she had it easy. At least she had already accepted they were going to die. Neil still had hope.

For the most part, Mike had only nodded while he and Bill came up with the plan. But Mike definitely understood what they were going for. Even better? He approved. And that was the kind of leader he'd been for HAL. He hired good people, let them figure out the problems, and gave them whatever resources they needed to succeed. In this case, they had all the resources they could want. The trouble was execution.

Sabotaging the halon systems came first. The halon tank was located in the secure area and surrounded by a metal shield. Getting past it required a pair of bolt cutters and some elbow grease. The real trick was disconnecting it. And, of course, bleeding the entire system.

Bill was still in his chair at the front of the lab. The old scientist was clearly spent. If they had to move fast, he was going to be more of a hindrance than Hoyt. When you pulled on her, at least her legs worked. Bill, though, had torn something. He wasn't going anywhere fast and he was too big for either Mike or Neil to carry. If things went to shit, Neil planned on just pushing him through the hall in his goddamned chair. He hoped like hell it didn't come to that. Every time he imagined doing it, a laugh tried to crawl out of his throat. If it did come to that, he doubted he'd be laughing at all.

Mike stood next to the metal shield, a large pair of bolt cutters in his hands. He faced the barrel at the other end of the room. *The* barrel. The M2 barrel. PPE's very own plague. Neil was closer to it, eyes focused on the orange ribs. They seemed to have, well, ballooned a bit, like something was pushing on them from inside. The image of tentacles bursting through the top and eating him flashed through his mind. He shook it away.

"You okay?" Mike asked.

Neil nodded. "Yeah. Just don't like being close to that shit."

"I know the feeling." Mike tested the handles of the cutters. They moved easily. The suicidally sharp, serrated teeth slid by one another as he closed it tight. "Yup. This will do just fine."

"So we cut the lock. And then we cut the pipe."

Mike nodded. "And then we pray a lot."

Neil pulled a mask from his belt. He'd managed to salvage two of the filtration masks from the storage cabinet. There were no more of them in bio-lab. Chem-Lab might have them, but he wasn't going in there. Standing this close to the barrel was bad enough. Being directly below the opening the M2 had used to escape? Fuck. That.

"Put this on," he said and handed a mask to Mike.

Mike looked at it and pursed his lips. "This is going to mess up my hair, isn't it?"

Neil laughed despite himself. "Yeah. Although I have news for you. It's already pretty messed up."

Mike hesitated. "So this stuff is toxic?"

Neil shrugged. "Depends on what kind of halon and what kind of exposure. If you bleed it wrong, it could kill us on the spot for all I know."

"Great," Mike said. "No pressure."

"None at all." Neil pulled on his mask and fought with the uncomfortable plastic straps. It pinched his skin and he gritted his teeth. He breathed through his nose. The air tasted like rubber.

"Yeah," Mike said. "That looked pleasant."

"Straps are the least of the problem." Neil's voice was muffled by the mask. "Wait until you smell it."

Mike laughed as he pulled on the mask. It was awkward because he was still holding the bolt cutters, but he managed just the same. The boss was nothing if not dexterous. He shook his head. "Feel like I'm breathing through a condom."

Neil nodded. He knew Mike couldn't see his expression, but he was grinning just the same.

"Well, let's see if we can screw this up. You watch that barrel."

"I will," Neil said. He turned so he could keep an eye on it.

He heard the sounds of Mike grunting and metal clinking. After a few seconds, the room echoed with the solid snap of metal breaking. He winced at the sound. The barrel didn't move.

He didn't think M2 was capable of hearing anyway. Otherwise, the creature would have found them long before this. Bill posited that maybe it was sensitive to sound waves as well as light waves. Neil didn't think he was right about sound, but light? That made more sense. How else could it "see" without actual eyes?

Or were those stalks with the orbs really some kind of visual mechanism he didn't understand? If the goddamned thing wasn't so dangerous, he'd love to actually examine a sample of its appendages. But that was impossible.

The real question, however, was whether or not the people outside, those *Federal* people, thought it was too dangerous to study. Based on what the voice had said on the radio, they wanted it for that reason. They couldn't have it. If they still thought they could control it after battling the M2 at Ben Taub, their judgment was obviously in question. You'd have to be a complete moron to—

The metal shield creaked and groaned as Mike pushed it open. Neil's thought train derailed at the sound. He held his breath as Mike walked inside the shielding. Through the gap in the shield, the huge, brushed metal tank looked as though it hadn't been serviced in a very long time.

A cloud of dust rose into the air. He couldn't see what Mike was doing, but he was definitely wiping at something.

"Can't even see the damned gauges," Mike's muffled voice said. "Remind me to get this thing serviced."

"Considering you're about to destroy it, that might be a good idea."

"Smartass," Mike said. His voice, filled with tension, had a trace of humor just the same. "I'm wiping these gauges so I can see the readings. But I have no idea what I'm looking at."

Neil shook his head. "Once you cut the feed line, it's not going to matter. Just stay the hell away from the pressurized gas. It's going to jet out at pretty high pressure. Might even cut a finger off."

"Great," Mike said.

Neil turned back to the barrel. He blinked. The lowest rib looked like it had bulged a little more. And then he heard it. A pinging noise. Something was hitting the barrel from inside. Didn't take a PhD to know what that was.

"Hurry, Mike. We may not have much time."

"What? I don't have time for a pee break?"

Neil shook his head. The rib pulsed. "I think whatever's in the barrel wants to get out."

"Fuck." More clanging from inside the shield. "Okay. I think I've got the feed line."

The barrel trembled. "Cut it. Now!" His ears rang from the sound of his own voice.

A sudden rush of air filled the room. Mike jumped backwards out of the shielded area. A blast of whitish gas rose to the ceiling with a roar. He couldn't hear anything over the sound.

Mike stumbled into him and Neil reached to steady the CEO. The bolt cutters fell to the floor and bounced. Then his skin began tingling. The tingling started to burn.

Neil put his hands on Mike's shoulders and led him through the secure door and back into the bio-lab. As soon as he closed the door, the sound of the pressurized gas escaping the tank disappeared, but the ringing in his ears was nearly as bad.

Mike stumbled forward and leaned against one of the lab tables. His shirt was ripped at the left cuff and his skin was red and raw. The parts of his face not covered by the mask and straps were blistered.

"You okay?" Neil asked.

Mike reached up and pulled off the mask. A long, thin swath of skin peeled off the side of his head where one of the straps had been. A drop of crimson beaded out of the wound, but didn't flow down. "Yeah. Just fucking dandy." He spat a wad of phlegm to the floor.

Neil pulled off his mask. He hadn't gotten the full dose of the nitrogen/halon mixture, but that didn't mean his skin wasn't itching like mad. He pointed to the sink. "Wash your skin. Try and get that shit off of it."

Mike said nothing as he headed to the emergency sink. He placed his face in front of the large shower head and pushed. Water welled out and sprayed against his skin. He gave a short-lived scream and then simply shook beneath the water. When he ceased the flow, he turned around and looked at Neil. "Well, that was bracing."

"Cold?"

Mike shook his head. "Not until you get that shit off you. Then it's freezing."

Neil stepped past him and followed the same procedure. Mike hadn't been kidding. The water seemed warm for the first few seconds and then was icy cold. He fought through the discomfort until he'd bathed his face, arms, and neck. When he stepped away, he was freezing.

"Brisk," he said through chattering teeth.

Mike leaned against one of the tables. The man was in fantastic shape, but he looked as though he'd just run a marathon through hell. "That was step one. Right?"

Neil nodded. "Yeah. But I think we have another problem."

Mike rolled his eyes. "Now what?"

He pointed toward the secure room. "The barrel. It's moving

inside the barrel. I think it's trying to break out."

Bill giggled. And then he belly laughed.

"The hell is your problem?" Mike asked.

Bill held his head in his hands as he laughed. The sound in his throat abruptly died and he looked up. His lips were set in a stony grin. "It can't—" he searched for a word, didn't find it, and shook his head. "Dissolve? Dissemble? Absorb? Hell, I don't know what it does. But it can't do that to metal, right?"

"From what we've seen, that's correct," Neil agreed.

"But it *can* grow solid appendages. Sharp ones at that. I'll bet that's what it's banging against the inner metal."

"Yeah?" Mike asked. "So?"

"Simple physics," Bill said. "How could it possibly do much damage unless it can get leverage? It would have to be pressing against at least two points of the barrel to make it bulge."

Neil blinked. The rib had been pushed out on one side, not all the way around. But he hadn't checked the side facing the wall. And he sure as shit wasn't going to walk close enough to check. "So what do you think, Bill?"

"Maybe it's more corrosive to metal than we think. Maybe it needs time to weaken it." Bill pointed to the chem-lab and the pipes leading to the dispensing station. "Those pipes are thick, but not as thick as that barrel. If it's doing damage to the barrel, what's to say the stuff trapped in the pipes isn't doing the same?"

Neil bit his lip. He tried to imagine what the M2 was doing in the pipes. Once the vacuum pump was connected to the barrel, its contents rushed into the pipes and whatever didn't fit there remained *in* the barrel. So was it one contiguous organism? Just spread out over the ten meters of piping and the barrel itself?

"Oh. Shit." Neil scratched at his arms. "That's bad."

"Okay," Mike said. "Maybe I'm stupid, but I don't get it. We're going to burn the goddamned stuff anyway."

Bill nodded. "And the sooner, the better."

*   *   *

"Wish I'd taken up knitting," Jay said. "Then maybe I'd carry some needles on me."

Kate sighed. "And how exactly would that help?"

He shrugged and clicked the knife in his hands. The tiny, gleaming razor edge jutted out a little further. They'd found the knife in one of the many toolboxes. It had worked well on the last remaining portions of Kate's chem-suit. Once they'd torn it into strips, he and Kate took turns with the knife as they liberated the metal threads.

The room was growing colder, not warmer. Instead of just smelling of dirt, debris, and mold, the new building's lab area also smelled of rain. The storm, the first cold one of the season, was out there. They couldn't hear it. They couldn't see it. But Jay damned sure felt it.

Several long, thin metal threads lay atop a strip of cloth from Jay's t-shirt. Kate wound them together with nimble fingers. The piece of metal had to be wide enough to make a firm connection to the contacts. Jay also wanted it to be thick enough to not snap.

He looked up at the ceiling. The creaking sound was more frequent now. More disturbing. The sound of something being dragged through the ducts. They didn't have much time. And Jay didn't think they'd have more than one shot.

Maeve wasn't asleep, but she had her eyes closed. Her foot twitched with nervous energy. Jay hoped the meds were finally helping. If they could kill the M2, maybe the CDC would even let them out.

Kate finished winding the threads together. Jay studied them and then checked the rest of their supplies. Strips of cloth. Check. Bits of paper scrounged from the floor? Check. Charged high power battery? Check. Metal for the contacts? Check.

"Well, I think you made Eagle."

Kate blinked at him. She opened her mouth and then started to giggle. "I was never even in the Girl Scouts."

"Well, doesn't matter," Jay said. "That's a fine smorgasbord of burnable materials."

"Is that the technical term?"

"I could have said flammable shit. Would that have been better?"

She punched him in the arm. His bare skin stung from the blow. He faked a wince and then laughed. "You punch like a girl."

She hit him again, harder. This time the wince was real, but the laughter was louder.

"Adults," Maeve said. "You guys are more immature than I am."

A metallic shriek echoed in the room. The three of them flinched. Jay turned and looked up at the ceiling. There was no ductwork immediately above them. *Thank god for small favors*, he thought. But just a few meters from the circle of light, ductwork criss-crossed the ceiling.

"Okay," Jay said. "That was well-timed." His shaky voice matched the trembling in his hands. "So, Kate, it can't pour out on top of us. So where do we set the trap?"

She looked up and followed the ducts as he had. Kate bit her lip. Jay tried to be patient, but it was agonizing. He couldn't think. If the M2 was coming down the ducts from the second floor, it could drop nearly anywhere. Or could it?

She nodded to herself and then pointed. "See that vent in the middle?"

He followed her finger and then blushed. Of course. The ductwork met in the center with a register. The register wasn't yet complete. Hell, the metal vent covers hadn't even been affixed.

"How long will it take us to start the fire?"

He shrugged. "A minute or two. I think. I never did it with a battery this big. Only ever used a 9-volt."

She blinked at him. "You think this is going to work on this kind of battery?"

"I hope it will." He cleared his throat. "Unless you have a better idea?"

Kate sighed. "No. I don't."

Another metallic shriek echoed through the room. A dull thudding noise followed.

"Shit," Jay said. "It's in the ducts."

"Well, light this shit!" Kate yelled.

He picked up the wound wire and jammed one end into the negative contact hole. When he let go, the wire sprang back out. "Oh, fuck," he said.

"You mean it's not going to work?" Kate asked. Her wild eyes bore into his.

He growled, put the metal back into the hole, and then stuffed one of the strips of cloth to plug it. When he let go, the wire stayed. He snapped off the plastic covering for the positive contact and did the same.

Jay touched the middle of the wire. The flesh on his index finger burned. He pulled it out and sucked on it. "Well, I think it worked," he said around his finger.

"Well, that's—"

Metal expanded. Aluminum and steel made to channel air buckled beneath incredible weight. Still holding the battery, Jay walked out of the circle of light.

"Jay?"

Her voice barely registered in his mind. Once his eyes adjusted to the dark, he saw the source of the noise. Jay's mouth opened and his eyes widened.

The metal ducts closest to the far wall were warped and dimpled. He watched as each successive duct sagged and lost its rectangular shape. M2 had squeezed itself in. *Jesus*, he thought, *how big is it now?* The sliding, dragging sound became a roar. The ductwork started to shake in the ceiling. Metal rattled. A bolt gave way and one of the duct connections buckled with a shriek.

"JAY!" Kate screamed.

He turned to her. She was screaming for him to start the fire. To do something. Anything. But his brain was slow. It took forever for his eyes to glance down at the cloth in her hands. Fire. He was supposed to start the fire. But she was so far away. And the noise was so loud. And—

The ground shook as something dropped from the ceiling. Jay turned back to the noise. Most of the ductwork had come loose and crashed into the concrete. A cloud of dust rose from the floor.

Jay stared into the dust. Kate's screams barely registered. He could hardly see anything through the motes hanging in the air. But what he did see unhinged him.

The ducts were a wreck of metal. They had collapsed into the floor leaving dented concrete and shards of steel in their wake. The very center of the line of ducts trembled. Metal squealed and then crunched as a black tentacle shot out through them. It descended and formed into a hook. It ripped along the duct seams like a can opener and then split apart.

The metal detonated as an impossibly black form rose from the wreckage. Appendages squeezed out of the ooze. Tentacles. Spidery legs. Stalks that ended with orbs darker than space. It stood on seven, one meter-high segmented legs. The appendages were several meters long and growing. A huge maw opened in the creature's midsection.

A circle of teeth appeared, their ends lighter than the gaping hole behind them. Its eyestalks waved and then stared straight at Jay. The thing seemed to roar, but was silent as death. Then it started to move.

Its spidery legs crackled and smashed through the remaining duct steel. Its talons clicked on the concrete floor as it scuttled forward. Jay was lost. His eyes were locked on the orbs. Lost within them. It was coming. He could do nothing.

His hand started to burn, but he couldn't look away. He gritted his teeth against the pain. And then something smacked him in the shoulder. He was dimly aware of movement, and then someone was wresting the battery from his hands.

Kate moved into view. She was running toward the creature even as it moved toward them. It was only five meters from her when she stopped, wound up, and threw the burning battery at the creature.

The cloth, Jay thought. *The cloth holding the wires must have caught fire.*

The creature's eyestalks all pointed and tracked the fireball as it flew through the air. The creature tried to back away, but it only managed a step. The battery fell into its gaping maw even as it tried to catch it with its tentacles.

For a moment, nothing happened. The creature stared at them, its razor sharp tentacles stretching toward them. Jay was still frozen in place when Kate turned and ran at him. She tackled him to the floor and then the world exploded.

The creature detonated in a fireball. Its tentacles didn't come off. They just ceased to exist. The same with its legs and the center that had once been a terrifying, razor ringed mouth. The fire spread out along the concrete floor, setting anything flammable alight.

Jay's mind finally snapped back into place. His hand screamed in pain and he was pretty sure Kate's tackle had sprained his ankle. Or broken it.

He raised his head and looked over her shoulder. The creature was gone. Only fire remained.

Kate rose on stiff limbs and offered him her hand. "You okay?"

Jay winced. "Sufferin' succotash, woman! You nearly shattered my back!"

"It was either that or risk you getting torched."

He took her hand. She pulled him to his feet. He hobbled on his ankle past her so he could see the carnage.

Dark smoke rose above the flames. "Jesus," Jay said. A massive scorch mark lay where the creature stood when it combusted. The concrete was stained and looked as though it was broken in places.

He stifled a cough and then failed. The smoke was starting to be a little too much. He turned back to Kate. "We have to get out of here."

"How?" she asked. "They've got the outer doors locked and blocked."

Jay stared at the stairwell door and pointed. "That thing is gone. We can go back upstairs, get into the NOC, and see if there's a phone or anything still working. Hell, maybe our cellphones will work up there."

Maeve groaned behind them. "We really have to move again?"

Kate said, "Hey, did you like the fireworks show?"

The girl smiled despite the pain in her shoulder. "It was pretty cool. I thought you guys were going to start a fire, not throw a hand grenade."

Jay laughed. "The cloth I used to secure the battery connections. The wire must have warmed enough to set it off." He stared down at his right hand. The skin was black in places, striated with crimson. "Shit." He looked at Kate. "Got anything in that med kit for burns?"

Her eyes stared down at the wound. "That looks third degree, Jay. Why did you just stand there?"

He blinked. "I don't know. It— It looked at me. Like it was—" He shook his head. "I don't know."

She sighed. "Let's table that for now. Let me get some bandages and see if we can find something for that hand."

* * *

There were three Bunsen burners in the chem-lab. The problem? They were in the chem-lab.

Neil and Mike walked outside into the hall and then stood at the entryway to the lab. Neil glanced at the glass wall. Bill watched them from his chair, his face a bit more pale than Neil liked.

He stared into the chem-lab. The distillation equipment was melted in places. The gaping, scorched hole in the ceiling was terrifying. The idea that, that thing, could just reach down and pluck them into its mouth was more than just a little disconcerting. He didn't want to go in there. But it was the only way, the only goddamned way, they were going to get through this.

And even then, the odds weren't exactly in their favor. The plan? Set fire to the M2 that was still in the dispensing station. Neil wished he could take credit for it, but it had been Bill's idea. Opening the barrel up and setting it on fire would be next to impossible if they didn't want to risk releasing it from its temporary prison. But if they managed to set the M2 on fire in the pipes, it should travel back into the barrel and ignite all of it.

Regardless of whether or not it worked, they were going to be in a world of shit. There was no telling what would happen once that much of it was alight. It could explode. It could do nothing. Or, more frightening, the M2 could just stream out of the pipe and kill them all.

They'd have to break the vacuum to force air into the system. Neil hoped Bill was right about that too. The pipes had a purge system to force air and clear them. But if they couldn't get it to go in reverse, it meant they'd have to drain the pipes *and* the barrel into the lab. At that point? All bets were off. Neil didn't want to think about it.

"How do you want to do this?" Mike asked.

Neil glanced at his worry-lined face. His eyes burned with something akin to anger. It actually made Neil feel a bit better. At least he had one pissed-off wingman.

"See that table over there by the distillation analyzer?" He pointed a finger toward it. Mike nodded. "There's a burner over there with an auto-igniter. The only problem is the tubing connecting it to the gas jets. But there are lots of gas jets in here. We just need to disconnect the burner, take it to the dispenser, reconnect it, and then figure out what's next."

Mike blinked. "Why can't we figure that out now?"

"Because," Neil licked his lips, "I don't know if the computer controls were damaged. If they were, we're going to have to think fast. If that thing comes back down here, we're not going to have a whole lot of time."

"That's easy," Mike said. "We turn on the gas jets, auto-ignite the burner, and let the gas do its job."

Neil gulped. "That could cause one hell of an explosion, Mike. I'm not sure we'd survive it if we were outside the lab, but we'll be blown to smithereens if we're inside when it happens."

"I don't care." Mike's eyes were hard steel. "I let that shit into this place. I'm sure as hell not letting it back out. We can't have this stuff out there. No fucking way." He shook his head. "If I ever see Simpson again, I'll kill him with my bare hands."

For a moment, neither man said a word. Neil tried to put the idea of them blowing themselves up out of his mind. Mike was right, of course. If the CDC or whoever the fuck had been on the radio was telling the truth, they were already losing a battle with an M2 entity at Ben Taub. Should the HAL sample of M2 get loose, there was no telling what would happen. If it reached the sewers, it could eventually destroy the city.

"Okay," Neil said at last. "I'm with you. Let's just plan on blowing ourselves up as a last resort, okay?"

Mike said, "I didn't say it was my first choice, Neil."

"I hoped that was the case." Neil turned back to the lab. "You know the plan?"

"Unhook the burner, take the hose, and meet you at the dispenser."

Neil nodded. "Right. Easy peasy."

"Easy peasy," Mike echoed. "Let's do this."

Neil opened the door to the chem-lab and stepped inside. The room stank of burned plastic and rotten meat. He stifled the urge to retch and suddenly wished they'd brought their gas masks. He was about to say something about it when Mike pelted past him toward the burner. Neil cursed and followed as fast as he could.

Mike made it to the burner station before Neil was even halfway to the sample dispenser. He slowed and looked up at the gaping hole in the ceiling. The hole exposed ductwork, pipes, and electrical wiring. He tried to ignore the feeling he was being watched through that hole and headed to the dispensing station.

The computer was still working. That was something at least. He brought it to life and logged in. The system took a moment and then returned with a login failure. "Fuck you," Neil said. The network was trashed. It couldn't contact the authentication server.

He clicked okay and then grinned. Because the scientists were always losing their passwords, Chuckles had set the labs up with connections to the network, but also with a root password. They were only supposed to use the root account if there was a network failure. Now was the time.

Neil typed it in and waited as the computer thought about it. The screen flashed and filled with a UI. From here, Neil could control most of the equipment in the chem-lab. Fortunately, there was only one item of interest on his mind.

He brought up the UI for the dispensing station. The screen flashed again and a new window filled the screen. Neil scanned the interface and looked at the system health bar. According to the sensors monitoring the piping system and the dispenser, there were no problems with pressure and the system seemed intact.

"I think we're in business," Neil said without turning around. "Everything's green and we still have pressure."

"Good," Mike said. "I've almost got this connection loose."

"Just don't turn on the gas jet by accident. That would be a bad thing."

"Noted," Mike said.

As Neil searched through the commands on the interface, Mike huffed and puffed behind him. The clinking of metal against metal was hard to miss. He hoped like hell Mike was being careful. If a jet came on while he was messing around back there, that metal on metal could deliver a spark that would blow them both to kingdom come.

At least M2 would die with us, he thought. Or hoped. He clicked through the menu and searched for maintenance mode. He found it and looked at the description. Neil nodded as he read it. He clicked a button and a new menu popped up.

They could bleed air from the system if the vacuum wasn't sealed. They could flush the system with water. Or they could force air into the pipes for a purge. As he searched, worry lines appeared on his forehead. What he was looking for, hoping for, wasn't there. The only way to get air into the system would also force the oil into the lab.

"Shit."

He barely heard Mike's footsteps behind him.

"Something wrong?" Mike asked.

Neil hissed between his teeth. "Like I was afraid of. The goddamned purge is one way only. We can force the pipes to empty through the nozzle," he said pointing to the metal and glass faucet, "in a purge. But that means we're going to bring all that shit into the lab."

Mike grunted. "No way to force it the other way?"

Neil shook his head. "I don't see a way to reverse it. The software doesn't support that and I've no idea how to jury-rig it." He thrummed his fingers on the table. "Shit."

Mike put the burner on the table and dropped the hose next to it. He pointed to a gleaming metal nozzle on the wall. "Is that the gas?"

"Yeah."

"Okay." Mike shuffled forward and put one end of the rubber hose on the nozzle. He fidgeted with it for a moment until he seemed happy. "One end in."

"Doesn't matter," Neil said. "We can't set what's in the pipes on fire. We'd have to somehow get the flame up into the pipes."

Mike ignored him and connected the hose to the burner. "Fuck that. We get some buckets or something from the storage area, flood the M2 into them and set them alight. It'll burn as it enters the buckets. No problem."

Neil stared at him. "You're out of your mind, Mike. We don't know what that shit will do once it's out of the pipes. It could just fly right out of the buckets and into our faces."

Mike shrugged. "But it'll die. Like us."

"Man," Neil said. "You really are pissed off."

"Yes. Yes, I am. I have two destroyed buildings, dead friends, and an army of assholes outside that are unwilling to help. So yeah," he growled, "I'm pissed off."

"Before we do that, let me think."

Neil stared at the vacuum pump mechanism. It was quite simple, really. The airtight connections at either end ensured no air could enter the system. Once everything was connected, the pump bled all the air from the pipes. After that? The dispenser end opened a valve and the fluid trapped in the pipes would flow through. When the valve was shut again, the vacuum in the pipes was restored.

But how to get it to go the other way? If he attempted to purge the system, air would flow through another valve toward the beginning of the pipe system. He pursed his lips. To perform a purge, they couldn't have the barrel connected anyway.

"Shit." Neil scratched his head. "Okay." He turned to Mike. Mike's eyebrows were raised. "Here's what we can do. We set the burner down, ignite it, and I set the dispenser to allow a very slow trickle of liquid. Once it starts catching fire, any additional M2 that exits the system will automatically ignite."

"And if it doesn't?" Mike asked.

"We'll let whatever's left in the barrel out into the lab. And we won't really have a way to stop it."

"So," Mike said, "either we leave this crap where it is, or we take our chances." He looked around the lab. "How many more of those gas nozzles are there?"

"Um, I don't know. Ten? Twelve?" Neil scrunched his eyebrows together. "What the hell you got up your sleeve?"

A slow, sadistic grin spread across Mike's face. "Help me find another hose. Two if possible. You're going to show me what to do, and then you're going to get the hell out of here."

"You're crazy."

Mike laughed and shook his head. "No. Believe me, I don't want to die in here. And you're going to have to get Bill and Hoyt the hell out of here. Get them to the building foyer. Hide there. If it comes for you, do your best to get away."

"That's a shit plan," Neil said.

"Got a better one?"

"No. I don't." Neil grabbed the burner and placed it beneath the spout. He exited the maintenance interface and brought up the main dispensing program. He could set a timer. He could set flow. How long would Mike need? He exhaled through his teeth. "Okay. Let's find those hoses first."

* * *

Neil and Mike were talking. He could see them waving their hands at each other. Something had gone wrong with the plan and Bill didn't like it.

His eyes kept wandering to what he could see of the damaged ceiling in the other lab. If they stayed in there much longer, they risked that creature coming down on top of them. Bill couldn't really imagine how they'd get away from it since it would be between them and the room's exit.

He was feeling a little better, able to catch his breath, and his heart had slowed down. If he survived all this, it was time to get in shape. 58 was no age to have a heart attack or simply croak from exhaustion.

CRUMP!

Bill flinched and stared toward the far wall. He waited for another sound, something to clue him in as to what had created the noise. It didn't sound like thunder. More like a gunshot from a very large caliber pistol. "Now what?" he asked aloud.

The radio on the table squawked. "HAL? This is control? Dr. Illing? Are you there?"

Bill walked to the table and picked up the radio. He fiddled with it until he found the talk button. "Dr. Illing isn't here. This is Dr. Field." He depressed the button. Grunted. Pressed it again and said, "Over."

"Dr. Field. Do you have any more casualties, over?"

"No. What was that noise, over?"

Pause.

"We're not sure. It came from building 2. We are investigating now. We have another team outside your building near the loading dock. They will come in to assess your situation momentarily. Over."

Bill blinked at the radio. "You mean you're coming to get us, over?"

Pause.

"We will be entering the building to assess the situation," the voice repeated. "Do not, I repeat, do not enter the secure area when our team enters. Any HAL personnel found will be treated as hostile. Do you understand, over?"

"Shit," Bill said. He didn't press the talk button. He stared back at the chem-lab. Neil and Mike were hooking up hoses to gas jets. He didn't know what the hell they were doing, but he had a bad feeling.

"Dr. Field? This is control. Please respond."

They were going to enter the secure area. They were going to take out anyone that got in their way. And there hadn't been a single goddamned word about saving the people inside. Great. *Our tax dollars at work*, he said to himself.

"Dr. Field?" the radio squawked again.

He pressed the talk button with a smile. "Control, this is Dr. Field. We are currently planning the destruction of the M2. We suggest your people stay outside until we're finished. Over."

He dropped the radio on the table and walked to the hallway as fast as he could. He had to let Mike and Neil know what was going on.

"Dr. Field? Dr. Field?" The radio was screaming at him as he walked out. "Do not—" The voice was lost when he closed the door.

Hoyt was still in there, but that didn't matter. He entered the hallway and made it to the chem-lab entryway as Neil was running out.

"What are you doing here?" Neil asked.

Bill pointed toward Mike. "They're coming in. For that shit. What is *he* doing?"

Neil shook his head. "Something really dumb. And something really dangerous."

"Well, we're going to have an army of assholes coming through the loading dock any second."

"Goddammit," Neil said. He turned and shouted into the chem-lab. "Mike! We have a—"

And then the fun started.

* * *

Mike wiped a sheen of sweat from his brow. *You're out of your mind.* "Shut up," Mike said to himself. He knew this was crazy. He didn't need some inner voice to tell him that.

The burner was set up. Neil had set the timer on the device for one minute. The stream would be just fast enough to keep a steady flow without dousing the burner. But just in case, Neil had started another burner on the nearest table. If he needed it, he could turn on a gas jet, light it with the burner, and use it like a flamethrower.

Neil had told him that the fire through the hose wouldn't shoot very far. And more than likely, the rubber end would melt damned fast. But it was at least something.

The counter ticked down. 20 seconds. He moved away from the dispensing station and stood next to the other burner. Four meters separated him from the dispenser that would release the M2. He held a hose in one hand, his other on the gas jet.

"Mike!" Neil shouted from the hall. "We have a—"

Three things happened at once. And none of them good. The vacuum pump groaned as it sucked M2 through the pipes. Mike was frozen between the sound of the pump and Neil's voice. Then? The secure area's loading dock door exploded outward.

The Bunsen burner beneath the dispensing faucet crackled and spit as the first drops of M2 hit it. The pipes groaned as something fought against the vacuum. More M2 drizzled out and then the little burner turned into a flame geyser.

Mike shielded his eyes as the red and orange flame reached all the way up to the faucet. Through the roar of the flame and Neil's screaming behind him, the sound of confused, panicked voices in the secure area caught his ears.

The secure area was drenched in nearly blinding light. Bulky shadows moved in. Some of them carried equipment. Others? The easily recognizable shapes of rifles.

Mike cursed and backed up. The fire had reached the dispenser. Metal squealed as it expanded from the heat and whatever was pushing on it from inside. The vacuum struggled to pull more of the substance through. Mike imagined it had grown appendages to grip the metal. He cursed again.

Those assholes in the secure area were here for one reason and one reason only—they were going to take M2 out of the building. They wouldn't save his team. Hell, they might even kill them. Regardless, he couldn't let that shit out of the building.

He had to break a pipe. Break the vacuum. Let the shit into the room and burn it. He looked around for something, anything, that could possibly break the pipes open. If he gave the stuff somewhere else to flow, he was sure it would.

Mike ran to the wall of lab equipment. The fire was getting larger, but not fast enough. That didn't mean the black smoke chuffing into the air wasn't starting to choke him. Through watery eyes, he scanned the items on the wall. He finally saw what he wanted and hoped it would do the job.

He pulled a large steel wrench off the pegboard. *This is going to be tricky, he told himself.* He pulled one of the lab stools beside the dispensing station. The heat from the fire made his skin prickle. He jumped atop the stool and eyed the pipe leading from the wall to the dispenser. He pulled back with both hands, and then swung the wrench into the pipe.

His ears rang with the clang of metal on metal and his arms trembled with the shock. He heard yelling on the other side of the wall, but it didn't matter. He pulled back and slammed down again. The pipe buckled and flakes of sheetrock fell to the floor. Someone somewhere was screaming for him to stop what he was doing and "right fucking now!" He didn't.

Mike took a deep breath, coughed on the acrid smoke pouring into his lungs, and then swung for the fences. The wrench head smashed into the pipe. Something cracked and the pump stuttered. He pulled back once more, ready to break the goddamned thing once and for all, and then he was falling off the stool and hitting the floor on his side.

His chest screamed in pain. He rolled over, screamed, and looked up into a masked face holding an assault rifle. The barrel was still smoking. He turned his head to stare at the dispensing station. The M2 wasn't pouring out of the spigot anymore. The stuff had stopped, the flame shortening and then disappearing back into its blue to yellow teardrop shape. He looked back into the gas masked face of his shooter.

"You. Killed. Us. All." He took in a wheezing breath. His chest felt like shrapnel and he couldn't get enough air. The sound of more yelling and screaming was growing more and more distant. So was the pain. Mike closed his eyes. He'd failed. It was the last thought before he blacked out.

* * *

There wasn't much to do now but wait. Kate sat against the wall with Maeve leaning against her. Jay sat on the floor resting uncomfortably against one of the tripods.

The med-kit was a mess. Dressing and wrapping Jay's burned hand required most of the supplies. Burn cream, antiseptic, and then lots and lots of gauze. Kate wondered if he'd end up losing the hand. If they didn't get access to some proper medical care, that was a real possibility.

Jay's eyes were closed. His foot flinched every now and then and the sound of his grinding teeth was annoying as hell. But she knew he was in a lot of pain. There wasn't much of a chance of it getting any better either.

He adjusted his legs and opened his weary, pain-filled eyes. "You think there's anything left of the M2 for them to find?"

She shook her head. After the fire subsided, and the smoke died down, Kate had walked around the perimeter checking for any remnants. Black soot and grey ash was all that remained.

"If it had DNA, maybe. But Neil didn't seem to think it has any at all."

Jay nodded, but didn't look convinced. He stared up at the ceiling for a moment and then said, "You realize this changes everything we know about chemistry and biology."

"And physics." Kate stroked Maeve's hair. "Don't forget that. Damned thing might as well have been a black hole. Stephen Hawking wouldn't believe it."

"True." Jay took off his glasses with his uninjured hand and stared at them. "It's amazing I can see anything through these."

Maeve yawned. "Uncle Jay? I don't think I ever want to see anything like that again."

"Me neither, honey."

Something banged in the stairwell. Kate turned her head and looked at the door.

"Mom?" Maeve asked. "There was only one of those things, right?"

Kate's mouth opened and then closed. Was there only one? Did another escape from the lab? Who the hell knows what happened in the chem-lab after they left. She pulled her daughter a little closer. "Yes. Only one." It could be a lie. Probably was. But it was the one she needed to say.

Another bang echoed in the stairwell. Voices followed it. Radio voices. Kate raised her eyes at Jay. He shrugged. Her nerves sizzled with a brief dump of adrenaline, but she didn't have much left. She was too exhausted to do anything about it. Jay looked the same— worried, but beyond action.

The door opened. A long cylinder with burning blue flame at the end peered out from the door. A blocky figure stepped through and scanned the room. It turned its head toward the circle of light.

The figure shook its head. A muffled, deep, baritone voice spoke. "Control. This is Hatherly. We have survivors."

Maeve started to cry. In a moment, Kate joined her.

EPILOGUE

Another quarantine started. Twenty-four hours of observation were required to ensure none of them were infected.

Once they were fed and given a place to sleep, Kate and Maeve had absolutely crashed. She wasn't sure, but it seemed as though people dressed in moon suits disturbed her dreams with ear thermometers and stethoscopes. She even half-remembered them taking Jay from the room. But when she awoke, he was back, his hand more expertly wrapped. He was snoring loud enough to wake the dead, two IVs plugged into his veins.

She rose from her bed and stifled a yawn. Maeve was still sleeping in the bed next to hers. Kate adjusted the gown, making sure her ass wasn't hanging out, and stretched her legs. Her calves were sore, her back screamed bloody murder, and half a dozen bruises ached.

A moon-suited figure stood just outside the room's airtight, plastic door. The figure carried a matte-black assault rifle and faced the front of the decontamination chamber rather than the room. She was thankful for that.

The idea they were being held in some secret government facility chilled her bones. Would they ever be allowed to leave? She didn't know. The room was covered in mirrored glass of some kind. She knew it was two-way. They were being watched. They were being studied. And somewhere else in the building, others probably were too.

The military-looking men that marched them out of HAL refused to speak about the situation in the labs or if there were other survivors. No matter how many times she asked, they ignored her. Now she wondered how much those soldiers even knew.

She poured herself a glass of water from a pitcher and drank it. After the never-ending night she'd had, it was the purest, most refreshing substance that had ever touched her tongue. She swallowed with greed. When the glass was empty, she poured another and drank again. *At least they have this.*

A beep echoed from outside. She looked up at the guarded decon chamber. Three lab-coat wearing people were in there with the guard. They weren't wearing moon-suits.

Kate frowned. *Now what? How long have we been here?*

The guard checked credentials offered by the group of three and then the room's door opened.

One woman and two men stepped inside. The woman carried a duffel bag. She set it on a table and stared at Kate. A lock of fire-red hair dropped down into her eyes and she absently pushed it away.

"Ms. Cheevers?"

Kate blinked and then met her gaze. She raised a finger to her lips and then walked toward the group. The lab-coated woman blushed and then nodded.

"We'd like you to get dressed, please," the woman said. "And join us outside."

Kate furrowed her brow. "Quarantine is over?" She was a little startled at the weakness in her own voice.

The woman nodded. "I'm Dr. Shannon Moore." She unzipped the duffel bag and pulled out a shirt, jeans, panties, a pair of socks, and sandals. "Afraid these are less than fashionable, but they're the best we could do on short notice."

The clothes were certainly WAL-MART specials, but she didn't care. Anything to get out of this gown. "I take it we'll never see our other clothes again?"

Dr. Moore's smile widened a bit. "I'm afraid you don't want them back. Not after, well, not after they were, um, studied."

"Right." Kate took the bundle of clothes. She pointed to an empty bed in the corner. "I'll change behind that curtain."

"Feel free," Dr. Moore said. "We have cameras in the room, of course, but I'll make sure your dignity is preserved."

Kate said nothing. She walked to the empty bed and, as silently as she could, pulled the curtain to hide herself. Despite what Moore had said, she didn't believe the cameras were off, much less that they had any privacy in here. Hell, she might never have privacy again.

When she was finished, she pulled back the curtain. Dr. Moore and her colleagues were still in the same place. They were whispering to one another, but stopped when she was a few feet away.

"Better?" Dr. Moore asked.

Kate nodded. She turned her head and looked at her daughter. "I don't like being away from her."

"I understand," Moore said. "I have a son. I'd hate to leave him like this. But this really is important. As soon as she wakes up, the guard will let us know and I'll bring you right back, okay? We're not going far."

"Okay." Kate narrowed her eyes. "If anything happens to her—"

Moore shook her head. "Nothing is going to happen to any of you. You have my word."

Kate searched the woman's eyes. They were as opaque as they could be. Either Moore was telling the truth or was the best liar she'd ever met.

"Okay. Let's go."

* * *

She sat in a comfortable chair at a stainless steel table. She gripped a steaming cup of coffee between her hands. Kate sipped it and relished the taste. After being asleep for— Wait. How long *had* she been asleep?

"Dr. Cheevers?" Moore asked.

"Yes?"

"Is something wrong? You look puzzled."

Kate blushed. "I was just wondering how long we've been here."

Moore said, "I'm not surprised. I'll answer all those questions in a moment."

"Okay. What are we waiting for?"

The door opened. Kate glanced behind her and then grinned. "Neil!" The bio-chemist practically ran to her. She rose from her chair and gave him a tight hug. "I didn't think you were alive."

Neil smiled and squeezed her back. When he let go, he brushed a lock of hair from her cheek. "Didn't think you were either." He looked around the room and then his lips tightened. "Where are the others?"

"Dr. Cheevers? Dr. Illing?" Moore said from the other side of the table. The two parted and looked at her. "If you would take a seat, we'll get Dr. Illing a beverage and we can discuss things."

Kate and Neil traded a glance. She walked back to her chair and sat down. Neil sat next to her. He sniffed her coffee longingly and they brought him a cup.

Two men walked into their room carrying laptops. They wore lab-coats identical to Moore's. Kate recognized them from earlier. They sat on either side of Dr. Moore, opened their computers, and then waited.

Neil pointed at them. "Do they have names?"

Moore laughed. "They do. But you don't need to know them. Yet."

Kate didn't like how she'd emphasized that last word. It sounded… wrong. Her heartbeat rose a little, but she did her best to push down a feeling of panic. Something was off here. Very off. Or maybe it was shock. Yes, possible. She was in shock. If—

"If we're ready to begin?" Dr. Moore asked.

Kate sipped her coffee. Neil followed suit. Moore seemed to take that as a tacit agreement.

She splayed her hands on the table. "First off, I want to explain some things and then I'll answer any questions I can."

I can, Kate repeated in her mind. Her pulse quickened again.

"I know you want to know about the rest of your team, so I'll tell you that they're safe. Dr. Field was transported to another medical facility because of heart palpitations. He's stable and his prognosis is good."

Neil let out a tremendous sigh. "Man, I thought he was dead."

"He's not," Moore said. "I promise. You'll see him in a few days."

"What about Mike?" he asked.

Moore's grin faded. "Mr. Beaudry's prognosis is a bit more severe. He was shot—"

"Shot?" Kate asked, her voice echoing in the room.

Moore thrummed her fingers on the table. "Unfortunate incident, really. I'm afraid Mr. Beaudry was about to do something that could have killed everyone in the room."

Neil narrowed his eyes. "No, ma'am. He was trying to make sure that shit burned so it never threatened the goddamned world."

For a moment, Moore said nothing. The tension in the air was nearly unbearable. Finally, Moore's grin returned. "That is debatable, Dr. Illing. Regardless, he's in critical, but stable, condition. I hope to have more news for you later today."

"What happened to Hoyt?" Neil asked. "She was in our group, too."

"Yes. Dr. Hoyt." Moore cleared her throat. "Dr. Hoyt is currently undergoing psychiatric treatment. Although she was not injured physically, her mind has been less than resilient in recovering from shock."

Kate and Neil traded a glance. "But she's alive?" Kate asked.

Moore nodded. "HAL buildings 1 and 2 are still under quarantine. It's unclear when we'll be able to release the facility back to civilian control."

Civilian control. The government owns it now, Kate thought. *And I'll bet HAL will cease to exist very damned soon.*

"We located Darren Strange. You'll see him in the next few days as well. I'm afraid he cut his feet quite badly and still runs the risk of losing one of them."

Kate hissed through her teeth. "Jesus."

Dr. Moore looked at Kate. "Dr. Hollingsworth will be fine as well. His hand is being looked after by a military burn unit and they will be monitoring him every hour. He'll probably need skin-grafts in the future, but for now, he's stable and will have no problem continuing his work in the future."

"Damned good to hear," Neil said. He glanced at Kate. "And I hope to hear how that happened."

Kate said, "Battery bomb gone wrong. Long story."

"As you said, Dr. Illing, we'd like to hear how all that happened as well." She tapped the table's edge. "You're probably wondering where you are."

"Um, yeah," Kate said. "Considering there aren't any windows."

"My apologies for that." Moore's grin returned. "We'll make sure you get out into the sunshine and air soon. For now though, we have to keep you inside the facility."

"Facility?" Neil asked.

Moore nodded. "We're at Ellington Field. This building was converted quite a long time ago in case of a significant outbreak. Afraid it's been hush hush for a long time. But after the Ebola scares, FEMA decided it was a necessary precaution. Especially for cases where transport of infected organisms or pathogens to other facilities presents a serious security threat. I think you'll both agree this situation qualifies as such."

"You're afraid to transport M2 somewhere else. In case it gets loose."

Moore nodded.

"Oh, shit." Kate looked at Neil and slapped her hands on the table. "They have it." He blinked at her. "They have the M2!"

Neil stared at her for a moment and then looked back at Moore, his eyes glittering with excitement. "You do, don't you?"

Moore said nothing.

He leaned back in his chair. "Of course you do. You brought that shit here. And that means we're, what, just a few dozen yards from the fucking barrel of death?"

Moore held up a hand. Neil was about to say something else, but stopped. Goose flesh broke out on Kate's arms. This just couldn't be happening.

"What you call 'M2' has been safely contained. You have nothing to fear."

"Bull. Shit." Kate leaned forward in her chair, eyes narrowed. "You didn't see what that stuff can do. You should burn it up and right fucking now."

"I disagree, Dr. Cheevers." Moore tented her hands. "First of all, we know quite well what it can do. We have both camera footage from Ben Taub hospital as well as eyewitness accounts. Not to mention the destruction at your buildings. And once your team has been debriefed, we'll know even more."

Neither Kate nor Neil responded. Moore gave a tiny shrug and continued.

"I understand you're both very concerned about this new lifeform, as we all are. But I want you to consider something. We have hundreds, if not thousands, of oil rigs around the world drilling in deep water. If there's another...encounter...we need to know how to properly deal with it. Especially if there's a way to simply destroy it before it becomes a problem."

"Just nuke the shit and take your chances," Neil growled.

Moore ignored him. "With that in mind, it's been decided that studying the M2 is worth the risk. We also know how to contain it. Should it show any signs of escaping its current containment, it will be immolated immediately."

Neil shook his head. "I wouldn't take that chance."

"That's unfortunate." Moore leaned forward in her chair, her grin widening. "Because we'd like your team to join us in studying it."

Kate and Neil exchanged a glance. She looked back at Moore. "What's the alternative?"

"You sign certain non-disclosure agreements and you'll be surveilled for the rest of your lives."

"Shit," Neil said. "Even if we agree to your terms, we'll probably be under surveillance until time ends."

"That's probably so," Moore agreed. "The difference? We're willing to pay you a handsome sum for a few months of work. Since HAL is currently unable to function as a business, I'm sure you could use the paycheck."

"What about Maeve?" Kate asked.

"Provided she agrees to the terms of her release, she'll be allowed back in the world. Look, you're not prisoners. But we have to keep this as confidential as possible. If the world finds out exactly what went on, and where the organism came from, it could very well destroy our way of life."

Neil sighed. "You're going to tell us to do this in the name of God and country, aren't you?"

Moore snickered. "If it helps. But really, I want you to think globally. Your entire team is more than capable of contributing to this project. And we'd rather not have to start all over. It's another, well, security risk. The fewer involved, the better."

* * *

They knew the room was bugged. They knew the cameras in the corners recorded every word they said. But that didn't matter.

A fresh pot of coffee sat in the middle of the table. Neil sat next to Kate and blew a cloud of steam from his mug.

"This is crazy." Kate poured a little cream into her coffee and then stirred it with a wooden stick. "I mean, they want us to just pretend nothing happened and start working with this shit like it's just some other oil?"

He shook his head. "I don't think so. I think that's exactly why they want us on the project. They *know* we're not going to do anything that might let it out."

Kate pursed her lips. "Maybe. But I don't like the idea of living with a bullseye on my back."

"I don't either. But I like the idea of someone else messing with that crap even less." He sipped his coffee. "If I'm working with it, I know someone else isn't. And I think we can help them at least keep it from getting loose."

"True." Kate played with the stirrer. The fake wood was bright and grained except for where it had touched the coffee. Some connection started to form in her mind. It was an idea. The kernel of a plan. She couldn't help but smile. She looked up at Neil. "So. Let's say yes."

ABOUT THE AUTHOR

A writer and Parsec Award winning podcaster from Houston, Texas, Paul E Cooley produces free psychological thriller and horror podcasts, essays, and reviews available from Shadowpublications.com and iTunes. For more than a decade, Shadowpublications.com has brought unabridged, original content to the ears of podcast fans.

While best known for his Parsec Award winning sci-fi/horror series The Black and The Derelict Saga, Paul also writes traditional horror as well as alternate historical fantasy.

He has collaborated with New York Times Bestselling author Scott Sigler on the series "The Crypt" and co-wrote the novel The Rider. In addition to his writing, Paul has contributed his voice talents to a number of podiofiction productions.

He is a co-host on the renowned Dead Robots' Society writing podcast and enjoys interacting with readers and other writers.

To contact Paul:
   Mastodon: @paul_e_cooley@vyrse.social
   YouTube: https://youtube.com/paulecooley
   Email: paul@shadowpublications.com

Want to know when a new book or podcast presentation is released? Join the Shadowpublications.com mailing list:
   http://mailinglist.shadowpublications.com

Made in the USA
Monee, IL
26 October 2023

45212060R00162